I0667288

Just For Michael
Bad Boys book Twelve

Christine Young

Chapter One

Virginia, July 1833

On this hot, windy day Clare Carter-Brown watched the sleek clipper until the white-tips of its sails were no longer visible. The sky was so blue, one could see from here to what seemed like eternity. Not one cloud floated in the sky. The vessel carried her older sister, Sophie Stewart, along with the rest of her family as they headed home to London.

She pulled in a deep breath of the tangy Atlantic Sea air savoring the moment along with her newfound independence. This was her home. Her sister, Sophie, and her husband were gone now, returning to their life in England with all their beloved children. She was by herself. Nonetheless, she didn't feel alone. The affinity she had for this land went far beyond the normal. The feelings traveled deep into her heart and soul, buried there. From the moment she left Virginia seven years ago, Clare knew she would return someday. America was in her blood. The land of the free, people said.

Clare twirled, her skirts flaring out around her slim ankles showing more than was appropriate. She didn't care. Let the world think what they wished. She was free, an independent woman, Sophie thought to herself with a knowing grin. She didn't know what she would do with herself. She did though. Link helped her with the promise he would never tell Sophie until she prospered. Following her dream, that's what she would do. He simply gave her the money she would need to get started. He helped her with other aspects of the business too.

Mayfair Racing and Stud Farm.

Her sister believed wholeheartedly she would return to England by the end of the summer. She wouldn't. Link Stewart supposed she would stay at Leslie Hall, his family's home. That wasn't going to happen either. Her intention was to march right up to Mayfair Hall then stake her claim to her inheritance. After all, the plantation was hers. Well, that would be in three months when she turned twenty-one. Link wasn't going to hold her to his wishes. She never promised him. When her uncle, William Brinkmeyer, passed on to greener pastures five years ago, Mayfair was turned over to her loving care. In the interim, however, the plantation hired a manager she would need to deal with.

She could barely stand the anticipation, the excitement of it all. Mayfair was hers. Beneath her ribs her heart hammered with eagerness to get on with her life. So excited, her palms sweated. Hastily, she pushed them along the fabric of her gown. While it was true she wouldn't turn twenty-one for another three months, she felt independent. As her guardian at this moment, Link held all responsibility for the estate. Nonetheless, he did not remain in Virginia to oversee her actions.

No, Link wasn't here. He was an ocean away, at least he would be soon. She did have his approval as well as monetary support until she started making a profit. Link Stewart, her brother-in-law backed her. He believed in her every bit as much as she believed in herself.

An agenda written in her head loomed at the top of her mind. There was so much to accomplish, so much planning. Clare walked away from the dock immersed in her thoughts, her mind clamoring with all the tasks in front of her. This area had not changed in the seven years since she was in Virginia. She walked past the alehouse where the men gathered to gossip. Hot toddies came to mind. Her brother-in-law used to spend time here so he heard all the rumors first hand. Most of them concerned her sister. Sophie had been known as the town harlot. She wasn't though. When she married Link, she was a virgin. Enough of those antiquated thoughts. They were best left alone, in the dark recesses of the past. Drudging them up would serve merely to depress her. Only the small-minded people of the town believed the rumors generated by her uncle. Well, perhaps not. Even Link believed those tales at first. Not much time passed, however, before he had second thoughts about Sophie.

So lost in reflections about the past, she walked right into Michael Flannigan. Michael was the manager of Mayfair Hall. She did think him to be a handsome devil. Also understood he would not be easy to deal with. Her first order of business would be to free all the slaves. When she did so, she would have another strike against her where the townspeople were concerned. Not only would she be the harlot's sister but the emancipator of slaves. That would almost be unheard of although several years ago the slaves at Leslie Hall were freed at her brother-in-law's command.

What she didn't comprehend yet was how Michael felt about slaves. She also didn't know if he would stand in her way when she took over the management. She was after all, a woman. Some men didn't like control wrested from their fingers by anyone let alone a female. From what she'd seen so far of Mr. Flannigan, he treated the plantation as his personal property. Clare felt certain she would have a fight on her hands.

"Hello," she said as she looked up into incredibly green eyes that reminded her of the soft moss in the glade where she used to spend a wealth of her free time when she was in England.

She smiled hugely at him. His shoulders were broad; his long, dark red hair could make a woman wish to run her fingers through the length. It was rakish, piratical perhaps. She saw him at the helm of his ship, his hands on the wheel, a leather thong tying his hair back. His legs long, his breeches molded lovingly to the prominent muscles. His chin was blunt, his eyebrows the same color as his hair. The chest she stared at was broad. Once, she saw him without his shirt. The sight managed to steal her breath from her very lungs.

"You should pay attention to where you're going," he told her, his hands resting gently on her shoulders steadying her. His smile was bold as well as arrogant, infectious too. His lips were full, sensual. A kiss would be heavenly. He offered an arm, "Where are you headed to now?"

The way his hands felt when he touched her sent an abundance of heated shivers throughout. Her breath caught in the back of her throat while she couldn't see to remove her gaze from his lean, hard features. She stepped away, unwilling to give over to the certain pleasure he made her feel. He kissed her once when they first arrived here. She liked the feel of his mouth pressed against hers. After that she decided kisses between them couldn't happen. The sensations were way too much for her to consider, heated her, sent that same fire to places she'd never thought of before. Those same perceptions left her weak kneed as well as breathless. Breathless, along with weak kneed was not a state she should find herself in while attempting to take control of Mayfair.

She didn't like the faintness he generated.

"We have a great deal of issues to discuss, Mr. Flannigan."

She meant to keep the relationship between them business, nothing else.

"Mr. Flannigan?" Michael arched a dark red eyebrow that was indeed perfectly sculpted. With that single action, he questioned her on a level she didn't understand. She employed him. He shouldn't be questioning her. "When did my name change from Michael?"

"Yes."

She meant to continue here as she planned. Giving into his charming ways was not going to happen. She was sure he could seduce her easily enough as she'd heard a few rumors concerning him involving the opposite sex. While he wasn't a lady's man, he wasn't celibate either. Clare didn't intend to become a conquest of his. She'd already given this man something she'd never given anyone else, a kiss.

"Michael," he murmured close to her ear. "Call me Michael."

His breath wafting across her sensitive flesh reaffirmed her need to keep this business-like. Distance from this enigmatic man was imperative to maintain her composure. He was a mystery she didn't wish to uncover. She stepped away, sifting in a staggered breath of air. Once again, her knees felt weak as if they would buckle. The man was too potent for her, too hard and unyielding. She had no idea how to counter his advances.

"Mr. Flannigan," she insisted as she suddenly realized he wasn't going to easily concede to her wishes.

She heard the breath of air he heaved into his lungs while she also saw the frown lines creasing his tanned forehead, obviously bronzed from days on end in the sun. Clearly, he was displeased with her stubborn insistence on using his last name. Becoming too familiar with a man she employed would be unwise. Damnation, she had to keep telling herself those words. If she didn't, she would give into him.

"Michael," he told her again, sterner this time. "Mr. Flannigan is far too formal. Besides, calling me by my last name makes me out to be an old man." Pausing for a moment before running a fingertip down the column of her neck. "After what we've shared? You must call me Michael. I'll have nothing else.

"Here is Duster," he said as they stopped in front of one of the horses that would make her stud farm a success. His mount, Gypsy, was tethered next to her stallion. Both stallions were from the best lineage, one that could be traced back to some of the finest horses ever. "I'll follow you to Leslie Hall. Did you know your trunks were deposited in the master chamber in Mayfair Hall?" He paused to look at her as if trying to discern her thoughts. "Ah, you do know. What should I think about that? Perhaps you do want to be closer to me than I previously assumed."

He slanted her a half-smile that made her stomach churn in a curious way.

Clare didn't think for a second he was asking her if she meant to take up residence in his bedroom hence sharing the bed. However, the look on his face was something she couldn't fathom. She wanted to see inside his thoughts. Wished she had more practice with men.

"You will move into the manager's cottage behind the plantation. It was one of the issues we needed to talk about. I would prefer to wait for this discussion until we have an office where we can speak privately. Perhaps we can curtail the conversation until we arrive at Mayfair Hall."

"No," his reply was succinct as well as to the point.

"You don't have a choice, Mr. Flannigan. I'm not conversing with you in front of all these people. Don't mean to speak until there is privacy." She found the calm serenity she wanted to proceed with was rapidly vanishing. The very look in his eyes challenged her, bringing anger to the forefront. She didn't want to deal with this man in anger. If she was to be successful in her dealings with Michael Flanigan, she needed to remain calm, indifferent to the sensual way he looked at her.

He flashed even white teeth, his smile telling her she was wrong about that. Of course, she understood he could refuse her request. Well, what she asked for wasn't a request; the words were more along the lines of a demand. Indeed, her words were meant as a command. If he didn't like what she was going to tell him, he could quit.

She had the control.

He wasn't in charge.

"We will see."

His large hands on her waist he tossed her atop Duster as if she weighed nothing at all. She wasn't tiny so why was he able to do that so easily? Why did she feel so helpless when she was with him? He meant to take charge. She wasn't about to allow such a nefarious action. Mayfair Hall was hers, hers alone. Sharing was no plausible option.

Helpless was not a feeling she needed or wanted. Nor did she want to feel weak-kneed or have her stomach turning somersaults when he smiled at her. Didn't want to feel heat tumble through her when his all-knowing gaze riveted on her mouth.

The next half hour they rode along the river in silence. She could think of nothing to say that wouldn't start an argument. The few times she glanced his way he looked straight ahead, crease lines still marring his broad forehead. What he was thinking was imperative for her to comprehend. Enlightening her to his thoughts was not something that seemed important to him. He also didn't appear pleased with anything she told him earlier. Well, of course the man wouldn't be delighted, you ninny. She thought for a moment to call herself more names as she did feel a tiny bit of guilt at what she was doing.

Pushing thoughts of the upcoming confrontation out of her mind for the moment, she let her mind wander to more pleasant avenues of thought. With the sun shining brightly, the heat kissed her face. She wanted to remove the hat shadowing her white features. Thought better of it before she changed her mind.

Unable to stop herself, in the process defying fashion along with good sense, she untied the ribbons so the hat dangled on her back. If she gave into this impulse too many times, freckles would ramble across her nose. Maybe the man didn't like freckles. She could only hope, as she needed some means to keep him at a distance. He slanted her a look, a fat grin on his handsome features. Heat rose to her cheeks again. Fire burned in places she didn't want to acknowledge.

Damn and blast, she didn't want to enjoy his blatant smile or even the twinkling green eyes of his that even now seemed to roam over her body. She tilted her chin before nudging Duster to a faster pace. Wind sifted through her hair until nearly all the pins fled the strands. Her hair streaked out behind her. She headed the horse along the banks of the river. He followed behind her, the sounds of Gypsy's hooves loud.

They passed Leslie Hall then turned toward Mayfair Hall. Michael didn't say a word nor did she. Explaining herself to her manager about where she meant to live was not part of the manager's job description. She would have to educate him as to his new duties. His first chore would be to move his possessions from the master chamber.

She was displacing him from a place he called home for the last five years. In his situation, she would be angry too. Empathy for the man would not do at all. She was sure he would take advantage of her weak, female thoughts. She meant to carry on now as she would in the future.

He would understand he would have to move in three months if not today. So, in that case what was the difference? They reached the newly furbished stables that would house her pride and joys. Her horses. Duster was a descendant of Fearnought who was a big bright bay horse very nearly sixteen hands high. Duster was of his size. He would be the stud of the Mayfair Hall Racing and Stud Farm. Duster filled a major portion of her dream. Her farm would grow and prosper.

She and Link discussed this in length, made plans together. She utilized all his ideas then beamed with pride when he approved of hers. Neither wanted to own slaves. At Leslie Hall most of the slaves were now freed. Leslie Stewart, the Duke of Southcliff, Link's older brother, didn't wish to have any part of slavery. This was all well and good. Nevertheless, the residents of Virginia, well this was a slave state. Slavery was acceptable to most everyone. They would not appreciate the freeing of an entire plantation.

To help make this stud farm a success, Link conspired with his friends as well as his business associates to find the perfect stud for her new adventure. This wasn't just an adventure; it was more her bid for independence along with a new life. As a woman no one expected her to flourish. She would.

When they reached the end of the road to Mayfair, Timmie the young black stable boy strode out to greet them. He grinned at her. One top tooth was missing. He lost it in a race when a competitor nudged him along with his horse into a ditch. The next race Timmie got even.

"Hello."

She dismounted before Michael could come to help her. Feeling his hands on her waist was sure to cause unruly sensations she didn't want to deal with before she spoke with him. Once again, she reminded herself this was business not pleasure.

"Brush Duster and Gypsy. Duster is here for the night. I'll be out to see to the horses when I'm done with Mr. Flannigan."

At her crisp words, she watched him bristle, a slight tick in the muscle at his jaw. Will he posture and get all out of joint? His displeasure coupled with her intentions would never change her plans.

He stepped up beside her, easily keeping pace as they walked through the huge front door. "Done with me?" he asked, repeating her words while his hand gripped her elbow turning her, forcing her to look at him.

To no avail, she tried to wrench her arm from his hold. He was too damn strong.

Michael no longer smiled. His face assumed an austere mask of what might be indifference. His gaze on her so unfriendly she nearly changed her mind. Nonetheless, his eyes darkened with his displeasure. She understood what this man felt was far from indifference.

Clare beckoned Old Suzzy. The woman was another one of the black slaves. She was tiny, barely reaching five feet tall. Her dark skin was wrinkled with age. She had the warmest big brown eyes Clare had ever seen. Several times the woman cleaned Sophie's wounds when their uncle hit her. Old Suzzy knew more about her life here than any other living soul.

"Miss Clare." She grinned showing a few missing teeth. Wrinkles crinkled merrily around her eyes. "Mighty glad to see you, Little Missy. We've been wondering if you would ever return. You here to stay?"

"Will you bring a pot of tea to the office, please? Maybe some of Delilah's strawberry tarts."

Clare would talk to Old Suzzy later. At this moment, she didn't intend to lose her train of thought. She needed to confront Michael, no,

Mr. Flannigan with strength, not hesitancy. She would not be talked out of her resolution.

Old Suzzy nodded before she took off down the long hallway to the kitchen. Clare took a moment to straighten her skirt. She walked into the office. She remembered William Brinkmeyer sitting behind the huge, oak desk. Her uncle would smile at her. Even then at thirteen she understood there was nothing good behind that smile. Uncle Brinkmeyer was an evil selfish man who cared nothing about anyone except himself. What she didn't know at the time was what he was doing to Sophie or how he threatened her. With his machinations he nearly ruined her. If not for Link discovering the truth, she would have never recovered from the viscous gossip.

Clare remembered a lot of things she'd rather not recall about that time. She hitched in a deep breath of air realizing she'd given Michael time to walk around her then assume an in-charge position behind the huge desk.

He did not.

Instead, he leaned negligently against the doorframe, legs as well as his arms crossed. This time he seemed to school his features. A lazy somewhat insolent smile plastered on his too handsome face. Clare didn't know what to make of his new position. He wasn't acting as she anticipated. He was too composed. She expected furious anger to erupt.

She sucked air.

This man would not give an inch. Who sat behind the desk would not matter to him. Certain that he didn't think she could manage the men who worked for her, she meant to convince him otherwise.

Old Suzzy brought in the tea along with the dessert. After Suzzy looked from her to Michael, she hastily scurried from the room. Michael pushed away from the wall then sauntered to the decanter of brandy on the sideboard. He poured himself a glass before he saluted her. So much was being said without words.

"What is this business you're going to enlighten me with?" he asked before he downed the snifter in one gulp. Michael set the glass down. His hands behind his back, his gaze insolent, he waited.

Deciding she needed to sit before her knees buckled, she poured her tea, adding a bit of milk and sugar. Behind the desk she rested both hands on its smooth top. The wood barrier gave her confidence. She sat; sipped her tea thinking about what she needed to say first. Silence thundered in the room. It seemed she could hear everything yet nothing. Even with the tea skimming down her throat, her mouth was parched.

Before she started, she tugged a bit of courage into her lungs in the form of oxygen. "Life around here will not be the same now that I've returned. I mean to take charge, to run the plantation as I see fit. This is my legacy."

She motioned with her hands.

"I gathered as much. How pray tell do you mean to change life?"

He poured more brandy. He didn't choose to sit.

Clare thought to start with the less controversial of topics. "To begin with we will no longer grow tobacco."

Intuitively, she watched his face. He was calm, showing no emotion at all.

His gaze never shifted. "The land would not take too much more of that crop. Tobacco sucks the life out of the dirt. Most planters rotate crops or allow the land to lay fallow. Your decision seems reasonable to me. I applaud your veritable knowledge of a working plantation. Did Link give you the idea?"

She drank in air at his audacity. "We won't be doing either." She placed a lemon slice in her tea then poured milk before adding a sugar cube. "I've other plans for the land." She'd already done that. Her tea was now tepid and far too sweet.

It seemed she caught his attention. "What do you intend?"

He appeared intrigued. His green eyes glittered with a golden sheen around the outside edges. His substantial mouth lifting into the form a generous person might call a smile.

"I'm going to free the slaves. Don't believe in slavery. Link gave me permission. Not that I need his agreement. Mayfair is my plantation."

When she was nervous, she talked too fast. That was what she did right now. He would know, would hear the anxiousness in the tone of her voice. Would understand he could easily assume the upper hand if that was what he wished.

"Good." After that statement which thoroughly surprised her, he leaned both hands on the desk she knew he usually sat behind during conversations of this nature. "What is going to happen to them? Without Mayfair they will starve. My God, woman, they are like children. Even though I approve wholeheartedly of your idea, you can't just pronounce them free."

She pulled herself up straight thinking he had no right at all to question her. "Link and I discussed this problem, not that the issue, right or wrong, has anything to do with you. I've set a course of action that will be followed to the letter. The plan I mentioned is exactly how the Stewarts freed the slaves at Leslie Hall. I believe that worked quite admirably."

"What brilliant strategy did the two of you come up with?"

His bland tone didn't surprise her. He was waiting for her to mess up before he jumped in with his opinions thereby assuming control. "Neither of you have lived in this part of the world. Nor have you any real knowledge of the slavery situation."

He would learn soon enough she made all the decisions from this point forward. "We will rent land to each family. If the people wish, they can plant crops as well as sell them. The choice is theirs. Your job will be to collect the rent on the properties after they have begun to make a living. The farm land will provide a decent living for anyone wishing to stay and thereby take advantage of what is offered."

"So far you make sense. Go on."

The acknowledgement was sweet of him. She didn't think he meant to be sweet. "We will build new homes for those who want to stay."

"What about the ones who don't? What will happen to them?"

He pushed away from the desk, pinching the bridge of his nose as he wandered around the room.

"I'm going to encourage them all to stay then I'll hire a person to teach them to read and write. They will need those skills to survive as well as prosper."

On the defensive now, she needed to turn the exchange around. Taking charge here was essential if she meant to run the plantation.

"Good luck with that. How do you expect to keep this place running without funds from the crops? Where is the coin going to come from to build new homes for all the people you've freed."

"Those are all good questions. However, I want you to know if you continue to manage the properties, your job description will change. You will be doing most of the teaching." She held up her hands, "Not the reading and writing."

"Figured as much." He sat down with another glass of brandy in hand, his long-muscled legs stretched out in front of him appearing totally relaxed. "I'm waiting."

"For what?" she asked, surprised.

Keeping her gaze from roaming the length of him was nearly impossible. When he was around, she had the devil of a time concentrating. Clare touched her lips recalling his kiss from a few weeks previous, the warmth, how he traced her lip with his tongue before plunging deep inside. She recalled his taste, his scent. That was a month ago, a mistake. One she wouldn't make again. There would be no more kisses between them…or anything else.

His grin was slow, lazy, his arrogance undeniable. It was almost as if he read her mind, knew her unruly thoughts. "My job description. Perhaps I'm to attend to the physical needs of the new owner since we are sharing a bedroom. I noticed how your pink tongue ran smoothly along your lips getting ready for the kiss you've been thinking about since we first met in the village."

"You!" Heat bathed her face, flames leapt within. "How dare you imply something like that!" She lost control, anger simmering deep and so very hot she had the urge to toss her cup of tea his way.

"Me, yes, who else? A moment ago, you were thinking about the kiss we shared the other evening. You know, the evening we watched the sun go down in the west. We shared a bottle of wine as well. Oh, did it happen nearly a month ago? You have a fine memory, Clare. Shall we see if the kiss will still taste as sublime as the first time?"

He stepped forward as if he meant to do exactly that.

She pushed away from the desk. "I have no physical needs you will attend to." Her breath stuck in her throat, her tongue on the roof of her mouth. In that one moment he took over the discussion. He made her recall in vivid detail that moment as well as the deep sensations he produced in her.

"You should understand, I won't share my bed with you unless you are naked." His gaze traveled the length of her before insolently settling on her heaving bosom. "You want me now. We can visit the master chamber. See if we are as compatible in bed as I believe we are. We haven't had a chance for anything more than a few stolen kisses. That night I had to keep looking over my shoulder to see if Link would turn up to rescue you. Not that you needed rescuing from me. I would never harm you. Have only our best interests at heart."

Clare understood the conversation turned to a topic she didn't comprehend too well. He was outrageous in his words. He was all male and powerful. She would do well to remember that fact when dealing with him. She needed to dissuade him from this line of conversation before the words traveled in a direction she could never contend with. Now, Michael assumed mastery of the conversation.

To get back on track was her immediate goal. She cleared her throat, a tiny little sound. "You will collect the rent monies, make sure they have seed to plant as well as the tools the men will need. They will most likely have to be instructed on what will be best for the land. I've heard wheat along with corn are good crops for the soil that has been tasked to the limit. The families may also plant vegetable gardens for their personal use if they would like to do so."

"You heard right. I'm sure we will think of other issues that might arise then deal with them together. Now, what are you going to do with the studs you brought in? What are your plans for the stable that has been reconstructed these last months since your brother-in-law has been in the states. I'm sure he didn't leave before he thought this endeavor was ready to be left in the hands of a woman."

She breathed a silent sigh of relief when he stopped pursuing this bedroom situation. Nonetheless, he maintained that arrogant air that only men would understand what was needed. He was wrong. She needed to dissuade him from that bit of male dominating thought.

"Mayfair Hall will no longer be a tobacco plantation. It will be a stud farm. A sign has been commissioned that will read, Mayfair Racing and Stud Farm. Duster has bloodlines going back to Fearnought. I've two pregnant mares both with lines that go back to Medley who was bred in England by Lord Grosvenor. Link has been busy, as he has lined up two mares that Duster will cover. We should make a great show of this. The men bringing the mares are each paying two hundred pounds, which is the going rate in England. I'm not certain how much that is in American currency."

"So," Michael tapped his long-bronzed fingers together before he joined them beneath his chin is a powerful steeple. "You've got everything figured out. Or…should I say Link has brought about this wonderful scenario for you. A woman cannot direct men to do her bidding. If she attempts such a feat, men won't obey. You need to come to terms with your femininity, which is beautiful by the way."

Enthusiastically, she nodded relieved he seemed to be taking this change in stride while she tried to forget the condescension in his tone along with his words about a woman's ability to lead men. Clearly, Michael Flannigan didn't believe women competent to run a stable such as this one.

"Link has been an immense help. However, the success will be up to me. My brother-in-law has confidence in my ability."

"Except the sharing of my bed." He leaned closer to her. "Link has nothing to do with that. I'm sure he would not be pleased if he discovered the fact. As you said, he is across the ocean with nothing to say about the matter. In this I will pursue my desires with no one to contest me."

"I've that covered also."

She felt prim and proper. After all, she was a spinster. She was on the shelf. While they discussed this new situation for Mayfair, she realized she would simply allow him to have the master chamber. The bedroom as it appeared now reminded her too much of Uncle William. She would not be able to sleep there.

"You do?" He sounded surprised yet at the same time a bit intrigued. His lips slowly formed into a generous grin.

Curtly, she nodded. "I will take the adjoining room. You may stay in the large room. I've no problem with that."

His curses shocked her to the tips of her slippered feet.

"Mr. Flannigan!" Her heart heaved against her chest. "I've been very congenial. You've no right to swear at me."

His scowl returned. He appeared dangerous and dark, his green eyes closer to the darkness of leaves on an oak rather than the soft green of moss she compared them to earlier. "Do you care so little about your reputation that you would bed down in the adjoining room?"

Blindsided, maybe more confused, Clare didn't understand what to make of his words. She blinked several times trying without succeeding to figure out what exactly he spoke.

"What does our sleeping arrangements have to do with my reputation? If we are sharing or not sharing a bed, who would know? Who would even care about what we do in the privacy of Mayfair Hall?"

She didn't want to feel quite so baffled. Didn't wish for him to believe she didn't understand what he meant.

She didn't.

"Are you stupid or naïve or both?"

He rose from the chair. His pacing took him in circles around the dark blue and cream Aubusson carpet. He paused at the window looking over the land, his hands clasped behind his back. For a few seconds he rocked on his heels.

Clare made a mental note to change the draperies. The fabric was too dark. The room needed a brighter look. He turned, a scowl creasing his forehead. His hands were fisted.

She wanted to understand what was traveling through his man's brain. Nothing he'd been telling her made sense. At first, he teased about taking her to his bed naked. The next thing she knew he was telling her if she slept in the adjoining bedroom, her reputation would never recover.

"I take exception to that. What is it that you want, Mr. Flannigan? What exactly are you trying to describe?"

His feet took him to a point directly in front of her. With a finger beneath her chin, he slowly lifted. His gaze bore into hers. Her breath caught in the back of her throat. "I should show you. God knows it's probably the only way you'll understand. You're too damn innocent."

Clare pushed away from him as well as the desk. "You ass..."

Her words trailed off when his large hands gripped her shoulders.

It didn't seem he was going to let her go.

He pulled her close. The scent of brandy caressed her as his breath whispered across her face. One month ago, he tasted of the sweet wine they drank, the white Bordeaux from the Stewart vineyard in France. She ran her tongue across her bottom lip, leaving a path of moisture. She did want another kiss, perhaps another one after that. Nonetheless, she didn't want him to know that. Didn't want to renege on her earlier plans to keep business separate from her personal life. At this point in time, she didn't believe he meant to give her a choice.

Damnation, she wanted that kiss.

With all her might, she pushed away from Michael understanding if they were going to maintain a working relationship, they could not dally. Sharing kisses would not be conducive to business. A personal relationship between them would prove to be distracting. Clare wasn't at all certain if dallying meant just kissing or if the word entailed more. Nonetheless, she didn't want to take the chance she would melt in the heat of his arms again.

One time was enough. A month ago, she turned into a little puddle. This afternoon was not going to see a replay of that frivolous evening. Her push seemed to bring them closer. His mouth hovered inches above hers. His brandy scented breath caressed her lips. "You want me to kiss you, admit to the fact." His voice was husky, a different sound from the norm.

She was shaking her head. Lifting one hand from her, he ran one hand through the length of her hair. He stared hard at her. A muscle along his jaw ticked warningly.

"No, no I don't."

"Tell me to keep my hands off you but don't lie to me. Kiss me, Clare. Kiss me like you did before, deep and hard, with all of your tongue involved. I want to taste your sweetness, feel your sultry heat the fire you spawn, the flames bursting. After that maybe we can talk in a more adult way about our sleeping arrangements."

"There is nothing to talk about. I don't want..." Her hands on his chest pushed. He didn't move.

"Oh, but I do believe there is a great deal of discussion to be had."

His lips found hers. Unable to help herself, she met his tongue with her own, delved inside the warmth of him. Clare wanted to cry with the desperate hunger he induced. She needed to put this man out of her thoughts. He was too big a distraction to her plans. If she gave him the chance, he would ruin everything. In order to prove herself, she would have to be strong.

When he lifted his head to look at her, to move a few strands of damp hair from her face she found her voice, "Stop, Michael, please...don't do this to me."

~ * ~

Well, hell, he didn't want to stop. There wasn't one doubt in his mind she liked his kisses. No, he wanted to keep kissing her until she agreed to marry him, until he couldn't breathe until he curled up his toes. Yesterday, after speaking with Link, he believed he had the three months until she turned twenty-one to convince her to his way of thinking. After that the undertaking would be more difficult for him to maintain the land he wanted, the land by birthright he should own.

Now she thought to take on her sister's shoes by sleeping in the adjoining room. If he had his way, she would never become the next harlot of Virginia. The difficult part of all this was that he did want her naked in his bed, her soft curves pressed sweetly against him. He wanted to give her a woman's pleasure. Needed to hear her howl at the moon when she climaxed, her silken white body beneath his. His emotions were in such turmoil he didn't know what to think.

He wanted to be a gentleman where Clare was concerned. Single handedly, she was making the job damn difficult

Hell, he wasn't a gentleman. Never had been. Never would be.

Link made it abundantly clear she was not to be present when Duster covered a mare. She was a virgin. Clare shouldn't see something so carnal in nature. Short of tying her somewhere, he didn't understand how he could prevent her from doing whatever the devil took her mind to do. From all she spoke of just now, she would make sure she played an integral part of this business, all of it, even the sexual parts. Quickly, he was learning she wasn't the type of woman to hold anything back.

When Link explained this dream of hers to become independent, well, he promised to give her that illusion if possible. Michael understood if she ran out of funds, he was to write to her brother-in-law immediately for more money. Clare's brother-in-law was going to use his substantial groats to keep her dream alive. Now, Link counted on him to be a silent partner in this ill-fated adventure of Clare's. Without a man's hands in the running of the business, her enterprise was doomed to failure.

The difficult part of all this was that he as well as Link prayed she succeeded. Neither had an iota of hope the adventure would, at least not without a man's interference, prosper. The other men would never take orders from her. Blast it all, she needed him to have a superior role in this undertaking of hers, needed to position himself at the helm.

He kissed the lass, felt her so very sweet curves against him.

After she asked, he stopped.

Even while lust surged straight to his groin so potent he had few rational thoughts, he set her aside. He was surprised he didn't toss her on that big desk and after that with her legs wrapped around his flanks teach her about a woman's pleasure. His imagination ran rampant. If he was going to succeed and see his dreams materialize, he needed to curtail his carnal thoughts concerning Clare.

Michael didn't want to stop and think about all these plans of hers. When he did, he realized Link supplied her with all she needed to make a success. Duster would bring top dollar as a stud. Two mares were lined up to test Duster's prowess. If he continued to advertise, there would be more mares standing ready within the week. He could race Duster as well as Gypsy. Duster was fast. Link told him the stallion did best at the quarter mile. Gypsy was in for the long haul. The stallion possessed a heart that never quit. The horse was quickly gaining an impeccable reputation in the racing world. While he wanted to race Gypsy, the problem was that he was just too damn big for a jockey. Link also made certain he understood that under no circumstances was Clare to race. She would try to do so. She would even lie if only by omission. He would have to be a step or more ahead of her to succeed.

He agreed.

She would try. He acknowledged that for a fact.

He grinned, a huge grin. Another possible tussle with Clare might be fun. "When do you want to begin telling the slaves they are free?"

She stepped away from him, wishing for more distance he felt sure. He strode to the big desk then sat down. For a few seconds while he tried to school his emotions, he shuffled the papers he'd been working on before he rode into town to meet Clare then escort her home.

"Timmie and Old Suzzy should be told first. They will help us with the rest when the time comes. Link thought we should start building the new homes before we do anything else. The freed men can help with the construction."

He agreed. "Over the last five years Mayfair has acquired no new slaves. Some have died. At this moment we have only twenty-five families. Twenty-five new homes will need to be built. What are you going to use for capital?"

Air shifted in then out of her lungs, her breasts moving provocatively beneath the bodice of the lovely blue gown she wore which each tiny breath. "Link wished to give me money for that. I told him no. I plan to use my dowry. The money is deposited in the bank in town. The funds are more than enough to cover the initial expenses then some. By the time I need more, we should have stud fees. Perhaps we can win a few races." She paused thinking about the funds there. "I'm not at all certain that Link considers that money my dowry though."

Michael leaned back, his hands resting on the desk while he played with the pen twirling the stem between his fingers. "Don't suppose it matters. Link made the notion clear to me, whatever money you needed would be supplied. The question now is what type of homes do you wish to build."

He watched the play of emotions across her delicate face as she thought about his question.

"Yes, well, they cannot be too fancy. They need to have a floor as well as two bedrooms and a kitchen, of course, a living area."

"Much fancier than anything they live in now. Have you seen the hovels they call home? I suppose I should have made improvements. However, the money was not there nor the permission. I've spent the last five years bringing the plantation up to standard. We've just begun to make a profit. Your uncle ran the place into the ground."

Michael watched her move around the room. The soft swish of her skirts gave him ideas he shouldn't have. She was graceful. Her hips rounded while her breasts were small. He wondered what color the tips were. He guessed a soft enticing pink.

She turned to face him. "I understand. Before my sister and brother-in-law left, Link made arrangements for the construction of the homes. The building should begin tomorrow. I do expect you to oversee this."

"What will you do with the overseer? The man who makes sure the slaves do their jobs?"

The man was evil. Once he discovered the man's true nature, he meant to fire him. Had not done so yet. The arrival of the Stewarts put a stop to much of what he planned. "You need to get rid of the man. I was making plans. Since you are taking control of the reins, so to speak, I suppose you will wish to see him."

"No, I don't wish to see Raynard or speak to him. My interest is with the racing along with the stud farm. You will tell the man not to come back. Give him a reasonable severance. Since there will be no more slaves, we will have no use for his services or his violence. I wish I could ask you to write some type of letter that would acknowledge his credentials. I can't."

"No, I would gag on the words. If you commanded me to do so, that would be my first act of disobedience. In most things I can be loyal. In that I cannot."

He watched her for a reaction to his words. Commanding men, for her, would not be possible. She was such a tiny, delicate slip of a woman. No man would take orders from her.

"Don't expect obedience necessarily. I do, however hope you will continue to give me an honest opinion. I know horses. I don't know anything about the workings of a plantation."

"Very well, advice I've plenty of. Shall we start with the freeing of Old Suzzy then Timmie so we can see how that will go?"

He was eager to begin this new chapter for Mayfair Hall. In time, all would come together as planned including the seduction of Miss Clare Carter-Brown. She could deny the fact until hell froze over. Nevertheless, she would be his by autumn, before she turned twenty-one if possible.

"Yes, that would be a good idea. After that will you show me around the plantation, especially the slave's homes?"

"I will call for Old Suzzy."

He stood then rang the bell that would bring the slave to the office, the soon to be servant. Michael understood the old woman would not be pleased simply because she wouldn't understand. This was the only life she knew. The woman had been born here. She would believe she'd done something wrong. His wording would have to be impeccable.

"She will be here in just a moment." He stood behind the desk. Clare appeared resigned to the fact that now he held the power. "Would you like me to tell her or would you appreciate the privilege?"

"Perhaps you should. It's been seven years since I've been at Mayfair Hall. Old Suzzy has taken orders from you while I was gone. If I tell her she is now a free woman, she will not believe her ears nor will she understand the implications to her new life."

Her voice was so calm and quiet the sound quite discomfited him.

To Michael, Clare seemed too damn serene when there should be a modicum of anxiety building. What she was about to do would have all the slaves on tenterhooks until they figured out what was now happening to them. It would also rally the town's people along with the other plantation owners against her. "If that's what you would like."

He tapped the pen he'd been toying with on top of the desk. Wished to whistle while he watched Clare's face turn pale with what he assumed would be anxiety. Well, hell, her skin was white to begin with. Now her skin appeared to be a death mask.

Old Suzzy walked into the room. When she looked between them, her face paled, if that was at all possible, the earlier smile vanishing. She clasped her hands in front of her. "Massa," she whispered her eyes drawing together. "Di' I do somethin' wrong?"

Michael sent Clare a look she might not appreciate. While he expected this, Clare did not. "Perhaps you would like to sit."

She dropped another shade closer to white. Old Suzzy sat, her fingers gripping the poor chair so tight the pressure turned her knuckles even whiter than her face. "Massa?"

"Rest easy, Old Suzzy. You've done nothing wrong. We want to give you a bit of good news," Clare said softly.

Her voice seemed to ease some of the suffocating tension swirling around in the tiny space.

Well, it seemed she couldn't keep her nose out of this situation. Clare touched the old woman on the shoulder if that tiny gesture could reassure her. The lady stiffened with the contact.

Might as well get this over with. "We, Clare and I..." he pointed to her.

She stiffened slightly tilting her tiny chin into the air. He cleared his throat.

"Neither one of us likes slavery. Another person should not own people. We plan on changing the plantation from farming to racing. In this case, we will have no need of slaves to keep the place running."

Old Suzzy promptly put her hand to her forehead. Her old eyes going vague and hazy, she slid from the chair to pool on the floor, her body still.

"Oh my God!" Clare blurted before she rushed to her.

She felt the woman's forehead. "She fainted? Is that a good or bad sign? Tears are running down her cheeks."

"A bad sign." Shaking his head at his stupidity, Michael strode swiftly to the kitchen to retrieve a basin of water along with a soft cloth. By the time he returned, Old Suzzy was sitting in a more comfortable chair moaning emitting gut wrenching sobs. Clare shot him a glance that pretty much told him what she thought. He'd gone about telling her about her freedom all wrong. The woman must have assumed he meant to sell her to another plantation.

Well hell! He jabbed his hands through his thick, dark red hair. Hair so dark it was nearly chestnut in color.

He crouched down in front of her, taking her elderly leathered hands in his. "We aren't going to sell you. Clare and I want to give you your freedom. We will pay you for working here, for serving us just as you've been doing for years and yes, years. You deserve more for your loyalty than being sold to another person."

Yes, she did merit more from them. He would contrive some way to give her something she would cherish as much as her freedom.

Blank, foggy, deep brown eyes stared at him. Apparently, she didn't believe those words. Either that or she didn't truly understand what his words meant. He would have to elaborate more.

"Don't want to work for anyone else." After what seemed an eternity, she was finally able to speak. "Want to stay here."

"You aren't going anywhere, Suzzy, unless you want to. This is your home for as long as you wish it to be so."

"I don't understand. I'm a free woman, Suh?"

Surrounded by his hands her bony fingers were shaking. She was thin and frail. If she had to leave, she would die.

"Does that please you? Your duties will be the same. The only difference is that you will now be paid to perform them," Clare said coming around to stand in front of her, her smile huge. "You can have a new home with the other people who choose to stay or you can remain in your room on the third floor. Where you want to live is your choice."

It still appeared she didn't comprehend all they told her. "You no going to kick me out? I've choices?"

"No and yes," Clare said softly tears spiking her lashes. "You're important to me. I remember when you used to help Sophie when Uncle William hit her."

Old Suzzy grinned back. "I want to keep my room. What will I do with the money you pay me? Never been paid before."

"No, don't suppose you have." Michael grinned, relieved now that she seemed to grasp her new situation. "You can do with the money you are paid whatever you wish. If you like, the first time you're paid I'll drive you into town. You might like a new dress or a bonnet."

She was nodding her head as if she thought over her new situation in addition was well pleased. "My children and my grandchildren will be freed too?" Her smile grew huge then suddenly she frowned. "What if they want to leave? You can't give 'em dat choice. 'Day can't leave me."

"Free men and women can go where they please. I couldn't stop them. You would have another choice to make," Clare said thoughtfully.

"I hope they choose to remain with us."

"May I go tell them?" she asked seemingly eager to spread the news. She stood, still a bit shaky around the knees, quickly sitting down.

"No," Michael picked up her hands again. "That is something I must do. This will come as a huge shock to some. Just as you didn't believe the good fortune, there will be others who don't understand. Can I trust you to keep the secret for a few days?"

She nodded.

"Good. I promise you won't have to wait long. Now, you're done for the evening. Clare and I are going to take a stroll to the stables. Want to talk to Timmie next. Perhaps I will contrive a better way to give him the message."

Yes, he hoped he could figure this out. Timmie would be embarrassed if he fainted.

A few seconds later Old Suzzy vanished up the steps to her room. Clare looked at him. He grinned ignoring the fact he bumbled the first telling of the news that would certainly shock the surrounding planters.

He held up his hands, laughing, "I know I did an atrocious job. Doubt if you could have done better. This freeing business is not going to be easy to explain. However, I'm more than eager to begin."

"No, I don't suppose the telling will be at all easy," Clare agreed with him, amusement clearly seen on her generous mouth. "I could not have done better."

He strode from behind the desk, holding his hand out to her, "Should we go see Timmie. If you think you can do better, please be my guest."

"Perhaps you've learned from your mistake." She laughed softly tilting her chin to look into his eyes. "If given the chance, I'm certain I would bungle the job worse."

"That is what I thought."

Her silver-gray eyes sparkled with amusement. As he watched they turned bluer.

Good lord, her hand felt so small, her fingers wound between his larger ones. The feeling was right. God, how he wanted her. When he looked at her the need to pull her into his arms for a kiss seared him. They needed to discuss her return to Leslie Hall before he did something he might come to regret. He didn't think he could stay away from her when she was one door away from him.

It was late afternoon. Heat still buffeted the soft grass around Mayfair Hall. Timmie would be tending the horses. They stepped inside. The air was cool, dark, shaded from the afternoon sun. Clare found the pail holding apple slices and carrots. Without paying heed to him, she approached Duster first. She rubbed his nose then whispered something to him. With greed, he took the food offerings before he nudged her. If he didn't know better, the horse grinned. She stopped at Gypsy next. He deliberated what she told him. Ah, but he had to find Timmie. He wondered what he would say to the lad that wouldn't frighten him to eternity.

Timmie was mucking out Jingle Bell's stall. He pondered on who could have given the little mare that atrocious name. The perpetrator must have been one of Link's many children since the mares came with the Stewarts. One evening, a glass of brandy in his hand, a glass of wine in Sophie's, she told him all about Link's children. How he adopted and loved all of them. The man had a heart of gold. The children were ones who had no home. Link provided love as well as shelter and food, all the necessities. The other mare that came with Clare was Maid Marion. In his mind it was a much better name.

"You about finished, Timmie?"

Michael rested one arm on the stall. He went over in his mind what he did wrong with Old Suzzy in his explanation. There had to be a better way. He should have explained her life wasn't going to change. Well, of course, everything she knew as well as expected would change.

Timmie nodded. "Just about ready to head for home. My stomach is rumbling hard. Practically smell dinner. He closed his eyes, my ma's a mighty fine cook. What do you need?"

Michael paused thinking and thinking, trying to form words that wouldn't terrify the lad. Well, the lad was nearing seventeen. He supposed Timmie was very nearly a man now.

"First, I don't want you to panic when I start speaking. You will always have a place at Mayfair. This will always be your home if you wish it to be. Clare will always need you to tend to her magnificent horses. Your duties will remain the same."

"Panic?" His eyes widened with apprehension. "Don't know what you are getting at, Suh."

"Promise me you won't lie down and start wailing or I won't give you the good news. Don't want to see you pounding your fists on the floor. I promise you the news will make you howl with delight."

Timmie nodded slowly, his breath seeming to be held tightly inside his chest.

Michael thought that to be a very good sign. "Would you like to be a free man, Timmie? Clare and I can do that for you. If you want to stay and work with the mares as well as the studs, I will pay you decent wages. If you want to race Duster and Gypsy, you can do so. In that case a portion of the winnings will be yours."

When the man didn't dissolve into hysteria, Michael was pleased with himself.

Though the young man's eyes seemed to be crossing while his smile grew fat. Perhaps he was getting the hang of the telling. For tomorrow he would work on his delivery. It would be the last time. He would have to make certain all understood their choices.

When Timmie sat on a stool, tears streaming from his eyes, Michael wasn't at all certain he did it right this time either. Mayhap he patted himself on the back a bit too soon.

"Why are you crying, Timmie? I would think you would be happy, perhaps dancing a jig or two. Do you want to remain a slave? A man should never be another person's property."

He thought maybe his words were too harsh. Michael couldn't imagine anyone not...well hell, the youngun' had to be happy.

"Never been happier, Suh." He sniffed before wiping the tears from his cheeks with the back of his sleeve.

"Good, good then," Michael patted Timmie on the shoulder, relief swamping him although now he didn't know what else to say. "Perhaps you could tender this happiness with something other than tears. Perhaps shoot me a big smile? Dance a jig?"

"Can I tell my ma and pa?" Timmie did grin. He smiled so wide his white teeth flashed; the missing tooth quite evident. "You goin' to free dem too? Every one of us?"

"No, Timmie not yet, not today. We do plan on freeing all the slaves. However, first we must build everyone a new home. Tomorrow, Timmie, we will have a meeting with everyone who lives on Mayfair lands. We will find out then how many people are staying so we will understand how many houses we will have to create for all our new tenants. No one will go into the fields. I'll be there before dawn to make sure of that. We will celebrate."

"I'll see to it dat we have lots of rum punch," Timmie said with lighthearted laughter. "If dat's okay with you."

Ah, so they were able to get to the rum punch. He'd have to think about someone confiscating the rum from the house. The thought of anyone sneaking inside to filch it stole his breath. Raynard would never allow the slaves rum. Yes, he'd have to think about that some more. Now that they were free, they could have all the rum they could afford to buy.

"I'll see that my cook supplies the rum punch. We won't drink too much though. Everyone will get a cup, no more." If they celebrated their new freedom too hard, he'd have a lot of drunk men to contend with.

The scream he heard next ripped him apart. It was Clare. She was screaming again and again. His big body shivered with terror as the sensation raced through to his heart. What the devil was happening? She was supposed to be close by listening and evaluating his performance. His breath caught while he tried to understand. Nothing made sense. Timmie and Michael rushed from the stables toward the loud yelling.

She sounded as if she were dying. His heart lurched to his throat. His booted feet pounded the hard earth. He was terrified. The shrieks didn't stop. He ran and ran, Timmie behind him, the lad's boots pounding along with his against the hard dirt. When did she leave the stables? Why did she leave him to contend with this by himself? He thought she would be there for him to give advice as she did with Old Suzzy.

What he saw made his blood curdle. His stomach rolled in endless waves of agony. A young woman, one of the black slaves, was strung up, her hands above her head. Her clothing was torn, welts from Raynard's whip lacerated her tiny body. Clare was on her knees in front of the girl, her arms crossed to shield her face. She must have tried to stop him from beating the girl to death. Raynard sent the whip against Clare, hitting her while she tried desperately to grab the leather from his hands. As she turned from him to protect herself, he saw that Raynard hit her back twice, the fabric of her gown torn by the stinging weapon. Blood pooled on her shirt. He must have hit her again in the front after she turned. She clutched her shirt with her fingers to hold the material together.

"Stop! Stop it now!" Michael roared as he raced faster toward the man.

He should have fired the man months ago. What the devil was going on here? Timmie ran behind him. Michael's rage was beyond anything he'd ever felt before. How dare this man hit an innocent woman?

When he reached Raynard, he hauled back his fist hitting him square on the jaw. The man crumpled. His large body sprawled on the ground. He hoped he broke his jaw. Michael turned to Timmie. "Run, fetch Mammy Jo, tell her what happened here. She'll know what to do. Find someone who can carry the girl back to her home. I'll have Old Suzzy go to her with some healing cream as soon as possible."

This tiny black girl couldn't be more than fourteen or fifteen. Why was Raynard punishing her? What could she have possibly done to deserve a beating? The overseer strung her up by her hands then laid into her with his whip. She was bared to her waist, her tiny breasts exposed for everyone to see.

Michael turned kneeling in front of Clare. He pushed sodden hair away from her face. She looked up, her eyes filled with pain as well as tears that fell on her lashes. "Cut her down, please. Cover her with something." Clare's voice trembled.

She got the words out before she moaned softly obviously giving in to her pain.

His hands fumbling with the ropes, he released the black girl. She fell to the ground, weak from the loss of blood. Timmie slipped off the shirt he wore then covered her exposed body with it. Michael covered Clare with his jacket. "I'll find out what happened here. Can you tell me?" he asked wishing he knew her name.

"I refused him," was all the girl said as she huddled, her arms crossed in front of her while she clung to the shirt.

Yes, he heard the rumors that Raynard eased himself with the slaves. For some reason, he hadn't believed the gossip. He was stupid. Of course, the man would believe they were his to do with as he pleased. They were property after all. In time, she would be all right. The wounds would heal. He didn't know if her mind would recover. She'd been maliciously abused. No one, not even a slave deserved treatment such as this. After tomorrow there would be no slaves on Mayfair.

Well, hell...

Michael hauled Raynard to his feet, his fist ready to slug the man again. This man deserved the punishment and more.

The man blinked at him several time. He looked confused. Appeared to not understand his fury. "What are you so fired angry about? She's just a little black whore. They are all the same, all harlots willing to give a man their body for something in return. Meant to be used by whites. When I'm done with her, she'll spread her legs for me."

Gritting his teeth together in his rage, he tried to calm himself, said the words as slowly as possible. "Get off Mayfair land now. Pack your things and leave immediately. Send someone here who can tell me where you will be staying in the village. I will see that you are paid through the month. If you know what is good for you, don't ever let me see you again."

Michael didn't ever remember being so angry he shook. The man had the audacity to wield his whip against Clare.

Clare held out her hand to him. He pulled her to her feet. She moaned softly. Staring hard at Clare, she said, "You will explain yourself after I've seen to the lacerations. He could have killed you. Why didn't you call for me or run back to get help? You knew I was close by. For that matter, why did you leave the stable?"

"Mr. Flannigan, I'm here."

The woman calling out was Mammy Jo. She stopped running when she saw the girl huddled on the ground, clutching Timmie's shirt. "Juney? Oh my. I brought Big Tom. He's going to carry Juney home. Don't you worry about Juney here. I'll tend to her. She'll be fine. Do you need help with your little lady?"

She fussed over the girl even when Juney was in Big Tom's arms burying her head in the enormous man's shoulder.

"No, I'll take her back to the house then tend to her myself." After that he would lecture her on her folly.

~ * ~

Biff Gideon and Busby Turnpin sat in the Deer Head Ale house sipping on the latest draught of ale created by the owner. Biff thought the brew was delicious. He ordered another pint. The owner experimented with different draughts monthly. Some creations were good, some not so tasty. This was one of his best. Two large pretzels sat on a platter along with what looked to be delicious crab cakes. There were bowls of hot melted cheese to dip the pretzels. Biff thought he'd died then gone to heaven, everything tasted so delicious. Heaven wouldn't take him. He knew that. Still, he could dream while he filled his stomach. He did so love to eat.

"Heard Link Stewart and his harlot bride left her sister in Virginia," Busby pointed out. "You remember the girl, Sophie? She used to take lovers to that cottage on their land. Brinkmeyer, her uncle never knew how to stop her. She wore harlot gowns, painted her face so she looked the hussy. Never understood why Stewart married her. He could have just taken her then left her when he grew bored. Doesn't make any sense."

"Yeah, I remember. She painted her face just like the women who work at Miss Bessy's place outside of town. Her dresses showed so much that if one looked close you could see most of her all the way to her pretty little navel."

"Saw Clare just this afternoon. Her face wasn't painted. She wasn't wearing a dress that showed off her womanly charms. Ah, too bad. She's a pretty little thing. Not much bigger than a minute. Kind a like my women to have a bit more to hold on to if you get my drift." Busby pointed out while he chewed on a crab cake. "Don't think the younger sister is anything like Sophie. She looks sweet to me."

"You don't think she's like her sister?" Biff asked as drool pooled behind his lips.

He didn't have to think very hard about Clare being naked and beneath him, all that soft white flesh in his hands. While his imagination zoomed in on the thought, his groin throbbed heating with raw desire. He was going to have to make a trip to Miss Bessy's place this afternoon. He tossed back his ale then pulled off a chunk of the pretzel before dipping the end in the melted cheese while he tried to calm his unruly body. Thoughts of Clare clouded his brain. Desperately he wanted her. He would have her.

"You mean a whore?" Busby tossed back his head then hooted with unrestrained laughter. "Nah, she's a pretty little thing. While Brinkmeyer was alive he kept her all gussied up in little girl clothes. She wasn't anything like her sister then although she could be now. Things like that tend to run in families. We should find out."

"Clare Carter-Brown was a little girl at the time. Did you see her in town the other day? She's a grown woman now. What I saw was a little flirt asking for a man to have his way with her. Why that manager of hers picked her up by the waist before helping her mount that stallion she was riding. He had this light of possessiveness shining in his eyes. Men don't think that way about a woman unless he's taken her. Mark my words that sweet little girl is no longer a virgin. I'd bet on that fact."

Biff was thinking that he'd like to see what she was willing to give to him that she was giving Flannigan. That little house where Sophie took her lovers was still standing.

She would be so soft and white pure as the driven snow. Her pretty white tits with pink tips would be big enough to fill his hands. Pure lust surged to his man parts. He groaned with the pleasure of it all.

"You thinking you'd like to be the stallion she was sitting on top of?" Busby chortled. "I know I would like nothing better than a good ride with her. We could share. What do you think of that?

"Wouldn't you like to pretend you're a stallion?"

Once more Biff thought about her creamy breasts tipped in soft pink. Yeah, he'd keep her for himself. It didn't even matter to him if she was well used. Flannigan probably had her already. He would share with Busby since his friend was clearly interested. "Don't mind sharing my women."

"Think we should ride on out there to see for ourselves if she's willing and warm? We should flip a coin to see who gets her first. What do you say?"

"Sounds like a mighty fine idea to me."

Chapter Two

When Michael stepped through the door to the master chamber, it seemed to Clare he wasn't thinking too clearly. He set her on the bed. As if to study her more closely he moved slightly backward. Pinching the bridge of his nose with his fingers, he squinted at her. At that exact moment, she understood she wasn't going to like his objectives. She acknowledged she'd been stupid. She wasn't a silly twit, as she understood she should have called out to him. Instead, she leapt into the fray against a big man believing she could render his arm useless. This action of hers was clear indication a woman can't order a man to do her bidding. Michael would make sure he pointed out her limitations. She would have to work extra hard so he would forget what she did today. Maybe a winsome smile or the dipping of her lashes would do the trick.

"Stay there!"

He pointed at the bed as if she would leap up then run from the room. She was hurt, damn it. A winsome smile wasn't going to sway him. He would see through any flirtatious attempt.

Where the devil would she go? She decided she would need more than a charming grin to deter him. What to do?

Clare didn't know exactly what he intended. All the way to the bedroom he'd carried her in his arms. His face was a mask of calm control, his anger buried beneath that same serene facade he presented her with. He didn't speak. In his arms, she felt his ragged breaths along with the rapid beating of his heart. She supposed he would want to know why she acted so impulsively. At the time her actions seemed right and true. She didn't know how to explain she sincerely believed she could stop the man. He would tell her of her stupidity. Damn it all she didn't need anyone to venture over that line.

Michael leaned out the door then hollered up to the third story where Old Suzzy lived. "Suzzy, I need you! Clare needs you. She's been hurt. Get down here as fast as you can!"

He turned back to look at her. Beneath his breath he swore. She heard several colorful words she didn't understand; another couple she'd never heard before. One of Link's adopted children came from the bowels of London as the boy used to tell her. He swore proficiently. None of these words had been issued from the boy.

"I'm fine, Michael. It's the girl. She was beaten severely. You have to go see to her. Timmie won't know what to do."

Her back and chest burned from the lashes she received. She pulled in a deep breath of air while her body shook with the agony ripping through her with just the slightest movement. She closed her eyes, hoping if she could ignore the pain, it would go away. It didn't.

On the bed he sat beside her. The mattress dipped. She felt the warmth of his breath as he studied her. "So were you. Timmie will make sure the girl is tended to just as I will tend to you. Mammy Jo is there for her."

It seemed he gentled his voice. His eyes were focused on the wound that slashed across her chest. "Put your hands down so I can see."

She was shaking her head. She didn't want him to see her naked chest, her breasts. This tableau was so embarrassing. Humiliation ripped through her as if a bolt of lightning had hit her. The whip cut through the fabric. "I can't. I don't want you to see me. You..." Her voice trembled.

He paced the room, swearing, cursing while he sat back. For a moment he waited, so very still as he watched her as if thinking, searching for the right words to use. "I need to assess the damage before an infection can set in. I promise...I promise I won't do anything that isn't necessary."

Once again, he gentled his voice. It seemed the calmer he sounded the angrier he was. He didn't appear furious. She understood he was enraged. She hoped he was angrier with Raynard than at her.

"Let Old Suzzy help me. She knows what to do. At least I believe so. I don't...you can't..."

She heard her voice, recognized the pleading tone. When she saw the glimmer of his eyes, she knew she wasted her breath asking. He would never give over the control to Old Suzzy. He was a man who'd made a decision. He would stick with that judgement. In too many ways to count he was just like her brother-in-law.

"No," he said softly as he pried her hands from the front of her bodice.

With her hands now by her hips, he looked. She couldn't read the thoughts behind his eyes. She didn't like the way he stared at her. Those beautiful green eyes of his shimmered before they turned dark.

When she looked down, she saw the swell of her breasts. He saw too. She swallowed the lump in her throat hating the pain sweeping through her, despising the fact he was looking at her breasts. That wasn't right. Where she looked, the wound burned. The wretched pain seared. She felt dizzy, the room beginning to spin.

As she swayed, he spoke softly. "Hold still. I know the lesions hurts. This will all be better soon." He tried to soothe with both the tone of his voice as well as his words.

"What can I do?"

Old Suzzy stood next to Michael waiting for the orders. Her gnarled hands were clasped tight in front of her. Her dark brown eyes showed concern in their depths.

"Bring me a pitcher of warm water and a soft cloth. Also heat up some of the willow bark and make a tea for her. Put some honey in the cup so the brew won't be quite so bitter.

He turned his attention back to her. "This is going to hurt. She will need to rest. Keep the tea brewing."

Tenderly, as if attempting to reassure, he brushed his knuckles across her cheek then down her neck.

Gently, he turned her so he could see her back. She heard the swift inhalation of his breath. He ran his hand across her shoulder then slowly down her spine, stopping where she felt pain. Her back was still covered. She understood she was bleeding. Just as the front of her shirt was torn the back would also be ripped.

"You can't take care of me, Michael. It isn't proper or right. You're a man."

She was weak, the pain raging more with each second. As if it would ease the agony along with the embarrassment she was feeling, she closed her eyes. Nothing helped.

"You noticed." There was no humor in his voice.

"What?"

She wondered what it was she noticed? She tried to think back on her words of only a few minutes ago. She couldn't remember.

At least for a moment, Michael ignored her while he observed. He pushed her hands aside as if he swatted at a fly. The front of her shirt was damp with her blood. She saw the red slowly spreading across the fabric.

"First, I'm going to unfasten your shirt then your chemise. Thank my lucky stars you are not wearing a corset. Though the damn contraption might have provided more protection for you. I don't want this to take any longer than necessary. Just be patient. Try to relax."

Relax?

"You can't take my clothing off, Michael."

Low in the back of her throat, she moaned. Clare didn't want him to see her pain. She didn't want him to see her at all. "I won't let you." Even while she spoke the words, her voice wavered to a thin wail.

"Won't look."

She wanted to believe him. Clare felt the backs of his fingers on her flesh as he began to unfasten the shirt. Warmth slid across her skin. She shivered. The buttons were in the front. She knew then she would have to deal with the embarrassment. He wasn't going to stop no matter her plea.

There were twelve tiny pearl buttons. The thought was inane. She tried to keep her mind off what he was doing. What he was going to do. He would look at her. She would be very nearly naked in front of him. He was a man. No man had ever seen her naked. Unless of course her father had when she was a baby. She didn't think that counted.

"Promise you won't look?"

The words wilted from her lips. Her head pounded. She'd never felt anything so horrible. She remembered when Uncle William whipped and beat Sophie. Her sister almost died that day. Link cared for her. He saw all of her. Sophie was different though.

He grinned. Soft male laughter flowed from his mouth. "Now, what do you think, Clare? Am I a gentleman or not? Of course, I won't look."

"That you're going to look. I've no idea if you are a gentleman."

The first day she met him, she thought him a handsome gentleman. Until now she thought about that characteristic as well as how the word fit him. He'd kissed her, stopped when she asked him to do so.

"Have to see the damage, Clare. Have to look." With his words, he tried to placate her. "Pretend I'm your doctor. This is all clinical nothing more. I'm not a man looking at a woman. I'm a doctor looking at his patient."

"You're not."

"No, nonetheless you can endeavor to pretend. Use your imagination. I suppose you do have an imagination. Do you ever dream?"

"Here it is."

Old Suzzy stood inside the room. She placed the two pitchers of water she brought on the table near the bed. The cloth, she handed to Michael. "I'll go back to the kitchen now. The tea will be ready in about ten minutes. I'll bring it up as soon as the brew darkens."

"Thank you, Suzzy. Before you do that can you bring tweezers? There are some in the drawer next to the knives. I've got to make sure all the fabric is cleaned from the wounds. Don't want any cloth left from her shirt to cause an infection."

Michael nodded concentrating on the task, his brows drawn close. The ribbons holding her chemise in place slipped through the eyelets. Tenderly, he parted the fabric. Dried blood kept the material held fast to her skin. He cursed. "I'm going to hold the damp cloth against you. Can you keep this in place?"

He pressed the fabric against her. He brought her hands upward. She held the cloth, felt the coolness against the heat of the wound. He needed the blood to soak away so he could bare her. His teeth gritted together when he heard her weak protest.

"No, Clare, don't think about what I'm doing. Don't object. You need to be tended to."

He couldn't lay her on her back or her front. One whip mark against her chest slashed across one breast then just beneath the other. It must have happened that way when she raised her arms to try to stop him.

Whip marks lacerated both hands. He would probably worry about those later. For now, he had to soak the fabric so he could remove her clothing.

Old Suzzy set the tweezers on the table then left. By the time the willow bark tea was brewed, he had her clothing off. For now, she sat in the middle of the bed, her arms crossed in front of her while she tried to hide herself from his view. Her attempts were futile at best. When she spread her fingers to cover more of her, cold air caressed her nipples where they peeked out between them. She slouched in an attempt to hide. The action caused the soft white mounds to overflow her tiny hands.

"Your front first, then I'll give you something to cover yourself with. You won't mind if I see your back?"

"It won't be so bad as this. Michael...they hurt, where he whipped me. Why would Raynard do something like this? Why would he whip that precious little girl? Nothing makes a wit of sense."

"I don't have an answer for that." His voice was harsh.

Clare knew he didn't like the fact Raynard whipped the slaves. "You should have taken the whip from him then flayed him alive. He deserved a beating."

From her waist up, she was a shocking shade of crimson. "Can you lean against the headboard if I place a pillow behind you? Let me know if your back hurts too much. You can always lie on your side." He pressed the damp cloth against her back. For several seconds he studied her.

She supposed he would decide if what he did hurt her too much.

What did she know?

"I'll try."

She managed to gasp out as her back pressed against the pillow. She gritted her teeth, ignoring the pain winding through her.

The contact hurt her. She tried not to show the pain to him. She wanted this to be over with sooner than later. No, she wanted it to be over with yesterday.

Once the fabric slipped from her, bared her to his view, he spent agonizing minutes with the tweezers. His brows were drawn tightly together concentrating on his task not her naked body. Clare closed her eyes. If she couldn't see him looking at her, he wouldn't be looking at her. The reasoning was anything except sound.

She knew he tried to keep from touching her. He didn't succeed. The tips of his fingers brushed across a nipple. Finally, he held one of her breasts in his large hand to finish his chore. She shuddered at the contact. The feeling was strangely pleasant.

"I'm sorry," he told her softly. "I would not wish this on anyone."

He finished bandaging her carefully. He sounded so very sincere. "You can open your eyes. Now, shall we see to your back? How is the pain? Ah, there is Old Suzzy with the wondrous brew, the amazing cure all. Drink it all. The tea will ease the pain though not your discomfort. When you are finished with the tea, you will lie on your side."

She drank first, grimacing as the bitter tea slid across her tongue. With his help she turned. He set one of her nightdresses beside her. She pulled the material to her chest covering herself. The damp cloths it seemed did the trick. His long fingers gently slid the fabric over her shoulders then down her back.

"When I am finished here, I will help you with the nightdress."

He proceeded with her back as he did her front. It seemed he anticipated her reply, with his finger to her lips "No, you will not argue."

She did. "I can put my nightgown on myself."

"I suppose that's possible. You can also rip the bandages from your body. If you did, we would have to start from the beginning. Is that what you wish? Now let me help. After I see to your hands I will go away until dinner so you can rest and ruminate about the dangers of attacking a man. The act was not well thought out, Clare. You reacted to a situation without thinking. Your impulsiveness needs to stop now."

His voice didn't change at all. He was calm, soothing. He was right too.

She didn't want to answer him. Telling him he could do whatever he thought right was not something she was eager to say. Her back took longer. She found she closed her eyes, concentrating on more pleasant things such as riding Duster along the riverbank with the wind flowing through her hair.

She breathed easier as she allowed her mind to wander. Ah yes, she thought again, wind swept through her hair. Duster's hooves churned the dark earth along the river. The stallion bolted through large puddles left there by the outgoing tides from the ocean. She laughed when the murky water splayed around his hooves. She would have to see to his cleaning when she returned. A seagull dove into the river to come up with a fish dangling from its beak. The scent of wildflowers filled the air. Sunshine beat down on her face. If Sophie saw her, she would tell her to wear her bonnet. Sophie wasn't here. For herself she didn't care about freckles. Seemed a small enough price to pay for the enjoyment of sunshine beating against her skin.

"I'm done. Now, Clare, we will get you into the nightdress. If you can't do the task yourself, well then, I will help. I've thought and thought, am willing to give you the chance."

The rough voice rumbling behind her brought her out of her musings. Her dream was a nice reflection. She would think on the vision again as soon as he left. "I can dress without help. Will you leave?"

"I would if I thought you could dress yourself without toppling over. Before you can put that nightgown on you must first remove the rest of your clothing. Your shoes and stockings along with your skirt and other underthings are still on your body."

All manly arrogance, he crossed his arms over his chest as he stepped back to wait for her.

She groaned softly. She had not thought at all. When she tried to sit, she found she could not even do that much less dress. The last thing she wanted was to have to admit to him he was right. Her back was still on fire, her head still pounding. The room seemed to spin lazily. Tears slipped down her cheeks.

"Clare, let me help you. I will do this chore as quickly as possible."

She nodded.

"Was that a yes?" he asked softly his voice tender holding the hint of surprise.

She nodded again. His strong hands beneath her arms, he brought her to a sitting position on the bed. He tugged on the gown she held so tightly against her chest. She clung to it embarrassed for him to look at her again.

"You have to let go."

She was sure she heard laughter in his voice. She wanted to hit him. If she did, she knew she would regret the impulsive action. Her fingers loosened as she was resigned to get this over with. In her entire life, she couldn't ever remember being so embarrassed or humiliated.

"Good girl."

Before she could blink the soft white material was over her head and pooling around her. The gown would cover her from head to foot. She closed her eyes. He was at her feet now undoing her slippers, removing them. His fingers were warm as they moved up her legs. Her garters were untied. He held her white stockings with the lace around the top as if they were a prize he won. Her skirt was unfastened. She felt the strangest warmth in parts of her, private parts. When she thought back, remembered those feelings the day he kissed her.

"Lift your hips."

She did so. Her skirt was on top of the pile of her clothing. He worked quickly with little contact. He stepped back, his beautiful long fingers on his hips, a slight seemingly tender smile on his lips.

"Your disrobing is complete. That was very easy now, wasn't it?"

"No, maybe for you."

"It isn't as if you have something other women do not have." He laughed, his eyes crinkling with the motion.

She didn't want to think his laughter was at her expense. She supposed his amusement was about her. She was certain he was no virgin. He'd had women in his bed. A wave of unexpected jealousy ripped through her.

Despite her pain, she felt indignation rise. She pointed at him, thought better of the movement as fire burst across her back. "Don't you laugh at me, Michael Flannigan! I've never shown myself to a man. This is a first for me. I don't like the fact you saw and touched me. You are the only one."

"Next time I see you, you will be more than willing. I promise you that." He smiled at her, his even white teeth showing. "Believe next time you will also see all of me. Would you like that, Clare? Would you like to see me as naked as the day I was born?"

She turned her face, unwilling for him to see her. He might read something into it that wasn't there. Arguing with him was impossible. Instead, she snorted, thinking of her sister and Link. They would always disappear together. She understood when they vanished the act had something to do with sex. She just didn't understand what that was. No, willingly naked with a man? That wouldn't happen anytime soon. The notion was too disconcerting.

He approached her with a cup. She assumed the mug was filled with this willow bark tea he had Old Suzzy brew for her. His features were taut with unease.

"Drink up, this will help you with the pain. This concoction will also help you to sleep."

He stepped back after he gave the cup to her, his arms crossed in front of his broad chest.

"I'm not sleepy." She told him.

"No but you are in pain. In order to heal your body needs rest. I'll check in on you later. Is there anything else I can get for you?"

"No."

She wanted to come up with something smart. She couldn't think. On her side she curled into a little ball. Well, she could try to sleep.

When she opened her eyes, the room was growing dark. The willow bark tea did ease the pain somewhat. From lying on her side, she found her arm was numb. Sitting up, she found the room spun a bit. She needed to relieve herself. As she put her legs over the bed, she hoped Michael would not choose this moment or the next few to make his presence known.

Michael would be angry with her for getting out of bed. What the devil would he expect her to do? No, the deed had to be accomplished, now or never. He told her he would see her at dinnertime. That moment had to be close.

Her legs unsteady, she was able to attempt the feat successfully. She was just sitting on the bed when he opened the door, a dark scowl on his face.

"What are you doing out of bed?"

Well, that was brash as well as to the point. Heat sprinted through her settling on her cheeks. What she was doing was not his business. She supposed though that an intelligent person would guess without making her say the discomforting words.

She looked down at her folded hands in her lap then beyond to her bare toes, hanging over the side of the bed. The bed was so high off the ground her feet didn't reach the floor. Suddenly, she felt so extremely tiny. His booted feet narrowed the distance. Looking at him was not an option she wanted to explore.

"Clare..." His finger was beneath her chin, lifting her face so she didn't have a choice. For a moment, she peered into his smoldering green eyes.

So as not to see him, she closed her eyes. With the heat of utter mortification filling her, ripping through her, she couldn't stand to meet his gaze.

"Open your eyes, Clare." His thumb traveled gently across her chin.

"No."

Suddenly his hand dropped away. She gasped while she waited for his anger to spill forth.

~ * ~

What did he expect when he asked? That she would blurt out that she had to relieve herself? This was one of the reasons he came to see her. It was almost dinner. He wanted to make sure she was comfortable. He acted the ass that she called him earlier. He needed to change the subject before she grew any redder with the heat of her embarrassment.

"How are you feeling? Do you need help getting into bed?"

He stepped back a few paces, watching her. Her face no longer resembled a beet. Now she was pale, ghost like. He didn't like the way she looked as if she would swoon any second.

"I can get into bed."

Slowly she slid her legs around before covering herself.

"Good. The pain, is it still bad? I've brought more tea."

He handed the cup to her then waited for her to drink.

"The stuff tastes awful."

"The pain?"

He was thinking now that he might have to pry all the answers he wanted from her soft lips.

"Bearable. Michael...?"

"Yes."

She was going to ask him something. He wondered just what that might be.

"Where are you going to sleep tonight?"

Michael tried to keep his grin from spreading across his face. "In my bed. Where do you think?" She paled even more if that was possible. He didn't want her to feel that way about the prospect of sharing his bed. Soon, by choice, she would sleep with him every night. He would have to ease her into that.

Clare turned her face away from him. If she wasn't going to be perfectly clear with him, he had no intention of telling her he meant to take her to the adjoining room. It was never his objective to ruin her reputation farther. He wished she would go back to Leslie Hall. In her condition that was impossible.

While she slept, he visited the Deer Head Ale house. He found an empty chair in a dark corner. Rumors were quite abundant about her as the men reminisced about her sister, Sophie. He didn't appreciate the fact she was equated with her sister even though Sophie was innocent. He wanted to yell at everyone she was an untried maid.

By the talk he overheard, he discovered that Raynard visited earlier bemoaning his fate as well as the method with which he'd been fired. The man told everyone they were sleeping together in sin. Raynard explained that he would see her tomorrow night. They'd made an assignation at the notorious cottage. She would spread her legs for him as well as take on other lovers. One man just wasn't enough for her.

Michael's gut curdled. Again, he wished there was some way to make her understand she needed to move back to Leslie Hall. There was only one solution to this problem that he could see.

She wouldn't agree.

He could try.

She was too damn stubborn.

He hated debating with himself. Michael decided perhaps a bit more honesty between them would be prudent. "Your question should have been where are you going to sleep tonight?"

"Oh...where am I going to sleep tonight?"

Wide eyed with what appeared to be apprehension, Clare seemed to gain some color as she began to realize they weren't going to share a bed.

"In your bed. I've a few things planned beforehand. Old Suzzy will let me know when dinner is ready. I've a bottle of wine. We can sit on the porch while we eat. There are a few issues we need to discuss before either of us retires for the evening. You're moving in here has created some disturbing scenarios."

"Like what?"

"Ah, here is Suzzy now. I'll retrieve the tray. Wait here. When I return with our meal, I'll help you to the porch. The weather is cool this evening, quite pleasant. You will feel a soft breeze from the river. Of course, when you are better in a week or so we can eat at the cottage."

Michael tossed that last bit out to see how she would react. The small house was romantic. The porch swing was nice. He wondered if she had any idea what her sister was reported to do at that place. If his math was correct, she was only thirteen at the time.

"May I go to my room?" Suzzy asked, a huge smile on her face as she beamed at them.

"Of course, I've got everything I need. I wish for some privacy with Clare."

Oh, yes, he wished for a great deal of privacy with her. Tonight, he wasn't going to be able to act on his feelings.

With different thoughts gnawing on his mind, he set the two plates of food on the tray along with the wine. When they started to talk, he didn't know what issue he wanted to begin with. Perhaps they should start with the whipping. He checked on the girl, Juney. She would be fine. Clare interrupted the whipping before Raynard could inflict too much damage. Unfortunately, it seemed the slaves were used to Raynard's whip. He should have known, should have paid closer attention to what

Raynard did. He was a careless fool.

To his surprise, when he reached the master chamber, Clare was sitting on the porch. She had even retrieved a robe from her room. Not one inch of her was left uncovered. For the evening, she donned her battle armor. Perhaps he should begin there. He would have to look at her wounds in the morning. He would see her naked again. For Michael seeing her gorgeous body wasn't an unpleasant thought. For Clare, well Clare wasn't used to men. Unable to help his feelings, a rush of pleasure at that thought rushed through him.

He needed to ask her to marry him until she said yes. Perhaps he would ask her once a day. She would believe he wanted her for Mayfair Hall along with the land. He did. Nevertheless, that wasn't the only reason. She was beautiful. In the short time he'd known her, he found he liked her better than any other woman he'd known. Now that he looked at her, saw the size and felt the texture of her breasts, he knew she would not be difficult to bed. Her curves were quite pleasant.

When he saw she was not in bed, he curbed the anger. His reason for keeping her there until he returned was selfish. He wanted to carry her to the porch. If he did so, the soft curves of her breasts would be pushed against his chest.

"You didn't stay in bed." Michael set the tray on the table. He ate out here often on the warmer nights. The porch looked toward the river. Below the veranda well-manicured gardens stretched for a few hundred feet. The scent of roses filled the air until he uncovered the plates of food.

"I'm not an invalid. I can walk from one room to the other," she spoke softly.

When she looked up, she smiled at him.

His heart melted. He liked her smile along with the two dimples he intended to kiss as soon as she was amenable. Her eyes sparkled. He thought perhaps she was going to laugh.

"Do not think to do too much too soon. While the lash marks didn't need stitches, you could open the wounds. If that happened, well then, I would have to repeat today's tender ministrations." He paused thinking about Clare along with the activities she loved. "Don't even think of riding." He presented her with his harshest voice.

She paled. A comment was not forthcoming as she slowly turned to face the river.

He couldn't believe he mirrored his words to her thoughts. "The devil, you were thinking that very thing. I will tell Timmie your intentions. After I do, he won't let you go off to hurt yourself."

He rubbed his hands along the back of his neck before rolling his shoulders with the hope of easing the sudden tension coupled with fear that she might do something utterly and completely foolish. She was impulsive. He understood that fact about her. Nonetheless, he would have to put a damper on her expectations.

"You would forbid me to ride?"

Her back stiffened perceptibly. Before his eyes, she grimaced with the pain of her actions. Still, she proceeded. "You've no right."

Michael was speechless for a moment. He thought she would be bright enough to behave. She couldn't possibly be so stupid she would think to do something so reckless.

"You're not a silly twit of a woman." He sat down beside her. "If you think about what has happened to you, you will agree with me. Perhaps in a week or so if all has healed nicely you can ride."

He saw her stiffen, watched as her defiant chin lifted a notch. At least he told her she wasn't a twit even though that was how she was acting at the moment. She was trying too hard to be independent, to run her life. While he waited for her to mull over his words as well as think about her body, he poured two generous glasses of wine hoping the alcohol would also ease her pain.

"You're right. I'm not a silly twit. However, I will know when I feel well enough to ride. Don't you think?"

In disbelief, he snorted. "You think riding will be tomorrow?" He arched a brow high wishing he could shake her until she found a modicum of sense.

"The pain is minimal."

She sipped her wine, as did he.

His was sweet and delicious. She looked as if she wanted to toss the contents in his face.

Clare needed to understand that the pain would come roaring back as soon as the effects of the medicinal brew wore off. He would make sure she understood. "It's the tea that makes you feel strong enough to ride. As soon as the medicine begins to dissipate in your system you will feel the pain again." He pointed his fork at her plate. "The fresh Atlantic salmon is delicious. Try the food. The amazing taste will take your mind off riding Duster on the morrow."

She forked a bite then chewed slowly. Her eyes very nearly crossing before she spoke again. "You will not dictate to me." Waving her fork in the air she continued, "I'm very nearly twenty-one. I've a mind of my own. If I want to ride, that is what I'll do."

We will see. "Three months." He chewed the boiled potatoes drenched in sweet butter as he savored the moment. "Three months until you come of age. You won't be considered an adult until then. Yes, what does that have to do with the pain?"

For a few seconds, she chased the peas around on her plate. She set her fork down. A second later she looked up, her eyes glistening, "Duster has to be exercised. There is a race in two weeks. He needs to be in top condition. Who will ride him?"

He grunted as he watched her renew her attempts to capture the runaway peas. When he turned his attention back to her face, "Timmie will exercise the stallion as well as ride him in the race. He will also ride Gypsy. They are entered in different races."

The devil, this was not a topic he planned on having with her tonight. She understood she wouldn't race. Indeed, she acknowledged the fact to him earlier in the day. He cleared his throat then set his fork on the table. He folded his arms neatly across his chest while he leaned against the back of the chair. "I was going to talk to you about your mad dash to help the girl. However, at this point I doubt if you would listen. You will continue to falter in your decision-making. I've no doubts about that. You are in need of a strong hand to help guide your choices."

"You bastard! What do you know of anything? I would do the same again. Raynard was beating her. He had no right to do so," suddenly, she spoke softly seeming more interested in her plate than him. "He would have continued until she fainted or died. I would not have a dead person on my conscious because I failed to do anything to help the girl."

"I understand that about you. There are other things though we need to discuss. Tomorrow morning, I will take another look at the wounds. You will follow my instructions."

She gasped her eyes wide, startled. "No!"

He meant to continue without heeding her declaration. "If you are lucky, there will be no infection. In that case, I won't have to look for another day. Hopefully, the flesh will heal without leaving a scar. The paste Suzzy made up for you should do the trick. I don't know what herbs she put into the mixture. However, Suzzy seemed to think if you continue to put the concoction on the wounds the medicinal properties would completely heal you. Of course, I will have to smear the mixture on your back since you cannot reach. You can do your front unless you wish me to do so."

"I don't want you to look at me!"

Her hands were winding in and out of the peach-colored robe she wore. Her soft hair curled provocatively down her back. "I can reach my back."

"Mayhap you are a silly twit after all if you actually believe that nonsense." He baited her.

What on earth could she possibly be thinking? Maybe she didn't care if her back was scarred.

Silence stretched between them. Michael wanted Clare to think about what he told her. He also wanted her to agree that he would have to look at her back because it was simply stupidity that caused her words to tumble from her sweetly pink lips, lips he needed to kiss. Even with a mirror she would not be able to do justice to the wounds. She could not possibly put the cream where it needed to go or massage it into the skin.

"I concede. You may examine my back. Nonetheless, you will not look at my breasts again."

In time he would look his fill. Her flesh was so white and soft. How could he ever resist? "See was that so hard? We might even meet half way before this is finished. I will allow that as long as there is no infection on your back. Agreed?"

This time he did permit his smile to slowly creep onto his face. She had a beautiful back. The surface would be more beautiful when she healed. She had two dimples at the base of her spine. Some day he meant to kiss her there.

"You will not give over on this?"

"No."

He topped off her wine knowing the wine would also ease the burning somewhat. The searing pain would begin again before she retired for the night. The willow bark tea would be more potent by that time. The pot had been brewing since this afternoon. Hopefully, she would sleep through until morning.

She lifted her chin a bit. "Is there more you wish to talk about? I'm feeling tired. Discussing things with you takes its toll on my stamina."

"You won't like what I have to tell you. The words will not be pleasant. However, yes, there is another topic that needs to be considered. We will have to figure out a means to stop the gossip before the rumors concerning you continue."

She downed the wine, emptying her glass. He refilled the delicate crystal thinking she might need the rest of the bottle. Maybe he should retrieve a second. He might need more also.

"Gossip? There is gossip? What about? You should get on with the telling then. I can handle most anything."

She arranged the folds of her dressing gown. Her enticing bare toes peeked out beneath the soft fabric. He thought he would enjoy kissing her toes as well as her dimples. They were delicate tiny things.

"I rode into the village this afternoon while you were sleeping. Went to the alehouse. This one in particular is notorious for spreading gossip. The men don't seem to have anything better to do than to talk about things that are none of their business. Seems to me they are more like old biddies than any woman."

He waited for a response. None was forthcoming. He tugged in a deep breath of air hoping he could relate what was said. Once more, he thought the men were like old ladies who also had nothing better to do. The men spoke of their conquests or the women they wanted. Clare was the woman they wanted now. Seemed to think she would let them have their way with her.

"The rumor that was bandied about...well, the men are saying that you are following in your sister's footsteps...where men are concerned." He wasn't certain what she knew about Sophie. Link would have wanted to keep her from learning about those trying events. "Because you are living here at Mayfair Hall unchaperoned, the men are betting as to who gets to be your second lover."

"Second?" she questioned sounding puzzled, her beautiful eyes widening with questions. Her head cocked to one side. "I don't understand. You are not making sense."

Well, that pretty much told him she didn't know anything about what good old Uncle William put Sophie through. "They are saying that I am your first lover, at least that is what the men believe. Gossip has created the fact I've been sleeping with you. They also think I would be willing to share your charms for a fee."

"You would sell me?" Her fists tightened while her eyes darkened with the anger she seemed to be feeling.

That was interesting. She didn't take issue with the part about him being her lover. "I can assure you I never share my women," he spoke blandly continuing his scrutiny.

He saw the swift rise of color on her cheeks. The rose blush didn't come from the excess of wine. The truth would come out now that she caught onto everything he said.

"You are not my lover."

Her indignation spilled over. She stood too swiftly, her hands on the table to support the abrupt move. She sat down just as quickly with a muffled groan.

The pain would return soon. The time had almost arrived for her to take that second cup of tea. First, he wanted to finish the discussion. "You know that as do I. Nonetheless, it is not what the good people living in the village as well as those in the neighboring plantations believe."

Her stubborn little chin tilted defiantly. "I'm not moving to Leslie Hall. You can't make me do that. I don't care a wit about the gossip."

If he wanted to assert himself, he could pick her up then carry her there. If he did that, she would undoubtedly come back. Besides he was beginning to like having her close. "Will you marry me?" This was the first offer. He understood before she finally agreed there would be many more.

He hoped not too many. Sometimes his patience wore thin.

Her shocked expression didn't surprise him. As if in a stupor her eyes glazed for a moment, she leaned forward. "What did you say?"

He hooted, didn't bother to give credence to her question. "You know what I asked you."

"Ask me again." She wiped her hands on the robe. Picked up her glass of wine then drank deeply.

"Answer me, Clare. I'm going to keep asking until I hear the right word. There is only one right word. If you answer incorrectly, I'll ask again."

"Why? Why would you want to marry me? You don't love me." She tossed that out as if the words were a true fact.

At the moment, the phrase was true. He didn't love her. Nevertheless, he was fond of her. He liked the way she sat a horse. Her breasts with the tiny coral buds could slake a man's lust. Although, those weren't necessarily reasons to wed.

Michael sat back, once more crossing his arms in front of him. "You love me. That is enough for now."

He didn't know if what he just said was true though he had a sneaking suspicion she was infatuated with him. He wasn't going to ask her again tonight. If she wanted to hedge around with stupid questions, so be it. Mayfair Hall was meant to be his. William Brinkmeyer stole the plantation from his father, just as Brinkmeyer increased his holdings by stealing from surrounding estates. The only one he couldn't get a hold of was Leslie Hall. No, Link Stewart outsmarted him.

"Was there anything else you wished to discuss?" She gazed at him over the rim of her glass, her eyes narrowed as if she loathed him. He knew that wasn't true. He understood women. Understood that first kiss to be a precursor of what might follow if he pursued physical intimacy with her. He was willing to wait.

"Mayhap I should take a look at your back." He grinned, watching her anger rise. As he held up his hands, "I'm joking. In the morning though."

"I'm riding."

That statement didn't need an answer. He would make certain Timmie would be exercising Duster in the morning as he would ride Gypsy. Michael assumed she wouldn't decide to ride one of the mares. They were both swollen, nearing the end of their time.

"We shall see."

Clare tossed her spoon at him. Hooting, he ducked. She pulled her back. He saw the pain, raw and bold seep into her beautiful eyes. To no avail, she tried to hide the wrenching agony from him. She wasn't able to hold back the soft moan.

"Drink the rest of your wine. You'll feel better."

It surprised him when she did so. He rose, poured her a cup of the cold willow bark tea. "Would you like me to heat the brew?"

"I don't want to drink that. The stuff is awful."

Once again, she tilted that defiant little chin of hers upward as if she meant to defy him.

So be it. Drinking the painkiller was ultimately up to her. He would never force her. However, if she didn't drink, within the hour she would regret telling him no. He held the cup out to her, waiting as he watched. Slowly, she lifted her hand accepting the tea.

"Drink all the liquid. As you well know, the tea along with the wine will help you sleep through the night. They will also ease the pain. Brandy might do a better job than the wine. Would you like Brandy?"

The heavy breath of air she let out was a forerunner to her acceptance. "I know," she said softly as she finally took the cup from his outstretched hand. "Do you think the tea won't be as bad if I drink it all in one gulp."

He held his laughter behind his teeth feeling immense sympathy for her. "It will be just as bad. Besides, I doubt if you can take that entire cup without stopping to breathe." Valiantly, Clare did the best she could.

He held out his hand to her. She accepted as he helped her stand. "Can you walk to your room?"

She sucked in a gulp of air, her hand on her belly. "I don't feel so well." She leaned into him.

He supported her for a moment then swept her into his arms, striding purposefully to her room. She drank the tea too damn fast. He wondered if he'd have to run for the basin when she tossed up all the liquid. She would have to relieve herself. Asking him to help would go beyond anything she could manage. He decided to take this matter into his own hands. He would give her stomach a chance to recover first.

Michael ran his hand very lightly along her back, saying soothing words. At least he hoped they would calm. Tonight, before he put her on the bed, he meant to kiss her. That would have to wait for a better time. He set her down on the edge of the bed.

"Do you need anything? Any help?" Perhaps she would ask him to help her to the bathroom.

Shaking her head, she looked to his room. The bathroom was there, beyond the door. She should have said something while they were seated on the porch. He decided he wasn't going to wait for her to ask simply because he understood she wouldn't mention her discomfort. Once again, he settled her in his arms. Silently cursing her shyness, he strode through the adjoining door. Without saying a word to her, he set her down in the bathroom then closed the door.

If she needed to relieve herself in the middle of the night, she would have to walk through his room. To wait for her he sat down in the chair near the fireplace. When she opened the door, her face was crimson. He was beginning to wonder if she'd ever have natural color around him. Once more, he carried her to her room.

"You will not ride Duster in the morning."

She nodded as if she understood that she wouldn't be able to ride. "Go away." Her voice was so soft and quiet he could barely here her.

He bent over and kissed her forehead then her cheek. This wasn't the kiss he wanted from her. Nevertheless, for now the brief peck on her cheek would have to do.

~ * ~

Two weeks passed rather quickly. It was the middle of July and the weather was despicably hot. They were at the races. Clare was flushed from the heat as well as excited about the upcoming competition. She could hardly keep her feet on the ground as she jumped up and down. The win would give them more credibility. Timmie was about to ride Duster in his first race. She crossed her fingers with a quick silent prayer directed upward. She had so much at stake. The lad looked splendid sitting atop the big bay horse, his riding crop in hand. This was a two-mile race. Gypsy would run later in the half-mile. Duster possessed heart; he would give the race his all.

Timmie was bent over, whispering to the stallion that nodded his head as if he understood every word. Timmie always charmed the horse, whispering sweet nothings into their ears.

Clare stood beside Michael clutching his arm, her fingers squeezing. He felt her breasts push against his chest. As of today, she had not answered either yes or no when he asked her to marry him. He hoped he was wearing her down. Wearing her down wasn't likely to happen anytime soon. She was a stubborn little thing.

Michael instructed Timmie to be aggressive. The jockeys would sometimes run their horse into another or hit an opponent with the riding crop they carried. Michael wanted to race. He loved the exhilaration of the moment. He could be as mean as any of the other riders. He was just too damn big his weight slowed his mount down.

No breeze flowed from the river to cool the blazing temperature. It seemed that any wind was from inland to the sea. Michael wiped the sweat off his forehead with the back of his sleeve. Clare's damp gown molded delicately to all her sweet curves he'd come to adore. Lord those days while he tended to the lashes she received were ever-present in his man's brain.

"Do you think Duster will win?" Clare asked as she stood on the tips of her toes to see over the crowds. "I can't see anything. Think we can move closer?" she asked as she jumped then craned her neck twisting for better angles.

"I do believe so. Suppose if you wish to watch, we'll have to find a better viewing place."

Michael took her arm guiding her gently to the front through the throngs gathered to watch the race. They both placed wagers on the horses. "If either one or both wins, the fact will be good for your business," he said enjoying the bright smile she flashed his way. "More of the owners will hire Duster to cover their mares. His bloodline is impeccable after all."

"The race is about to start."

He watched her breasts heave excitedly. His attention fixed more on Clare than the race. Nonetheless, Duster performed well, taking the lead from the beginning. He outdistanced the other six horses, keeping ahead at least a nose until the final twenty yards. One of the jockeys hit at another's horse pushing the rider and the horse to stumble. In the end, Duster won and Gypsy took third place.

The day had been agreeable. Michael arranged a private dinner at the cottage after they returned from the races. He brought wine as well as an assortment of foods that would tempt any palate. Clare decided to walk through the garden to the cottage while he finished seeing to the horses. He would join her there.

Her wounds were healing nicely. No infection had set in. The cream Old Suzzy gave her seemed to work on the scars. The day after the incident, Clare didn't get out of bed except to see to her needs. A week passed before she walked to the stables to ride. Timmie had to help her mount, Duster. She was so weak, she lasted ten minutes before she turned around to go home. Michael wanted her strong and feisty once again.

On his way to the cottage, he whistled, pleased with the day's events. They made money. The horses performed well. Two weeks had passed since his last proposal. He meant to ask again tonight. When he reached the front porch, Clare was asleep on the porch swing, her head nestled in the palm of one hand. This would be the perfect opportunity to check her injuries one last time.

He crouched down in front of the swing. She was breathing evenly, her breasts rising and falling gently. Her hair hung loosely around her shoulders. Her gown tied in front and was gathered around her shoulders. He tugged at the bow. Easily, the ribbon was undone. Lavender, he decided, must be her favorite color. He grinned knowing he could ease the fabric down without her waking. She appeared deeply asleep. Slowly, he pressed the fabric to her waist then undid the ribbons on her chemise. Her breasts were beautiful milky white globes. He recalled how soft they were. He felt a moment of guilt before he reminded himself, he was simply checking on her wounds, nothing more.

Well hell, he knew better than that bit of ludicrous mutterings in his befuddled brain. He should call this what it was. In retrospect, he wasn't sure himself what prompted him other than lust. He stared at her. There was no infection just as he knew there would be none. He cupped one breast in his hand weighing the soft mound, slowly ran his thumb across her nipple while he watched the tip harden with expectation.

Beneath his hand she stirred. When her eyes opened, they were slightly dazed with sleep. She was trying to figure out what was happening. As yet she wasn't fully awake. He kissed her softly, touching his lips to either side of her mouth. More than a month passed since he kissed her last. It had been way too long.

With his teeth he tugged gently on her lower lip. Dazed, she moaned slightly. He ran his tongue along the softness of her mouth before he delved deeper. "Open for me. I want to taste you," he murmured as to his surprise she took his advice.

Inside, she was moist and warm. Her body pressed upward against his as if seeking his touch.

His questing fingers continued to knead her breast, caressing the nipple while she arched against him. When his teeth tugged on her earlobe, she moaned softly in the back of her throat. Even her ear was tiny and delicate. His lips trailed down her neck then across her collarbone. He nipped the white flesh of her shoulder before soothing the mark with his tongue. His kisses grew hotter and hotter while she responded in kind, coiling then arching her sweet virgin body against him. Beneath him she curled. Small mews of pleasure echoed through her.

Michael knew the moment she woke completely. He allowed a small amount of air to whisper from his lungs.

Clare stiffened with a following gasp. "Michael!"

"Will you marry me?"

She scooted away from him. Reluctantly, he drew her chemise together. She was flashing him looks that he was yet to decipher. After that he settled her gown around her shoulders tying the ribbon. He ran his thumb along her kiss-swollen lips. Not as much as he would like, nonetheless she looked thoroughly kissed.

"You..."

"I just checked you for the last time. Everything is fine. No scars to speak of. Suzzy's cream is phenomenal."

He wanted to hoot at her look of chagrin.

"Of course I'm fine. I've been fine for well over a week now."

She pushed at his hands that were lingering on her shoulders. "You shouldn't have done that. Looked at me. Touched me."

He ignored her protest. "Dinner awaits us. Are you as famished as I am?" He rose from his kneeling position extending his hand to help her to her feet. "Are you hungry? He asked again. "I sent Big Tom to Leslie Hall for wine. Another shipment arrived from Bordeaux two days ago. Someone has to drink the expensive wine. Don't you think?"

"Yes, except for breakfast, we haven't eaten all day. I'm famished."

It didn't appear she was going to say anything about his unveiling of her bosom or the kisses. Perhaps that was for the best. He would have to give her time to adjust to his plans. After all, she must guess his intentions.

They stepped into the main room.

Big Tom poured the wine. After that he left them alone

During the meal, silence stretched between them. He gazed at her while he remembered how she felt and tasted, all that soft white flesh. She would stare at him then return her attention to her plate. He enjoyed watching her eat and drink, also liked watching her sleep. The thought of running his finger across her eyebrows crossed his mind. He wanted to enjoy all of her until he cocked up his toes. He wondered when she would bring up the kiss or the unveiling of her breasts.

She set her fork down before gazing at him her eyes a bit starry. Clare tempted him mightily. She ran her saucy pink tongue along her bottom lip unknowing what the sight did to him. She was impertinent as well as sassy coupled with a whole lot of spice, all that he loved in a woman. She would never be boring.

It seemed she searched for the words. "I liked it when you kissed me. You tasted all hot and...sweet."

He didn't expect her to admit to enjoying his kiss. His manhood swelled. "Did you enjoy my hand on your breast. Your nipple hardened. Do you think it would be nice if I kissed you there?"

For a moment her eyes crossed. She hesitated before answering. "Maybe...maybe I'd like that."

Begrudgingly, it seemed she admitted that fact.

"Clare, you in there?" A man called from the exterior of the house. "Come outside so you can play with us too. Your sister shared her favors. I'm sure you would do the same."

She stiffened, her eyes taking on a look of pure terror. "Who is that? Make him go away."

Michael cursed, felt the shuddering of her slender body against his. He didn't believe these men would possess the audacity to invade her privacy, a confrontation in town perhaps, never this.

"Sounds like Biff Gideon. He is one of the men I told you about who was wagering about you. Thought I was your lover. If he sees you like this, your appearance will solidify the rumors. Stay here, I'll send them on their way."

Her trembling hand rested on his arm. "What if they don't go away? What we do is none of their business or anyone else's."

"I will make sure they understand that you are not interested in them. I'm certain his buddy Busby Turnpin is with him. They are cowards. Nonetheless, they gain courage when they are together. While I'm around they won't do anything. You cannot be alone." He grasped her by her shoulders. "Don't go out there! Will you heed me in this advice?"

Not waiting for an answer, he strode outside, his fists clasped tightly. More than anything he wanted to shove his fist into Biff's jaw. He sucked in a hard breath of air; furious his plans for this evening took a decided turn downward. Perhaps with a bit more wine, he could retrieve the ambiance. He doubted that would happen.

"Best the two of you get on your way. Clare isn't interested in either of you." He slashed his hand through the air while he scowled at them. "In any case, her wishes don't matter. I don't share what is mine. Clare is mine. Best you find another woman to dally with one who might want your attentions."

"We'll pay you for her. Got a dollar here just for you so we can see her sweetest charms. Think those breasts of hers are as lily white as what she shows us in her low-cut gowns?"

Biff's words were slurring. Busby appeared nearly ready to fall from his mount.

A dollar, for Christ sakes, she was worth far more than a dollar. A whore in town cost more than that. "Not interested. Get out of here!" He stepped from the porch to put emphasis on his command. "Do I need to get my rifle?"

Biff backed up his horse, his hands held out in front of him. "You don't need to get mean about this. Never hurts to ask. Well, when you do get tired of the little woman, your fancy piece, you can send her our way. We'll entertain her, keep her satisfied for a real long time."

When he felt her small fingers close around his arm, he cursed. "Do you never listen? You should have stayed inside."

"They are talking about me as if I'm for sale." She sounded equal parts terrified as well as angry. Beside him, she stiffened. "I'm certainly worth more than one dollar."

Chapter Three

Michael took her by the arms then set her inside. "You should not be out here," he mumbled as he watched the men ride away. "By showing yourself, you cemented all their thoughts. Your hair is disheveled as is your gown. Nothing is where it should be."

She wanted to kick him. "How?"

He held her close. His hands settled on her waist. Slowly, he pulled her close so close she felt the hard ridge of his manhood against her. Knew in that instant he wanted her. The fact didn't answer her question.

One hand cupped her cheek. Tenderly, he ran his thumb across her bottom lip. Her breath caught in the back of her throat as she tried to breathe, the sensations so extremely potent she could barely inhale.

"How do I know? I can see your lips swollen from the few kisses we shared. If I can see, so could Biff and Busby. They will want you more now that they understand we've been together. Truly, you should learn to listen to my sage advice."

"You still make no sense, Mr. Flannigan. We haven't been together. You kissed me, that is all. Even I understand that is not the same as making love." Though she thought she would truly like to find out the difference.

He would if she asked him.

"Ah, my little pigeon, what do know about making love?"

He trailed his hand down her neck then back up to cup her chin in his large hand.

Inadvertently, she touched his calloused thumb with the tip of her tongue. She sipped in air. The caress was not enough. Her heart thundered. "I..."

"You told me you liked my kisses. Should we try another kiss?

Perhaps I should touch your breasts one more time since you didn't seem to know if you liked that novel sensation. What do you think? I could run my hand up your leg all the way to your female mound. Would you say yes, or no?"

Clare had no relevant thoughts in her head that now seemed filled with musty cobwebs. Once inside, he bade her sit on the fur rug by the fireplace. It was too hot for a fire. He poured more wine then set the glasses on the hearth. He opened the big front doors that would let in the breeze from the river. After that he opened the opposite windows.

The wind felt delightful on her hot skin flushed from her humiliation she felt from this encounter with Biff and Busby as well as his kisses. She touched her cheeks with her fingertips. He clasped her hands in his. He moved fluidly when he walked. His hips narrow, his legs long and lean. Clare loved looking at him. Thoughts of seeing him naked brought fierce heat to her cheeks.

"Do you have an answer or should I experiment with what you like as well as don't.? You did tell me you like the way my mouth felt framing yours."

Gently, he touched each side of her lips with his.

Sheepishly, she grinned feeling as if he misrepresented what she told him pulling back a smidgen. "I said I liked your kiss. That was all."

Studying her, he drank long and deep before setting the glass back where it belonged. "Shall we try my version of that kiss you liked? Would you like that, Clare?"

"I think maybe, yes."

Clare caught her bottom lip with her teeth while his hands slipped around her neck. Innocently, she pressed against him, her soft length molding perfectly to his body. Tenderly, his thumb brushed her cheek. She did like the feel of his hands upon her, his mouth as well. She should tell him no. Link would not be pleased to find them so, when her brother-in-law thought she was living somewhere else.

Naively, she opened for him without his asking, as she wanted the sensation of his tongue moving inside her. He kissed her again and again, hard and so very deep. With his lips, teeth, and tongue, he created dizzying sensations. Lightly, he tantalized her with nips and tugs with his teeth. His teeth grazed her shoulder then bit. She gasped startled when she felt the ties of her clothing slipping through eyelets.

It was happening again. He found so many delightful ways to give her that melting sensation. She was too cautious of Michael's warm muscled length next to hers to pay any attention to the crackling fire or the bear skin rug in front of the hearth. Her fingers found the buttons on his shirt. When the fabric was open, she ran her hands across his lean hard chest. Where she was soft with curves, he was hard and sculpted.

Once again, he was gazing at her breasts, the tips hardening as if he willed that to happen. She liked the way he made her feel all warm and swelled, on fire with liquid heat. This time when he gazed at her she felt different. When he tended to her injuries, he looked at her with apparent disinterest. His gaze at this moment was anything but impartial. His eyes were a deep dark green startling in the rapid change of color as they flowed over her. He stared at her, let his gaze drift to her waist then casually back to her breasts.

"They are not overly large nonetheless they are nice. The shape and texture, well, I find those two characteristics without flaw. When I draw them deep into my mouth, I will relish their taste immensely."

Clare gulped air. She wanted him to keep touching her even though she understood his doing so was wrong. She wanted to look at him without a stitch of clothing. She'd never seen a naked man. Neither Sophie nor Link told her anything that would help her make this mad decision. All she understood was that she wanted him needed him desperately.

Unable to come to terms with her actions yet needing to touch him, she placed her hand on his arm. "Michael."

"Hmmm..." His teeth grazed the tip of her breast then bit gently.

She squirmed against him, gasped. Her breath caught in the deep dark recesses of her throat while her fingers wound into his hair, tugging him closer. She felt things she never felt before. "You shouldn't."

"Shouldn't what? Just relax, feel me while I feel you. It's right to do this." He turned his attention to her other breast. His roving hand slipped lower, touched her ankle then her calf.

"Do that, Michael. Touch me in places. I don't want you to stop.

I know you should. We are not lovers. We aren't married. This shouldn't be happening."

His hand stopped on her upper thigh. Slowly, he withdrew, tenderly sliding down the length of her leg. "No, you are right. We shouldn't get this out of sequence. I want to be your lover as well as your husband. What do you want, Clare?"

"You..."

"Will you marry me?"

"Michael."

"All you need do is say yes. One word then I'll give you pleasure. Once you understand a woman's pleasure you won't want to ever be out of my bed."

She hit him on the shoulder. "You are arrogant."

"Perhaps I will give you pleasure even if you don't say yes. Not tonight though, tonight you need to come to terms with everything we do together that you like. I can show you more if you ask nicely."

She understood she shouldn't allow him liberties. Her body trembled when he caressed her. He was skilled. She would give him that.

Michael slipped his arm around her. He pulled her so her head fit in the hollow of his shoulder. His body was warm and hard. She liked the way his arm around her gave her protection. Safety in his arms was something she needed to feel. Why, she wasn't certain. Perhaps it had something to do with her parents. At that thought moisture filled her eyes. She pushed the unwanted sensations away yet she couldn't shake the unwelcome thoughts.

"My parents died when I was thirteen," she murmured unsure why she was telling him this. He couldn't possibly be interested in her sob story. "I barely remember them."

"Seven years ago. It must have been dreadful growing up without a mother," He was soothing her, running his calloused finger up then down her arm. She felt comforted by his attention.

"Sophie tried in every way she knew how to be a mother to me. At the time, she was only seventeen. I think she tried to protect me from Uncle William. She was terrified he would do to me what he was doing to her. At her expense, she protected me from his evil."

"Brinkmeyer is or was a horrible man. I've heard some of the things he did to your sister." He paused seeming to think. "Do you want to talk more?"

Idly, he continued his exploration running a fingertip along her shoulder, coaxing her to ask for more of his gentle persuasion.

Earlier he pulled her chemise as well as the bodice of her gown back together. The thought was odd though. When he was caressing her and kissing her, she didn't feel one moment of embarrassment. It wasn't at all like the time he played at being her physician. Of course, she knew he wasn't. At that time her embarrassment swamped all other feelings. Now...now she didn't understand her behavior.

All she felt this afternoon was heat and a strange need for more of his kisses. She didn't understand what that entailed even while she did understand he should stop. Clare didn't believe she could ever tell him no.

"Before Link married Sophie then set both of us on a ship to London, uncle William beat her nearly to death. He used his fists on her. When that didn't satisfy him, he lashed her until her back as well as the backs of her legs were bloody. What transpired to her was nothing like what happened to me two weeks ago. She nearly died. Even without your tender care I would have been fine.

"I was deathly afraid Sophie wouldn't live. Link protected her. He married her so William couldn't get to her. I think he loved her even then. Now you are protecting me from those horrible men."

Love was what she wished for, a love just like Sophie's and Link's.

"Was this the cottage where she brought the men?" He held up a hand when she pushed away from him to refute his statement. "I know they came here. I also understand they were drugged. Brinkmeyer was blackmailing the men to get his hands on their land. As with my father, he found a way to gain this plantation. They are all weak men."

"Yes, he made her meet the men. She didn't want to. Sophie had to paint her face as if she was a harlot because she always had bruises on her face." She was ranting, babbling on and on, she knew it. He must realize how hard this was for her. "Sophie never had sex with the men.

Always, another woman, one of the slaves who came to the men had sex with them. Until Link was brought here, no one realized Sophie wasn't the woman beneath them."

"I do understand Brinkmeyer's motives. He wanted more land, always more land. His greed was overwhelming. Brinkmeyer stole this plantation from my father, cheating him to do so. My father was weak though as the others were. He gambled then lost. The deed was as much his fault as it was Brinkmeyer's. I never forgave my father or your uncle. Never will."

"So, you want me so you can have what you always believed should be yours."

Clare didn't like the thought that she wasn't good enough for him to want her for herself. Wasn't' the woman he would love. They worked well together. Maybe she should tell him yes next time he asked her to marry him. As the days passed it was becoming very clear he was in charge, in total control of this endeavor of hers. The match would not be so very bad. He would make her burn.

Yes, they worked well together. They both cared immensely for the land as well as the horses. He loved horses, as did she. There was more in common between them than not. Maybe they could do well together. She always hoped for love.

His breath whispered across her face as he sighed deeply. "Yes and no, Clare." He slipped a finger under her chin before lifting gently. "You are beautiful. I find your body more than attractive. You're intelligent. I like that in a woman. If you want love from me, I don't know if I can give that. Love is just lust by a different name. What I can promise you is that I will give you a woman's pleasure. If you want children, you can have as many as you wish. I won't hold back your dreams. Except maybe the one that puts you in Duster's saddle for a race. A woman jockey cannot race against men. Not because they don't have the skill. Hush now, it's because women don't have the strength. If there were rules, perhaps I would relent. No, don't argue with me when you know what I say is true."

"The main reason you want me to marry you is so you can own Mayfair Hall again."

She wanted to howl at him. Howling would never help her. Michael was a stubborn man. If he thought love was lust, so be it.

"The main reason I suppose. I doubt if I would ever consider marriage for any other reason."

Michael wanted to be honest as well as sincere with her. She deserved as much, mayhap more. He was trying.

"For me, after I saw how much Sophie and Link love each other I vowed never to wed for anything less than that same love. Nonetheless, I will consider your proposal simply because a union between us makes some sense to me."

"Well, that is better than no answer at all. Which is all I've received from you so far."

He kissed her again, the caress light and teasing this time. He didn't deepen the intimacy. Instead, he pulled back.

She wanted more.

He couldn't give her what she desperately longed for.

He kissed her on the tip of her nose. "If you want me to kiss you as before, we won't be leaving this cottage tonight. In addition, you will lose your virginity. From all you've told me it's my conclusion you're not ready for that. You mean to give your innocence to the man you intend to marry. Although, I do know I could make you forget to tell me no."

"You would seduce me?" She laughed then a small giggle erupted at the absurd notion, which on second thought might not be so ludicrous.

The sound seemed to please him. He grinned.

"No, sweet Clare, I would call my actions sweet talking as well as coaxing you to my way of thinking. However, Little Pigeon if you ask me outright, I would never refuse such a request." He stood, holding his hand outstretched to her. "Come, take my hand. Let's go back to the house. The evening is growing dark. Believe we've had enough revelations for one day. All that information taxes my poor man's brain."

What he said was true. She spilled part of her heart to him tonight. Michael was little more than a stranger. Somehow, in such a short time, he managed to hold a part of her soul in his big hands. Of all the things that surprised her the most, she trusted him.

Clare didn't understand.

Stepping out into the night air felt refreshing. He held her close, his arm over her shoulder. Together, they walked through the rose scented garden. His warm body so close to hers, felt more than right. The hard, lean planes and angles of his body felt delicious.

The day had been magical. They won their first race. There was more money in the bank. Tomorrow a mare would arrive. Duster was scheduled to cover this mare. Gypsy would cover a different mare in two days. With the proceeds they purchased a mare with bloodlines tied to Sir Archie, the best thoroughbred in North Carolina. She was a three-year-old, ready to be breed. The sense of accomplishment soared through her. The day was a good one.

When they stepped into Mayfair Hall, the magic vanished. All hell seemed to have broken loose. Old Suzzy was downstairs treading from one room to the other, wringing her hands, small mewling sobs wracking her aged frame. Big Tom stood by the main doors waiting for Michael. From the slave quarters she heard wailing along with shouting.

"What's going on?" Michael seemed to take charge with ease as he asked Big Tom.

Clare backed off seeing she didn't have one idea how to proceed. By the scene, it was apparent something bad had happened. She wasn't needed here. All she wished for was to run to the slave quarters. She wanted to make everything right. If she did so, Michael would be furious with her. Waiting, she stood her ground, her hands clasped tightly in front of her.

Big Tom spoke slowly. His deep voice resonated in the narrow hallway of the mansion. "Raynard, the son of a bitch, came back to get the girl, Juney. Her father put up a fight. For his troubles he got the whip along with two broken ribs. Old Raynard told the man just because you freed him didn't make him any better. Told him he was scum. The color of his skin would label him a slave now and for always."

"The girl?" Clare stepped around Michael. She had to know. "What has happened to her?"

Clare's stomach rolled churning horribly. By the look in Big Tom's eyes, she had a pretty good idea.

Michael put out a hand to stop her. His voice harsh when he spoke to her, "You're not going anywhere, Clare. You can vanquish that notion right out of that pretty little head of yours. I don't want you hurt again. Don't want to see the fear in your eyes. Don't want to have to tend to wounds that shouldn't be there in the first place. You will behave yourself."

She wasn't about to listen to him. "I..." She swallowed down the words hovering on the tip of her tongue. She wanted to go, to help in any way she could.

Michael stopped midstride, his hand placed on her shoulder. He bent so they were eye level, "Unless I get your vow that you will stay inside this house until I return, I'll tie you down. That's a promise I intend to keep. Though it's not something I wish to do. Don't make me." His voice was harsh while holding a wealth of assurance. "Clare?"

He didn't trust her. She understood why. Promising was not something she wished to do. Nonetheless, she didn't want him to tie her anywhere. By the harsh, threatening look in his eyes, he meant every word he spoke.

His glare penetrated. He didn't look too happy to wait for her word. She knew he wanted to leave, to search for the girl as well as Raynard.

"Promise," she told him reluctantly, her hands behind her back.

"If I see you out there tonight, I'll send Big Tom for you. At least that man can follow orders. He will bring you back here then stand over you until I return. While I'd much rather have his help in this, you are too important to me to leave to your impulsive, reckless behavior." Michael strode into the office. From the desk drawer, he brought out a pistol then stuck it in his waistband. He collected bullets. He slipped a long knife into a leather holder he lashed to his leg.

To Clare, it appeared he was going into combat. Clare watched him walk out the door. Her hands were clasped beneath her chin. She turned to Old Suzzy who shook her head as if she was certain Clare would disobey.

"Don't you do it, Little Missy," Suzzy said while glaring at her. "If you do, you won't like wat' goin' to happen next."

"What happened to the girl?" Clare asked softly while she hoped for the best. She knew the best wasn't going to happen in this case.

"Raynard took her. She fought him. Her nails scored his cheek. She even hit her knee to his groin. Not hard enough to drop him to the ground. He hit her good across the jaw. She crumpled. Just like that she wilted to the earth. Old Raynard picked her up off the dirty ground then heaved her over his shoulder. That man's not good. He's pure evil. There's no way around this. Master Flannigan is going to have to put a bullet through that man's evil heart or he'll keep coming back. Next time he'll come for you. Raynard hates you. Said so himself. You mind what I say. You, Little Missy, need to watch out for him more than anyone. Your man's right in keeping you in the house. Best you behave yourself. It's not goin' to be safe for you around here unless the master gets rid of dat man. He means to do so. I could see the cold determination in his eyes." Old Suzzy started her pacing again. She looked up and stopped as if she forgot something important. "Timmie trailed them. He'll know where dat man took her."

Clare followed suit. She walked in circles around the office until she couldn't see straight. Perhaps, if she got a bit closer to the disturbance without leaving the house, what she might overhear would help her discover what exactly was going on over in the slave quarters. She wasn't going to break her promise to Michael. She wasn't going to sit idle either. If she could find the way, she would help. These were her people. She cared for each and every one of them.

After a few more seconds of thought, she poured herself a generous snifter of brandy. After that she walked to the master chamber. Once on the porch she stared toward the slave quarters. The hollering and wailing died down. After another hour, she didn't hear much. She saw lights weave in out of the construction site. Once in a great while, she caught sight of a shadowed form. She wasn't going to learn anything this way.

The small homes were not completely built yet. Though the families were sleeping in them at night, cooking outside during the day. All but one family decided to stay. Already some were planting fall along with winter crops on their plots of land. The major cash crops couldn't be planted until next spring. Although if the winter wasn't too harsh, there would be money sooner for the new farmers. The profits from the last tobacco shipment had been divided between the families who stayed.

Fighting the urge to run as fast as she could to see, to better understand the situation, she sat down on one of the chairs on the veranda. She wrapped a blanket around her shoulders to ward off the cool breeze coming from the river. Old Suzzy knocked softly on the door, a tray in hand.

"Thought you might be hungry tonight. Although I know Big Tom brought a powerful lot of food to the cottage. You and the master might have worked that off."

Heat rose to her cheeks at Suzzy's meaning. She coughed slightly. Her body stiffened as she thought of what Suzzy told her. What the older lady thought she knew. Everyone must believe they were lovers. The truth was they only kissed. If she faced her feelings head on, she would admit that not much more time would pass before he seduced her.

Well, he said his actions would be coaxing to his way of thinking. The end result was the same.

She knew better than to believe a seducer of an innocent. The tray was filled with all kinds of delicacies. There was a plate of deep-fried oysters along with two different types of soft goat cheese. Fresh berry tarts with flaky crusts tempted her. She realized she didn't eat much of the food Big Tom brought to the cottage. Her stomach had been tied in knots. She broke off a piece of bread. The bite tasted full of yeast, fresh and hot. The bread wouldn't stay that way much longer. She tried something of everything except the oysters. All tasted delicious. After that as she helplessly waited, all the food sat in a lump in the pit of her stomach.

It wasn't as if she wanted to eat. Her stomach churned and rolled just thinking about that little girl. She tried to push those horrific thoughts from her head. The girl wasn't much younger than when Sophie was being mistreated. Uncle William could have insisted she entertain men in the cottage. Her reputation would have been ruined, stained for all time. If that had happened, she would not have returned here. She arrived here demanding her inheritance, making changes in everyone's lives. Clare wasn't at all certain she had that right.

Time dragged by. She finished the glass of brandy fifteen minutes ago. Her eyelashes drooped. The day had been filled with excitement along with magic. She was exhausted. Waiting was hellish. She curled her legs beneath herself tugging the blanket closer. A moment or was it an hour later she jerked awake.

Walking into his bedroom, she told herself she would lie down until he came, until he told her what happened. If she fell asleep on her bed, he would never wake her. Before she settled on his big bed, she changed to her nightgown thinking he might not return until the morning. After all she needed to be comfortable.

On the far side she curled up, her face resting on her hands. It was easy for her to imagine him stroking her. She felt positive she dreamed. His fingers brushed the hair away from the back of her neck. She felt his lips there, touching lightly caressing her, his teeth scraped gently across her shoulders. Felt sensations deep in her core grow as she pushed back against the warmth that seemed to heat her body from the inside out.

She heard a masculine chuckle. His fingers closed around a breast, stroked the hardened tip. She'd fallen asleep again. Michael seemed to like to wake her this way. He would tease her now with all that he wanted to offer. If she didn't ask him to make love to her, he would draw back.

Clare turned over, still dazed and sleepy. She framed his face with her hands thinking he was the most beautiful man she'd ever seen. "First you can kiss me then you have to tell me what happened. If you found the girl or if you killed Raynard, I need to know."

Clare didn't recognize the sound of her voice, husky with desire for something she didn't yet understand.

"Since I found you in my bed, I felt certain you decided to accept my proposal."

He kissed her on the tip of her nose then laughed. He flopped onto his back, his hands beneath his head totally unconcerned about the fact she was in his bed in her night clothes.

"I wanted to know the news as soon as you came home." She pushed herself to a sitting position against the massive backboard as she looked down at him. "Didn't think you'd wake me if I weren't in your bed."

"You thought right. Good God, it's three a.m."

He rolled off the bed then walked to the tray where he poured himself a glass of water.

She watched him drink deeply. "Michael?"

He turned slowly, "Nothing good happened."

He ate a berry tart then another. For a few minutes he partook of the leftover food on the tray until it seemed he was sated.

"You will keep looking." She guessed they didn't find Raynard, understanding it would now be too late to save the girl from the misuse she would surely find at Raynard's hands. "You can't stop. If you do, he'll kill Juney."

"For Raynard, yes. We found the girl, bloody as well as bruised. She couldn't walk. Clare, she was horribly brutalized. Her mind won't ever be the same. At the moment, she stares at her mother with glazed over eyes while she sits and moans softly. She rocks back and forth, tears filling her lovely eyes. The man needs to be lashed to death, castrated first. Perhaps with time along with love, she will improve."

Sensing his need, Clare held out her arms to him. He came to her. She felt the wetness of his tears seep through the fabric of her nightgown. His huge shoulders shuddered with the weight of what transpired of all the things he saw. He wept for the girl who would carry the abuse to her grave.

Michael looked at her, raising his face from her shoulder. "Big Tom and I...we hoped to save her. Prayed we would find her before that man could hurt her." Tears spiked his dark lashes. "She says she wants to die."

Tenderly feeling the pull of his emotions along with his need for her to hold him, she pushed a wayward lock of hair from his eyes. "You will find him. You won't stop until you do so."

"You must take care. I don't want you going anywhere by yourself. Big Tom will shadow you. Because of what you did the other day, you're in grave danger. He hates you."

"He wouldn't dare harm me," she spoke without thought.

If Raynard assumed he could get away with hurting her as he did Juney, he would most likely murder her. Hurting a previous slave was one thing, a white woman something completely different. She didn't truly believe she was in danger from Raynard. "What will you do now?"

"When Timmie finds him, we will grab the magistrate. We will see him in the jail then a trial. I guarantee you he will be put away where he can't hurt anyone else. Doubt not. Even if the girl was still a slave, I would see that man punished."

"Then I can train Duster while Timmie is otherwise engaged?"

Michael frowned at that. She understood he didn't want her participation in any part of the training.

"I will think on it."

~ * ~

The mare arrived that morning. Michael was pleased with the arrangement. Clare remained busy in the house helping plan the meals for the week. Their cook, Delilah, was amazing. The dishes she created were astonishing delicious as well. He tasted the oysters last night. Even cold they went down smoothly.

He wondered if Clare ate any of the oysters the evening before. Perhaps that was why he found her in his bed. She didn't want to leave him. The aphrodisiac might have taken hold a tiny bit. He was afraid if she stayed where he found her, he would make love to her. Until she told him she would wed him, he didn't want to have sex with her. However, he did have plans to give her pleasure. Mayhap in another night or two he would coax her to that point. If she climaxed in his arms, the startling pleasure might give her reason to say yes to his marriage proposal. A man could always hope.

Raynard had not been found yet. Timmie returned to help with the horses. The mare would stay three days. Duster would do his stallion's duty each day. Michael rubbed his hands together in anticipation. In some ways he wished Clare would not obey him in this. He wanted to see the look on her finely sculpted face when she watched Duster cover the mare. He didn't think the sight would frighten her. What he believed is that she would be very curious, perhaps even wonder what he looked like.

The idea pleased him.

Ah, he'd seen her nearly naked. Maybe it was time to show her a bit more of his body. Doing so was only fair.

"You ready to begin?" Timmie stood beside him, rubbing his hands together as if he felt as much excitement as he did. "This is a big day. I sure am ready."

"Duster seems excited, the little mare flirtatious. Look, she wants him," Michael said blandly as he watched the stallion raise his head. He whinnied, prancing as close as he could get to the female. She sidestepped, teasing Duster who reared on his hind legs.

Timmie brought him to the mare as the stallion's head bobbed in anticipation of what he was about to get. Michael chuckled behind his teeth while he thought of Clare watching the exhibition. Duster bit her on the neck then her flank as Timmie maneuvered him around the mare. The mare pranced seeming eager for the mating ritual to begin. Big Tom held the mare steady with soothing words coupled with a strong hand.

"Yes," he murmured, "it's just about your turn. You just do what comes naturally and all will be fine. Just you wait and see."

Michael felt her presence before he saw her. Deep inside, his body tightened with his anticipation. Just as he expected she couldn't stay away. Clare stood in the shadows about ten feet from him. She was watching. With her slender brows drawn tightly together, her expression filled with intense concentration. He chuckled to himself thinking he should bring her to him put his arms around her while he let her feel the heat of the drama that would be enacted in front of them.

Her curiosity did get the best of her. Timmie looked to him as if he noticed Clare too. Timmie understood Clare was not supposed to be present. Well, she was. As far as he was concerned, she would stay. He would be pleased to see her face when the stallion entered the mare. Michael also wanted to feel her reaction to the mating.

With his hand held up for Timmie to wait, Michael strode to Clare. When she spotted him walking to her, she backed up a step, running into the solid wall of the stable.

"Oh, no…"

She was shaking her head, holding up her small hands. If he guessed right, she was thinking of an excuse for her actions. In her very sweet, impulsive way she would make up something so outrageous the excuse might be believable.

He held out his hand to her then grasped her by the wrist tugging her toward him. "Don't agree with your brother-in-law in your case. Think you should watch. Come along now. This will give you some insight into what we will do together in the not-so-distant future. You won't be quite as innocent after you see Duster cover the little mare. You do want to further your education, don't you? That's why you are here, right?"

Inside he was laughing, enjoying her obvious chagrin. She'd been well and truly caught. Now she would pay the price. He would keep her with him until Duster was finished with the mare.

Now, she stood in front of him. His hands rested on her shoulders Massaging her tight muscles. He bent low so he could speak to her in a whisper. Distracting Duster was not something he wanted to do.

"Little Pigeon, you will enjoy this. I promise. The sight is not for most women. You are different though. I don't believe watching will have harmful consequences. You won't be afraid."

His breath wafted across her neck, the tiny hairs moving slightly. He felt her shiver, wondered at the meaning. Hoped the shudder was because she was excited.

Now his arms were wrapped around her with his hands resting placidly on her small belly. She pushed back against him. He squeezed his fingers Massaging her softness relishing the moment. She squirmed when Duster mounted the mare.

She must feel his member hard against her backside.

The mare screamed. Clare quivered, her body stiff against his. "Relax and enjoy the moment. This is the beginning of your dreams," he whispered once more against her ear touching the lobe with his tongue then nipping gently.

A soft mewling sound rippled from her. Michael suddenly had second as well as third thoughts about her watching. Again, he felt her stiffen. What she was thinking was paramount in his head.

Unable to understand what drove him, once more, he whispered close to her ear, after taking another small nip at her lobe. "Will you marry me?"

Clare didn't move now. Her soft body was frozen and still against the hardness of him. She was so very calm, so serene. He was petrified while he waited for her to respond in some way. If she would speak, he would feel better. His intent with her was not to traumatize her. He wanted to feel her woman's petals, to know if she was wet and swollen for him.

Time slipped by while Duster finished his duty. Both horses were led to their respective stalls.

For the longest time, she didn't move.

In his arms, she turned then placed a slender white hand on his cheek. Her saucy sweet tongue danced across her bottom lip, tantalizing him. "Is that the way we will do it?"

Her eyes were wide pools of gray. In his arms her body trembled slightly.

When we will do it? The thought echoed in his man's brain. She wasn't traumatized. No, she acted as eager as the little filly.

He felt relieved.

Wanted to laugh that he'd been worried about her.

Like a spring, she always bounced back up. He was laughing. She frowned at him then pushed on his chest. His hands were molded around her adorable backside holding her tight against his heavy arousal. He hadn't seen her tiny butt yet. Somehow, he knew the soft rounded cheeks would please him immensely. Yes, she satisfied him more than he ever thought possible.

Soon, you randy goat, very soon.

He kissed her, probed into the moist hot depth with his tongue, deepened then deepened the caress until she sighed opening even farther for him, tempting him into her sultry heat. She tasted warm, deliciously sweet. She burned him. He felt the raw passion generating within her openness. Just as before when he squeezed her soft belly, he did the same to her rear. She pushed closer as if she wanted more sensations.

Her soft moan of sexual pleasure surprised him, delighting him. She was more passionate than he ever expected. Timmie stood in front of them, shifting his feet, his eyes on the ground. Slowly, Michael broke off the kiss. He brought his attention to the young man who flushed with embarrassment while he didn't seem to know what to do.

"Sir, they are," he swallowed, his Adam's apple bobbing up and down beneath his chin, "taken care of. Should I take Duster for a ride?" he spoke, his gaze solidly on a point between them.

When she heard his voice, Clare gasped. She hid her head against his shoulder, her fingers digging spasmodically into his muscles. Her tension radiated from her into him. He would have to do something to regenerate the mood. Doing so might not be too difficult. She was so very passionate.

He cleared his throat while he shook off the hunger he felt for this delightful woman. "No, Clare and I are going for a ride. She would like to ride Duster if he's agreeable after his sexual fling with the beautiful mare."

Timmie blushed crimson, probably to the roots of his hair and the tips of his toes. That surprised Michael. Timmie was young though. That gave him pause. Perhaps, he'd never dallied with a lady.

"Sir, I'll stay with the mare a bit longer. She's heaving. Duster might have been too enthusiastic in his endeavors." Timmie spoke slowly keeping his gaze focused anywhere except on them.

Michael wanted to tilt his head back. Wanted to hoot with laughter. As he thought of the mare, he also wanted to watch Clare's heaving breasts before the day was over. He decided he would do that very thing as soon as he found a bit of privacy for his endeavors.

"Should we ride to the cave?" he asked more ulterior motives on his mind coupled with thoughts of isolation.

He would make sure he took an extra blanket. Perhaps he'd visit Delilah to see what she could put together in a basket for them to eat. Perhaps more oysters. His grin was devilish.

She looked at him, a tiny scowl marring her forehead. "Don't like caves." Her words were curt. "They are cold and dark. The shadows give me the willies. Things like mice and spiders live in caves." As if to emphasize her words she wrapped her arms around herself then shivered.

He knew for a fact she lied. What he didn't understand was why. The first month she was in Virginia, she rode with him to the cave several times. They walked inside. She never complained. The dark interior seemed nostalgic to her. At least that is what she told him. That sunset they watched when he kissed her for the first time, was near the cave. The river would be warm enough to take a swim, perhaps in the buff. Now he was dreaming.

"In that case, we'll walk in the patch of wildflowers nearby. Most should be in bloom by now. We can swim if you'd rather not walk into the cave." He didn't quite understand why she was acting so peevish.

"The bees will bother us. The river will be too cold to swim."

She was pulling back from him. That was unacceptable.

This wasn't like his Clare. He didn't like to think she was backpedaling.

"Clare, what is wrong? My God it's July. The river will be perfect and cooling after the hot ride."

He was perplexed by all the excuses. She was doing an about turn of face. One moment she acted as if she wanted him, now this. It wasn't to be had. She would explain herself. He needed to get to the bottom of her strange reticence.

"Link was right. I shouldn't have watched."

She fidgeted. He still held her against him. Mayhap this was just embarrassment doing her talking.

"Why did you?" he asked wondering what she thought.

She shook her head, denying everything. Her shoulders lifted slightly suggesting she wasn't going to answer or she didn't know.

He felt certain he could answer that for her. "Because you were curious, weren't you, Clare? Your inquisitive nature spurred you to discover what would happen. You wanted to know more because you understand it's only a matter of time before I come inside you. Seeing that part of Duster frightens you. So, now you are backing off."

Gently, he smoothed his hand along her spine, stopping at each vertebra. He thought of slowly kissing each one. Getting his mind back on track was going to be harder than he thought it would be.

"Are you that big?" her voice wobbled on a high note.

Now, he understood better what was bothering her agile mind. Her hesitancy coupled with her distress and curiosity was endearing. He wished he could ease all her fears with a single word. That wouldn't happen with words only when he slipped inside her to prove they would fit together with precision.

"No, Duster is a stallion sixteen hands high. I'm not that big." He tried and to his amazement kept his laughter behind his teeth. She was truly afraid.

"You're big though. Aren't you?" It seemed she didn't want to end this conversation.

"Yes. When you see me naked, you'll wonder how I can possibly fit inside you." When he watched her face drain of color, he understood he said too much. "I will though. I won't hurt you. I can promise you that."

Well hell, he couldn't, shouldn't have said the words. The first time would give her pain. Even though he was far from inexperienced, he'd never made love to a virgin before.

"I won't look at you. You can't possibly be telling the truth."

Her saucy chin tilted up. Her chin was slightly pointed. It was also just as small and delicate as the rest of her. She could wield that look with aristocratic precision as if she was born royalty.

"I assure you when the time is right, I will fit." He smoothed a finger down her nose. After that he touched her soft moist mouth. "Shall we ride?" He thought of another delightful way to ride. In time, he reminded himself.

When need be, I can be a patient man.

"I see Timmie saddled our horses," she murmured as he loosened his hold on her. "I will ride with you."

"Looks as if that is true." In such a short time with this untried woman, lust seemed to rule all his actions along with his words. Beneath his trousers he was hard as steel. He didn't mind. Not with his Clare. Strange how he thought of Clare as his.

He helped her mount while he thought about her questions along with the obvious assumptions. He supposed it would be best to keep everything sexual out of their conversation for the time being. They could mount that particular issue after their ride, after the delicious oysters along with a glass or two of the sweet Bordeaux Delilah packed.

At a gallop, she rode in front of him. The pins in her hair

separating themselves from her scalp. He liked the way her auburn hair flowed out behind her. The flying tendrils weren't just auburn. No, there were so many different shades he was hard pressed to name them all. He thought of counting the different shades while she slept beside him.

With the widening of the path, he rode next to her. She was an excellent horsewoman. Her body seemed to move as one with her mount. The skirt she wore billowed with the air showing her knees. Another part of her he would examine more closely with time, especially the backs then the fronts after that all the delicious flesh up to her thigh and beyond.

Every day for more than two weeks he asked her to marry him. He supposed, he needed to speed up the process. By September he intended to be married. Mayfair Hall as well as Clare Carter-Brown would be his before her twenty-first birthday.

They stopped in front of the cave. She did appear apprehensive. Once the horses were tethered, he spread the blanket. The basket of food sat on the edge.

"Are you hungry?"

"Not right now." With her hands swinging in time with her stride, she headed to the river. She slipped out of her boots then tucked the hem of her skirt into the waistband showing long white legs.

He imagined those perfectly shaped legs around his flanks.

Perhaps she didn't want to swim, just wade in the cooling water. He followed suit, removing his boots then his shirt. He wore his breaches. If he swam, he preferred to do so naked. In the buff, that was the only way to swim. However…after this morning that might be too much too soon.

Clare kicked up water with her feet. Some of the drops landed on her. She giggled seemingly delighted. When she turned to look at him, there was a wicked glint in her eye. She splashed water toward him challenging him to join her.

"Witch," he murmured for his ears only, watching her, understanding she meant to play with him, with the water.

Well, he did mention swimming. If she wound up drenched, she would have to remove some of her clothing. The thought was heady. Lust yowled through him with a mind-boggling pace.

With purpose in his mind, he strode to the river. Two feet in, she dipped her hands into the river, splaying a heavy spray of water onto him. Drops careened down his face along with his shoulders. The water cooled his body but not his ardor.

"You think I'll let you get away with that?"

His hands were on his hips. She was grinning at him. Purposefully, he stepped forward, his intent to one end.

Clare cried out a loud squeal then ran, picking up her skirts, water spiraling away from her feet. Nearly knee deep in the river, she couldn't run fast. She stumbled, her arms waving wildly.

He was upon her before she could get more than a few feet away. Leaning toward the bank, his arms wrapped around her they tumbled into the water which now was only inches deep. She laughed. He turned her so his back was pressed against the bottom. Her legs straddled him. He chortled, so very pleased with the quick outcome then bringing her close to kiss her open mouth.

"You're all wet."

He brushed the long strands of soaking hair from her face. Her lashes were spiked with moisture. Droplets touched upon her lips endearing her precious face to him even more.

"So are you."

She bent close, swept her tongue along his mouth. He opened for her, played with her burgeoning emotions. He didn't intend to allow this heady moment with her to pass without taking his suit one step closer to its ultimate achievement.

He pulled her to her feet unsure of what he was about to do or why. They were both soaked through to the skin. Held in his arms, he waded with her until he was almost hip deep in the water. With a great heave, she flew through the air, her arms whirling. A second later she rose from the depth, laughing, pushing her hair from her face. Her bodice pressed against her breasts, revealing all her sweet and spicy charms. So far this afternoon he was delighted with her.

She struggled through the water, stumbling then righting herself. Still, she moved forward, toward him. "Cad!" she cried out laughing and hitting him on his chest. "I'm soaked."

"You started this. I simply finished the game which means I won."

He grabbed her wrists held them behind her while he kissed her again and again. Her soft curves pressed tightly against the hard angles and planes of his body. "Wench, we need to dry ourselves. Did you think on that before you started the game? You will have to remove some of your clothing so it can dry."

He grinned at her. Saw her nipples so delightfully revealed beneath the thin fabric of her shirt. She wore no chemise. He wondered what was beneath her skirt. He supposed he would discover just how many petticoats she wore if any.

"No, just wanted to get you damp, a few drops. Didn't think you would throttle me, after that dump me into the water. Didn't think I'd end up saturated to my skin."

Against him, he felt her shiver. "I'll wrap you in the blanket I brought or if you choose, I'll keep you warm. Your body against mine. Enclose you in my arms."

"The sun will warm and dry us soon enough. There is no need to strip naked." Her chin trembled when the sun dipped behind a cloud. The goose bumps on her thin arms belied the fact she might be cold with the sodden clothing against her skin.

"Come along then, if that's what you want. I'm certain you are right."

He held out his hand. She was sure to change her mind soon enough. Autocratically, making the decision for her would not aid his cause.

They walked hand in hand to the blanket. She pulled on her shirt, tugging the fabric away from her breasts. After that she bent over to wring out her hair. Water soaked the ground. A good thing the sun was hot. Her skirt slipped from her hips. She pulled up the blanket to wrap it around her. She was clad in frilly white drawers. Very clearly, before she covered herself, he saw her woman's mound framed beneath the wet silken cloth.

"You are right. I'd like to eat now. What did you pack?"

She sat beside him, not close enough though.

He waggled his eyebrows, smirking. "Oysters…"

Clare cocked her head, her pretty eyes questioning the food choice. He knew in that instant she had no idea the renowned aphrodisiacal characteristics of oysters.

"Don't understand you." She rummaged through the basket finally bringing something out. "Prefer the tarts."

"They are a tiny bit sweet and a lot tart, just like you." He wanted to laugh, to howl with the pleasure of her.

She grimaced at him. Nonetheless, she didn't seem to concern herself with his proclamation of her character.

"That's not very nice," she murmured as she took a bite, powdered sugar, coating her lips.

"Come here," his voice grew husky with the raw passion passing through him in ribbons of the sweetest pleasure while he studied her.

He wanted to share that ecstasy with her. She was half dressed, what better time than this very moment to show her how much he could please her.

Hesitating for a moment, she finally moved toward him. "All right."

After the softly spoken affirmation, she was in his arms. He wished he had a second blanket to spread so they could lie down.

"Try an oyster first."

He plucked one from the basket. She tipped her head up. The oyster slid from its shell. She swallowed then pursed her mouth grimacing.

"You don't like them?"

"They are not my favorite. The tarts taste better. I was just wondering why you waggled your eyebrows at me." She pulled the blanket closer as if to protect herself. "What is it you are not telling me?"

"Have another," he told her while he ate two.

The wine was poured.

She sipped thoughtfully peering over the top of her glass. "Are they supposed to taste better with wine? You're not making any sense."

He sat down his elbow resting on his bent knee. "It's not the taste of the oyster that is important. The effect they have on a person is the relevant factor."

"What is relevant?" She tilted her head a bit sideways before she caught her bottom lip with her pearly white teeth.

Clare looked so adorable he wanted to squeeze her tight then never let go. He wanted to taste that bottom lip of hers, suck it into his mouth then play with the softness. He brought his attention back to the conversation. He tugged on her hand until she sat. "Ah…have you heard of aphrodisiacs?" He watched different expression play across her face as she tried to understand his words.

She continued to sip. When she looked up, she was swirling the liquid left in her glass. "No. What is an aphrodisiac?"

"Your education, Little Pigeon, begins now."

He winked at her, thrilled as well as appreciating this conversation more than he probably should.

"Don't be so damn illusive, spit it out," she said angrily as she seemed to lose all patience with him.

He chuckled appreciating her irritation. He loved all her moods; saucy and spicy, tart, and sweet. "My, my, you're swearing. I like that. If that is what you wish, an aphrodisiac is meant to enhance sexual pleasure. If a woman is not willing, a bite of oyster might change her disposition. If she is willing, it might make her more appreciative of a man's enthusiastic attentions."

It seemed she thought over his words. "Do you believe that nonsense?" She appeared truly baffled. "A food can't possibly do what you've described."

"You've had two of the little marine animals. Do you lust for me? Does your breath pant and heave with desire?"

She threw the last oyster at him. The marine vermin hit him square in the chest, falling to the grass. He lunged for her. She giggled as he flipped her over. He felt her soft curves pressing against him. Her legs were parted so she straddled him. The blanket slipped from its location around her waist. His hands pressed her closer to him. The hardened peaks of her breast pushed against his chest. When she moved slightly, they flounced across him tantalizing every male part of his body.

"That, my dear, will gain you punishment or perhaps a boon. You must pay for tossing things at me. That oyster could have injured me. What should I ask for?" Michael didn't have to think long. He knew exactly what he wanted. "A kiss, Clare, you have to kiss me."

"That's certainly not a punishment. I like your kisses." She paused for a few seconds. "I adore the way you taste."

She pressed her lips against his mouth then moved back, a warm smile gracing her features. She appeared satisfied as well as a bit smug as if she controlled this scenario. She would learn soon enough she did not.

He shook his head at her. "Didn't I teach you better than that? I thought surely," he paused to run his knuckles across her face then down her neck stopping when he reached the tip of one breast, "well, I suppose more lessons are needed."

His hands rested firmly on her backside. The blanket no longer covered her. He slipped his hands beneath the drawers she wore to meet naked flesh. It was almost where he wished to be. She was so soft yet firm. Her skin was silken to his touch. He squeezed, let his fingers slip between her parted thighs until he found sweet swollen woman's flesh. This was heaven. He closed his eyes, absorbing all the sensations into his raging body.

She squirmed against him. "Michael…?"

"Yes."

He parted her woman's flesh then held still as she seemed fascinated by these new vibrations that must be coursing through her.

She pushed against him. "What are you doing?" she asked her voice whisper soft a hint of desperation in her tone.

"How do you feel?"

He needed to stop her questioning. How to do so was the immediate problem. He meant to try whatever came to mind. He found the tiny pearl of her greatest pleasure, touched and caressed the hard nub until tiny feminine sounds rippled from her. Her purrs of pleasure delighted him.

She cried out, squirmed then coiled moving her supple body against his arousal raising raw desire in a lightning flash. "Hot. I feel hot."

"Anything else?"

Her slickness coated his finger. Sweet nectar poured from her raining down on his hand. He slipped one finger inside her, pushed deeper, deeper still until he touched her maidenhead. He groaned low in the back of his throat. He wanted nothing more than to plunge inside her sultry heat, become part of her then introduce her to the fairy-tale that would soon follow. He wished to look upon her face see into the depths of her gorgeous eyes when she climaxed in his arms.

"Just hot and different where you are touching me, swollen, maybe wet."

Another tiny mew escaped in a soft ripple from her lips as he moved within.

He brought his finger to her cheek, touched her there. "That is your wetness, the honey of your desire. You're ready for my sex just as the mare was ready for Duster's." He wanted to be back inside her. "You're very small. Your body was stretching so I'll fit. We will take this so slow you will beg me to cover you."

"Michael, I think you should stop now. I don't understand what you're doing. Don't think I should let you. Michael, it feels sinful. Wicked."

"Sinful? Even wicked? I like that. Stopping, not yet. Not until I give you the first taste of a woman's pleasure. Would you like that, Clare? I won't come inside you nor will I break the membrane that proclaims your innocence. Technically, you'll still be a virgin."

"How can that be?" She was panting as he moved his finger in a heady rhythm inside her.

"Kiss me, Clare. You will soon see."

~ * ~

Raynard watched the couple cavort in the field below him. Loudly he cursed, swore then shook his fist in the air. He muttered to himself then paced the hilltop where he looked down upon the man and woman he credited for all his problems. He could barely contain himself. The black slave he took the other day didn't satisfy him. Now that he'd seen this woman no one else would do for him.

"She's a bitch." Yes, she would get her comeuppance. Because of her he lost his job. Because of her the slaves were given priority. He was a wanted man because he dared force a slave.

He swore again livid with all that one woman took from him. He was just the man to show Clare Carter-Brown how a real man took his woman. Once he found her alone, she would beg him. One way or another he would have her. The deed was just a matter of time.

He stared hard at the couple below him, could not keep his eyes from them. Her frilly white drawers high in the air while Michaels hands were beneath them, touching her intimately out in the open for anyone to see. Doing what he wanted to do. Ah, he could just imagine how she would feel, all that lush soft flesh in his hands.

"Watching the two lovers play?" Biff Gideon spoke to Raynard from atop his horse. He was leaning a forearm on the saddle horn. "Thought you were wanted by the law. You seem to be moving about very easily. Looks as if you've been watching the show."

"I am. Going to get the girl first. Before I finish with her, she will understand what it's like to be with a real man not a sniveling Irishman." Raynard was gritting his teeth, his insides churning. "How dare she?" he muttered beneath his breath, "How dare she waste her charms on that sorry excuse for a man?"

"When you get her, let me and Busby know. Want to taste her honeyed gems too. If she's handing out her favors, I'm going to be right there getting my fair share. Wanted her the moment I saw her walking down that gangplank with her brother-in-law and sister. She ignited a flame inside me I can't quite seem to douse."

"Flannigan doesn't seem like a man to share his woman," Raynard said while he watched Michael flip her on to her back. She no longer straddled the man. He was on top of her now, heaving. His mouth descended, took hers while another hand played with a breast then lower beneath her drawers. He heard her screams of pleasure.

What the devil? He wasn't taking her. His britches were still secured. Maybe they weren't lovers yet. He could still be her first. His mouth watered in anticipation. He would show her who was in control.

He would.

Yes, he would do exactly that.

"Michael told me as much the other day, when I offered to pay him for her use. Offered him a whole dollar, more than enough in my mind. Busby was with me. He tell you what I just said? Michael turned me down flat," Biff said, while he stroked his chin thoughtfully. "Maybe I didn't offer him enough. She is a fascinating little piece of baggage. An experienced whore would get more than the sum I offered. Perhaps I will propose a bit more. The man might find himself persuaded to change his mind now that he's about to sample her."

"What you going to do?" Raynard asked still watching the tableau below. "I want to get her alone. You'd have a better chance of that. Why don't we work together, you me and Busby? We can all profit from a deal between the three of us."

Biff stroked his chin again, his gaze focused on the pair below them. "It will be much easier for Busby or me to get closer to her. Don't think they'll believe I'm dangerous to her even though we did offer to teach her the finer points of a sexual encounter."

"He's sucking on her tits. You think she's got big ones? It's hard to tell all those damn clothes she wears all buttoned up to her chin. Can't see anything this far away." Raynard wanted to let Flannigan know he was watching. Nevertheless, he didn't dare show himself. Flannigan would stop what he was doing and come after him. God, when they were rolling around in the river he got hard as steel. If it was possible, he was still growing harder. Raynard was surprised he didn't take her there in the muddy water.

"Big ones, nipples soft and pink," Biff said wistfully. "Bet those tits of hers more than fill a man's hands." He adjusted himself in the saddle. "Next time she comes into the village if she's alone, I'll grab her. Shouldn't be too much trouble if you lie low, Michael will ease up on her guard, Big Tom. How do I get a hold of you?"

"For the time being, I'm staying in the Anderson shack. It's about ten miles east of the village. No one will think to look for me there. The hovel is falling down around my ears. It's not fit for a human. At the moment, though it's all I've got."

"I know where it is. You stay put up there. If you want our plan to work, don't you dare show yourself. When I get her, we'll have a real party. I'll bring Busby. It'll be just the three of us along with the haughty Miss Clare. Might even get a hold of some rum punch. We can drug it a bit so she'll beg for us to take her. She'll be all glassy eyed and willing to spread her legs for all three of us."

Raynard grunted as he rubbed his chin. H needed to shave. Was not one to like stubble on his face. He might do that for the girl, shave. But then he might not, a few stubble burns on her silken skin might please him.

They watched as Michael pulled Clare to her feet. He swept her into his arms, the blanket lying on the ground. They walked into the cave. If he could corner them inside that dark dank place, his chance with the girl would happen sooner than later. To ease the discomfort, he rubbed his crotch. Nay, they would be back outside sooner than later. He sat back watching. Minutes ticked by. Raynard thought he should go in after them. He waited too long.

They were outside again. Michael set her on the blanket, poured her more wine. They still wore their clothing. Even though Clare wasn't naked, she had very little on to cover herself. Once more he wondered at that. He always made sure his women were naked.

Michael stood, shaded his eyes with his hand. The man searched the hill. Raynard slunk out of sight. It would never serve his purposes to be caught. Biff turned his horse with the same idea.

Chapter Four

Clare didn't understand what was happening to her. Michael's finger slid inside her then there were two. She wanted more and more, more of the same but something else as well. She cried soft tiny incoherent sounds while he stroked her. His thumb caressed a place that made her go wild. He didn't stop. She climbed higher and higher still. Her fingernails bit into his shoulders, scraping flesh. She arched against him, twisted, frantic with her hunger, beseeching with her body. It seemed she undulated beneath him.

"Easy Clare, relax now, just let me…"

His mint scented breath whispered across her lips. His mouth molded with hers. His tongue played and danced inside just as his fingers were doing the same. "You are so hot and wet. God, I need you."

He released her mouth then cast his attentions lower, sucked a breast into his mouth, so deeply she thought he must hold all of it. His tongue flicked across her nipple then he bit gently. She yelled then moaned softly writhing against him, feeling his hardness touch her belly. Her body was spiraling to ever greater heights beyond anything she'd ever known. As a fierce hurricane that flew through these parts, the wind-swept storm he created grew wilder, hotter then, fiercer still. A firestorm raged within. She felt out of control as she realized the control lay in his skillful hands. He commanded, demanded her to give while he deftly sculpted the magical scenario.

Unexpectedly, ripples of ecstasy erupted, pulsed, throbbed. Deep spasms centered in her core, ragged spiraling then strengthening still higher. She didn't know anything like this could happen. The sensual eruption of sensations kept going on and on. She whimpered, pleasure overpowering all her senses. His fingers moved within her, a pace that didn't stop, a swiftness that controlled, generating raw hunger deep inside her pounding body. She cried out as he absorbed the sound into his mouth. Blackness then blinding light ripped in erotic patterns in her mind. She quivered as the pulsing stopped. Exhausted still in the after affects, she vibrated. Shuddering her pleasure, she clung to him.

Slowly, it seemed he brought her down from that heavenly pinnacle where she soared so very high. Beneath her shirt he ran his hand along her backbone stopping to caress each separate vertebra. He kissed her softly his tongue lightly traveling across her mouth. Braced on his forearms, easing his weight from her he grinned seemingly pleased with himself as well as with her hungry response filled with raging desire she couldn't deny.

"You are very sweet, Clare. Did you like that as much as I did?"

She was just now regaining her breath, her eyes glazed over with the novelty. She didn't think she could move. "What happened to me? What did you do? Michael?" Well, she understood what he did yet she didn't.

"Gave you the most wondrous feelings on earth, Clare. You just experienced a woman's pleasure at my clever hands. The gratification is even more exquisite when I come inside you. At that time, I'll have those same pleasures too. When I empty myself inside you, I'll also bring you to ecstasy. Did you like what we did?" He repeated the question.

"All right," she said softly his eyes dark with something she didn't understand but wanted to do so.

Liking what he did to her woman's body was an understatement. She touched his lips with the tip of her finger.

To her it seemed he couldn't help himself. He beamed down at her. His smile broad. His seeming satisfaction undeniable. The timing of the question impeccable, "Will you marry me, Clare? Do I need show you again how your life will be every night for the rest of our lives?"

In order to think better, she closed her eyes. Clare understood he wanted to hear the word yes. She couldn't say that one word at least not yet. The only excuse she had, "You don't love me," was all she could manage to say. More than anything she wanted to give in to his desire, to the hunger, the tempest, the ragging storm. Maybe she had enough love in her heart for both of them.

His answer to her was a low groan. He brought her to her feet, swept her into his arms. Whispering into her ear, "We're going to the cave now. No, don't shiver in disgust. The interior is not all that scary a place. It's dark, yes. Nonetheless, your eyes will grow used to the blackness. I want to show you what I've discovered." His low voice was intense, penetrating.

She didn't know what to make of the seriousness. Clare hoped there wasn't some hidden intentions to his words. She hesitated. "If you insist."

"I won't let you be afraid." He kissed her forehead then smoothed her eyebrows with his thumb. "I will protect your virtue inside the cave just as I did out here."

His lips were warm, invitingly soft against her skin when he kissed her lips. She recalled the powerful feeling he just generated within her. He told her she could feel that way every night for the rest of her life. The devil, she wanted to tell him yes, she would marry him. She held back still wishing for the words that would tell her he wanted her not just Mayfair Hall.

What was he going to do now? She pressed against him, her head in the hollow of his shoulder. "I'm not truly afraid of the cave unless we go so far inside, I can't see the light."

She had the heady feeling he meant to do exactly that.

"Just hang on to me. I won't let anything happen to you." They strode farther into the cave. "Don't understand why I need to show you this. Something happened out there…I think someone watched us. The thought terrifies me. If someone is watching us, I think we can guess as to the identities." Tenderly, he ran his hand along her arm. "This is just a precaution, nothing more."

"They…are you sure? We were…?"

"Yes, we were," his low voice rumbled against her chest. "Don't like to think about that." As if to give reassurance, he hugged her close. "Nothing is going to happen to you. I won't let it."

She didn't want to believe someone watched while she and Michael were so intimate. He was doing things, lightly touching then caressing. Was he still coaxing? She didn't think so. His strokes seemed more as if he soothed her shattered senses.

Her mind clouded. She thought of Biff and Busby. Thought of those two men watching. After that her mind blazed to Raynard. Inside, fury grew to epic proportions. She tried to tamp down the rising anger. Nothing worked. She seethed.

"What are you going to show me?"

Her mind swam with different scenarios. If someone observed them as he touched and caressed her intimately, they should leave here now. They shouldn't be walking through the cave. They should go back to Mayfair Hall.

"How to get out if you ever find yourself trapped. I've a bad feeling about all that has been happening. We haven't found Raynard. Biff and Busby are supposing things about you they've no business to assume. Raynard can be dangerous. Biff and Busby are fools. Nonetheless, that fact doesn't make them less dangerous. They are men and because of that fact stronger than you. If threatened or attacked, you need alternatives."

"If that's what you think best."

She had no other words for the situation. In any case even if she refused, he would do as he pleased. Held in his arms, she didn't have a choice. She wasn't about to walk outside without him by her side. In this she would accede to his wishes.

He laughed softly squeezing her shoulder. She imagined his amusement was at her easy compliance. She would allow him this show of control he seemed to insist upon. For a few seconds she held her breath. The air rushed out suddenly.

Once they passed the entrance to the cave, he set her down, "Come here," he told her as he led the way to a dark corner.

When she peered down the corridor, the long, intimidating hall was black as sin.

Michael rummaged in a depressed area of the solid rock. He held up a lantern along with a box. After he lifted the lid, he pulled out several sticks that appeared at first glance to be friction lights. With them, he lit the lantern. Holding it high he reached out for her hand.

"Stay close." He whispered.

She didn't know what else she would do. They didn't go far before they turned down another corridor. "This one is marked with paint as are all the other corridors where you will turn. If you follow the markings, you will come out on a small pool. The opening leads to the river. If you ever need to get away from someone or something, I don't want you to feel trapped inside this place. Come in here if you need to hide from someone, the cave is safe. It could be your refuge from trouble."

His words caused a ripple of shivers to infuse her body. This was remarkable. She had not thought of anything like this. She would have never explored. They didn't walk far. Several minutes later they made another turn then another. They stood in front of a small pond. The surface rippled with the movement of the river beyond. She bent over, testing the temperature of the water. It was cool to the touch yet warmer than the river. Questioning his intent, she looked to him.

He seemed to have the answer to her unspoken question. "Depending on the level of the river you can either walk out or swim." Michael hesitated a moment. "Do you swim?"

Her breath held deep inside, she nodded.

"Good. Assumed as much by the way you played in the water." He pointed to the sides of the pool. "When the river is lower, there is a path along the bank, once outside turn to your right. You will have to walk along the beach for about a half-mile before you can turn inland. When you are there, turn north then east. Not too much later you'll find that field of wild flowers with all the buzzing bees. Or…if something happens that you need to flee to the cave, wait here for me to find you. Remember…I will always find you, come for you. Hold on to that thought if you are ever in trouble."

It seemed he saw her shivering. Michael pulled her into his arms. His lips found hers in a brief hard kiss that reassured her yet did little to warm. "I don't know what to say to that as I don't want to believe I would ever find myself trapped in this place. Don't want to believe anyone would want to hurt me."

"I don't want to imagine that fact either. We both understand that Raynard will blame you for his downfall. After that you have Biff and Busby to contend with. Either of those men might want to corner you in a place they believe you can't run from. If the river wasn't so high, I would lead you out, show you everything. We're just beginning to dry. So, another swim would hardly be practical. Don't think you should get wet again. Come, let's finish our picnic unless the wild animals finished off the food for us."

"Are there wild animals that like oysters? Do you suppose the aphrodisiac would affect them the same way it did us?" Unable to help herself she giggled.

"Imp," he teased her. "Of course, it would. Why do you think so many animals like shellfish?" he paused, turning her, tilting her head so he could look into her eyes. "Does that question mean you believe in the sexual powers of aphrodisiacs?"

She hit him in the stomach but not too hard. Nevertheless, his obliging groan gave her reason to smile. He slipped his fingers through hers. Markings also showed the way back. After they stepped outside, Clare breathed in deeply of the clean fresh air. Inside, the cave the air was stuffy, stagnant with no breeze to sweep away the odors that had probably been there for centuries.

In the open, he stared at the hillside above them. "No one is there."

"How do you know?"

"Hairs on the back of my neck aren't sticking up. I would not have touched you so intimately if I'd thought someone was watching. You understand that. Tell me you do."

"Yes."

"I felt their presence after the fact."

They ate more of the delicious food enjoying conversation along with the sunshine. Michael poured her more wine. She curled up next to him, her head on his chest. His back was propped against a rock. The feel of him so close, so protective, the need to sift in the fresh air felt natural. She needed to breathe in the moment. Her hand swept across his chest. He was so hard and flat. Her fingers exploring his belly seemed to jerk him awake. She'd thought for a moment he'd been sleeping.

"If I were you, I wouldn't do that." His lazy drawl surprised her.

Ignoring his comment, she shifted her fingers a bit lower. His hand closed over hers before bringing her questing and curious fingers higher to settle on the middle of his chest.

She felt precocious just as she had when she started the water fight. She wondered if a woman could seduce a man. Someday she might feel brave enough to try. "Why?"

"You should not be so very inquisitive. If I were to take your virginity in the process, I would also take away your right to choose me as your husband. I need you to pick me not be forced by something I did."

Startled, she pushed away to look on his face. "Why?" she asked again.

There was a wicked gleam in his eyes as well as a devilish expression on his face. "Because I would take that right from you. I would write to your brother-in-law explaining what I did, that I broke through your maidenhead. He would arrive back in Virginia to see you wed."

"That's despicable."

He grinned down at her his smile broad. "No, I've given you fair warning. Tell me, yes, Clare, before we are unable to stop ourselves. Before all my manly control vanishes. Your body is enticing. Captivating. At times I yearn to ravish you. You are passionate beyond what any man could expect or even imagine. This afternoon you would have let me inside you. We both understand that for a fact. You would not have told me to stop."

She frowned at him, her brows narrowing. "I did let you inside me." She felt confused, frustrated too.

"Not the way I want to be. Not in the way that would give me good reason to write that letter to Link. Not in the way that might conceive a child. When I come inside you, I won't withdraw. When my rod finds its way deep within your velvet sheathe, you will have given me the answer I seek, or we would have lost control. Unless you push me over the edge with your wandering hands as well as that avid curiosity you possess, my loss of control won't be something you have to worry over."

Her fingers moved lower. She was touching the waistband of his buckskins so tempted to test his words. He was right. She was curious. "Like this?" She grinned at him. She wanted to laugh at the pained expression on his handsome features. "I would like to feel what is beneath the fabric. Want to see that part of you that wants to be inside me."

"Clare." Once again, he stopped her hand. "I warn you unless you are ready to say yes, don't do it!"

Reluctantly, she brought her hand back to his chest even though more than anything she wanted to touch him, to see him enlarged as the stallion was. Eventually, giving him a yes answer would happen, just not now, not today. She had too much to think about. She didn't wish to give in to his manly ego too soon. Before she could marry Michael, she would have to come to terms with the fact he wouldn't ever love her. All he wanted from her was Mayfair. If she didn't own the plantation, he would never care about her.

"Are you waiting for love words, Clare?" he asked his voice whisper soft his tongue leisurely teasing her ear. He brought her fingers to his lips for a sweet kiss. The caress was brief, still poignant, still heating her body from the inside out.

She pushed the desolate feelings from her mind. Dealing in reality was the only way for her to proceed. "You've made it abundantly clear you don't think love exists. I happen to disagree with you. My sister and Link are very much in love. I'd like the same for myself."

She wouldn't tell him how she felt even though he must guess at the truth.

"Do you love me, Clare?"

He sucked a finger into his mouth then another. He smoothly bit each one before releasing it from his lips.

In the back of her throat a moan of pleasure mingled with a delicate sigh. She imagined the denial. Would have to lie to him. "It's just lust I feel for you, nothing more. That's why it's so damn hard to resist my curiosity. Want to know what is behind your pants. My hunger for your body is impossible to put to the back of my head. I do want to touch you, kiss you, taste parts of you that you refuse to show me. It's not fair that you touched me intimately then won't allow me to do the same."

His heavy sigh then groan left her questioning once more. "Two entirely different scenarios exist here. I can bring you pleasure without ruining you," he grumbled softly. The sound was followed by a low moan. "Now, I could coax your ecstasy again or we could ride back to Mayfair. However, I'm afraid you would not be in control. If I'm going to leave you with a choice about our marriage, I can't allow that."

Clare thought better than to push this after what he told her about the letter he would write. If she wed him, the marriage contract would be on her terms not the ones he elaborated just now. She didn't want Link hightailing his body across the Atlantic to see to her wedding. No one was going to make her say the words that would commit her for life to this man or any other one. This was all about free will.

"We should ride back. I'm not ready to pledge myself."

She let out a wistful little sigh that made him smile.

"You wish for me to give you your woman's pleasure again. However, the stakes are too high. Am I right?"

"Yes and no, I was thinking about that feeling of yours. I don't want anyone to see us, see me in your arms. See you touching me so personally. It's too private. What if that horrible man was Raynard watching or those other two men? I couldn't handle the thought they saw me nearly naked."

A frown deepened on his face. One perfectly sculpted eyebrow arched upward seeming to contemplate the possibility of just such an occurrence. "Neither could I. Nonetheless, if any of them were here, they are gone now. Before we sat down, I scanned the area. Big Tom was supposed to ride out to the cave. He would have warned us if a man or men were out there. Perhaps he scared them away. If Big Tom saw Raynard, the man might meet his demise at the big guy's hands."

"Big Tom? He follows me everywhere. I feel uncomfortable to know I've a constant shadow that's not actually attached to me."

"A shadow that's not attached? Interesting. Do you suppose one could sew the shadow back onto a person's feet so the darn thing would then be attached?" he questioned seemingly amused with the caricature. "I've never heard of such a notion. However, the situation is as you descried. For now, Big Tom is your unattached shadow whenever I'm not around to be with you." He pushed a few strands of her unruly hair from her face. "Don't wish anything to happen to you."

They rode back to Mayfair Hall. She felt disillusioned as well as uncertain about her future. Clare understood she would have to make a decision soon. He would continue to coax and sweet-talk her until she wouldn't be able to stop his lovemaking. He would keep asking her to marry him. What did it matter that he didn't love her? She had enough love in her heart for both of them. Marriage to Michael Flannigan was what she wished for with all her heart.

Perhaps love would come.

Not if he didn't believe in the unmanly concept of love.

She decided then and there if she could, she would take the decision out of her hands. She would tempt him until he did make love to her. Could a woman coax a man bent on resistance into making love to her?

The thought had its possibilities. She recalled his reaction to her exploration. Perhaps she could seduce him.

"We should get back."

His curt words hurtled her back to the authenticity of the here and now.

She didn't want to leave. Returning to Mayfair meant leaving this glorious day behind. Clare understood she should have said yes today. She was afraid he'd withdraw from her. If he did so, his departure would not suit his purpose. If he ceased his attentions, he would never own Mayfair Hall. A feeling of loss as well as confusion sped through her.

If he did withdraw, she would have to take matters into her hands. She would set the course, having made up her mind today that she would not tell him what he wanted to hear concerning the proposal until she was good and ready to do so. Instead, she would show him how she felt. After all it was his words that spurred her rebellious thoughts. She would play into his hands. If he didn't write, she would. However, she would put her seduction of him off for a while. She didn't want Link to feel as if he had to set sail again so soon. Her sister didn't need to be present for her nuptials.

After they reached Mayfair, Michael spent time with Timmie discussing the racing schedule as well as the training and exercising of the stallions. Aimlessly, she wandered around the big house lost in her musings. Delilah was in the kitchen preparing dinner. Old Suzzy was dusting the parlor. She felt useless at the moment. Upstairs, she stopped in her old bedroom. It seemed to be a cubicle compared to the massive master chamber and the adjoining bedroom she used.

Outside on the patio, she sat on a chair looking out on the great expanse of land. She tucked her feet beneath her. She held the pillow that had been on the chair in front of her. She thought of the little boy who had his home ripped away from him. As a man, he wanted his home back. Would even marry a woman he didn't love to gain his dream. She couldn't blame him. If put in his shoes, she might do the same.

In the distance she watched clouds build on the horizon. Thought of the thunderstorm that would reach them soon. Gusts of wind swept through the gardens. Tree limbs swayed. Birds chattered sensing the coming tempest. The scent of rain filled the air. She loved these moments, the storm, the lightning along with the thunderous booms that would rupture the very air a person breathed.

Old Suzzy brought a pot of tea. "There's a storm a brewin'. Best you think about comin' inside soon. The way that wind is pickin' up it'll blow you off the porch if you're not tied down. You're such a little bit of a woman. Need to put some meat on your bones."

"Don't believe the wind is quite that strong."

Clare laughed softly as she watched Suzzy shuffle from the porch muttering to herself about the little miss who didn't know what was good for her.

Perhaps she didn't.

Suzzy stopped before she left, boldly pointing a finger at her. "Best you accept that man's proposal before he gets tired of saying the words. You need a strong man to protect you. With that temper of yours, never know what could happen if you anger the wrong man."

Clare gasped startled. She wondered how Suzzy knew about his proposals. She imagined Suzzy knew most everything that went on around here.

"She's right. You know that." Michael stepped on to the veranda, a wide grin complimenting his striking features. He kissed her on the forehead. "Best you tell me yes right now. As you well know, I'm the strong man who will defend as well as safeguard you from that fiery temper of yours."

"Have you been telling everyone?" She mushed her lips together thinking he had no business doing so. She felt annoyed with him. She wanted to tell him what she just thought.

"No, I think Old Suzzy overheard us one day. You well know there is no privacy in this world especially in this house. When you think you're alone, you're not." He hollered at Suzzy. "We'll have our dinner here on the balcony. I'm famished. No tea for me. Bring a couple of bottles of wine."

"With that tempest a brewin'?" she tsked. "Now don't dat just beat all? Dinner where all the elements can come out and drown them." she tsked again, "Two bottles of wine. Might be what you need to convince her to tell you right."

Clare thought it might just beat all.

~ * ~

Old Suzzy knew what she was talkin' about. A few minutes later, lightning hit the ground near the river. Thunder reverberated through the hot summer night. White-blue flashes slashed across the heated summer sky one after the other. Michael sat beside Clare, wrapped a protective arm around her pulling her close.

"You're not afraid of storms? Are you?"

While he had other ideas about how they would pass the time, he was indeed famished. His hunger wasn't for food though. No, it was for Clare. Earlier today she tormented him with her inquisitive exploration of his body. Now, he needed to discover more of her. He wanted to make love to her, plunge deep inside her tight sheathe.

"No, are you?"

She turned a dazzling smile on him before she rested her head in the hollow of his shoulder. She did fit him to perfection. He did want her more than any woman he'd ever known. Could only imagine how he would feel buried deep inside her. Those thoughts tormented him night and day.

He cleared his throat not wishing to give her news that would worry as well as frighten her. He had no choice in this matter. "Raynard was seen this afternoon. Big Tom saw him on the bluff. Took off after him. Raynard's a wily devil. He managed to get away. He disappeared into a corpse of trees. By the time Big Tom got there it was if the man vanished into the hot summer air."

She hissed in a breath of air. The knowledge was too much. She clasped her fists tight. "Raynard, he saw us, didn't he?"

"Possibly. Tom saw him near the cave riding away. Seems he was headed inland. Must have found some place to hunker down for a spell. If he hasn't found shelter, he'll be miserable tonight. There's a storm brewing, a big one if that thunder and lightning we just heard means anything. Big Tom rode into the village to tell the sheriff. I might have to leave soon."

"He's still a threat to all of us, isn't he?" she shivered. Michael's arm tightened around her. "I don't regret what I did. Just wish he hadn't raised that whip to the girl."

"Let's not worry about him right now."

His finger traced her jaw then down the silken white column of her neck. More than anything he wanted her acceptance of him as a man. He needed her to realize they were good together better than good. That desire and passion seething between them were more important to a marriage than love. Good God, he hungered for her every time he set eyes on her. He didn't know what love was. Nevertheless, he sure as hell knew what love wasn't.

After a long roar of thunder, he stared outside. With his hands behind his back, he rocked on his heels. He enjoyed a good storm. Hurricanes were different. Tonight, it seemed the natural elements opened up on them. He was heartily glad he wasn't caught beneath this storm without shelter. He hoped Big Tom reached town. He should have plenty of time with Clare before he would need to leave. The posse would take time to muster.

Hail pounded on the part of the balcony that wasn't covered, the thundering noise drowning out every other sound. Where they sat, they were protected from the onslaught. With Clare nestled softly in his arms and covered by a warm quilt, they viewed the tempest. At this moment with her sweet curves pressing against him, he would relish the storm more so if he wasn't going to have to leave her.

"I always loved storms," Clare murmured as she pushed against him seemingly needing to get closer to the warmth he offered.

Her hand rested on his chest. He covered her fingers with his large hand. "Sometimes we would go to the beach house my Uncle Cam owns. The storms there would be wondrous coming in off the Firth of Clyde. Spray from the ocean would hit the rocks billowing sometimes almost to the porch. The scent of the salty ocean air would sting my nose. One of the children Link adopted, his name is Johnny, would run down to the rocks. He could have been washed over into the turbulent waves. He tempted fate too many times to count, as he wasn't afraid of anything or anyone. Before he met Link, he was a pickpocket. Link found him at Vauxhall Garden. The boy was fearless. Link saved him from Newgate or transportation to one of the colonies."

"You admired him? Does he still pick pockets?"

Michael wasn't at all certain why he felt jealous. He supposed it was the tone of her voice. She seemed mesmerized by the telling of the story. He could understand she cared for the lad. That fact didn't please him.

"Good God, no, to both questions. He teased me mercilessly. One time I threw my glass of milk at him. The boy grinned as if he enjoyed the mess. One day I told Link I wanted a punching bag so I wouldn't take my frustrations out on him." She lifted her delicate shoulders before she grinned at him. "He's at oxford now. Wants to become a solicitor of all things. No, Johnny is no pickpocket though he still possesses the necessary skills."

Feeling a bit at a loss, he smoothed his hand down her hair. "You tossed an oyster at me," he murmured thoughtfully, watching her as her eyes darkened with what he was beginning to realize was hunger. He wouldn't mind letting her feast on his man's body any time she wished to do so.

"I did. Didn't I? Well, you're different. You're not ten years old. He did things like sneak into my room to steal my drawers. He would tie them outside his window just to embarrass me. Link would scold him every time he was informed of the little devil's prank. Since Link and Sophie didn't live with us, that wasn't very often."

"How old were you?" He was chuckling now thinking he'd like to steal her drawers right off her. He could do so now. She wouldn't protest. He would hold them for ransom. A few kisses would be nice for payment. His hand wandered to her legs.

Nonetheless, jealousy still swept through him. When he voiced his thoughts, her eyes darkened. "I would take them off you right now. Slip my hand up your skirt. When my hand reached your soft belly, I'd slide my nimble fingers beneath the fabric then tug them to your knees after that off your ankles. What do you think? Should I do that?"

It appeared she meant to ignore his suggestive words. Her eyes did cross for a moment. "Seventeen. You won't. I won't allow that to happen." She laughed as his hand lingered suddenly on her ankle. He massaged gently inching along her calf.

Everything about her was small and delicate. Her bones were so slight and fragile he could break them without much pressure. "Not tonight, though I would like to do just that." His fingers inched upward until they were behind her knee while she squirmed slightly. Perhaps there would be time. "Are you remembering this afternoon? I'm not going to propose to you again tonight. Think I should wait awhile. If you change your mind, feel free to chime in a sought after yes. If you don't want to say the words, why, you could just come into my bed naked. That would tell me you were ready without speech."

She sucked in a swift breath of air when his hand teased the soft flesh of her thigh. He wondered if she reacted to what he was doing or the fact he wasn't going to propose. Let her think he lost interest. He would never lose interest in this woman. She was his.

Perhaps he should make love to her tonight. If he did, the deed would be done, her maidenhead pierced through. That would be nice since he was fast losing patience with her along with himself. His body reacted to her when he looked at her. At this moment in time, he was hard as steel. Beneath his doeskins, his arousal pulsed, leapt each time she touched him or pressed her breasts against his chest. It had been all he could do this afternoon not to take off his trousers then push into her. When he closed his eyes, he had no trouble imagining the moist heat of her body surrounding him. She was heaven and hell to him all encased in one tiny feminine package.

He reveled in her woman's pleasure. The expressions on her face when she reached the pinnacle sent his body spinning. Hearing her moan her pleasure then cry out his name was something he wanted to hear until he stuck his spoon in the wall. At this moment, with his wayward thoughts running rampant in his poor man's brain, he was hard pressed to contain himself.

Suzzy brought dinner to the balcony. The plates were loaded with slices of pork seasoned with rosemary, asparagus from the garden Delilah planted. Hot rolls along with the sweet strawberry jam that was made this June finished the meal. Yesterday, he raided the wine cellar at Leslie Hall. He brought back several bottles of Bordeaux for their consumption.

They ate and drank in companionable silence. The storm raged around them. When he finished, he sat back replete, his hands resting on his belly. He watched her finish her wine. Over the rim of the crystal, she slanted him a provocative look that left him reeling. She tapped her fingers on the base of the glass.

"What are your plans for the rest of the night?"

"Just enjoy your company for as long as I can. I've a feeling we'll have company soon."

"All right. Who?"

"As I said earlier, Big Tom went to the village to tell the sheriff about Raynard. There might be a posse tonight. I might have to leave."

Michael cursed when he saw the riders on the horizon. He didn't want to leave Clare. Had plans on sleeping with her through the night after they were sated on the food as well as the wine they shared. As he just explained to Clare, he wasn't surprised to see them. He expected something like this to play out before he retired to bed. In any event, he'd hoped the posse's arrival would have been tomorrow morning.

Even though the display of lightning was winding down, this was not a night to be out battling the elements. The rain would undoubtedly continue to fall for the next few hours. He counted eight men along with four hounds. Tonight, they were hunting man. Didn't know how the hounds would help. The rain would have washed away any lingering scent. Still, there was an off chance. These hounds were magnificent in what they did. Most of the time they tracked runaway slaves. Now they followed the scent of a free man who raped a young slave girl who had been set free. The hunt seemed fitting this time. He was eager to see Raynard pay for this crime as well as all the others he committed.

"Why are they here? You said Raynard? I believed he would get away with the crime." Clare stood, her hands now on the balcony railing. Her body shook with what he felt certain was confusion. She turned to him, looking for an answer. "Do you think they found Raynard? Is that why they are here?"

"No, they're hunting him. As you know he was spotted earlier today. I'm going to have to go. I'll join the men tracking him. They don't do anything like this in London? You will get used to our ways, I'm sure." He pulled her into his arms. He kissed her hard before setting her away. "I hoped they wouldn't arrive until morning. Wanted to spend the entire evening with you."

She touched her lips with a slender fingertip, her eyes blazing with passion. "How long? How long will you be gone? What if Raynard comes here?"

His gut curled at the thought. He didn't believe the man would be so stupid. One never knew. "Raynard will not. If he does, we'll be right behind him. Timmie will sleep in the parlor."

"All right."

Her voice was calm and serene.

Even while he tried to see into her emotions, he prayed she was truly that calm. He shook his head as he strode into the bedroom to grab a jacket along with a great coat to ward off the rain. He hated knowing she was terrified. Raynard would not come here. He was certain of that. "Wait for me in here, in my bed. I want you to be there for me when I get back. I want to know you want me as much as I do you."

Her reputation no longer mattered to him. People in the village talked, they talked about them. Rumors abounded that they were lovers. What did it matter if the gossip was true or not? In time they would be more than just lovers. Men wanted her just as men wanted her sister because they believed her a whore. No, they wanted her because she was exquisite. The loveliest woman anyone of them had ever seen. The other was simply an excuse. There were a lot of differences in the two situations. Clare wasn't flaunting her body so her uncle could gain more land. Clare just wanted what she thought to be her inheritance.

All he wanted was Mayfair Hall.

No, that wasn't all. He wanted Clare. *She's mine.*

When he reached the stable, Timmie had Gypsy saddled. "Sleep in the parlor, please. Go to the stables every other hour or so. One is nearing her time. The main house, Clare being inside, is of the utmost importance to me. I don't think this is a diversion to get to Clare..."

God, he didn't know what to think. Raynard could be doing anything. He would be out there watching, waiting for the posse to leave. Raynard used to ride with them. He would understand their habits.

"Thought you would say that. I will keep a wary eye. I've sent for my older brother. He can help keep an eye on your woman as well as the mares. We'll take turns watching the horses. They are hunting Raynard. He was seen headed to the old Anderson property. It's a ways to go. Take care. I'll make certain no one gets into the main house."

Michael reached the group. Big Tom sat on one of the new mares they bought from North Carolina a week ago. He wished Big Tom were staying at the house instead of riding with them. The big man couldn't do so. They needed him here.

Clyde, the sheriff, rode in the front leading the posse. They would spend the night tracking the man he fired only a few weeks ago. He not only fired him, he humiliated him. A man didn't take kindly to something like that. Raynard would seek his revenge. Part of that vengeance would be directed toward Clare since she was the main source of his problems.

The hail from the thunderstorm cooled the air. He buttoned his jacket then slipped into his great coat. They rode hard, pushing the animals to their limit. Rain continued to fall. The trail muddied. Beneath him Gypsy heaved. Clyde raised his hand calling a halt. The hounds were useless, at this point confused. Suddenly, one howled at the sky, racing off in a different direction. The dog returned a few minutes later.

They'd been riding for hours. He was cold, exhausted as well. To his dismay this seemed to be a fiasco. Tonight, they would not find Raynard. Still, they continued. Another hour slipped through time. The

108

men were closing in on the old Anderson place, a rundown shack. He prayed this would end. Somehow, he knew this hunt would not. Raynard was no fool. When he heard the posse, he would leave. Hell, he could have heard them before they got within sight of the shack, the pounding of the horses' hooves, the baying of the dogs.

At the small hovel where Raynard was supposed to be living all was quiet. The only sounds were the usual night noises coupled with the steady drip of the rain. The men dismounted easing their muscles. Everything was dark. Michael was positive no one was inside. The shack was rundown. One wall had collapsed on the far side. Rain ran through the open roof. No one would stay here unless he was desperate.

Clyde motioned for them to dismount. "Raynard," he called out. There was no answer. "Raynard! Come out now!" The sheriff, pistol drawn pushed aside the door.

It was as he expected. The man was not stupid. He understood he was hunted. He would never return here. Where could he go?

"I thought we would find the man here." Clyde said as he wiped his brow with the back of his sleeve. "We've been on a fool's mission. He knew..."

"Knew we were coming for him?" One man asked. "That thought makes me think of so many other scenarios."

"How the devil would he know something like that?" Biff asked, clearly perplexed by the idea. Yet there was an underlying note of annoyance in the man's voice. "This is the last place I would have thought to look." Now, the man sounded defensive.

Michael felt his stomach churn, his thoughts boiling. All this time was wasted. He knew then that this man was allied with Raynard. Biff would have told him the posse would come out here. He wasn't positive how he knew Biff leaked the news. He just did. This man wasn't to be trusted, not that there should be trust after what he said about Clare.

"Why?" Michael asked hoping to hear something that would give him more answers to this relationship between the two men. "What do you know that we do not?" He turned to Biff, seeking a response.

This was the man who offered him a dollar to bed Clare. He should be strung up by his thumbs along with Raynard. There was no doubt in his mind where this man was concerned that he was guilty of aiding as well as abetting an enemy.

Biff sent his horse to step backward. He pushed his hat back off his face. "Don't know what you are talking about. What are you implying?"

It seemed he tried to bluster his way out of the accusation humming on the air. As far as Michael was concerned Biff showed his true colors.

"You know exactly what I'm implying," Michael ground out as he approached the man. "You told Raynard the posse was formed, told him also we knew where to find him. You're after Clare. We both know that for a fact, as is Raynard. You have joined forces with him. Tell me if I'm wrong."

Clyde appeared from inside the shack. "Raynard was here. He isn't now. Doesn't look as if he'll be coming back. We're going to continue looking."

The time for Michael's confrontation with Biff passed. He would have another time.

Of course, he wasn't in the hovel. Earlier today the man saw Big Tom just as Big Tom saw him. Somehow, he was told more bad news. News that his hiding place had been discovered would have been the next bit of information. Raynard was most likely watching them at this very moment, just as he observed him with Clare this afternoon. Had Biff along with Busby watched them also? His gut churned with the fear that perhaps the men were plotting together. If they were, it would be more difficult to capture Raynard.

Michael wanted to race home. Needed to make certain Clare was all right. That Raynard wasn't, even now, forcing her. He feared for her more now than when he left. He tugged in long breaths of air while he attempted to steady his nerves along with the hammering of his heart.

The hounds bayed. It seemed they all had the same idea as they took off toward the river. Few sounds could be heard over the barking of the dogs. What night animals stirred here probably took cover from the constant rain. The forest from here to the river was thick and dark. A man could hide with ease in this place. Not with the dogs on his scent, no one could hide from the hounds.

"Looks like the dogs caught his stench," a man said looking in the direction they were going.

Michael tossed a look at Big Tom. He wanted to tell him to return to Mayfair Hall. His woman needed protection. They didn't need all eight men here. Big Tom nodded seeming to understand what he wanted. He tipped his hat to Clyde then turned his horse to go in the other direction.

"Clyde," Michael began, catching the older man's attention. "Big Tom's going back to Mayfair Hall. I need him there."

A knife of fear slashed through him. Perhaps he was being nervous over nothing. The hounds weren't going toward Mayfair. No, they were headed in the opposite direction.

That fact didn't matter to him. All too well he understood how Raynard thought. Michael had no idea why he felt obliged to continue on this ill-fated quest. Years ago, he made a commitment to Clyde that he would be here if he needed assistance. The only times he refused were the times they were after runaway slaves.

This wasn't the case. Raynard needed to be stopped before he hurt someone else.

A few hours later they reached the river. At this spot, the river ran fast as well as deep. For a man as well as a horse the crossing could be deadly. Raynard would have to walk along the bank until the water grew shallow. Raynard must still be mounted. If not, they would have caught him by now.

The dogs lost his smell. Michael, just as everyone else understood he waded for a ways then crossed to the other side. Of course, he could have stayed on this side expecting the men to assume the first scenario.

Their sheriff wasn't stupid. The men split up. When the hounds finally found the odor, the trail was on the other side of the river. Now Raynard headed back toward the village. If he continued on this path, he would end up near Biff Gideon's plantation. There could be no place for him to hide. The slaves certainly wouldn't give him shelter out of the rain. They couldn't search a man's home without reason.

The chase lasted three days. They continued to catch clues of his whereabouts that would end with no hint of the man. Several times they doubled back. The men weary from the constant riding gave up the hunt. Eventually, Raynard would surface. Clyde left men to guard the Anderson shack. All had been done that could be done.

When they reached his home, he left the group. The rest were headed toward the village. Grayson, the manager of Leslie Hall, would be the next man to leave the posse.

Wearily, he dismounted from Gypsy. He took a moment to stretch some of the kinks from his stiff muscles. He was sore in places he didn't know existed before this. He was hungry as well as exhausted. They spent the nights under the stars, sleeping on the cold barren ground. Each man took turns hunting as well as foraging for the food they ate.

Timmie was waiting for him, taking hold of the bridle as he dismounted. "Everything is just fine here, no problems. The little missy has been to the stables every day to check on the mares. Neither one has delivered their foal. It's just going to be a matter of time before both do. Best you get some sleep before that happens. I'll call for you if there is any change."

"Thanks."

"No reason to thank me. Just doing my job." Timmie's teeth gleamed white behind the wide grin.

"Well, in my mind there is. The fact that you're loyal is reason I could stay away, do my duty. You and Big Tom have my gratitude. Now, I'm going to mosey on up to the house and get some of that shuteye you insisted on, first a bath though. Maybe I can sneak a bit of food from the kitchen."

"Delilah will bat your hand away just as if you're a recalcitrant child. You just wait and see."

"Naw, the woman has a soft spot for me. Besides she's got to know I'm starving for some of her cooking."

Michael whistled softly as he made his way to the kitchen. As he thought there would be, a few slices of soft bread waited for him. He grabbed a piece, slathered it with sweet butter then two-stepped his way to his bedroom.

Michael thought of a hot tub of steaming water. He thought of Clare washing his back. No, perhaps Clare would join him in the tub. He grinned. That perhaps was asking too much under the circumstances. She was still shy. With time that fact would change.

It was dawn. If she slept in the bed in the master chamber since he left, she would be there now. He wanted to see her in his bed, her beautiful auburn hair spread around her and across his pillows, his covers pulled over her. No, she usually braided her hair before she went to bed. If he had his way when she wed him, that particular practice would have to stop.

It seemed Old Suzzy must have heard him arrive at the stable. When he stepped into his room shedding his clothing, the tub was out. Several of the house servants were bringing hot water. No, Delilah must have heard the posse then gone to get water. She was always in the kitchen this time of day. He was surprised she wasn't there when he nabbed the hot bread off the serving tray.

Quickly, he finished disrobing. He settled into the hot water relishing the heat. Breathing in deeply he took a moment to look at the woman lying on his bed. There had been times over the last few nights he felt frozen to the skin. Especially, the first night out when it seemed all the weather could dish out was rain. The ground had not only been cold but the earth was wet.

Michael closed his eyes. Minutes ticked by as the hot water kissed his skin. He settled his head on the back of the tub. He didn't hear the footsteps. The first indication she was beside the tub was the soapy sponge rubbing gently across his chest then the sweet smell of gardenias embraced every sense he possessed.

He groaned low in the back of his throat as he absorbed her soft caresses. This was heaven to be welcomed home in this manner. He couldn't wish for anything more. When she washed lower, a fierce surge of longing rippled through him.

Her voice was smooth, a sultry soft purr against his cheek. "I wondered if you would ever come home. Thought you must have run off to some other state. My goodness it's been three nights you've been gone. How could one simple man elude all of you along with the hounds for so many hours? The fact doesn't make sense."

"We didn't find him." He let a long breath of air rush through him.

As she moved lower, he stilled her hand. "Not this morning, just wash my back," he said softly. "I'm too tired for anything else." He leaned forward so she could soap the muscles on his back.

"Would you like me to wash your hair as well?"

He nodded his approval. Until he slipped into the hot water, mud along with dirt covered him. She caressed him as she washed, the motion eased his strained muscles notwithstanding his burgeoning desire. Despite the fact he was exhausted bone-deep, her nimble fingers continued to arouse him. She massaged his shoulder muscles. Some of the soreness from sleeping on the hard ground the last days vanished. When she finished with his back and shoulders, she soaped his hair. Her fingers kneaded his scalp. Unable to help himself he groaned again all the while wishing this moment when it seemed to him, she would say yes, he could do something about her desire.

Clare brought him a towel after she rinsed his hair. He understood she wanted to see him naked. Someday her curiosity would get her into trouble. Perhaps this was the morning for that. A morning when he was so tired almost all he could think of was sleeping, sleeping with her, nothing else. He didn't have the energy to make love to her or bring her to pleasure.

She held the towel up, waiting for him to step from the tub. He rose. Water sluiced from his shoulders then down his legs She let out a tiny puff of air, her eyes wide. He was fully aroused. He didn't think she expected that. He didn't expect to be aroused either.

"You're beautiful." Her words were whisper soft so gentle her gaze resting on his. "I didn't know what you would look like."

He felt heat rush to his face, as he'd never been called beautiful before. Embarrassment was not something he was accustomed to feeling. "Is your curiosity assuaged now?"

He couldn't help asking the question, his grin widening as he watched the amazement in her eyes the way her gaze unwaveringly stroked his body. He wanted to toss his head back then roar with laughter. He didn't.

He saw her swallow as he wondered if the gesture was from fear. For a moment, she lowered her lashes. No, he didn't think she was afraid of him, not his Little Pigeon. Her curiosity coupled with her impulsiveness would drive her to learn more.

"Not all of my curiosity. Not until you make love to me. I want to know what will happen, how you will feel inside me. I know some of what we will do, not all. As you bade me, I watched the stallion with his mare."

He took the towel from her hands. Dried himself along with his hair. He pulled the covers of the bed down so he could climb in. "Will you join me tonight? Just to sleep?"

He wasn't at all sure what she would do though he understood what he hoped for. She nodded a small smile on her face. "I've waited for you. Been worried about you. I'll come to bed with you. Will you hold me?"

Clare climbed into the other side. She wore her innocent nightgown buttoned to her throat. The fabric covered her toes when she stood. He thought that when they wed, he would buy her a silken confection he could see through. Something he would delight in removing from her soft white body.

She set her head on his chest after he wrapped an arm around her tugging her close. He wanted to make love to her. His hand roamed across her breast delighting in how the crest hardened for him. He moved lower until he widened his fingers across her soft belly. His fingers spanned her hipbones.

"If you want to go to sleep, Michael, you should not be touching me like that. If you continue to do so, I will seduce you, coax you with my soft woman's body until you cannot say no to me. I will hold your man part in my hands. Caress your member until your rod is as hard and aroused as you were in the tub. Don't doubt me."

"I believe you," he groaned.

He didn't like the fact. He could barely keep his eyes open. The chore seemed insurmountable.

"What will it be? After the fact you can write Link. I suppose I'm saying yes," Clare said softly as she brushed a wayward lock of dark red hair from his forehead.

~ * ~

Timmie paced the length of the stable then back. Big Tom sat on a stool near one of the foals sipping hot black coffee. It was the kind of coffee he loved. His wife made it for him every morning before he left for work. He didn't like anything extra in the black stuff. Just loved the rich dark brew along with the way the coffee made his innards feel in the morning. By the time he would finish his second cup, the jolt of energy ripping through his big body was something he enjoyed immensely. The coffee made him feel as if he could conquer the world. Today he might have to do just that. Timmie heard the master ride in along with the posse. When the young man informed him, he sent the lad to the kitchen so Delilah would know to heat water. Now they would wait for Mr. Flannigan to arrive at the stable.

"What are you going to do now?" Timmie asked as he stepped in front of him his hands stuck in his pockets. "The mare is going to drop that foal anytime now. Got to tell Mr. Flannigan. He's going to want to be here." The lad looked to the house then back to him.

"Mr. Flannigan just got into bed a few minutes ago. He's been gone three nights. We can't wake him before he manages to get a bit of shuteye. We can wait a little while longer. Maid Marion isn't going to go into labor in the next few hours. If she does, I'll go rouse him. If he's with the little missy, we might have to get Old Suzzy to help us out." He lifted his shoulders, felt the fabric of his shirt stretch across his back.

"I don't know about that. He's going to be furious with us if something happens to the mare or the foal and he's not out here to oversee everything. He's like that, Mr. Flannigan is. Well, you know that for a fact."

Timmie rocked on his heels, his thumbs in his belt loops now. His panicky energy was apparent.

Somehow, he needed to find a way to calm the young pup down. "We'll survive his wrath. You worry too much," Big Tom said blandly as he tossed a bored grin Timmie's way.

He would get him soon. His boss needed at least three hours of sleep before he roused him. The mare wasn't in labor yet. Oh, she showed all the signs of getting ready for the big event. She was restless in the stall as well as sweating. Big Tom laughed when she curled her top lip at him, sneered at him, she did. The gesture was just like the female persuasion. Yes, she was showing all the signs. The birthing wouldn't be long now.

Timmie jabbed his hands in his hair. He looked out the door then back to Big Tom. He started down the path to the house then turned around. "Don't like this. Don't like rousing him one little bit. Hope you know what's right."

"As long as she's just getting ready there is no reason to bother Mr. Flannigan. When she starts her labor, I'll get him." Big Tom wondered how many times he would have to tell Timmie the same thing. "Why don't you take Duster for a ride? The race coming up this weekend is important. Don't you have to train the two stallions?"

When Big Tom finished speaking to Timmie, he looked up. Old Suzzy was shuffling into the stables carrying a tray he hoped was food for them. His stomach grumbled appreciatively when he caught the scent. She brought them some delicious looking plum pastries. She refilled Big Tom's coffee cup with the brew from the main kitchen. It wasn't as good as his wife's though he didn't say no. At this point, any coffee was good coffee.

"Thanks, Suzzy, this was real thoughtful of you. Is everything okay up at the house?"

"All's right and dandy. You two just make sure the massa gets wind of this happening before it's too late. He's not going to take kindly if he misses out on the birthing. You two make certain he doesn't bring the little missy with him either. She don't belong in dere. No, she doesn't. Don't know what that man's been thinkin' when it come to her wellbeing."

"Nah, he wouldn't do that."

Big Tom knew though that Mr. Flannigan let the little missy watch Duster cover one of the mares that was brought here. That wasn't well done of him. He couldn't question him though. It was, after all, the master's business. Big Tom didn't understand why he wanted her to see something like that. It wasn't right. No, siree, it just wasn't right.

"He did and we both know that for a fact. He let her watch Duster and dat mare go at it. All the squealing and nickering could have frightened her to death especially when Duster nipped the mare's neck with his big white teeth. That wasn't all either. Mr. Flannigan had his big hand on her belly. Didn't want to look. Nonetheless, I had to take care of the stallion as well as the mare. There were times my eyes riveted on those two and what he was doing to her. She was letting him too. Her eyes were closed, a dreamy expression on her pretty little face. Doubt if she had a clue as to what that man's mind was thinkin'."

The mare shifted her weight then got down as if she was readying herself for the birthing. A few seconds later, she rose again. The foal was Maid Marion's first. Jingle Bells time would come soon. Big Tom was sure of that fact he just hoped she didn't decide to go along with Maid Marion and give birth today. If that happened, this place would be in chaos, no doubt about that. He sent a silent prayer heavenward that all would be well.

Timmie assumed his pacing again. He walked from one end of the building to the other. Every so often he stopped to run his hand along Gypsy's and Duster's nose. Big Tom sipped his coffee wishing the brew were stronger. He set the cup on a nearby stool. He rose then stretched. His long strides took him outside. The air was hot, the sky an endless blue. This morning there were no clouds to cover the sun and ease the heat. Looking up to the second floor, he didn't see activity. No, Mr. Flannigan had only been in bed for an hour. He needed more time to rest. No matter what Timmie or Old Suzzy said, he wasn't about to interrupt his sleep.

The flash of yellow striding purposely down the walkway to the stable caught his attention. It was the little missy coming to the stable all bluster coupled with no common sense. Big Tom grinned. He would have thought she would be in bed with her lover. Well, Michael probably fell asleep before she could properly welcome him home. He wished they'd get married. The two of them belonged together. He didn't understand what was holdin' 'em up.

"Hello, Big Tom. How is Maid Marion doing." She flashed a smile his way, one that must melt Mr. Flannigan's heart when she sent that grin to him. "Is it her time yet?"

She walked past him before he could stop her. Not that he could lay a hand on her even though he was a free man now. No, the only way would have been to step in front of her. He didn't dare do that either.

This was too much, much too much, this woman thinking it was all right for her to watch a mare giving birth. She shouldn't be here. He turned to take off after her. When he caught up to her, he didn't know what he should do. She stood in front of the mare's stall. Her hands were on her hips looking the mare over. She was smiling, grinning from ear to ear looking as pleased as if she downed a glass of rum punch.

"You shouldn't be here."

He knew his voice was too gruff. He didn't want to be that way to her. Nevertheless, he didn't want to give her the wrong impression. This was a man's domain. This woman was feminine to the tips of her delicate little toes. He'd heard Michael mumbling one day about her delicate toes. The information didn't surprise him. He shouldn't have repeated the thought. His Mercy wasn't delicate at all. She was strong and sturdy. He wouldn't let her see either the mare being covered or the birthing before they were wed. After all, she was also a woman. This was unheard of.

When she turned to him, her hands were on her hips, her voice firm. "This is my place, Big Tom. Don't you forget that fact. I own Mayfair Hall. I'll go where I please. All the coin going into this endeavor is mine. Will remain mine until I wed." She stopped suddenly a strange expression on those fragile little features of hers. "Perhaps I won't ever wed. Don't want what's mine going to someone else."

Chapter Five

Clare pushed up on her forearms. For several seconds she stared at Michael. His eyes were closed, dark lashes lay against his tanned flesh. She laughed softly. Here she was ready to give herself to him and he slept.

The sun was just peaking its golden head over the eastern horizon.

What did she expect? Most likely he had very little sleep in the last three nights.

Now, he was snoring ever so softly. She wondered if she could look at him again as she wanted to see him, all of him. He was naked beneath the covers. She watched him climb into bed. His sex had been hard, standing at attention as if he wanted her. Would his rod still be hard?

She didn't know.

Her curiosity was getting the better of her. She had to see for herself.

Slowly, she pulled the covers to rest on his thighs. Unable to help herself, she reached out to touch him then hesitated for a moment. A tiny ribbon of fear or was it excitement surged through her. What if he woke up? What if she touched him and he didn't like what she did? He was limp. His member was nothing as it had been after his bath.

This was passing strange. She touched him intimately. He was soft, dark red hair surrounded his rod. He groaned, moved to pull her into his arms. She wrenched back surprised as well as frightened. His hand fell to the mattress. She wondered what he would think of her looking at him, taking her fill of all his male beauty. This wasn't something she would tell him. So, what she did now wouldn't matter to him because he would never discover the truth.

Nevertheless, she decided she didn't want to tempt fate any farther. Not wishing to disturb him, she curled up, her back to him. She pulled a pillow to her head.

Dawn along with the crow of a rooster woke her. She sat up, stretching. He was still asleep, still softly snoring.

One of his large legs was across her thighs. His hand cupped her breast. He wasn't moving. Still, she felt his lips on her ear while his deep sleeping breaths fluttered her hair, tickling her cheek. Without waking him, she tried to move his hand first. Almost as if he teased her, he squeezed slightly, flicking his thumb across her nipple. Her body reacted.

"Michael?" He didn't respond.

"Michael, are you awake?"

The silence except for his soft breathing unnerved her. He acted as if he was awake. His leg moved on her. She reacted as if he coaxed her. Her body quickly became aroused. After the episode at the river, she knew the sensations for what they were.

"If you're awake, I'm going to turn my head then scream in your ear."

Nothing. It was uncanny these feeling she was having. He groaned. After that he moved his leg. She was suddenly free. He no longer touched her. His long body was no longer sprawled atop her. He turned over baring his long powerful back to her.

Somehow, she felt as if she lost something precious. Yes, she did like the way he felt against her. Her nightgown was hoisted to above her thighs. It was strange. That never happened when she slept alone. Had he done that to her? Reluctantly, she left the bed.

All her plans for last night were thwarted. By allowing him to take her maidenhead, she was going to show him that her answer to his proposal was yes. To decide to stand in front of him naked took all the nerve she possessed. In the end, she'd not been able to remove the nightgown. If he could have kept his eyes open, he might have done the deed for her.

Perhaps tonight.

She didn't know if she could regain the brazenness needed to think such a thing let alone accomplish disrobing in front of him. In the adjoining room, she rang for a bath. Quickly, she washed then dressed in one her favorite gowns, a bright yellow muslin. Twirling in front of the mirror she was pleased with the way she looked. Old Suzzy helped her braid her hair then wind the long strands around her head in a coronet.

Waltzing through the kitchen on her way to the stables, she grabbed a hunk of piping hot bread fresh from the oven. She didn't want to take the time to eat a real breakfast.

"You need to sit down and eat your meal, Little Missy. You're going to waste away to nothing. You're all skin and bones now. The massa won't want a woman with no sweet curves to hold onto." Delilah was finishing the cooking chores while waggling a finger at her.

The eggs and bacon smelled wonderful. She just didn't want to take the time. "Thank you, Delilah. When you get a chance can you have someone bring a cup of tea to the stable, please?"

"Well, all be, that Little Missy just won't sit herself down long enough to eat proper. I'm going to have to talk to the massa about that. Bless his soul, he'll make sure you eat proper."

As Clare left the kitchen, she felt Delilah's gaze sear her back. With too much to do today, she just wasn't hungry. Above her the sky was bright and blue. The sun was a huge golden orb sitting just above the horizon to the east. The day was an absolutely beautiful one. Chickens were plucking grain tossed out by one of the servants. An old goat munched on blackberry vines near the stables. The dog that lived here when she first arrived as a thirteen-year-old snoozed by the fence. She tried to whistle as she strode to see what the mares were doing. Whistling was not something she could do well.

Once inside, she was met by frowns from the two men who took care of the horses. She didn't think Michael had the presence of mind to forbid her entrance if one of the mares was birthing her foal. He wouldn't have thought that far ahead. Before she reached the mares, she fed Duster an apple treat, rubbing his nose then telling him what a magnificent male animal he was. She did the same with Gypsy.

Michael wouldn't appreciate a good nose rub even though in her estimation he was a magnificent male animal. Nevertheless, she bet he would like to be told he was magnificent or perhaps splendid. He might relish a good back rub. She'd have to think on that.

Perhaps she shouldn't pander to his vanity. She enjoyed his vanity, all his male arrogance. With Michael the concept wasn't overdone. It seemed an integral part of who he was. She enjoyed him when he laughed. She loved the moments when his voice rose in anger. She relished everything about him including his gentleness.

Again, she thought about the man who stole her heart. She didn't believe his vanity to be more than who he was. When she finished giving all the animals treats, she walked to Timmie and Big Tom. She expected to be tossed out of the stables on her rear, told this place was a man's domain. They didn't move to do so. She supposed the reason was because they'd been slaves a few weeks ago. The rules were different now. They wouldn't understand they now had more privileges. Getting past ingrained beliefs would be difficult. She did own this property, the horses as well as the entire building. Would do so until she wed. That was a staggering thought.

If she chose to stay put, neither would lift a hand to remove her. She grinned knowingly.

"Hello, Big Tom, how is Maid Marion doing? Is it her time yet?"

She stood at the stall, watching the restless mare. It wouldn't be long now. No, another hour or two then she would labor to bring the foal into the world. Excitement surged within. Her breath raced with anticipation. This foal would be the next generation at her stable. She hoped both mares gave birth to males. In her mind, she was counting the money she would earn from the stud fees. Mares she could also breed. Link would send her another stallion, one with impeccable bloodlines. Perhaps one descended from the great, Byerley Turk. Yes, she would ask Link to find a stallion of that magnitude for Mayfair Hall and Stud Farm. With the winnings from the races along with the increasing stud fees she would have the money to pay him back.

Once again, her roving thoughts gave her reason to pause. If she wed, the coin would be Michaels. The fact women couldn't have their own money wasn't fair. Sometimes life wasn't fair. She needed to come to terms with a few things before she made any more decisions about marriage. Children were something she'd always wanted. Wedding a man was the only way she could have a baby. Ah, Michael was a good man even though she knew first hand he could be a very bad boy. Still, she needed more time to think. She was heartily glad; he was too tired last night. Eagerly, she would have let him make love to her.

"You shouldn't be here," Big Tom said, his voice too gruff. "I don't think Mr. Flannigan will want you in the stable when it's her time. Nevertheless," he held up his big hands, shaking his head to keep her from speaking, "I don't want to give you the wrong impression. However, this is a man's province. Women do not belong under these conditions. You've already seen more than you should. I'm looking out for your best interest. Mr. Flannigan will agree with me."

Clare rounded on him, hands on her hips thinking he overstepped his bounds. She wanted to make sure he understood her point of view. Mayfair Hall was not Michael's yet. She meant to take advantage of the few remaining moments that the place was still hers. With that thought in her head, she knew she made up her mind about his marriage proposal. Running this place, making her dream come true would need a man at the helm. It was her wish that she would have a hand in the decision-making. She prayed Michael would give her a say. That was just the point of all her worries. She would have to pray for the best.

She spoke directly. "This is my place, Big Tom. Don't you forget that fact? I own Mayfair Hall. I'll go where I please. All the coin going into this endeavor is mine. Will remain mine until I wed."

She stopped again sweat covering her brow. The thought of marriage turned noxious to her. Confusion assailed her. Again, unwilling to set all her dreams aside, she said, "Perhaps I won't ever wed. Don't want what's mine going to someone else."

Even if that someone else was Michael, no, she had to do more thinking on the matter. It was a good thing he was so exhausted last night. If not, she would have given the man her virginity. This morning she would have had second thoughts. The extra thoughts would have been too late because Michael would have written to Link. Link would insist on a marriage. She vacillated from one extreme to another.

Life was better this way. She gave herself a month to come to a conclusion. A month wasn't that long.

Clare spent the better part of the next two hours moving between the stable and the main house. She checked on Michael who was still soundly sleeping. Maid Marion was not in labor even though she was obviously uncomfortable. In the kitchen, Clare finally sat down to a breakfast of ham and eggs. The meal was delicious as was the second cup of tea to which she added honey and lemon. When she walked back to the stable, Big Tom decided it was time Michael learned Made Marion was in labor.

"I will wake him," she told Big Tom smiling, understanding the man's chagrin. He didn't believe she should be in Michael's bedroom, shouldn't see him sleeping. She comprehended exactly what the man was thinking. Big Tom's opinions didn't bother her over much. No, it was what everyone else in this little part of Virginia thought about her. In this case, Big Tom and Timmie were different. They respected her, wanted to protect her. At least she assumed they did. She wanted to yell at them that he wasn't her lover. Didn't because she understood it wouldn't be much longer until the title owned her.

"I can go for you," Big Tom blurted out with a disapproving look in his deep brown eyes. "A man should wake him. It's not right you go into a man's bedroom when he's sleeping. What will people think?"

No one except the people who worked here would know, probably only the servants who were employed in the house. "Don't worry about me, Big Tom. You don't have to protect me from Michael." She turned without further word. "I've been in the room before with him. He hasn't touched me. My virginity is intact."

Well, that was more than she should have said when she saw his eyes widened to dark pools of embarrassment.

Once again in the kitchen, she looked over the array of food. This time she ordered a huge breakfast along with a pot of hot coffee for Michael. He most likely wouldn't eat the food. After that she strode up the steps wondering how she was going to wake the man if he was still soundly asleep.

She didn't have any ideas. Earlier, she touched him intimately. He didn't wake. If she tried that again, the action might end badly considering her new reservations about marriage along with the resulting indecision.

Opening the door slowly, she hoped he would roll over and say good morning to her with a cheerful smile. When she did step into the room, he was on his back, one arm thrown over his eyes, still snoring. He didn't look asleep. Didn't appear awake either.

What to do?

She rubbed her hands together, indecision clouding her muddled brain. Clare stared then stared some more. His beautiful chest was bared. The sheet covering him just below his navel. She wished the fabric were lower as she wanted to see his man parts again. Desperate for air, she tugged some into her lungs. She was afraid if she tried to wake him, he might have other ideas. On the other hand, if he wanted her...

Letting that thought slide was in her best interest. She considered Mayfair Hall. Thought of her stud farm that she wished to own independently. Was reminded of the way he played her body giving her sensations she'd never known existed. She wanted children. Perhaps she could have both. No, she knew different. Bewilderment settled deep in her belly. He wasn't about to make love to her without a solid commitment.

Michael was purposeful. He was a man who knew what he wanted then went after his goal until that target was his. Clare understood she was his target. She could be just as determined. Clare wanted both Mayfair Hall along with the man in front of her. She wanted to hold his babies in her arms. Damn the fact, she loved him.

Slowly, very quietly she walked to the bed. Her heart wrenched inside her chest when he moaned. The fabric covering him slipped lower. She recalled what he looked like. Her breath caught in the back of her throat. For several seconds she closed her eyes willing her heart to stop racing.

"Michael?" she spoke softly while she inched her way to the bed.

He didn't move. She didn't believe he heard her. The bed dipped when she sat down. Clare set her hand on Michael's chest, which was furred with soft very dark red hair. The hair was silken, curly. She wanted to run her fingers through the softness.

The mare was about to go into labor. He needed to wake up now. He would want time to tend to his needs. Still, she wished she could steal a kiss, a quick kiss with no repercussions one that would say good morning, nothing more.

Careful not to wake him, she bent low, touched his lips with hers.

His mouth was moist and warm. The moan she heard was a deep rumble. The sound made her jump back. When she did so, she stared into his deep green eyes, vibrant eyes. They were dark with passion now just like they always were when he kissed and caressed her.

"Clare."

One of his large, very strong hands held the back of her neck. He tugged her down.

She felt his breath across her cheek. His hand massaged her where his fingers held her. She swallowed hard. He tugged again.

With no balance, she sprawled across his chest. He flipped her over. She was now beneath him, her legs spread. His weight pressed her down while his legs were between hers. He swept his tongue across her lips. With the tip of her tongue, she touched his. She understood exactly what he wanted. Her body responded arching frantically against his. One hand remained on her neck pulling her closer. It seemed he didn't want her to draw away from him. He wanted the kiss to go on and on.

For a brief moment, long enough to say the words, he ended the kiss. "I'm glad you came to me. I was lying here thinking of doing this." He kissed her again then again and again, ravishing her mouth with his.

The hem of her skirt began to inch upward. His hand rested on her backside. She squirmed against him feeling his arousal against her belly, the steel-hard length of him so different from what she witnessed earlier this morning. The need to tell him about Maid Marion vanished. His hand slipped beneath her drawers. She jerked up, his big hand sending rolling sensations of pleasure throughout. His hand pressed against her naked flesh.

His tongue pushed against her lips. She opened her mouth for him, spread her legs wider. While he pushed inside, she tasted him, tasted the strong black coffee he must have had before she came into the room. Inside his mouth was hot and dark, sultry, and erotic. He tricked her. He must have known she was there from the moment she walked into the room.

The cad.

Her hands wound into his hair, holding him close. His fingers, now that they no longer needed to hold her steady, inched the bodice of her gown over her shoulders. Cool air flowed against the newly revealed skin. In a few seconds her breasts touched upon his bare chest. The sensation was heavenly. Then his questing fingers played with her more intimately, stimulated her until she was wild and frantic, bucking up with her need for him. Oh, my, oh my...no, no, no.

Michael was taking the decision from her hands. She needed to stop him now or the time would have passed. He pulled back slightly to look at her. His lips were moist, shiny with the moisture from their shared intimacy. Slowly he bent to flick a hardened crest with his tongue. With obvious relish he bit gently. A tiny mewl of pleasure sifted from her lips into his mouth. Her body tightened with need only he could assuage.

Clare felt the ripple of pleasure pulse and shimmer through her body. She pulled him closer, needing more so very much more while she arched against him. Her fingernails dug into his shoulders. The woman's ecstasy he brought her to a few days ago was almost hers. She felt his hand on her belly. He slid it lower until his fingers spread her swollen hot folds before moving gently inside.

"Michael!" she cried out his name.

Her body heaved against his fingers as he searched her intimately. One finger then two slid deeply inside her. His thumb played with a spot that seemed to spiral her higher and higher. No, she wanted his member inside. Wanted him to take her innocence. Wished for him to teach her all she wanted to learn. *Not now.*

"I like the way you cry out my name."

His low throaty voice sent her higher. His fingers explored deeper. She was beside herself, wanton and desperate with need.

The spasms built then built to a deeper more intense level, spiraling, and spiraling. She was about to detonate. "So hot," she whispered. "So....Michael do something. I can't..."

She wailed with her pleasure. He sent her over the edge. Her body was so out of control she could do naught but let him have his way.

Not that she wanted anything else.

Against him, she wilted, whimpering softly as he soothed her running his hand along her back. "Easy, Little Pigeon."

"Michael..." She was limp, unable to move a muscle.

She had to tell him what was happening in the stable.

"If you wish we can take this one step further. Say the word, Clare," his whispers were next to her ear. His breath hot and sweet against her.

It would not take much to send her to another crescendo of pleasure. "I do. We can't."

After that, coming to her senses was not an easy feat.

He didn't seem to listen. The sheet slipped lower. Her drawers were slowly sliding down her legs. In a few seconds he would be inside her. She understood what he wanted. He wasn't going to stop unless she gave him an adamant no.

"What do you mean we can't?"

His strong hands gently kneaded the roundness of her buttocks. His fingers continued their casual exploration of her intimately. He was sweet-talking and coaxing. He would have his way. No, no, no…not right now.

Clare tried to push away the sensations he created, truly she did. She found she couldn't speak as he pushed her to the plateau of delight she began to crave again. Telling the big man no was impossible at this point. Something needed to happen. All was out of control. Her mind was a mass of spider's cobwebs.

"Mr. Flannigan. Mr. Flannigan." His name, along with the pounding feet taking the staircase two at a time wrenched both of them from the haze of euphoria surrounding them. She whimpered. Moisture stung her eyes. She was well and truly ruined. Someone would see her compromise.

"No…"

He groaned so very low in the throat. The sound was of a desperate man. He tugged her skirt to her ankles. The footsteps she heard had to be Big Tom's. They were too loud to be anyone else's. The fist pounding on the door gave credence to her original thought.

"Big Tom won't come in until I answer. He sounds urgent."

Michael rolled to the side. He tugged up her gown. "Nothing I can do about the drawers." He stuffed them beneath the pillow. Go sit on that chair." He touched her lips with a fingertip. "We will finish this later.

Nothing I can to about your mouth either. The way your lips appear right now is a dead giveaway as to what we've been doing." He grinned at her. "Your hair is a delightful mess that only a lover would appreciate."

"Mr. Flannigan!" Big Tom's pounding sounded even more urgent.

"I don't understand why Big Tom is here."

Maid Marion must have made a turn. She must have begun her labor.

She tugged on his arm, giving him her sole attention. "I came here to tell you that Maid Marion is about to go into labor. You made me forget everything."

He did. The moment he kissed her she forgot her intentions.

"Clare!"

For a moment he sounded outraged. She needed to defend herself. "You didn't give me a chance to tell you. This situation is not all my fault. When you kissed me...then you...then...after that..."

She closed her eyes her body shuddering with the remembered pleasure.

He chuckled softly. "Made you forget your mission, did I? Can't say I can complain about that. Certainly, she won't have finished by the time I get out there."

Michael rose from the bed. His arousal so evident she wanted to reach out and touch him. Wished she could learn how his sex would feel deep inside her.

A deep breath of air filled her lungs. Slowly, achingly so, she let the oxygen slide out of her lungs. "You know you did."

She sat then pressing the creases from her daffodil yellow gown her eyes downward.

"I'll be out in a minute. Clare just told me why you are pounding on the door. I'll be in the stable soon. Go on. Go back to Maid Marion."

With relief, unfettered relief, she heard Big Tom leave. Now, she watched Michael dress. He winked at her. "Are you coming?"

"You will let me be there when she births the foal?"

His question had been unexpected. His show of faith in her made her sparkle from the inside out. Maybe if they wed the marriage would not be all one sided.

He lifted his broad shoulders, his muscles flexing. "I made you watch Duster covering his mare. There is no reason why I wouldn't share this the birth of a foal." He held up his hands when it seemed he thought she would protest. "Just listen. Childbirth is something women should know about. Secrets aren't good for a woman or a man. A long time ago, I watched a young woman struggle to give birth. The doctor did nothing to save her because she was a slave. She meant next to nothing to him. He believed her life worthless. Not only was she a slave but female as well. The owner merely went to the next auction then bought another female. I knew naught about childbirth. If I had knowledge, neither the woman nor the babe would have died. After that I read as much as I could on the subject. I made it my duty to see the slaves were protected from bad doctors. I would see you protected. Knowledge is power. You should know what will happen to you after we've made love, when you are about to deliver my son or daughter into this world."

"You will allow me this privilege?"

She was overcome with the knowledge he would allow something like this even though everything he told her made perfect sense. A woman should understand childbirth. Watching a horse though was hardly the same thing.

Gently, he touched her on the chin, a smile gracing his handsome features. "When you give birth to our child, we will both be there. We will both be responsible for the babe's life. I'll be solely responsible for yours. Now, while I finish putting on my boots, you will fix your hair. Tie those soft auburn locks up with something, a pretty ribbon maybe. Hopefully this birth will not take more than the normal amount of time."

Quickly, she found a hair ribbon that would keep her hair in place. "How much time would that be?"

"From the start of the real labor to the end the birthing should not take more than an hour." He held out his hand to her beckoning her to come with him.

She sucked in spoonful of air. "Neither Big Tom or Timmie will be pleased with your decision. They will scowl then shoot you dark looks."

Her hand held by his, he started to leave the bedroom. She ran along beside him. His strides were wide apart. By the time they reached the stable, she panted, her breaths heaving with the exertion of keeping up with him. She doubled over gasping for oxygen.

Before untoward looks could be exchanged or words said, Michael pointed out, "Clare owns this place, all of it. She wished to watch the birth. I encouraged her. A woman should know these things. It is unseemly women should be kept in the dark about something that concerns them so profoundly. Men, after all, do not give birth to babes. Why should a woman be left ignorant of something so important in their lives?"

Well, Clare thought, that was forward thinking. She wanted to applaud the little speech. Instead, she watched transfixed as Maid Marion pushed the new foal from her womb. The process seemed too quick, so easy. She knew from Sophie's pregnancies, births for women were not so fast. The sight was miraculous. She felt in awe of what transpired. A renewed determination to have children of hers and Michael's settled deep inside her.

She didn't know what to tell him. He rapidly broke down all the barriers she built to keep from wedding him. She thought on the man who forced her from England. He pursued her would not take no for an answer. At times she'd been afraid for her virginity. Michael was nothing like that. She concentrated on what was right in front of her.

Maid Marion took care of the tiny male horse. She was proud of the mare. Michael seemed to know what to do although the mare took care of the details. Not much time passed before the foal stood on wobbly legs.

"We will call this one Canter," she spoke softly still somewhat in awe of what she witnessed.

"A good name," Michael agreed.

A hushed silence filled the stables. Now, she stood with her hands folded in front of her watching, mesmerized by the miracle that just enfolded in front of her. Old Suzzy appeared with glasses filled with champagne for each of them. The elderly lady stepped back a look of appreciation for what happened here on her grizzled features.

The men toasted. She joined in, all the while thinking about the magical lovemaking she shared with Michael this morning. Her heart leapt to her throat when he turned then winked at her.

~ * ~

All Michael wanted, at the moment, was to hold Clare in his arms again to celebrate the birth of the new foal. If labor hadn't started when it did, he didn't have a doubt in his mind he would have made love to Clare this morning. The woman was so hot and willing beneath him less than an hour ago. If Big Tom had not pounded up the steps when he did, the man would have been too late to stop him from breeching her maidenhead. Too late to stop him or too early to save her from the assurance he wanted, the declaration she didn't want.

Well, there would be another time.

More convincing or cajoling was necessary on his part.

He believed for sure that before he left with the posse to find Raynard she was planning to come to his bed. Perhaps tonight she would wind up in his arms again. Maybe she would welcome him to come inside her. He held visions in his imagination of her coming to him naked.

"Timmie," Michael turned to the young man. "Will you train Duster now, Gypsy later? We need them both ready for the races on Saturday. Since Gypsy doesn't have the impeccable bloodlines that Duster has, he has to gain a sterling reputation."

A huge grin split the young man's face as he nodded before he turned to saddle the huge horse.

To Big Tom, "It doesn't matter if you disapprove of a woman watching the birthing process of her horses. I don't. I have my reasons. They are sound. If you don't agree, that's fine with me. Men don't have to have the same views."

Big Tom nodded.

"I'm going to go for a ride." Clare's hand was placed softly on his arm when she spoke. "I'll be back by lunch. I'll take Midnight. She needs a good run. These last few weeks she's been getting fat, lazy as well."

"Take care. You said you're taking Midnight?" he asked as he retied the ribbon holding her hair back. It seemed his mind had become distracted. "Your lips are still swollen from my ardent attention." He traced his thumb along her moist lower lip. Her eyes were wide. "I'd like to toss you over my shoulder then scale the ladder to the loft. Up there we could finish what we almost started earlier this morning. I've got the uncanny sensation something would interrupt us though."

Michael didn't have to close his eyes to see her soft white body pressed beneath his, her thighs spread to welcome him. Her breasts filled his hands, the tips a tender pink. He almost felt as if he could taste her now. Gardenias, the scent of Gardenias always surrounded her. Everything about her was sweet and saucy. In so many ways she challenged him to think about life differently. He liked the fact she questioned him.

With all his heart he meant what he told her of childbirth as well as his feelings about the birth of their child. To have children with her left him with longings he couldn't understand. She was his forever then on into eternity. He felt a soul deep connection to this little lady.

Frowning, he thought of another woman in his life, Jillian Whitehead. She loved him until she didn't. Loved him until she learned that he didn't own Mayfair Hall. The thought of her disturbed him, made him compare her with Clare. The two didn't measure up. Clare was nothing like the other woman.

A moment later, he smacked the palm of his hand to his forehead. She rode off alone. He hadn't thought. No one, not even Timmie or Big Tom were with her. This wasn't to be. How could he forget about Raynard? How could he not remember the lust in Biff's and Busby's eyes? Neither the foal nor the mare could be left alone at the moment.

He cursed then cursed again.

"Big Tom!" he shouted loud enough they would certainly hear him at the new quarters they were building for the families. "Big Tom!" Long strides guided him to the entrance.

For a huge man, he ran fast. "Massa," he gasped out less than a minute after Michael called for him.

"Stay here. I've got to find Clare. In all the chaos, I let her ride off by herself."

He was a fool, an utter fool. Visions of Raynard coming upon her left a hollow dark pit in his heart. The image of Biff taking her on the hard ground made his stomach lurch. He nearly doubled over in pain. Sweat beaded on his forehead.

"Yes, I saw her. She's been riding by herself every day since you've been gone. I never thought. You think the man would have the nerve to grab her?"

"My overseer, ex-overseer, would do anything for revenge including taking her in broad daylight. That's the kind of man he is. During the last few days, I came to believe Biff and Raynard were working together to grab Clare. Both men want her. Saddle Gypsy, I'm sure he's rested enough. I'm not going to gallop him, just let him set his pace."

Michael cursed silently while he stared out the door, his heart pounding frantically. He didn't think he would recover from the scare until he once again held her slim little body next to his.

While Big Tom saddled Gypsy, Michael paced the length of the stable then back. He swore beneath his breath then aloud. Frustration along with fear eating at him he swore then cursed his forgetful memory. The simple chore of saddling the big stallion seemed to take forever.

"Here he is," Big Tom said, as he handed the reins over to him. "Find her. Bring the little missy home. She'll be fine. We won't let her out of our sight again."

Michael nodded understanding there were no guarantees. He mounted. Gypsy seemed to understand the urgency as he picked up the pace. He tried to remember where she usually rode. If he ever knew, he wasn't sure.

The devil, neither man would try something in broad daylight. He needed to pray that was true. Midnight might be able to outrun most stallions. Michael wished she was mounted on Duster. Anyone trying to catch her wouldn't stand a chance against the stallion. Clare could ride better than most men. She was also lighter than most. She liked a good race. Not when her life was at stake, though.

He started up the riverbank toward the cave. Seagulls swooped down to the river then back. Ducks lined the banks. Some searched for food in the water. A lone heron stood in the water where the ripples lapped against the mud. Sweat dripped from his forehead, along his cheek then down his neck.

The day was hot, blistering. She would have taken off without her hat. He liked the freckles that danced across the bridge of her nose, charming freckles, ones he wished to kiss. If she weren't careful her white skin would burn.

Unlike the past few days, no dark clouds loomed out to sea threatening a storm. The sky was cerulean blue. He reached the cave without seeing Clare. At that moment he decided to go inland. There was a trail where Timmie used to train the stallions. Clare would be aware of the path. Nonetheless, he liked the idea of her out in the open rather than surrounded by dense forest where she would have no way to escape a man.

By the time he reached Mayfair Hall again an hour had passed. If nothing happened to her, she should be headed home. He turned inland, finding the trail used for training. Timmie pulled up seeming surprised to see him.

Michael pushed his hat back, "Have you seen, Clare? She went ridding by herself. I don't like her being alone" He held his breath while he watched Timmie nod an affirmative.

"Saw her a while ago. She told me she was going to head toward Leslie Hall. Thought she would stop by and have someone bring a few bottles of wine over here for dinner."

"Where was she when you saw her?" He kept his breath inside his lungs while he waited.

"About a half hour ride inland from here. There's an old animal trail. The route is not used much. The place is all wild and overgrown. I'd bet my last dollar she's on that one. She likes to take Duster over the jump."

His gut clenched when he realized the trail Timmie spoke of. If anyone wanted to kidnap her, she would be easy prey. Once more, Michael reminded himself she could outride most in this territory. She could outride Raynard and especially Biff and Busby who were blundering idiots. Why then, didn't the thought make him feel better?

He rounded Leslie Hall then set off on the track where Timmie said he would find her. If he continued this way, he should meet up with her. Minutes seemed as hours while he searched. She could be home, safe and very, very sound. He should return to see if this mission of his was necessary.

He sipped in air as Gypsy ran faster. A bad feeling seemed to fill the air.

His nerves tightened. His body tensed.

All seemed wrong. Silence overpowered the forest. There should be all types of noises, animals, wind whispering through the leaves. Now, he heard nothing, nothing at all as if an evil spirit possessed the land. He was not superstitious. Nonetheless, the land always spoke.

Michael kicked Gypsy in the sides. They raced forward as branches licked at him. He didn't care. Something was so wrong, the air seemed deadly, menacingly so. His fear might not be real at all. He ducked a large branch that would have claimed his head then slowed Gypsy to a walk. The horse had a lot of heart. Nonetheless, it wasn't his intention to run the great beast into the ground.

If he didn't see anything in the next ten minutes, he was going to return to Mayfair Hall. It was possible Clare changed her mind about the wine, also possible that she made her way to Leslie Hall before he did and somehow, they missed each other. There was more than one path between the two plantations.

It was that moment when he saw Midnight standing in a small copse of trees. A wall of stones resembling an old fence ran across the trail. This was the jump she liked to take Duster over. Blood dripped down Midnight's leg. His heart leapt to his throat.

"Clare! Clare!" Where the devil was she. "Clare!"

Midnight nickered. When he saw the slash on his foreleg, he was afraid the horse would have to be put down. Clare wouldn't leave the horse. Yes, she would. She was going after the horse drawn apparatus they used to take Gypsy and Duster to the races in other towns. She knew Midnight would not be able to walk that far without doing more damage. Mayfair Hall was her destination. No one grabbed her. They wanted her demise instead.

Dismounting, he walked to the horse. At that second, he noticed the sharp edge of a scythe jutting up near the wall of stone. Midnight's blood was on the deadly sharp blades. He peered over the wall to make certain Clare wasn't lying unconscious. This misfortunate happenstance was not an accident. Someone put the scythe in her path.

He didn't know what to do.

Guessing he should wait, he strode to the horse, stroked his nose, telling him he would be fine, whispering encouraging words that would have no meaning. A poultice would be put on his leg. Mammy Jo would fix a healing cream. Clare and Timmie would come for him. He was a fine lad. In a daze Michael continued murmuring the nonsense words.

The sound of the trailer along with the horses lumbered along the narrow trail. They would have to go the long way since the trailer would not have been able to go over the wall. Waiting was hard. He didn't have patience. He acted. To him this was hell.

Michael spotted them. Timmie drove. Clare sat next to him. At least she wasn't hurt. No, it was Midnight that was hurt because someone wanted Clare or Duster to be put out of commission. His nerves seemed to unravel all at once. Too much happened this last week.

"Michael!" She shouted. "You're here. I'm so relieved. Timmie told me you were looking for me. I'm glad you waited with Midnight." She ran to him, throwing her arms around him.

Yes, he was here, expecting her so he could lecture her about taking precautions. She was a woman with a woman's strength. After this minute, he wasn't about to let her go anywhere without him. He wouldn't forget. No, this was a relief. She was safe. His emotions so mixed, he felt certain his head would split. He didn't know whether he was coming or going.

"I was worried about you," he spoke calmly while they slowly led Midnight up the ramp to the trailer. His heart pounded. His nerves seemed stretched to the breaking point. He didn't know where this air of calm came from. He wanted to strangle her one moment. The next second he wanted to crush her against his chest. "We will take him home, fix him up."

"Mammy Jo will make this seem like a chicken scratch. Midnight will be fine. Big Tom says he knows just the recipe that will heal him the quickest and if it's not what Mammy Jo thinks is best why then he will bow down to her expert skills. As we speak the healer is mixing the potion in the kitchen with Delilah supervising. The cream will be ready as soon as we're back at Mayfair. She even told me she'd be waiting in the stable for us. Everyone wants to help."

Clare had everything organized. That was good. She was excellent. All their people were coming together.

By the time Midnight was patched up, Michael was ready to relax with Clare. If he could pick up where they left off this morning, why, that would be exceedingly nice. He had plans, big plans for this evening. He grinned. He thought of all her soft white flesh for him to caress and kiss. Tonight, the yes to his proposal would be on her lips.

Together they both checked on the new mother and her foal. All was fine on that front. Clare fed both Duster and Gypsy an apple slice. Timmie would stay in the stable for the next two hours to watch. Big Tom would relieve him when the time came. So, the night would go.

He wanted to hug Clare close, whisper in her ear. Wanted to touch that sensitive spot behind her right ear, or was that spot on her left ear? He had time to figure that out. When he took her hand to walk to the main house, she moaned softly as if in agony. After that burst of pain, she slumped to the ground curled up in a tiny ball.

"Clare?" Michael didn't know what to think. He crouched down beside her while his heart thundered in terror. Her face was pale as death. His voice shook when he asked, "What is it? Are you hurt?" All he wanted was to shelter as well as protect Clare. He ran his hand along her back. "Clare, tell me."

He was doing a damn bad job of protecting. This was the second time he failed.

Tears spiked her dark lashes when she looked at him. Ribbons of moisture slid down her cheeks. Her eyes were deep pools of pain the silver streaks glistening in the muted light. It didn't seem to him she could talk. "Are you hurt?" he repeated more for his benefit since he wasn't positive, she would tell him.

She nodded her head then with a weak nearly murmured word. "Yes."

After that she closed her eyes. He wanted to fix everything, take the pain into himself. He couldn't do that until he understood what was wrong.

Michael moved closer to her, afraid to touch her yet knowing he needed to thoroughly examine all of her. He looked at her ankles, so tiny and small. She was fragile delicate in her form. Smoothing his hands along each leg, he watched for her expression to change. He understood if he touched the injured area, even lightly as he continued his exploration, her face would tell him where she was hurt.

The position of his hands changed. He caressed her arms then her rib cage. Why he waited to see if she possessed broken or bruised ribs was beyond his power to think. If she fell from the horse, something would be bruised or broken. It wouldn't be just her ego or her adorable backside. He knew more than her self-esteem was hurt.

Clare sucked in her breath when he touched her ribs. A soft painful moan whispered from her lips. With the gentle contact she closed her eyes. Barely able to move, she grabbed his wrist to stop his exploration. All her gestures seemed to do was cause her more pain.

Each rib he examined, he watched. He looked up to see Big Tom hovering over them. "Big Tom, ride into town for the doctor. I'm going to have your brother watch the mare and her foal."

More tears slid down her cheeks. "Michael," she paused seeming to sip in air, "it hurts. I can't move without pain. I can't even breathe."

Each shallow breath must cause her more agony. "I know you hurt; understand you won't be able to walk. I'm going to carry you to our room. This will hurt too. Nevertheless, this is the only way. Now hush, don't say anything more. Just close your eyes. I'll do everything for you. When the doctor gets here, he will examine you to see if there are other injuries."

"Don't want a man looking at me," she whispered her voice thin, pain so very evident with each word. "Don't want anyone to touch me except you. Please, Michael. I don't want a doctor. You can help me."

"All will be fine."

He was worried about her. She might need more help than he could give her. He needed to know if there were internal injuries that he didn't have the knowledge to deal with.

"No. Michael, my shoulder hurts too," she managed to gasp out while he scooped her as gently as he could into his arms. "You have to put me in my room not yours. What will it look like to the doctor when he comes if I'm in your bed?"

He didn't give a damn what the picture looked like. Rumors and gossip be damned, "No!" He supposed this moment was his turn to become negative. He wasn't about to move her around after the doctor left. "Your shoulder hurts too?"

When he stared at her shoulder for a moment, he realized she had dislocated it. With her broken ribs this would truly hurt her when he jerked the arm back into the socket. The sooner he did so, the less swelling would occur, the less the action would hurt. The doctor would do the same.

Walking through the house he called out orders to both Old Suzzy and Delilah. By the time he set Clare on the bed both women were behind him. He turned, his body seething with worry, apprehension for Clare. The disapproving expression on their faces didn't do anything to change his mind. This was where Clare belonged. Damn them all. Damn their supercilious opinions. Clare was his.

"Will you both hold her? I'm going to set her shoulder. What I have to do is going to hurt like hell. She'll scream. Wouldn't do this if I didn't have to. The sooner the better."

He wished he realized what happened to her when Big Tom was still standing beside him. Putting her shoulder back into the socket would have been easier with Tom holding her.

Sweat broke out on his forehead. He grasped her arm. A few moments later her scream filled him, turned his stomach sour. There was nothing to do for the pain though. He issued more orders for willow bark tea along with bandages. Binding her ribs would help ease some of the pain though not all of it. Every time she moved the agony would burn deep inside. The doctor would want to look at her. Perhaps he acted too soon when he ordered Big Tom to ride into the village. Well, he couldn't rescind the order now.

As gently as he could manage, he lowered her bodice to her waist.

After that, he pulled the satin ribbons of her chemise through the eyelets so he could push her chemise off her arms. More than anything, he needed to learn what happened. Why the scythe was left there. His knowledge would have to wait. He felt certain Raynard was behind the accident. While the man might want to force Clare, he wanted revenge more. Neither Biff nor Busby would want to kill her. Not for a moment did he believe the sharp-edged tool was meant for Duster.

Old Suzzy stood at the door her hands clasped tightly in front of her. "Do you want help?"

There was definite censure in the old woman's voice. He understood the disapproval. Soon the condemnation wouldn't matter since they would wed.

"Set the bandages on the table. You can leave."

The older lady would never gainsay him even though he felt the condemnation sear through him. His servants, all of them, would do everything they could to keep him from ruining their little missy. In such a short time they came to love her as if she'd been with them forever. Hell, they'd seen her when she was only a young child. Watched her grow.

He wasn't going to ruin her. He was going to marry her.

He smiled. Yes, he did have plans. He had big plans.

Michael heard the loud harrumph then the sound of footsteps echo behind him. It would take at least a half hour for the doctor to arrive. He wasn't about to wait to bandage her. Nor, was he going to let the man examine Clare. She didn't want another man looking at her. Now, after observing her, he knew enough to understand she had no internal injuries. In any case, if he was wrong, they would surely begin to show by the time Big Tom returned. He felt as if the emergency subsided.

Clare was naked to the waist. Her body beginning to bruise, she had one broken rib and two were bruised. Quickly, he bound her tight. When he finished, he walked to her bedroom. After he returned, he slipped her maidenly nightgown over her head then fastened all the buttons.

"If you lift your hips, we can rid you of the gown you are wearing. I'll slide the dress down your legs. You'll be more comfortable."

She nodded then did what he requested. He undid her garters, removed her shoes and stocking.

"I had to leave him there." Her voice quivered with pain. "Didn't want to, you know. Was so afraid something would happen to him while I was gone. Is he going to live?"

Surprised, he looked up. "Midnight? You did well. The horse could not have survived the walk back to Mayfair. Yes, I believe Mammy Jo can concoct some excellent potion to heal his leg."

"Someone wanted to kill me or Duster. I always ride Duster over that trail. The scythe was never there before. I rode him two days ago. We took that wall without a hitch in his stride." She drug in a breath of air then winced at the pain. "Why?"

"Here it is, Massa. Put honey in the brew just as you told me to." Delilah stood at the door, a cup of steaming willow bark tea in her hands. "I'll leave the rest to steep. It will be stronger in a few hours."

Good God, he felt as if they'd just done this a few days ago. Well, several weeks had passed. Raynard had been the cause then just as he was certain he was the reason now. They had to find the man before anything else happened to Clare.

"Delilah, I would appreciate it if you no longer called me Massa. Call me, Sir or Mr. Flannigan."

"Yes, Suh."

She curtsied then left the room, her disapproval at his actions written clearly on her face.

The condemnation would have been no different if he'd taken her to the adjoining room. He would have done the same. He would have stripped her, seen her beautiful soft breasts even though he tried not to look at them. He would have bound her ribs. He would have removed her dress along with the rest of her clothes. He didn't see anything he hadn't seen before. Nonetheless, before this afternoon what he'd seen and touched had been between the two of them. His servants knew nothing about their private lives. At least they didn't condemn Clare. He bore the brunt of their wrath.

They were alone now. She sipped her tea. Soon she would sleep. He would deal with the doctor when he arrived. As he knew he would have to turn the man away. She tried to smile at him. The gesture was halfhearted at best. When she lifted her shoulder slightly, she grimaced in pain even though she tried to hide what she was feeling.

Even though hiding the agony was impossible to do so, he wanted to take the suffering from her.

"Tell me everything that happened. After that, I'll leave you alone. You can sleep, rest, and heal."

She set her head back on the pillow while she closed her eyes. "As I told you, I rode Midnight on the same trails where I exercise Duster. We always take this jump. The leap is not difficult. The big stallion soars effortlessly over the wall. Midnight has taken this wall before with no incident. We were headed over when I looked down. I saw the blade. Tried to lengthen Midnight's stride so he'd miss the blades."

"It was too late to do so," he finished for her, understanding at the moment, her anguish was for the horse not herself. "You could have done nothing different. You appreciate that fact, don't you?"

"If I'd known a second before, he would have missed the scythe. Midnight would have easily cleared the wall as well as the knifes left there."

"You must have fallen."

"Yes, when his forelegs hit the ground then his back legs, he reared up," she admitted. "I was unconscious for a while. Don't know how long a minute maybe more. When I got my bearing, Midnight stood looking at me as if I could fix everything. Well, I set off for Mayfair Hall that instant."

"You didn't know you were hurt?"

Unthinking, she lifted her delicate shoulders until she grimaced realizing the gesture was a foolish mistake. "Didn't feel a thing until I knew Midnight would be fine."

~ * ~

Damnation, Big Tom paced in front of the doctor's office. It was closed. The man was off somewhere delivering a baby. What was he supposed to do? He stuck his hands in his pockets. He sauntered down the boardwalk looking in every direction as if he could conjure the doctor. His thoughts centered on the little missy. She was hurt bad. Hurt real bad. He had to do something.

The doctor's wife told him he most likely wouldn't be back until late this evening or early tomorrow morning. This was the woman's first labor. It would take time to deliver the tiny babe. Her husband would most likely stay the night since he wouldn't drive home in the dark.

Why did birthing take so long for women when the deed took less than an hour for a horse? Nothing made sense. He didn't know what to do, as he didn't want to deliver the bad news to his boss now, not his master. Big Tom smiled broadly. This was good, as what was happening here was also new to him. He'd never been a free man before. He could make decisions for himself along with his family. There was a new home being built for him. He earned a wage even though he'd yet to be paid.

He wanted to saunter into the alehouse then order something to eat and drink. All too well, he assumed that despite his new status he would be kicked out because of the color of his skin. For the present it was enough that he was free.

Well, there was nothing to do now except go back to Mayfair Hall. As he rode from the stable, he heard the little missy tell her man that she didn't want a doctor. Perhaps this was a good thing. His wife didn't like to have anyone except himself look at her.

True enough, maybe what happened here was for the best. Tomorrow, if the doctor got the message, he would come right out to the plantation. The doctor would discover that Mr. Flannigan took care of the little missy. Big Tom didn't like the fact the doctor would discover her in his boss' bed. No, Michael would stop the man before he got the chance to see anything was amiss. He would think of her reputation. At least Big Tom hoped he would.

Mr. Flannigan should wed that woman sooner than later. That's for certain sure, he should make the talk in town stop before people looked at Clare in the same light as her sister. He heard the people whispering behind his back as he strode to his horse. He saw Biff Gideon, rocking on the balls of his feet, his tiny hands behind his back a smirk on his face. His jowls hung to nearly his shoulders. His eyes were black as midnight.

In this town he was a powerful man. A black man, even a free black man, didn't go up against the money.

"What are you up to, Big Tom?" Biff called out while he waved him over to him. "Want to talk to you."

Answering that man was not something he wanted to do. As a slave he would be expected to explain himself if he didn't obey. As a free man he had the option of turning his back then walking away. He decided he didn't want to push his luck, as he'd only been a free man for several weeks.

"Fetching the doctor."

The fewer spoken words the better as far as he was concerned. He wasn't about to tell this man what happened to the little missy. Her fall wasn't Mr. Gideon's business.

Damn, Biff appeared concerned. The look seemed genuine. That surprised him a bit. Even though he overheard the little missy speaking with Mr. Flannigan about Biff and Busby wanting to have her for a dollar. His bargaining for the little missy wasn't at all something that should have happened. Didn't he know she wasn't for sale now or ever would be?

"What do you need a doctor for out there? You've got Mammy Jo to fix up all you black people."

Biff was probing, his question easy to answer.

He wasn't a stupid man. He knew what Biff tried to do. In this instance or any other, he wasn't going to be taken off guard. "Not my place to spread gossip. If Mr. Flannigan wants you to have the answer to your question, he'll tell you. I'm just the messenger."

Big Tom mounted. He clucked to the horse to move on wishing to be away before there could be another question.

"Don't want to have to ride all that way to find out. Why don't you just tell me?" Biff shouted at him.

"Why don't you go home to your wife? I'm sure she would welcome you with open arms."

Big Tom pushed the horse to a canter. He didn't look back, however he heard the man curse. It was a well-known fact that both Biff and Busby frequented the house of pleasure just outside of town. Now they wanted the little missy too. That wasn't going to happen. The boss should make certain sure no one touched her except him. If he married her, she would be safe.

By the time he rode into the stable at Mayfair Hall, all seemed back to normal. Timmie was brushing down Gypsy, murmuring sweet nothing in the stallion's ear. The stable smelled of leather and linseed oil of hay and horses. The scent was nice, normal. He handed the reins over to Timmie thinking he needed to get the message to Mr. Flannigan.

"Where's the doc?" Timmie led the horse to his stall then waited for the answer. "Expected him to be with you."

Big Tom turned then holding the bridge of his nose, wishing he had different news, "With a lady who is giving birth. Can't be here until tomorrow morning at the earliest. Got the impression from his wife, he wouldn't travel after dark. The way things are going around here, can't say it's a good idea to do so. Mr. Flannigan's not going to be happy."

"The doc's not going to be here?" Michael asked standing behind him. "Probably a good thing since Clare told me she wasn't going to let him examine her. Said she didn't want a man touching her."

"How is the little missy?"

Big Tom ignored the last statement. She seemed to be all right if Mr. Flannigan touched her. After all, she was going to be his wife. In his mind, no one else should see her. Mr. Flannigan knew what to do.

"She will be fine in a week or two. With two bruised ribs and one broken one along with a dislocated shoulder, it's going to be a while before she's riding again. Clare's not going to enjoy bed confinement."

"Was it Raynard who left that wicked scythe there?" Big Tom clenched his fingers, anger rolling through him. If he could, he'd strangle dat man with his bare hands. "We got to find dat man before he does more harm."

"Believe so. Doubt if Biff or Busby would have an interest in hurting Clare," Timmie said as he walked to meet them.

"Forcing a woman entails pain," Michael said as he gritted out, his face flushed with anger. "But no, they wouldn't hurt her that way. If Clare wasn't an excellent horsewoman, she could have been hurt much worse. She might have died along with Midnight."

"Died." Big Tom echoed the words. "She could have died. We've got to take much better care of our little missy."

Chapter Six

Clare drank enough willow bark tea to make her feel as if she was going to float away. That and the wine Michael gave her, some brandy too, was all he would allow to ease the pain. Two excruciatingly long weeks passed, two long and very boring weeks that found her in bed for most of the long minutes of each day. Michael would visit when he could. He ate dinner with her every night. A few times near the end of the second week he carried her downstairs so she could sit on the shaded patio in the back of the house.

Now, she sat on the veranda outside the master suite, waiting for Michael. In the meadow beyond, she watched Timmie put Duster through his paces. The stallion was magnificent. He won the last two races he was entered in. Gypsy placed third in one and fifth in another. That wasn't quite the reputation she and Michael hoped would bring more mares to the stud farm. Duster covered three more mares last week. They were making money. Soon she wouldn't have to use the funds in the bank to keep the plantation afloat. So far, she'd not had to ask Link for more money. She was proud of herself along with the hard work at the plantation. The black folks who stayed were thriving.

The houses for the newly freed people were all built. Many of the families planted gardens for their use. Some winter crops were planted where the tobacco fields had once been. A small school provided education to any of the folks including the adults who wanted to learn. Michael employed a man from the village to teach anyone who showed up at the schoolhouse. All this happened by her direction even though she couldn't supervise.

When he wasn't at work, Michael spent the majority of the two weeks hovering over her. He was solicitous. She wanted something more from him. July turned into August. The days were hot and muggy. When the breeze floated from the river, the evenings were nice. She wanted to go to their summer retreat. Michael told her he wanted to make love to her on the fur rug by the fireplace, perhaps this winter when the flames could flare within.

"Here is dinner for you and the massa." Old Suzzy walked onto the balcony carrying a loaded down tray. She smiled at her. "Got lots of tasty items here; fresh watermelon and grapes, along with cheese and ham slices also tomatoes and cucumbers. Delilah just took out a loaf of hot bread. We've got sweet butter along with fresh honey from the hives."

The elderly woman seemed sure of herself, so unlike the days when she was a slave. She walked straighter; her chin higher. Despite the wrinkles around her eyes, they were sparkling with happiness. She smiled more often except when she was looking at Michael with disapproval. Clare understood both Suzzy along with Delilah thought he took advantage of her. He didn't do anything she didn't want him to do. If she protested this living situation, he would bow down to her wishes.

"Did someone go to Leslie Hall for the wine?"

The ambiance of the evening needed to be perfect. She wanted to figure out how to seduce Michael, how to let him know she was ready to accept his proposal of marriage. He'd been so protective of her even the last few days he'd not kissed her still so afraid he might hurt her.

She didn't know the first thing about seducing a man, an experienced man at that. He would probably laugh at her bumbling attempts. She hoped all she needed to do was to put on the negligée Sophie gave her.

"We've got a whole cart full of that sweet red Bordeaux you and Massa like so much. More than enough for tonight as well as tomorrow night, maybe the entire week."

Heat flooded Clare's face. She saw a silly grin on Old Suzzy's face. The woman certainly understood what she planned. She thought of the way Michael made her feel when he touched and caressed her. Clare's heart leapt, sultry warmth filling her.

"Thank you, Suzzy," Clare murmured while she studied the tray not quite ready to meet the elderly woman's eyes.

She did look up. "Have you seen Michael?"

She'd been wondering when he would show up or if he would continue to avoid her. The last two nights since she began to feel better, he waited until it was late to come to the bedroom. The hour was still too early for him to quit work. Perhaps another half hour and he would be here to join her for the evening meal.

The dinner was light fare meant for a hot evening. She'd given Delilah carte blanche to the menu. Everything would taste divine. Clare rose, smoothed the folds of the lavender lingerie Sophie gave her before she left telling her the sheer gown was meant for her wedding night.

Well, in her mind, tonight was the precursor to her wedding night. She wanted Michael to see her as a woman not an invalid who needed his care. When he made love to her, the act would seal the proposal. Unless Michael changed his mind about the marriage, she hoped what she did would serve that purpose. Since the accident he quit asking. A dollop of fear swept inside straight to her stomach. What if he didn't want her?

On shaking legs, she rose to pour herself a glass of wine. She stretched a bit to ease the stitch in her side that was still a bit sore. The rib that had been broken still gave her pain. Not as much as the thought that Michael no longer wanted to marry her. No, the man was predictable. Even if he didn't truly want her, he wanted Mayfair Hall. Marrying her was the only way he would achieve his dreams. While she hungered for Michael more than anything she'd desired in her entire life, she didn't want to be a consolation prize.

In time, if she was lucky, he might come to love her. Even if he didn't, she had enough love in her heart for both of them. She prayed her love for him was enough to sustain their relationship. Tonight, yes, tonight she wanted him, hoped to experience that same pleasure he initiated her to weeks ago. If she had her way, he would make love to her.

Sooner than she expected Michael appeared in the bedroom. She didn't look at him. Nonetheless, she heard his boots on the hard wood then the sound of him bathing. He would be surprised to see her in the filmy negligée. Surprise might be on her side.

She drank half her glass of wine before setting the crystal on the table. The heady brew simmered in her stomach. When the wine finished with her stomach, she hoped some of the heady effect would go to her head so she would have the courage she needed. If she was going to show herself to this man, she needed more bravery than she usually possessed. While she wasn't naked, she knew he could see most of her.

In the tub, he whistled slightly off key. Sometimes his whistling sounded as if each vibration was the same note. Well, she couldn't make music through her lips at all. Who was she to criticize?

"Clare?"

He stood beside her, looking down at her, a different expression on his masculine and well-chiseled features. He wore only his buckskins. She forgot how broad his chest was, how his muscles rippled with each movement. His body was whipcord lean. She wanted to trace the line of hair that disappeared beneath his pants.

Open mouthed, she gaped at him. When he saw her, she thought his eyes would certainly pop from his head. He frowned at her, crease lines slanting across his broad forehead. His perfectly sculpted eyebrows rose in an arch above his eyes. He poured himself a glass of wine. She wanted to understand his thoughts. He hid them too well.

"Should you be...?"

He stopped short as if he didn't know what he was going to say.

The direction of his obvious feelings displeased her. She was tired of the bed if that was what he implied, tired of doing nothing. Of course, she wouldn't mind the bed if he was making love to her. "I should be here. I'm no longer an invalid, Michael. My ribs only give me a tiny bit of pain. The last few days I've been bored to tears."

She felt a slow rise of anger. Quickly, she tamped annoyance down. Ruining tonight with an argument would not give rise to the end of her plans.

As if he didn't hear her the first time, he asked again, "Does your broken rib still give you pain, Clare?" He lifted the lid on the tray as if he tried to ignore her. "Dinner, I see. Wine and a beautiful negligée meant for what? You aren't trying to seduce me. Are you, Clare?"

It was just like Michael to go straight to the point. "Some, not much." She ignored the part about seducing him. Perhaps if she were lucky, he would take over that particular role. She could always hope.

Hope she was certain had nothing to do with this.

He dished up a plate for her, handed the food to her with a stern expression on his face. "I'm famished." His gaze settled on her bosom. "Are you as hungry as I am?" His words implied so much more.

He wouldn't see a lot of her, not with the robe covering the nightgown although the fabric of both was diaphanous. Yes, she was hungry. So nervous all day about this evening, she barely ate. Now, that he was beside her she didn't know how she felt.

She smiled at him. Her following words stilted. She could barely think or form a coherent thought. Within her fingers the fabric of her gown twisted. "Thank you."

He sat down his plate of food in front of him. She watched him swallow. His Adam's apple bobbing as he did so. His shoulders and neck were stiff.

"You look nice." He told her as he picked up a slice of cheese.

While he chewed, he watched her, seemed to study her.

At this point, she wasn't at all sure what to say. Again, she settled on, "Thank you. You look nice too."

Well, that exchange was ridiculous. To her he always appeared nice, handsome. She wiped her sweaty palms on the pelisse. Her stomach curdled. Eating another bite of food seemed impossible.

With his fork, he pointed to her plate. "You should eat. You might need your strength later." He winked at her flashing her a roguish smile.

She gasped at the shock of his gesture. *He winked at me? What did that mean?* Well, eating was her intention. She wanted to eat and drink. Nothing changed, doing so did not seem so easy. Her stomach rolled contentiously. "How was your day?" seemed innocuous enough.

The air between them smelled stilted and motionless. Everything she planned was going awry simply because her nerves were getting in the way, fraying more with each second. She needed to change the tenor of the moment. Didn't know how. She fiddled with her eating utensils.

He leaned back while he seemed to thoughtfully chew a piece of bread and ham. When he finished, he crossed his arms over his chest. Once again, he stared at her. "Believe the question would be how is the night going to be? I do imagine this evening will be quite to my liking.

What do you think?"

She felt heat surge inside her. The sip of wine slithered down her throat in a tasteless stream. "Hot," she whispered.

Heat engulfed her. She wasn't certain if the sudden rush of color to her face was heat from embarrassment or something else, perhaps anticipation of what might come her way.

"Hot is good," he murmured, closing his eyes briefly. "Heat even better if the inferno flames." He drank the remainder of his wine. "Would you like more?" He held up the bottle, a confident, all-knowing smile painting his face. If she had another drink, she might relax.

Unable at this second to speak an articulate thought, she nodded. He filled the glass. She didn't touch the glass. Instead, she stared at the liquid contents. What had she gotten herself into? She acted like a brazen hussy.

"Are you finished eating?" It seemed her voice squeaked.

She stared at his lips. They looked warm and moist. She remembered how soft they were. She ran her tongue along her bottom lip felt the wetness left there.

He nodded yet he didn't move from the chair. Now she felt certain she would have to do this all on her own. "I was thinking that tonight we could walk in the garden. Would you like that, Clare? Well, no you would have to change out of the beautiful negligée. What do want to do with the rest of the evening? Do your thoughts have anything to do with that sheer confection you donned for the evening meal? Did you mean to entice me? Is the negligée for my eyes only?"

Michael asked even though she was positive he knew what she planned. He alluded to the notion earlier. She rose then walked to the railing while attempting to sort out the simmering emotions that stretched her nerves so tight she feared they would shatter. At the moment they were skittering out of control. Her hands clamped tightly around the solid, smooth wood. Thoughts of him, of his kisses swamped her until she wanted to turn. She wished she could throw herself at him, into the embrace of his strong arms.

After that, she thought of the man she ran from. Wesley Brown was his name. No one except her knew anything about that man who cornered her in the woods near her home. She didn't even tell Sophie, her sister. As soon as she could get away from him, she leapt on her horse. The stallion she rode was fast as well as sure-footed.

She heard his laughter. Heard the words that haunted her until she came to Mayfair Hall. The man yelled at her that he would have her soon. She had to leave England. It was what she wanted. She would never go back, unless Michael was with her.

The soft touch on the back of her neck channeled her thoughts to Michael. Perhaps she wouldn't have to do everything. His lips swept softly across her nape.

"I've wanted to do this for two weeks now. Do you think you are finished with getting yourself hurt? Your bruises serve to frustrate a man. Seemed these last days it was devilish hard to even get a kiss."

His hand pushed aside her hair. His lips touched the tender spot behind her ear. He continued his investigation exploring more of her.

In response her body quivered. Her knees might not hold. She tightened her grip on the railing. Slowly, the robe began to tumble down her body. He pushed on the shoulders of the robe guiding the material downward. The silken fabric pooled on the floor behind her feet. The silver moon that stood out a few hours ago was covered with clouds. Except for the meager light behind her they were veiled in darkness. No longer would he be able to see her. A breath of relief sighed from her. She wasn't sure if she was ready for him to see all of her.

The palms of his hands lightly passed over her breasts, stimulating her sensitized nipples. She gasped in a new breath of air. He continued his quest lower, down her thighs then back to her breasts. His hands cupped them, tenderly squeezed. His thumbs explored more evocative spots. She pushed back against him.

"Do you like this, Clare?" he asked his voice so husky and deep she wanted to know what he was thinking. "Do you like my hands here, cupping your beautiful, white breasts? I want to taste them too."

"Do you like this?" she asked unable to stop herself.

Of course, he liked stroking her. He was a man. She wanted to turn in his arms. Her body becoming so vibrantly alive, she needed more.

"Does this mean your answer is yes? Don't tease me, Clare."

He kissed her newly bared shoulders. His teeth found gentle purchase. "Your shoulder is healed? There is no more pain? I wouldn't want to hurt you."

One of the ties holding her gown up was slowly pulled free by his teeth. He kissed her there where there was nothing but flesh. After that he moved to the other shoulder to do the same. Her gown slipped down the length of her body. The fabric moved against her hardened nipples. Lower still as the diaphanous gown now pooled around her feet. She was naked. He was fully clothed.

Once again, his hands explored the path they took earlier, passed over the curve of her hips down her legs then higher. Rendered speechless, she knew she needed to answer him. Words stuck in her throat. Anyone out there could see her. Her body hummed to life with each pass of his hands along the length of her, always stopping to brush against the hardened crests of her breasts.

It seemed he read her mind. "It's too dark. Only I can see you, Clare. Don't worry that anyone watches."

He feathered kisses across her back, down her spine as his hands pressed against her belly, his long fingers spread from hipbone to hipbone. "You are so soft and white. All white except the tight hard crest of your breasts and your woman's mound. I haven't seen all of you, just bits and pieces. You are lovely, Clare, a man's dream, at least this man's dream."

"I'd like to see you," she whispered to him as she tried to turn in his arms.

His hands on the curves of her hips, he held her still.

"Only if your answer is yes." Gently he bit her shoulder again then the other after trailing kisses along her back. "Is it yes, Clare? I would know the answer before I might not be able to turn back."

She nodded, her voice soft yet resilient. "Yes, Michael. It's a yes. I want to marry you, only you."

He turned her. Sometime between finishing eating and when she walked to the railing, he had unlaced his pants. Her breasts pressed against his hot flesh felt the rasp of his hair rasp against her nipples. She wanted him needed to see all of his body.

"Tomorrow then, we will tie the knot."

Pressed against him, she ran her hands up his back, feeling his muscles as they flexed with her touch. "Tonight?"

A gust of wind blew around the porch. She shivered thinking how rapidly the weather changed. They needed to go inside. It didn't seem that was his intentions.

"Come, let's have another glass of wine. I'll get a quilt." He smiled at her, his finger beneath her chin lifting until she gazed into his eyes. "I want to hold you while the weather does it's best to discourage us."

"You are wearing trousers. That's not fair at all," she told him wishing he would do something to change that. The heat of embarrassment flowed through her. So much so she wanted to see his sex. To see that part of him that was so different from her.

His lips brushed softly against hers while he slipped his tongue inside her open mouth. His tongue swept inside. The caress was wet and so very scorching. He kissed her then kissed her again. He held her so very close. She knew she wanted more.

When he parted from her, he whispered, "Perhaps you should do something about that little problem." He stroked with his tongue along her mouth then pulled on her bottom lip with his teeth.

"You want me to..."

She didn't have an intelligent thought in her head. When she touched the fastening of his buckskins her knuckles against his flat belly, he sucked in air. She stopped, her fingers trembling with the weight of what she was about to do. Her hands rested on the laces. "What did I do? Did I hurt you?"

He laughed softly, "Nothing yet and no, there was no pain." He straggled kisses along her jaw before exploring down her neck. "Go on. You can do this." His hands cupped her backside, pulling her closer.

Her fingers pressed tightly against his belly. Against her he was hardened. She gulped air wondering what he looked like, wanting to discover him yet afraid. While she fumbled with the laces, his hands ran the length of her back then down again. She pulled the last ones free. Hesitantly, she looked at him. Held a deep breath of air inside her lungs for too long.

"What should I do?" she whispered as she looked at him truly looked at him for the first time without turning away embarrassed.

Dark red whirls of hair curled on his chest. As her gaze drifted lower to where her fingers seemed to be stuck, the hair thinned. She needed to explore farther.

"Whatever you want? What happens next is up to you," he answered, his voice soft a hint of amusement tinged his words.

It didn't seem to Clare he wished to tell her anything. At this moment, she didn't know what she wanted. No, she lied to herself. She wished to see all of him. He looked at her, all of her. She wanted the same. With another gulp of air, she pushed the buckskins down his legs. His thighs were solid muscle yet that wasn't what caught her eye. With the removal his trousers, his sex jutted out pointing at her as if his member had a will all its own. Perhaps it did.

At the sight her breath caught in the back of her throat. For a moment she thought her knees would give out. His hands circled her waist, holding her upright. She wanted to touch him, reached out then brought her hand back. When she looked up to see his eyes again, he grinned at her.

"Perhaps you should finish the job. If the house caught fire, I'd be hard pressed to run."

Bending over, she pushed his buckskins to the floor. He stepped out of them. Now he was as naked as she was. She stepped back to look her fill. "You're beautiful, Michael." She ran her tongue across her mouth. "I want you. Do you want me?"

Deep in the back of his throat, he groaned. He didn't answer. She didn't have one clue as to what to think. When he turned away, she thought she would shrivel up and die from humiliation. He didn't like what he saw. Clare felt swamped with doubts of herself.

She picked up her robe feeling as if she needed to wrap it around her shoulders. Covering herself, hiding from his assessment became a very real need.

His hand touched her shoulder, stopping her. Tenderly, his fingers squeezed. "No, I want to look at you. It would be nice not to rush this first time, as we should get comfortable with each other. Don't you think?"

"I don't think." Her voice wavered, confused at a loss for thoughts. All she wanted now was to hide behind as much material as she could find.

"Don't think. Just feel. Let me do the thinking," he murmured softly close to her ear.

So, very close she felt the whisper of his breath. She tried to swallow her fear. "All right."

Clare didn't believe she would ever feel comfortable naked around him. This was not something she'd ever thought about. He handed her a fresh glass of wine then retrieved a blanket from the porch swing. She also didn't think she could stop thinking about all the differences between them as well as about what they were about to do.

"Let's watch the storm, drink some more wine. I would like to run my fingers over every sweet inch of you then I'd like to do the same with my lips as well as my tongue. You are so soft and white. Your bountiful curves fit my hands."

On the swing and beneath the blanket, Michael pulled her close. He proceeded to do just as he explained to her. It seemed he would make all his wishes come true.

"This is difficult. I..."

Her mind was a befuddled mess. Her body trembled with each pass of his calloused fingers. While she wanted him to pursue this course, she also didn't.

She felt his man's body against her. The hard muscles of his chest and belly, he wasn't soft anywhere except perhaps his lips. His hand rested on her upper thigh. He roamed higher, exploring, investigating. He stopped just before the apex of her thighs. She had this strange urge to part her legs for him. The jolt of pleasure surprised her. She wanted to touch his sex. She didn't dare.

"You can do whatever you want with this man's body," he murmured as he found her hand beneath the blanket.

He saved her the decision by bringing her hand to his belly. She understood moving her hand lower would be up to her. "Touch me. Caress me anywhere that pleases you."

"Are you sure?" Her voice squeaked. She didn't sound normal.

"Positive. The touching shouldn't all be one sided. I want to feel your hands and mouth everywhere. Stroke me, Clare. Run your sweet pink tongue wherever you wish."

Tentatively, she ran her hand along his member. The length was silken steel, so very hot. His rod throbbed and pulsed beneath her fingertips, changing in shape as she caressed him. She heard the sound, the soft groan rumble upward from his chest. Clare was certain the sound was pleasure he felt. When she looked at him, his eyes were closed, his lips pulled back showing his teeth as if his body was fraught with pain.

For a moment, she pulled back, hesitating before she caressed him again. "Michael?"

"Perhaps this isn't such a good idea as of yet." He placed her hand on his chest. "Drink your wine. We'll take this farther in another moment."

She felt a moment's set back unsure of what she did wrong. He seemed to realize her confusion.

"Sweetheart, I might explode if you keep touching me. I don't want that to happen until I'm deep inside you, until I can feel your body pulse around me."

"Oh."

She still wasn't certain what he meant. What he said might be a reason, other than her ignorance, to please him. For now, she would accept his declaration. They both stared at the landscape. Lazily, with his fingertips, He continued to roam her body. Perhaps she would explode if he continued this path. Her body reacted violently to each simple stroke.

Rain spilled from the sky. The water began as a soft drizzle. Now, the drops pounded on the balcony's roof. They were deep inside the veranda. Still, with the cresting winds, water began to seep inside where they sat. He topped off her glass. She wondered what she could possibly do next. Closing her eyes, she thought on all they shared before as well as now.

She didn't wish to go inside. Wanted to feel the brunt of the storm while she absorbed the feel of his heat next to her. When the first drops hit their toes, he wrapped her in the blanket then set her inside the bedroom.

"Go to the bed, I'll get the food and wine. Bring everything inside." Once more he stood in front of her naked. He seemed so oblivious as if this was all normal.

Wrapped in the blanket, hiding from his gaze she picked up their clothing then rushed inside. A howl of wind shook the house, the open shutters rattling with seeming displeasure. This wasn't a normal storm. It also wasn't a typical show of lightning and thunder above them. The storm matched her turbulent emotions.

Michael set the tray of food on a table near the bed. He started the fire that was laid out for them. Embers popped as the flames began to catch on the dry wood. The night had taken on a decided chill. She had not expected to need a fire tonight. The day had been hot, hotter than most. The wind came from the southwest. What did that mean? Most storms traveled the coastline in a northerly direction. This was most likely not a hurricane.

Unclothed, wrapped in a blanket, she wasn't sure what to do with herself. The seductive atmosphere had been severely doused by the tempest. She sat down on a wing chair in front of the fire, curling her legs beneath her. When she looked at him, he was shaking his head, his grin wicked. Her heart skipped a beat then started again pounding furiously beneath her ribs.

"Get in the bed. I'm not going to give up our closeness now just because of the howling winds. While we drink our wine, I want to feel your soft curves press lovingly against me. Want to feel them until I can stand the sweet ecstasy no longer. After that I'm going to explore you again then again. After you climax sweetly due to my expert tutelage, I'll come inside you. You will be warm and dark, hot as well as sultry. I will learn all your secret places. Since you've known no lovers, your sheathe will be small. I'll try not to hurt you."

She wanted everything he said, wasn't too sure about the last part. Nonetheless, she didn't know what to say. Everything she thought of sounded wanton, brazen in its wickedness. Under the covers, she pressed against the backboard. His movements were lithe and graceful. Finally, she blurted. "I want that too."

Christine Young

Smiling mischievously, he sat down beside her. They drank the wine while the storm grew outside their cocoon of warmth and security. She was a bundle of seething nerves. Didn't understand why he didn't proceed. After all, she gave him all he wanted.

Did she?

"Tell me what you are thinking." He smoothed her bottom lip with his thumb all the while he sipped the liquid in his glass.

"I...," She moistened her lips following the path his thumb roamed. "Well, when I first saw you naked, I thought you were beautiful. Didn't believe any man could be built so fine. My next coherent thought was that you would never fit inside me. You looked huge to me."

His long sigh gave her reason for concern. Now, he looked worried, his eyebrows drawing together. He crushed her in his arms. Kissed the top of her head. "What do you know about making love?" He kissed her forehead. Soothingly, his hand ran the length of her arm then back.

"Well." She looked to her clasped hands, after a moment's pause back to him. "Not much. As you know I watched Duster cover the mares. You know that. After that all I understand is the way you touched me before," she repeated nervously. "For some reason, I doubt if what we do will be the same for us as the horses. I know you will give me pleasure. After that..."

"At times it can be. Not the first time though. Just as when we were by the river I'll see to your pleasure. You won't be disappointed."

"If not like the stallion, how will you do it?" Her hands trembled while she clutched the blanket.

"I'll show you later. You do know this first time together I might hurt you. There is nothing I can do about that. You are a virgin. You have a thin membrane inside you. When I come inside you, I will break through the tissue. I don't want to give you pain. From what others have said, the first joining will hurt."

She grimaced at his words. "Well, then after that there is to be more pain? You will stretch me inside that will also hurt."

"Most likely, I'll be as gentle as possible."

It seemed he was gritting his teeth when he spoke. She could

161

almost hear them gnashing together.

Clare understood he was loath to tell her anything. "I'm glad you're not mincing words. Although at the moment, I'm not sure I can go through with this. Will there be pleasure too. You remember when you didn't come inside me? You made me..." She didn't know how to explain the things she felt that time. All she did know was that she wanted more of that same exquisite pleasure.

"I hope so. I'll bring you to your climax first."

I hope so. Those words frightened her. She wanted the pleasure not the pain. "Do we have to do this tonight? Tomorrow might be better."

Now, she thought her idea of presenting herself in the negligée was premature. She should have taken into consideration more facts. At the time she didn't know those facts. Perhaps that was what men counted on, ignorance.

"It will happen tonight or tomorrow. Might as well make the best of this evening you planned. I will do my absolute best to please you." He sat against the backboard. "When I saw you tonight, waiting for me, the sight stole my breath. I knew then you wanted to wed me. For tonight just tell me yes or no."

After a long pause, "Yes."

~ * ~

When Michael saw her wearing barely anything, he understood this was the night. Anticipation along with the feeling that his dreams were about to come true filled him with infinite pleasure. Lust for this lovely woman-child settled in his loins. He would have to make sure she knew that she meant more to him than the winning of his ancestral home. He cared very deeply for her. In such a short time Clare became precious to him. Her wants along with her needs were at the forefront of his poor man's brains. Twice she'd been injured. He prayed he would never have to nurse her back to health again. Mayfair Hall had been his family's since before the revolutionary war. Tomorrow the plantation would be his to hold for his ancestors.

He thought of the woman who taught him what love wasn't. Clare was nothing like Jillian Whitehead who cared for no one except herself. His gaze drifted to Clare. While he understood he might never love this woman, he cherished her, felt a deep-seated need to see to her happiness. When she bestowed that bedazzling smile of hers in his direction, he thought his heart would stop beating. The devil when she stood in front him, watching Duster cover the first mare, he wanted to come inside her, wished he could touch her womb with his sex.

Tonight, he might do just that.

First, he needed to ease her maidenly fears. They were real and heartfelt. This lovemaking was all new to her. She understood only what he already showed her. Before this evening he'd done nearly everything except come inside her. He touched as well as stroked her intimately. Felt the rain of her desire slick his fingers. His nerves seemed to stretch as thin as hers appeared to be, the burden of doing this right centered in his gut then radiated outward.

He set her glass of wine on the table beside him while he wondered how to proceed. For the first time with this beautiful lady, he was reluctant, uncertain of how to forge ahead. Getting this over with wasn't an integral part of his plan. Nevertheless, the thought had its advantages, playing at the forefront of his befuddled man's brain. Once her membrane was no more, he could show her pleasure, all types of ecstasy. He had plans for them, plans that he meant to last a lifetime.

Michael wasn't certain where to begin. What he was certain of was that she needed to be so frantic with her hunger she would forget her fears.

"Will you kiss me, Clare? Show me everything I taught you?"

He supposed that was as good a place as any to start. He loved to kiss her. Loved the way she tasted, the scent of her the feel of her silken flesh.

When she moved against him, the tips of her breasts brushing softly against his chest, he stifled the groan building inside.

"I do like to kiss. Kissing makes me hot, makes me feel tingling in certain parts of me I didn't understand until you pleasured me. Are you going to do that first?"

Her question was guileless. Her inquiries were straightforward.

"Yes, I plan on doing exactly that. Your kisses also give me pleasure."

They gave him immense pleasure. He wanted to kiss her and kiss her until there was no more breath left in his body or in hers. In years and years when they grew old together, he wanted to lie in bed with her and kiss her, give her immense pleasure as well. After children her body would change. She would give him just as much satisfaction then as she did now.

She braced herself, her hand resting square in the middle of his chest. Just that simple touch sent lust swamping him. It would be all he could do to hold himself in check until he could make sure she was ready to take him inside her velvet sheathe. Never before had he felt such a rise of passion, so fast and hard he couldn't breathe.

Soft, moist lips touched upon his. She swept her tongue across his, touching and teasing begging for him to open. Begging wasn't at all necessary. He opened for her, accepting her inside of him. She played with him, dancing, and dueling until he could stand no more.

He cupped his hand behind her head, pressing her closer, tasting the sultry heat of her deeper then deeper still. Assuming control, he kissed her and kissed her. Her fingers wove into his hair clenching tightly. It seemed she tugged him, closer still. Her body arched against his, her breasts swaying provocatively, sending tremors of heat through him, a tempest that could never be doused. Still, he continued his ardent onslaught of his mouth upon hers.

With his teeth, Michael tugged on her bottom lip as he slowly grazed the inside with his teeth while he pulled away. After that he soothed her lips with his tongue. Tiny sounds, soft mewling noises of ecstasy rippled from her throat. He kissed her until she moaned into his mouth, until she pushed against him arching to get closer.

With his lips fastened to hers, kissing and kissing still, one hand grazed the tight hard peak of her breast. Her hips bucked and coiled seeking more from him. He grinned. Pulling back, he gazed at her allowing his ardent perusal to fasten on the milky white jewels with soft pink tips that beckoned for him to taste and savor. Her breasts were so sweetly curved and full. He knew the taste of her, remembered so well.

The sweet scent of gardenias wafted from her silken body.

"They beckon to me, your lips. A man couldn't wish for more than what you offer."

Clare blinked a few times. Her eyes were glazed over with raw hunger. "What? She queried softly, her voice soft and seductive, just how he enjoyed hearing her. "What beckons?"

"I'll show you."

His mouth closed over a puckered tip. He suckled until he thought surely; the entire soft curvaceous mound was inside his mouth.

She tugged his head, pushing him closer. He spread his hand on her belly, kneaded the softness he found there. When his fingers dipped lower to find the moist feminine folds, she arched against him, twisted. Her hands roamed his back then around to caress his chest touching upon each of his nipples.

Hot and wet, once she described herself to him in those terms. He slicked his finger along the crevice between her thighs, felt the opening to her body that was slowly growing ready for him. With ease he found the tiny nubbin that would give her the delight she sought. He touched her there, moved his finger slowly until she whimpered softly.

"Open wider for me."

He rose up to whisper the words next to her mouth. When she did as he bid, he kissed her again, swept his tongue deep inside her mouth to be met with hers.

Her knees hugged his hips. Gently he slipped one then two fingers inside her core widening her. So silken and hot, drenched with her honeyed-nectar, he groaned. Until he touched the barrier he hoped wasn't there, he continued the exploration inside her slowly moving his finger deeper before withdrawing. The barrier held strong and firm when he tested the thin membrane. She was tiny. He was afraid he would hurt her in more ways than one. Her body needed to adjust. He was afraid only time would allow that.

Kisses spent along her body left her panting her desire. Slowly, he moved his mouth lower then lower still until he reached the apex of her thighs. While he wanted to taste her, he decided to wait.

"Michael..." she moaned his name. "I need..."

More than anything he relished the sound of his name, the soft breathy way she spoke. He could listen to that his entire life and never grow bored. He prayed it would be the same for her. He understood what she required. He would show her soon.

His sightseeing brought him lower, kisses along her inner thighs after that behind her knees. Her delicate toes gave him good reason to spend moments there.

By the time he worked his way up her legs and reached her hot swollen petals she was frantic with her hunger, arching and bucking wildly. With his hands beneath her adorable butt, he brought his mouth to her folds. He sucked and licked, giving attention to the sweet pearl that would eventually send her over the edge. Over and over again, he kissed and laved then bit gently until it seemed she was beside herself.

Using his forearms to lift, he brought her higher. For a moment he paused to look at her. Her hands were fisted, her eyes closed. He needed to see her when she climaxed.

"Open your eyes, Clare."

She did. He watched her as he once again gave his attention to that part of her that would bring her the delight she would learn to crave. With his tongue he came inside her. He turned his attention again to the hidden nubbin.

"Let it go, Clare. Let me give you the pleasure you seek. Relax and enjoy."

He continued the onslaught of her senses.

"Michael...! She cried out as her body tensed then heaved. In his hands her hips jerked. "Michael..."

She bucked and coiled against him, her body shuddering the release he expertly orchestrated. She was writhing, pulses shimmering through her body. He needed to be part of that.

"I'm coming inside you, Clare."

He eased inside, feeling her body tighten around him, her snug sheath giving him all that he desired, as her body seemed to draw him deeper. "God, you're so tiny."

Michael gritted his teeth praying he would not give over to his thirst too soon. All he wanted was to bury himself as deep as he could within her silken heat. Holding back with all the foreplay aroused him to a point he'd never felt before. Rapidly, his body was losing control.

The tiny whimper he heard stopped him cold. The sound wasn't one of pleasure but pain. She climaxed but now she responded to his sex penetrating her. He would have to carry through with this in order to move on. If he didn't, she would always fear their joining. He needed to show her even though there would be pain this time, there would also be pleasure.

"Michael?"

"I'm so sorry."

He butted against that barrier that proclaimed her innocence wishing the skin gone. Closing his eyes, warding off the guilt he was feeling, he burst through. He filled her now. God, she was so tight, so very small. He didn't want to give in to the hunger that threatened to ruin this union for her.

She cried out, her nails biting into his shoulders. He tried to stop, to allow her time to accommodate his size. Desperately, he tried to hold back. That feat was impossible. He exploded within her narrow sheathe, pushing into then withdrawing to do the same again and again until he spent himself inside her.

When he climaxed, he fell upon her, the weight of his body pressed against her petite frame. His breaths came in deep sharp pants, his heart pounding frantically.

By the time he calmed himself he braced himself over her, looking down on her face. Tiny diamond teardrops of moisture spiked her lashes. Tears slipped down her cheeks. She caught her bottom lip between her teeth.

Finally, she opened her eyes. "I didn't like that last part, Michael. It wasn't good for me."

"I understand. When I come inside you again, the connection won't hurt. I promise."

He brushed damp hair from her eyes. God, he hoped he spoke the truth to her. While she stretched for him when he was deep inside, he didn't know if that was enough for next time.

"Don't want to do that again," she murmured gulping air while it seemed she tried to push away the tears. "At least not the last part. Is there any way you don't have to be so huge?"

"No, I cannot change my size."

If he wasn't so worried about her as well as the next time they made love, he would have laughed. In regards for the next encounter, he kept the chuckle behind his teeth.

The words at first alarmed him then he realized she thought sex with him would always cause pain. She would have to learn to trust him. He smiled, dropped a quick kiss to her lips. Next time he would move slower. He would stretch her slowly so she could accommodate him.

"You will come to beg me."

He discovered he was still heavy and full inside her his body responding to the soft pulses she unknowingly inflicted. If he didn't miss his guess, she was still aroused. Making love to her a second time so soon would not be something he could be proud of doing. Slowly, he pulled out of her. He grimaced as she flinched with the pain.

"I doubt that." Her voice was firm, stubborn as well. In defiance, her chin tilted upward.

He rolled off her. When he looked at her, her virgin's blood mixed with his seed was on her inner thighs. Well, the tempest outside matched the one within. Unable to hide his body from her, he was still fully aroused. The wind howled around the eaves. Rain still poured from the sky. The weather fit his mood. Turbulent. Unsettled.

A few steps took him to the pitcher of water. He picked up a soft cloth before dipping it in the water he poured into the basin.

Standing in front of the bed, he smiled at her. "I'm going to wash the blood off."

Her eyes widened as she pulled her legs together then tried to gather covers around her. "No. No, I don't think so."

Tenderly he smiled. "I have tasted every charming inch of you, Clare. You're going to become my wife tomorrow."

He stepped forward, meaning to begin now, as he would continue the rest of their lives together.

When he reached her, the covers were pulled to her chin. He sat next to her on the bed. "You can't bathe me. I won't allow it."

"Do you wish to sleep with the stickiness of my seed coupled with the blood between your legs?"

Well, the question was a bit harsh even to his ears. He didn't want to play tug of war with the covers either.

It seemed Clare realized what she didn't want when she shook her head. However, she had not yet to come to terms with what was going to happen.

"I would do it myself."

The covers did slip a hair. Her creamy white shoulders peaked above the quilt.

This was something he needed to do for her. He tugged in a deep breath of gardenia-scented air coupled with musky woman and sex. The scent gave his lust a jolt of pure pleasure. Good God, he wanted this woman again, this instant. He wasn't a randy stoat. He could control himself. Perhaps not.

Sitting on the side of the bed the damp cloth in his hand he bathed his sex. Watched her eyes shimmer as she watched him cleaning her blood from his member. After that he strode to the basin to rinse the cloth. When he returned, her eyes were huge pools of dark blue reminding him of the storm swept Atlantic.

"It's your turn, Clare. Let the covers slide then open your legs for me. This will only take a second. When I finish, we can eat more of that delicious meal Delilah sent our way. I'll open another bottle of wine. We can talk about what happened just now along with what will happen next time I make love to you."

She shook her head again. He wasn't about to give in to her. Nonetheless, he wished for her to give over to his suggestion with a willing mind. He ran his fingertip along a bared shoulder then found his way across the top of her breasts. She sucked a gulp of air. Her eyes widened, while she sent her pink tongue sweeping along her intoxicating lips.

"No, let me do this." The tone of her voice pleaded with him. "I don't...Michael truly."

"This is the only time I will have to wash blood from between your legs. I want to see if you are hurt more than normal."

Good God, he didn't know what more than normal meant. He also didn't know if this would be the only time. He prayed it would be. He didn't intend to push himself into her until she was ready. When she had a child, there would be blood. He intended to be there for her.

Slowly, as if his argument convinced her she allowed the covers to dip down to her waist. He finished for her, baring her legs, which were pressed tightly together. A spurt of tenderness for her slashed though him with near blinding speed. He reminded himself that all this was new to her. Smiling fondly, he waited for her.

"You aren't going to let this go, are you?" she bit out even though she also sounded resigned on some elemental level.

Grinning, besotted with her he shook his head. The sight of her swaying breast, her nipples slightly swollen from his passionate attention sent another powerful upwelling of longing to his rod as well as tenderness. She did it to him again. If she didn't stop her unknowing seduction of him, he would no longer have charge of his body. He would take her this instant.

A long slow breath of air shivered from her lips. "All right." She closed her eyes as he gently pushed her legs apart.

At the sight of her, he sucked in his breath. He had not thought there would be so much blood. An outburst of guilt flooded his senses. Quickly, he bathed her then covered her so she would be more comfortable. He wondered if she would ever feel comfortable enough to walk around the room naked while he watched. More than anything he wished for that.

With the wine poured along with a single plate of food to share, he sat beside her. Their shoulders touched. Through the terrace door, they watched the storm howl and moan. Saw the rain slash its fury against the panes of glass.

"We might need to batten down the hatches," he murmured as he thoughtfully sipped his wine.

Getting up to do so would set them back. While he was gone, he felt certain she would take the time to cover herself not in the negligée she wore earlier but in that prim old maid nightgown of hers.

"This doesn't sound like a normal storm," she said seeming to agree. "Are you going to fasten the shutters?"

"You're right. I don't believe this howling wind is at all normal. While this tempest is not a hurricane, I do believe it's close. The winds are coming from the southwest. Most the hurricanes around these parts blow straight up from the south. Stay here, I'm going to shutter up the house."

"I'll help."

She started from the bed.

He grinned, smiling tenderly at her. "You'll have to put more on than the robe you were wearing when the evening began."

He spoke while he pulled on his buckskins. As he feared she would don her armor then be reluctant to remove the gown. In his mind, the only way he wanted to sleep with his soon to be wife was naked.

"I'll just run to my room."

The sight of her white curvaceous backside pleasured him. Her legs were long and sleek even well-muscled for a woman. All of her was white such a beautiful alabaster. Ah, he would like to make love to her again tonight. To hear her howl with her pleasure would also delight him. She returned in a few minutes. Her nightgown caressed her slender form while she pulled on a robe that would also cover her from her chin to her delicious toes. He meant to taste them again.

Michael wondered how difficult it was going to be to remove the new articles of clothing, perhaps not too problematic as he could sweet talk and seduce with the best. He was a good lover. She would discover that fact soon. A long whoosh of air left his lips. No matter what happened next, he was going to sleep next to her. She would be naked, crushed against the solid wall of his chest. His thoughts pleased him. He hoped Clare would be satisfied as well.

Clare shuttered all the inside windows. He took the outside. By the time he finished his hair was dripping. The great coat he wore was nearly soaked through. When he entered the bedroom, she sat on top the bed still in the nightwear he meant to remove, sipping a glass of wine. Seeming content, she nodded at him. Light from the single candle danced in her eyes, created a warm glow on her skin.

Over the top of the crystal, she grinned at him, her smile wide as well as infectious. He hoped she forgot the pain of the first mating. Prayed she would be willing again very soon. With long strides he walked to the bathroom. When he returned, he was towel drying his hair. In front of her he stripped then dried himself.

Seemingly fascinated she watched.

A few moments later, he sat down on top of the bed next to her then poured a glass of wine. Leaning back, he closed his eyes thinking of the best way to remove her clothing. At the beginning of the evening, he'd not thought this would have to be done a second time, so much for the tempest blowing outside. He supposed he could simply ask her.

"You don't intend to keep wearing that horrid nightdress. do you?" he asked while he stared at the long row of buttons he might enjoy dealing with while he kissed tender flesh each time, he unfastened one.

A silver lining could always be found when the notion of removing clothing leapt to his mind.

Her small pink tongue whipped across her lips leaving a dewy trail of tantalizing moisture everywhere it touched. Once again with little provocation hunger flooded him. If this rush of pure raw desire didn't stop with each tiny look, she would be the death of him before the evening ended.

"Do you expect me to sleep naked? Haven't we already done all there is to be done?" She appeared surprised when she asked the question. Her eyes widened perceptibly. "I shouldn't have asked," she murmured while her fingers wound into the soft fabric of her robe.

"Maybe you shouldn't have. Yes, I do mean to sleep naked. Will not do so alone."

If he accomplished what he was thinking about, he'd be deep inside her when he finished the last button. If he did so, would he hurt her again? A virgin was beyond his experience. He would have to proceed with caution, test the waters while he moved slowly. Would have to take each moment into consideration.

"I'm cold."

To Michael it seemed a ploy. Nonetheless, it wasn't good enough for a gentle answer that would douse her ploy. "I'll warm you. Now, will you take this off or would you like me to have the honors."

At this moment he hoped she would give him the opportunity.

She seemed fascinated with her toes. Well, he was captivated with them too. Hell, he was spellbound with every part of her. "Yes, I should do so."

Several seconds passed while she toyed with the buttons. The fasteners seemed to be immovable beneath her shaking fingers.

He felt certain she was thinking of ways to prolong this adventure. Relaxing against the backboard, he placed his hands behind his head. "You having trouble? Would you like a bit of help?"

She looked up, her eyes startlingly wide, the turbulent blue simmering with emotions. "No...I a-am perfectly capable." Yet the gown was still fastened to the point beneath her chin.

Quickly, he brushed her fingers aside, his patience having ended. This second seduction of his woman would happen now. He set her on her back then fanned her hair across the pillow. Now, he straddled her, his sex jutting toward her.

He tapped a finger on his chin pondering several scenarios. "Now, where to begin? Believe at the top is always the best strategy."

With each button he unfastened, he kissed her, nibbled, and laved. By the time he was able to push her gown over her shoulders she was purring, her hips arching upward searching for the satisfaction he could give her. His little Clare was wanton perfection.

"Lift your hips."

When he touched her petals, she was hot and slick with her desire. Her body bucked frantically against his hand as he taunted the glossy bud he found beneath curls guarding her sex. He slipped the gown from her body; let the fabric land on the floor in a pool of virgin white.

"You are no longer a virgin. Hence you have no need of a gown such as this one. Perhaps it is meant for the ragbag."

He tested her readiness, slipped two fingers inside. She was larger than the first time. She was moving, taunting him, pleading for her release.

"Please, Michael..." Her fingers dug into his shoulders.

Watching her for a couple of seconds, he was a man well satisfied with his woman. Slowly, with infinite care he pushed inside her hot velvet sheath. Inch by precious inch he gently began to fill her. No grimace of pain met his ears. She didn't flinch as he came deeper and deeper inside her. Didn't tense when he was so deep inside her, he touched her womb. Her core kissed his rod, licked with lightening pulses that couldn't be denied.

"Do you hurt anywhere?" Michael held his breath waiting for the answer he wanted to hear, needed to hear.

"Please, Michael. I want you...make the sweetness happen again."

She did beg. As he brought her hips higher, he filled her more deeply. When he touched her womb again, he closed his eyes for a second. Now, now was the time to show her this act between them would never hurt her again.

While he began to move, slowly at first, he listened to her, tried to stay tuned to her responses. Beneath him, she frantically coiled and arched. He understood her need as well as his own. Harder and faster, he pushed himself into her until she cried out. He covered her mouth with his, molded and framed her lips while he took her climax inside him. With a howl of his own, he spent himself inside her.

Beneath him she trembled, her body still responding still moving as if he could give her more. He soothed her, running his hands along her back. Slowly, his rod slid from inside her warmth. This was heaven. Together they rolled so he held her close, her head tucked into the hollow of his shoulder.

"Was that better?" he asked while he ran his finger through her hair. "Did I hurt you?"

Her hand rested on his chest. "You know you didn't. Yes, you were right. I might want to do that one more time."

With a slanted eyebrow and a wicked grin, he studied her. "One more time?"

"Maybe two."

"We will see."

~ * ~

Raynard huddled in one of the outbuildings at Biff Gideon's

plantation. The building seemed to be meant for storage. Old desks along with chairs as well as other pieces of furniture were stacked one upon the other. Rain pounded on the roof above while he pulled the horse blanket around him to keep warm. His stomach rumbled. When he stopped at the main house, Biff sent him here. Told him it wouldn't do at all if anyone saw him. Well, who the hell would be out on a night such as this one?

"This is all that girl's fault. If she hadn't come to Mayfair Hall, all would be just as it was two months ago. As it was, he'd been in hiding since that day. While he wouldn't mind plowing her belly, he preferred the slaves. They were more submissive. Fighting with the lady beneath him was no fun. He liked them pliant to his whims. The slaves were too terrified of the repercussion he always inflicted to act different.

"You in here, Raynard?" Biff called out as he sauntered toward him.

Raynard held the lantern high. It was about time the man came to see him. He left a message hours ago with one of his slaves. Stupid slaves, they could never do anything right. He was so hungry his stomach rattled from the emptiness. Hunger didn't suit him either. He should have just left the territory. It would not have been too difficult to find another job. If he'd done that, he wouldn't be sitting in this isolated place listening to the wind howl and at the whim of a rich plantation owner. All they had in common was the girl. Raynard didn't think that was very much. He could always cut and run when the tempest finished yowling its fury.

"I'm here." Raynard stood, stalking toward the man who almost wanted the same as he did.

Second thoughts, curse them, assailed him. If Biff knew he wasn't in this wholeheartedly, he'd boot him into the wings of the gale. If he were caught, he'd pay dearly if Michael didn't kill him first. Just as sure as this storm wasn't going to let up anytime soon, he was certain the girl meant more to Michael than he pretended.

Though he did need to see Clare Carter-Brown brought down to the level a woman was born to be at. The task would never be easy. Somehow, she won the hearts of all at Mayfair. She became their little missy.

The woman acted too high and mighty. He wanted to taste her then toss her to Biff who would then hand her off to Busby. Maybe they would pay him the dollar he offered earlier. Flannigan could have her when they were done with her. He only wanted that if he wouldn't die because he sampled the goods.

Before that he needed to see Flannigan ruined. The man possessed the audacity to fire him. Hoped to see the arrogant manager of Mayfair Hall run out of town, tarred and feathered in the process. Raynard watched Biff stride toward him. He was just as arrogant as Flannigan. He supposed wealth bred arrogance.

"Did you bring me something to eat? Could use a bottle of wine too. I'm a starving man," Raynard grumbled.

"Yes, you shouldn't be here. It's too dangerous for both of us if you get caught on my property. You do understand if your discovered, I'll disavow any notion that I knew you were here. Will tell people you were using the building to hide. That, of course, would be the truth of the matter. When are you going to grab the girl? I'm beginning to lose patience."

"Understand perfectly. Did you bring a slave to ease myself with? No, I see you haven't." He let out the breath he'd been holding. Well, hell, he never truly expected Biff to give him one of the slaves for the night.

"I'll grab Clare when I get the chance. Don't exactly have a face that will be overlooked if I'm in town. If you want her, you might have to find a way to grab her yourself since I'm a wanted man." He looked around Biff to take a second look to see if he brought a woman for him. "No, can't say that I'm surprised. What do you want me to do? Don't have anywhere to go unless you know of another shack nearby. Have to stay here whether you like it or not. At least it's warm and dry. The law doesn't have a reason to search here for me."

"No, this place here is most likely the safest. You can stay in the back room. There is a bed. The rest is up to you. I want you out of here when the storm passes by."

"Yeah, that's what I was afraid you were going to say. I'm not going anywhere. Going to stay here until I get my revenge. Did think about leaving the county. Changed my thoughts seeing I can't stand the idea of Flannigan getting everything."

Biff stood with his hands on his hips a sour expression on his face. For a second he looked to the door. When he turned his attention back to Raynard, "After tonight, you'll have to feed yourself. Can't risk anyone seeing me come to this building. We no longer use this space for anything."

"Suppose I can steal food. If I do that, people around here will start asking questions you won't want to answer. Best you find a way to keep me comfortable. Send one of the slaves to me. She can bring me food. Do it tonight. If you make me happy, I'll be more likely to do the same for you."

Raynard watched the older man shift from foot to foot. He was clearly displeased. Well, too bad. Biff got himself into this because he lusted after the girl, Clare, thinking she was like her big sister. She wasn't. He was certain of that fact. Clare wasn't a trollop.

Still Raynard believed the best way to seek revenge on Michael was to hurt Clare. Forcing her to his way would be a pleasure. If she didn't fight, he amended. He rubbed his hands together. He saw enough of her tender white skin to know having her beneath him would be a real pleasure. In so many ways, white flesh was always better than black.

"Bring me a girl tonight. If you do, I'll guarantee you that you'll have Clare."

Biff didn't answer. He did nod. Perhaps by the time he finished eating he would be able to satisfy himself in another manner.

He picked up the food Biff brought him before sauntering to the mentioned room at the back of the building. When he looked beneath the lids covering the food, he was surprised to see the succulent shrimp, along with tender green beans. Other delicacies adorned his plate including scalloped potatoes in a cream sauce. Before Biff left, he handed him a bottle of wine. He would have preferred ale. Nonetheless, he meant to savor this meal. Too many days passed that he had to forage for food. He didn't think berries along with mushrooms would ever appeal to him again. Not that they did the first time.

While he ate, he sifted through a plan. It wasn't a good one. All he knew was that he needed to find Clare alone. Once he had her, he could tie her up in that cave. If he closed off the entrance, she would die in there while Flannigan tried to get her out. That plan wouldn't satisfy Biff.

Ah, it wasn't the best scheme. However, he hoped the plan would work. After all, what Biff wanted wasn't important to him. When he left her there, he would have to hightail himself out of the county. It wouldn't take long for Flannigan to figure out who was responsible. Perhaps he could even steal the horse. Duster was his name. That would put an immediate stop to Flannigan's plans for the stud farm. Its future depended on that stallion.

He sent his head back and hooted with laughter.

Chapter Seven

Warmth enveloped Clare's body. A soft sigh rippled from her throat. Content, she snuggled against Michael. Her bottom pressed against him. His arousal pulsed against her backside. She held still. With a deep breath of air, she let her mind wander to the night before.

Michael taught her desire along with raw hunger, all of that leading to dazzling ecstasy. Taught her about lust after that along with secret pleasure so pure and sweet she longed for more. No words of love were spoken between them. While she knew Michael didn't love her, she now understood he wanted her to ease his body with hers. Was lust so different from love? She decided she would take his idea to heart. Since she wasn't about to offer her love for him on a silver platter, she would tell him she lusted for him.

She thought love would be a fine thing. For now, she would settle for all those brazen emotions he introduced to her.

Ecstasy.

Enchantment.

Blazing raw craving.

Love, she knew that was never in the offing from the beginning. Perhaps love for them never would happen. Well, she could settle for lust if she had to do so.

In time, over the years, love might come. More curious things had happened. She pondered that thought for a few minutes before she gasped for air. Wrenching her from her thoughts, his hand cupped her breast, a finger flicking across the hardened tip of her breast. With quick and heady speed her body reacted to his tender advances. She supposed this was lust.

His lips found their mark against her neck, nipped, and sipped as he directed a scorching path across her shoulders. While he toyed with her nipple the fingers of his other hand slid between her legs, played with that part of her that enticed her to the enchantment and rhythm of his loving.

Her moan of pleasure surprised her. She pushed back against him. Felt his sex jut against her. Raw hunger enveloped her. "Oh..."

His fingers delved intimately, massaged, and kneaded. She arched against him. Twisted. "Are you eager for me. Can you take all of me inside you now?" His low throaty voice caressed her.

The whisper of his breath along her shoulders aroused and excited her. She thought it must be obvious how enthusiastic she was for his entrance into her. "Please," was all she could say.

From behind, he pushed into her, filled her with his steel-hard length. Within seconds, spasms seemed to spread within her before he even began to move. While she pushed back against him, his hands held her hips. His fingers gripped, guiding her, encouraging her to set the pace.

"Michael!" She cried out his name as he pushed harder and faster, deeper still deeper than she thought possible. She felt his seed flow into her.

His loud yell followed. Spent once again, Clare closed her eyes. He lazily ran his hand along her arm. Once again, he cupped her breast in his large hand. She heard his long breath of air as the sound flowed across her shoulders.

He moved higher, his lips against her ear, murmuring, "That was well done of you, my soon to be wife," he whispered close to her ear, his tongue touching inside. "You're turning out to be a wild, fantastic lover. That was immensely satisfying. Didn't expect you to be such an excellent student. I'm very thrilled. Believe we will suit well together."

What he told her was true, more than true. He stroked her so expertly all she could be was crazed. He pushed her until she was frantic with hunger for him. Even now, she hoped he would teach her something new, perhaps a new way to pleasure him. She did want to kiss his shaft, lick, and nibble until he was beside himself with desire.

He nipped her ear. "What? Nothing to say? I would have thought you would have some argument for me. Didn't expect you to be a brazen hussy."

In his arms she turned then punched him in the shoulder. "That was not nice of you. I'm only what you make me."

"Clare, you are wonderful. A man couldn't ask for anyone more delightful in bed than their wife." He grinned from ear to ear. "Of course, at the moment you are only my lover. Should we change that title today? What do you think?"

"Your words didn't say I was wonderful. I'm no more a brazen hussy than my sister was."

With one of his long-tanned fingers, he touched the tip of her nose. She stared at his mouth, looked at the moisture. Longed to kiss him before making love one more time.

"Ah, but my words did say you were wonderful. I want my wife wild as well as frantic, twisting with her passion beneath me when we are making love."

His lips found hers, molded them underneath his. He sent his tongue inside her before he groaned. When he pulled back, he brushed strands of her hair from her face.

"You are as sweaty as am I. Another go around might not be prudent. It's our wedding day. Are you pleased with the man who will be your husband until one of us kicks up their toes?"

"Indeed, if you make lust to me every night then I will forever be pleased until you stick your spoon in the wall."

He frowned at her. "Make lust?"

She grinned wondering if he wanted to hear love words. Maybe she had the way of things with him.

At the knocking on the door, he stood. He slipped his dressing gown on then belted it. When he opened the door, Old Suzzy stood in the hall with a tray of food blatantly showing a look of disapproval.

"Thank you," Michael said as he took the tray from her, seemingly unwilling to acknowledge the sentiment. "Will you send a message to Ezra that I would like to see him in the parlor at ten. How is the weather? Has the rain stopped? Well, no, I can still hear it battering the windows."

"Ezra?" she questioned. What you need dat man for?" she asked the question yet the light in her eyes told a different story.

He looked at Old Suzzy, grinning from ear-to-ear. Clare must be in total dishabille after the night. He grinned. "Today is our wedding day.

Since the storm seems to still be pouring buckets of water on the earth, I thought we would have Ezra wed the two of us today." He held up his hands as she started to protest. "I understand the good folks in town won't consider us properly wed. Nonetheless, I will. When the storm is over, Clare and I will have Reverend Jones say the words also. So, we will have two weddings, one at our home with the people we truly care about in attendance, also one in town to stop the gossip."

Suzy grinned broadly. "I knew you'd do the right thing by our lil' missy. Ezra will be here at ten o'clock sharp." With that said she quickly turned, heading down the steps.

"Your words pleased her," Clare said as she held the covers to her chin. "When she first saw me, she was frowning her condemnation."

"Our people have sought this marriage since you moved into Mayfair. Of course, they will be pleased, as are we. Would you enjoy a bath?"

Clare nodded. Between her thighs she felt sticky with his seed. Thinking of a wedding her heart did a tiny jig. She didn't have anything to wear, not that the fact mattered. When she left for Virginia, she never thought to marry. Didn't believe there would be a man to snag her heart.

Now she intended to spend the rest of her life showing Michael Flannigan just how much of her heart he owned. "Yes, I'd like a bath. Do you want one first?" She set her eyes on the tray of food. Her stomach rumbled hungrily. It seemed the night before all they did was drink the wine. She supposed she should be happy she wasn't sick.

"I'll take a bath then dress. I'll wait for you down stairs."

Slowly, he rose. When he turned to look at her, she wickedly returned the favor. Heavens, she could look at him forever without batting an eyelash.

Watching him bathe would be nice. Looking at him was more than pleasant. He rang for the bath. While they waited, he drenched a scone with honey. He handed the bread to her. The food was delicious. She drank the coffee he poured for her. The brew was heady and strong. She felt invigorated, excitement for the day coursing through her.

Over the rim of the cup, she stared at his mouth. He lifted an eyebrow seeming to question her. After that she allowed her gaze to drift lower. When she saw his reaction, she slipped her tongue along her bottom lip. She grinned at him.

"If you don't wish to be late for your wedding, you should be careful as to what you are staring so intently at." In turn, his gaze focused on her bosom.

Beneath the covers, which she held tight to her with her arms, the crests tightened. Her breasts swayed. She almost moaned. This staring was something she should not have begun. Filing away the sensation for a later date, she looked away.

"You are too beautiful, Michael. I want to see all of you all the time." She held her breath when he stood, his dressing gown now sliding to the ground. His arousal jutted from him.

"We could make this fast. You did find your release this morning just seconds after I entered you."

Clare held out her arms for him. "I believe we can try to do this making lust thing faster." She flew to him.

"The water..."

The knock on the door stopped them for a moment only. After Michael donned his dressing gown and she fled beneath the covers, he let the servants into the room. In the bathroom, they filled the tub. As soon as they left, Michael strode to her. He pulled her from the bed.

"Wrap your legs around my hips."

She did.

He surged inside her fast and hard. So deep, she wanted to yowl with the pleasure of it all. She pulsed around him, sobbing her pleasure. He drove inside her over then over again.

"Michael! Oh, my...Michael..." After she climaxed, she buried her face in the hollow of his shoulder. "I can't move."

She thought of all she needed to accomplish before the ceremony.

Still deep inside her she thought he meant to bring her to that place of raw ecstasy again. Finally, he pulled out of her, his arousal still blatant.

"You are going to be the death of me." He set her on the bed. "Eat. We will have all the afternoon to explore as well as pleasure each other. After that, if it pleases us, we can do the same tonight. There is no work until the rain stops. We cannot exercise the horses." He handed her the robe he divested her of the night before.

Clare watched him stride into the bathing area. For a moment, she thought to watch. She didn't dare. If she gave in to her desire, they would never get out of the room. The marriage would take place at ten. Reverend Ezra, the people of Mayfair called him, was a free man long ago. He was also an ordained minister. On the plantation, he prayed over all the births as well as the deaths. He performed all the marriage ceremonies.

This was good.

She liked this plan of his.

In the adjoining room, she searched her armoire for a proper dress. She brought two ball gowns neither would do. When Merry Stewart wed Devlin, she wore a beautiful white gown that molded all her curves. Clare fell in love with the gown then commissioned one to be made for her even though she didn't believe she would ever have the opportunity to wear something so revealing. Actually, the gown covered all of her.

It was so simple. Instead of white, Clare had hers made in a pale ice blue. The gown was form fitted to her. It showed every curve she possessed. Thirty blue covered buttons, tiny buttons, traveled down her back to the base of her spine. Merry told her that Devlin kissed every spot he uncovered. Well, that was what Michael did last night when he unfastened her prim nightgown. He might do the same tonight with the wedding gown. She shuddered; anticipation coupled with lust flooding her senses. He wasn't even looking at her.

When she returned to the master chamber, Michael was out of the bath. He was dressing. His breeches were black, his shirt a fine white lawn. He donned a dark blue frock coat before pulling on his perfectly shined black boots.

Her eyes widened. She'd never seen him dressed so fine. "You're beautiful." *I love you, Michael Flannigan.*

"How long before you're ready?" He stepped close to her. One of his long fingers lifted her chin. Tenderly, he kissed her on the lips. He was ginning at her. "Don't dare do more than that. If we do…"

If he did, they would not be downstairs for the wedding on time. "An hour, give me an hour. I'll be ready then."

"You found something to wear?" A dark red eyebrow arched

upward in speculation. "I was afraid you might have to wear that splendid lingerie from last night."

She wished to cosh him over the head, nodded instead. For the first time since last night, she felt a wave of shyness tumble through her. More than anything she hoped he liked the dress she chose. He never commented on her gowns, only the britches she wore in the stable. Her day dresses were serviceable, far from provocative.

"I did," she tilted her head slightly, slipped her tongue along her lips knowing what the gesture usually did to him. "You will have to wait to see the gown. Don't want bad luck if you see me before the ceremony. If you would send Old Suzzy up in about thirty minutes, I could use her help."

He grinned lecherously. "I could help. Would love to help you into your wedding finery."

Shaking her head, laughing softly at his declaration, she stepped away from him. Trying for indignation, she told him, "No, your help would be no help whatsoever. You are better at undressing me than dressing. Send Old Suzzy to me please. As it stands, you've seen me before the wedding. Don't want more bad luck."

He kissed her again, this time on her forehead. Swiveling on a boot heel a wide grin on his debonair face, he left. The door banged shut behind him. Her hands were clasped beneath her chin, her gaze focused on the door for at least ten seconds, willing him to return. She tugged in a long deep breath of air, hoping for calm to permeate her emotions. She didn't believe she'd be calm until this was over and done.

Suddenly, she was aware of the time. Her heart thundered. Goodness, she had only an hour to bathe then dress. Usually, she wore little to no makeup. Today she would use something to darken her lashes as well as a bit of color for her lips, her cheeks as well.

With a great rush of air, she exhaled. The new bath water was steaming in the tub. She found the heat relaxed her strained muscles. Until she found a moment alone, she didn't realize she was sore from all his attentions. She wondered if she would be able to walk tomorrow if tonight went the same as last evening. She supposed if he had his way, the night would be the same. She wouldn't mind.

In exactly thirty minutes, Old Suzzy knocked on the door. "Dis is one of duh happiest days of my life, Lil Missy." After her spate of words, she cackled. "Suh, he told me, he did, to give this to you. It was his mother's a long time ago." She held out a beautiful sapphire necklace. The three blue gems hung on a silver chain, each sapphire surrounded by diamonds. "Massa wants his bride to wear this for him."

Clare couldn't help but gasp. Her eyes widened feeling disbelief. "It is something blue. I had not expected this." Truly, she didn't think any of the traditions would be followed today. The wedding was meant to be expedient nothing more. In a way this was as much a joining of the business part of Mayfair as it was two people. The necklace was the first truly romantic gesture Michael ever made.

"Yes, it is. Mammy Jo wants you to carry dis with you. It will do as something new. She likes to crochet lace around handkerchiefs. She sells them in the town. Dis one is for you. And...Delilah is giving you dese garters to wear. They have to be something borrowed. However, she says if you want to keep them you can. She has no use for them. Dey can be borrowed during the ceremony then yours afterward."

As if she were still a little girl at Christmas, Clare clapped her hands together all the while jumping up and down. She folded the elderly lady in her arms hugging her tightly. "Thank you, thank you with all my heart. I don't think...well people are so nice. All of you, my new family, I didn't expect anything." She was overcome with emotion.

"Now, don't you go and cry. Dat won't do. No crying won't do at all on dis happy day. Turn around now. We'll get everything done up nicely."

Old Suzzy stepped back after fastening the necklace. She tisked when she studied the line of buttons down Clare's back that needed fastening. "Dat man's not goin' to be able to get you out of dat beautiful gown. What were you thinking child?"

"I won't allow him to rip it," she said softly thinking he might do just that. "He will have to be patient I assume. Do you think that's possible?"

Clare couldn't imagine Michael showing patience when it came to lovemaking.

"Well, dat might be askin' too much of any man, especially a man like Mr. Flannigan an' on his wedding night to boot."

"Michael won't want to tear the gown. He'll be careful."

No matter how many times she said the words, she wasn't at all certain they were true. She remembered their mating of less than an hour ago. No, patience would be difficult for both of them.

Old Suzzy stepped back, her hands on her hips, shaking her head as if she was looking at a crazy woman. "I'll just have to wait outside dat door for you to come get me. If he can't undo all those tiny little buttons, I'll be waitin' for you. You hear? Those big hands of his...no, he won't be able to get past the first one."

Clare nodded, believing she was most likely correct in her assumptions. "Now why don't you fasten them?"

Twenty or so minutes later, just before the hour she was given passed, Clare walked to the parlor. Sam Grayson from Leslie Hall stood at the door. He smiled at her as he held out his arm.

"I'm going to give you away," he told her his grin wide. "It's what Link would have wanted. Too bad your family can't be here. Do they know you're getting married today?"

No, she needed to write to them. They would be disappointed not to be with her. Having just returned to Scotland, it was not reasonable to think they would make the voyage back. Besides her decision nearly blindsided her. She'd been so very determined not to wed.

Delilah stood in the entryway as well. "I'm going to be your matron of honor if that's alright with you." She handed her a bouquet of flowers, a mixture of different colored daisies.

Clare nodded. The flowers were something else she never expected. Edward Grayson from Leslie Hall stood next to Michael by the big fireplace. She supposed Edward was the best man. They were definitely a rag tag group. Timmy and Big Tom sat on strategically placed chairs along with Old Suzzy who took her place after leaving her with Grayson.

Mammy Jo sang. She stood near the fireplace, her hands held together in front of her. Her voice was beautiful. The song was not a traditional Scottish song for a wedding, nor was the tune, Irish. Still her voice was loud and clear, powerful, so sweet and pure. Her voice stirred something inside her. Mammy Jo hit notes that were filled with heart and soul.

She watched Delilah, walk slowly to the fireplace where the men stood. She saw the appreciative look in Michael's eyes when his gaze rested on her. He didn't smile though. He appeared grim, maybe nervous. She wondered what he thought of the gown. She wore nothing except her garters and stockings beneath. Michael was sure to appreciate that fact if he knew.

Well, she was so nervous she could barely walk. She couldn't imagine what Michael was feeling. She sipped in a short draught of air. It was all it seemed her lungs could hold at the time. She fidgeted with her hair, pushing a few curly strands behind her ears. "I'm so glad you are here, Grayson. Hold me up, please. My knees are threatening to give way. Don't know if I can put one foot in front of the other."

The low masculine chuckle both unnerved her and gave her confidence. He would do as she asked. She looked over the people in attendance. They were her employees, her friends now. Except for Delilah they were all black people. They were free, could live just as they wanted. She was proud of that fact. No one should be a slave.

"This wedding will be over with before you can blink. Link told me I should keep an eye out for you two children that something such as this might happen. You're going to have to write to your brother-in-law soon."

"Yes." She ran her tongue between her lips. Yes, writing was a good idea. It surprised her that Link thought she might marry Michael. The thought vanished as her gaze settled on her groom. Writing would be unimportant if she fainted and the result was no marriage. Would the wedding stop? Well, of course the ceremony would. Michael would wake her up with a dash of cold water. After that they would proceed as if nothing happened.

Delilah waited off to the side. After Grayson reached Michael, he handed her to him. She gave Delilah her bouquet. Michael took her hands in his. They were large and warm. Gently he squeezed as if he understood she was terrified. When he smiled at her, she knew everything would be fine. He mouthed the words. *You can do this. I've faith in you.*

His gaze focused on her mouth before slipping to her bosom. He winked. She almost giggled. He was so outrageous. She also felt the swift infusion of heat to every part of her. The tips of her breasts hardened in anticipation. Good Lord, she hoped no one could see what was happening to her body beneath the gown that molded unforgivingly every curve.

The ceremony was over quickly. He slipped a ring on her finger. She wondered when he had time to buy the piece of jewelry. When Reverend Ezra told her he could kiss the bride, his lips molded firmly on hers. His hands on her back pressed her against him. She felt the hard ridge of his sex against her belly. A tiny mewl of pleasure escaped her lips.

Wickedly, he swept his tongue across hers. Unable to resist, she opened for him, felt the devilishly tender movement of his tongue inside her. "Brazen hussy," he whispered. "Wouldn't want you any other way."

With that done, he pulled away. While he stared at her for several seconds, he brushed his thumb across her lip seeming to swipe away the moisture left behind.

Cheers resounded in the parlor of Mayfair, their people rejoicing their marriage. The moment was good, filled with happiness. Suddenly, it seemed chaos reigned. Delilah along with Old Suzzy bustled from the kitchen to the parlor. One carried trays of food, the other bottles of champagne straight from France. They poured everyone a glass, liquid bubbling over each one. Grayson and Edward helped distribute the drinks. She smiled at the room, everyone was laughing and talking. It was all so good.

When everybody held a glass of the bubbly drink, Edward cleared his throat. He held up his glass. "Here's to the new Mrs. Flannigan. While this pair created a few scandals on their road to happiness, we are all genuinely happy as well as relieved they finally decided to tie the knot. We no longer have to look in the opposite direction when Michael gets possessive." He tipped his glass and drank.

"Here! Here!"

Everyone followed suit. Clare leaned into him even while a wave of heat suffused her. When she looked into the deep simmer of his green eyes that now seemed more the color of the dark pine needles than the mossy glen she first thought, she whispered softly hoping he was the only one who heard. "I lust for you, Michael."

He choked on his drink, a few drops splaying outward. She wiped one from her nose.

Michael drank the contents before leaning close to whisper, "You will pay for that, Mrs. Flannigan."

"I hope so," she murmured.

~ * ~

"I'm exhausted. Who would have thought a wedding would consume so much energy?"

Clare leaned onto Michael's chest. Beneath his frock coat, she rubbed her hand down the front of his shirt. He tossed the coat on a chair then loosened the tie around his neck.

Michael looked at his wife of only a few hours. He was pleased. He relished the feel of her, all of her. As an untried woman she somehow managed to do him in with lust. She knew that. Might even use the fact to get her way about things. He wouldn't mind in the least, as he would understand the blackmail attempts.

"You're also a wee bit tipsy, Mrs. Flannigan." The sound of his last name coupled with the single word Mrs. gave him a few more good reasons to smile. "Finally, you're mine. All mine."

She didn't answer right away. Decisively, "Just a *wee* bit tipsy, Mr. Flannigan. Does that change what you plan for tonight? Should I cease to celebrate our marriage? What would please you the most?"

"Not in the least. A bit tipsy has untold possibilities."

He kissed the back of her neck, grazed his teeth across the sensitized flesh. He was delighted in her rapid response. When the time came to consummate the marriage, she would be wet and swollen for him. He meant to tease her mercilessly to that point where all she could do was beg. "What changes everything is that damn line of buttons down the back of your dress. Did you pick this gown out for today in order to torment me? Torture is not nice of you."

Not for one second did he believe his statement. His intention was to use those tiny blue buttons to thoroughly seduce his blushing bride, perhaps torment her a *wee* bit.

Clare set her head against his chest then placed her hands around his forearms. He'd rolled up the sleeves of his shirt. Her fingers felt nice. "Old Suzzy said she would unfasten them for me when the time was right. All I need do is ring for her. She told me she'd wait for the summons." Her fingers traveled along his skin sending fire racing in their path.

"Not on your life. I'm going to have my wicked way undoing each one of those wretched little torture devices. I promise you I won't rip your gown. It's beautiful except the way the fabric molds to every sweet curve you possess is meant for my eyes only. When I saw you...Jesus, Clare. I was sure I saw all of you yet I saw nothing. Every man in attendance saw the same." He wasn't sure if he was enraged or jealous.

She pushed her adorable little bottom against him. "Did you lust for me?"

Despite his best effort to remain calm, he groaned. He wanted to fondle every part of her. Wanted to forget the fact that all she felt for him now was lust. He liked it much better when she spoke of love. He'd much rather hear her tell him how much she loved him.

What to do?

"Witch."

He sipped a tender spot behind her ear. Felt her tremble. He placed his hand beneath her breast. Even covered with the fabric he teased the nipple, pushing enticingly against the material. Ah, both were eager for his attention. At this moment he needed to forget what she was making him feel. Forget that he wanted to toss her on the bed. If he did that now, they wouldn't surface for air until the *wee* hours of the morning. He cleared his throat.

"Would you like food or do you want to proceed to the bed?"

Michael wasn't sure why he gave her a choice. He wanted to clear up a few things before they played.

"Food would be nice. I do believe I'd like to watch the sun dip behind the hills before we retire for the evening. I find I've a wealth of energy even though I'm also exhausted. Today was trying in so many ways yet fulfilling also. Finally, the rain isn't falling. We can enjoy the splendor of the evening."

His fingers tightened on her shoulders while his trousers grew tighter in anticipation. Without too much thought he could change her mind about what she wanted. Decided on prudence to rule the moment. Waiting would increase the pleasure. "Food it is."

Old Suzzy and Delilah had left a tray of appetizers for them, all leftovers from the party after the wedding. Everything was delicious. She ate little during the feasting. He supposed she was as nervous as he was. A person didn't get married every day. He was content the wedding night happened last night. She made the decision even when he thought for an instant to wait. He also supposed they should speak of a few things before they lost themselves in each other's arms.

Her back to his chest, his arms wrapped around her, they stood on the balcony just as they'd done the night before the storm hit. The water level rose nearly to the gated fence surrounding Mayfair. They wouldn't go into town tomorrow. No, they would have to wait until the land dried out some before they could seek another minister.

"It will take several days for the water to recede," he told her touching his lips to a tender spot behind her ear he discovered the evening before. "We will be isolated here until the roads are dry."

"Grayson told me he and his son took one of their small rowboats to get here this morning. Leslie Hall is closer to the river. Not close enough for flooding, nevertheless closer than Mayfair. Has it ever flooded here?" She turned to look at him, her hands sliding along his arms.

"Not that I know of. We are located far above the flood plain. The slave's homes are behind us, even higher as is the stable. Timmie told me the horses were all doing fine."

"I assumed as much. If you'd been afraid for them, you would have spent the night with them instead of me."

"You're right, of course. Duster is much more valuable than a mere wife," he kept his tone bland while he nipped her ear, touched inside with his tongue.

She pressed against him, moving her hips as if she wanted to see if he was as hard as stone.

Indeed, he was.

"That is very true, more valuable than a husband also. Do you like my gown?"

He wondered when or if she would ask. She would know he'd have deep feelings about its fit. "The gown is seductive as you well know. There is no other way to describe the way the fabric lovingly hugs your body displaying you daringly. The cut leaves very little to one's imagination. Leaves nothing to my imagination since I've seen every sweet and tender inch of you. Wherever did you get it?"

The moment he saw her in the doorway to the parlor, lust spread from the tip of his head to the ends of his big toes then back to settle in his groin. During the ceremony it took forced concentration to keep from acting on that fact.

"Merry, my sister-in-law, wore a similar gown to her wedding. I saw the dress. Knew I had to have one. Didn't know if I would ever be able to wear the dress. Link didn't know I bought one just like Merry's. He would have had a fit."

He thought over what she told him. Wasn't sure he believed every word. "You knew you had to have one exactly like hers. Where have you worn the gown, Clare? Be honest." He gritted his teeth at the thought. "You understand this dress is not meant to be worn in public. No man except your husband should see you in this."

A wave of jealousy swept him. He thought of the men downstairs who saw her today. It wasn't to be. Maybe he should burn the gown.

"Merry's fiancé, an English duke, had the gown designed specifically for her. When he saw her in it, I do believe he had second and third thoughts about his design. Although the only people at the wedding were family, he still thought more than once about how he displayed his wife. At first, he thought only of himself and how he would obviously like to look at her. At the time, Merry didn't know he was a duke. She believed him to be a horse breeder. He kept so many secrets I was afraid they would bury themselves in them."

"Ah, is that who Link sought out to find Duster as well as the mares? This horse breeder who was a duke?" He stroked her arms, wondering how she would be able to remove the sleeves. They fit her tightly, clung to every precious inch."

"Yes. Because of the way the gown hugs my body, I couldn't wear anything beneath except my stockings. I'm practically naked, Michael."

His mouth watered, yearned to taste every unclothed part of her. That would have to wait a few more minutes. "You told me that bit of information just to arouse me. Perhaps I should pull up the skirt. I could test the waters, so to speak. See if your nectar spills over my fingers."

He liked that thought. He liked it very much. She could straddle him. He would still be able to undo each tiny button.

"Is it working? This arousal of yours?"

She tried to turn in his arms.

"No."

His hands rested on her belly. He felt the tremor, the soft shuddering response as he pressed. He thought about a child that might be growing inside her as they teased each other. The idea was splendid; if not now, then soon.

Slipping his fingers between hers, he led her to the porch. She sat on a plump cushioned seat. He placed food on a plate before he refilled her glass, not with champagne but a nice sweet Sauterne from the Stewart vineyards. It was truly very good, a nice dessert wine. It was made from the sweetest grapes.

He walked from the porch to ring the bell for Old Suzzy. Another hour might pass before he would unfasten each delicate button one at a time, lingering over each newly exposed part of Clare. He meant to take his time with each sensitive piece of flesh he uncovered. He was also certain that Merry's husband had the same thoughts when he designed the dress. It would be the only reason to have something so exquisitely revealing fashioned for ones soon to be wife.

After Old Suzzy left shaking her head and mumbling about him ruining dat purty gown, he filled his plate topping off his glass. He sat beside his new wife. Her eyes were closed, as she seemed to soak in the evening, the ambiance he created. The feeling was heady, pleasing as well. They would do well together.

Michael stretched out his long legs, his glass resting on his lean belly. He didn't want to look at her until this conversation finished. If he did so, they would end up on the bed. She could entice him with her bedazzling smile. She would do other things to assume control. He would have to hold firm. He was the person in charge, at least at the moment.

"Are you cold?"

He made the mistake of looking at her. Saw the tight buds of her nipples pressed against the fabric. He wanted to taste, to suckle until sounds of pleasure rippled from her so kissable lips.

Clare allowed her darkened lashes to fall across her white as alabaster cheeks. "A little, not too much. Perhaps you could warm me."

She stared at his mouth, moistened hers with the tip of her exquisite tongue leaving a glittering trail of tempting moisture behind.

He wanted to taste her essence coupled with the sweet Sauterne. He brought her the quilt from the bed then settled the fabric around her shoulders. His hands lingered on sensitive flesh. He meant to entice her as much as she tempted him. This small barrier might keep his errant thoughts from straying. Staring at the rushing river, he sat down again. This was not going as he planned. His body was in tune with hers. Desperately, they needed each other now, not in another thirty or forty minutes.

The confrontation would have to come sooner than later. Once they were done, they could move on to more pleasant endeavors. He hauled in a deep breath of air, watching her intently before letting the air go as he spoke the words. "Mayfair Hall along with everything in it is mine now."

While holding his breath he waited for an answer unsure of how she would react. She could yell, rant and rave to no avail. He stated the facts. When a woman married, all she owned went to the man. He would agree. The tradition wasn't fair.

Serenely, as if she didn't hear the words, she inhaled a long deep breath. At this time, it seemed she searched for the correct words. Setting her glass on the table then placing her hands in her lap, she graced him with a tender smile. "I'm not a silly twit nor am I stupid, Michael. When I decided I wanted you more than my dream, I understood what would happen." She spread her arms wide to encompass the land. "It is my hope you allow me to share with you the pleasures we can find here on this plantation turned stud farm. Hope you will seek me out for my opinion once in a while."

Hell, and damnation, she didn't have to give up her dream. "Your advice will be listened to. You know horses. I've come to understand that over the months you've been here. Your only flaw when it comes to running the farm is that you're a woman. To me that fact is not a flaw. To others it most certainly is."

With her fingernail, she tapped the bottom of her glass. After that she studied the tips of her toes. When she looked at him, she spoke slowly, "I want to ride Duster in his next race."

He knew her demand would come, just not this soon. All of him stiffened in fury. "No!"

Even though he understood she would eventually say the words, he was shocked at her audacity. A woman racing was unheard of. Just as Link told him, he would need to take every precaution against her slipping around him to ride the damn horse.

With his resounding no, Clare didn't skip a beat or blink. In the same serene tone, she continued flaunting her attributes. "I'm lighter than Timmie. Also, I sit a horse better. He can still race Gypsy. Although over that distance the race might go better if the jockey was lighter also."

"You will not race at any time on any mount! Is that clear? Don't think you can get by on this issue. I've made up my mind. You will obey me."

Once again, he recalled Link's words. He shook his head, would have liked to shake Clare instead. Link did tell him this might happen. Told him to look out for her trying to do what she pleased. At least Clare asked. She could have mounted Duster in the next race if she had not given herself away. In all the confusion, she would have an easy time of deceiving him. Too late he would have discovered her ruse.

"I will keep trying to convince you. Doubt it not. You haven't heard the last of this." In defiance, her shoulders were stiff, her chin tilted upward.

"The answer is no. I'm your husband. You will obey me in all things. I know what is best for you."

First, she snorted. It was a very unladylike snort. Michael didn't believe she cared. "Look at me," she said softly. Her voice was a siren's call.

To what ends he didn't know. What he did understand was that turning his gaze on her wasn't in his best interest. He didn't want to look at her, at least not until he felt good and ready. If he did, she would find some means to do him in. Oh, he knew her well enough. She would have some underhanded ploy up her tight sleeves to find a way around him.

When he did turn his eyes her direction, he said in the calmest voice he could muster. "You will not race Duster at any time. I will not change my mind. I will never allow you to put yourself in harm's way."

"All right." She sipped her wine then set the plate and glass on the nearby table. "Whatever you say. You are my husband. I pledged to obey you. It's just that in this instance it's devilishly hard to submit. Especially since you're wrong in this instance."

That was exactly who he was, her husband. He was in charge of everything including her. She would follow his dictate in this matter. He smiled a smile he didn't feel. "Glad you see things my way."

He still believed she was planning something he wouldn't like. Ah, but he was beginning to understand her more thoroughly. He would have to watch her quite close to ferret out what exactly she schemed.

She smiled prettily at him. More clearly than ever, he understood in that instant she wasn't giving in to his directive, not by a long shot. No, she did have something calculated that would unman him. He couldn't allow that to happen. Placidly, she sipped her wine again. Pointedly, she stared at his crotch over the top of her glass.

He adjusted his trousers thinking he would like to get into something more comfortable. The inherent problem in this scenario was that he didn't want Clare in something more comfortable, not just yet. No, he still needed her covered from her nose to nearly her chin even in this charming, husband-seducing confection.

"What will my spouse allow me, his dutifully submissive wife to do? Plan menus? I assure you I've no reason to take one of Delilah's tasks from her. She does it so well. She never gives us too many oysters."

His eyes crossed. What the devil was she contemplating about oysters?

"Or…would you rather I just stay in your bed waiting for your whipcord lean body to pleasure me? While that would be agreeable for a time, I'm positive I would grow bored with that as well as you making lust to me."

He gritted his teeth. At this very second, he needed to drill home his point. "Lying in my bed, waiting for me would be preferable to racing against men. As you well know, the races are dangerous. Grown men get hurt all the time. There are no rules even though there should be. You are too small to compete against the power and strength of a man," His teeth clenched, his jaw ached. He downed the glass of wine he poured himself. "You can do whatever you did before we were wed, muck the stalls if you like, exercise Duster daily as you always do. Until Raynard is found, you cannot do any of those things alone. You must have Timmie or myself with you at all times."

"All right." The serene calm tone was back. Her hands were tightly entwined resting in her lap.

He didn't know how to handle her. She was an enigma to him. He wanted to yowl at the silver moon that was now shining just above the horizon. He yearned to shake her until he understood exactly what was swimming around in her woman's head. Michael wondered what exactly she was plotting. "We have two mares coming at the end of next week. Damian Andrews is bringing them from his ranch northwest of Baltimore. Believe his son is coming with him. I've told him they can stay in the guest room at Mayfair."

"Are you asking me or telling?"

Her smile once again unnerved him. She was acting strange.

The air of serenity in the midst of their argument stopped him cold. He didn't know how to proceed. He believed she would do as she pleased. Being one step ahead of her was perceptibly a necessity.

"Neither, since I didn't believe you would say no, suppose I'm telling. If you don't want them here, I'll find a place in town for the man and his son." He wondered if she would continue to make all these little things so very difficult. Pondered the thought that this might simply be her way of retaliating about the racing. He doubted if she ever obeyed her brother-in-law. Link probably let her behave just as she wished. The man had too many children too many responsibilities.

"Very well, I don't mind at all, if you trust them that is. We have more than enough room."

"I trust the man. He has a sterling reputation. Now, would you like to continue as the boss here or would you like me to take over the duties for you? The men are coming to me with questions. As you probably assume, the directives will be heeded completely if I give them. I cannot assume the same for you even if the words are the same."

"Can there be two bosses?" She lowered her dark lashes for a moment before she looked at him again. "You've already explained to me how a woman cannot order men. Well, they can try. Nonetheless, as you just proclaimed, it is highly unlikely the men will obey me, a mere woman. I bow down to you."

"One boss. However, what part would you like to play in the running of Mayfair Stables?"

"As when I first arrived, I don't want any part of the handling of the freemen, their crops or whatever it is they will plant. I want you to oversee the collection of the rent money as well as pay them for their service. As to the horses, all I expect is for you to share any new developments. I understand all the bartering of fees will be done by you, the man of the stables. Will that work?"

"Don't see why not."

Well, they covered most of what he intended. He still had not told her about Jillian Whitehead. He didn't want to. With him the lady was a sore topic. The woman lived two plantations away. She had the most annoying habit of showing up here unannounced. The fact she had not done so for months on end surprised him. Ah, well, when she left last time, she was furious with him. He'd had the audacity to turn her sexual innuendos down, the blatant boldness to call her what she was, a whore.

"I want to get into something that isn't so restrictive." She tipped her glass emptying the contents in the process. She stared at him, this time from head to toe with no particular interest in any single part of him. "I'm too cold to stay out here much longer. The sun has set as you can see, the breeze chilling despite the fact it's still summer."

It seemed telling his new wife about Jillian would have to wait for another time. He was now more than eager to pursue more pleasant avenues. "Yes, as would I. Although nothing I am wearing is quite so formfitting as your gown. How would you like me to disrobe you?"

She jerked. Well, he surprised her with that question. He wasn't too certain why. Tomorrow, he would make it a point to ask.

Once inside he slipped off his shirt. His next move was to unfasten his trousers. He wasn't going to remove them just yet. What he craved right now was to give her a peak at what she would see later. No, he had some very tiny buttons down the back of Clare's gown to see to their undoing. He grinned. A full day passed by since he was deep inside his wife.

Clare sat on the bed. Her gaze pointed at him. "Are you positive you don't want to ring for Old Suzzy to undo the buttons. She did promise me that she would make certain nothing was ruined. Since you dislike this gown, you wouldn't plan on damaging it would you?"

He didn't dislike the provocative piece of clothing that it was. What he didn't like was other men seeing her succulent curves so unashamedly displayed. Savoring every delicious moment was in the forefront of his mind. "Need to uncover each tender sensitive spot with kisses. Would you like that, Clare?"

He witnessed her shudder.

With a broad smile, he sat down beside her. Slowly and very carefully he unwound her braids that lay in intricate circles around her head. When he finished, he sifted his hands through the silken strands.

"Every part of you delights me." He brushed the pieces of hair over her shoulder. He kissed her nape before he bit gently. "I like the way your woman's body responds to me, only me. Shall we go on? Would you like another glass of wine, Clare? It's best if you're relaxed."

"Michael...I want you to take off this dress!"

He grinned. He moved his hands along the front of her dress his palms brushing her hardened nipples caressing her as he explored. When she purred softly, he unfastened the first tiny button, spreading the fabric away from her neck. His teeth grazed the exposed skin. After that, he laved the spot with the tip of his tongue.

"I like the way you taste."

The next button came undone with his nimble fingers. Once more he grazed then sucked. He nibbled and kissed. The process continued until she was moving against him twisting in his arms. Her body sought satisfaction. Her petals would be ripe and swollen with heated moisture. She would be slick with her need for him.

He was pleased. Many, many minutes later all the buttons were undone. He gazed on her back, the spine so straight. He kissed each tiny vertebra one-by-one. She pushed back, her hands on his thighs squeezing. Sometime between the first button and the last, she sat between his legs. Even while he spent the time to unfasten the gown, he brought her gown up so the soft fabric bunched around her hips.

Her body was so white, her curves lush and full. He slipped his hands between the fabric of her gown and her skin. In a moment he cupped her breasts, assaulted her nipples with his fingers. She'd thrown her head back, her long neck beckoning to him. She moaned again, soft purrs rippling from her throat.

He brought his hands from their coveted spot. With his fingers he caressed her thighs slowly romancing higher until his hand covered her woman's mound. He pressed there, slipped a finger along the crevice between her legs, massaged and tempted evocative tissue. Found the sweet, secret jewel that would bring her so very high she would soar.

"You are so hot and wet. What do you think Clare? Are you ready for me?" He removed his hand to bring his fingers to her shoulders. "It's time we removed the gown altogether. I want you naked."

She nodded. "Yes, that would be nice."

Michael chuckled softly while he wanted to howl with the pleasure of her. He pushed the sleeves down. They were tight but they seemed to slowly glide away from her silken flesh.

"When the entire gown was settled around her waist, "Lift your hips for me." She pushed on his thighs to move higher. The gown pooled on the floor around her bare feet. He pulled back the covers to the bed. "I'll pour you a glass of wine."

As he walked away from her, he peered over his shoulder. Her eyes were wide the blue a very deep dark color. She caught her quivering bottom lip between her teeth.

Well hell, she was so aroused, he didn't think she would be able to wait. She would wait. He wanted to continue the foreplay until she begged him for her release. In her way, she already was begging. He groaned when her gaze drifted to his crotch.

"You need to take your clothes off now."

Her beautiful breasts with the very large rose-colored nipples swayed enticingly while she moved to put pillows behind her back. She leaned against the headboard the large tips jutting toward his lips. He was pleased she was no longer shy around him. He would take this beautiful sight with him throughout his life.

"Suppose I do."

He set the newly poured wine on the tables then stripped. His arousal was blatantly obvious. She licked her lips. He wasn't going to wait for the wine.

~ * ~

"So, you want this Clare person for your next lover. I want Michael now that he owns what should have been his in the first place. Couldn't marry him when he was dirt poor. He was born on Mayfair, groomed to take over the plantation which was in his family for many years."

She tossed her head while she stared at Biff Gideon. The man wasn't anything like Michael in his physique. Nonetheless, even with his huge paunch, he would suit her for tonight. He possessed all the necessary male parts to give her pleasure, ease her needs. She sipped her wine.

The man drooled when he stared at her beautiful bosom provocatively displayed for him. If he stared, she didn't mind at all. Her large endowments were made for a man's hands, for his perusal. He was a man, with a man's sex. As far as she was concerned that was all he needed. She didn't know if he would give her pleasure. It didn't matter. She could see to that specific aspect of the evening if necessary. She craved for him to come inside her sooner than later. The sweet hot friction he would create beckoned to her. They could talk after they enjoyed themselves.

"At the moment I want you, Biff, not Michael. You know that too. Also, you know what to do to me. You own your plantation. Too bad you've a wife. We could have dealt well together, you and me."

He held out his hand. She placed her small fingers in his beefy ones. She moaned softly hoping the sound would help arouse this man who was always a bit slow.

"Should we do this then talk?"

He rubbed one hand down his enormous belly stopping for a moment at his crotch.

She watched the sway of his belly with a moment of revulsion. "Maybe I've changed my mind. Don't know if I want you right now, Biff, darling. During the past years you've overindulged. You're not the man you used to be. Your rod isn't even at attention yet."

She turned to walk to a chair near the fire swinging her ample hips hoping to entice his arousal. Of course, she wanted him. However, she didn't believe it necessary to stroke his enormous ego. Eventually, he would rise to the occasion.

"You're still a tart, aren't you?" He followed her. "What your preferences are doesn't matter. You came to see me, to seek my help. I'll have you when I decide the time is right. If you believed you had a say in the matter, you were wrong."

When she turned to look back at him, she slanted him a flirtatious smile. "I make the decisions about my body, Biff, not you no matter what you'd like to believe."

She liked the loving to be a bit rough. She knew Biff did too. If she taunted him enough, he'd lose control. He always lost control. As a man he would be frantic for her. "Maybe you should send for Busby. I could have both of you at the same time. She knew he would like that. The bulge in his pants finally began to grow. Yes, she thought with the two of them she would surely find pleasure, at least a small amount.

She thought of Michael. While he was gentle, she always had the most amazing climaxes. The man always thought of her needs first. He would do for a husband as well as a lover. First, she would have to discover a way to rid him of Clare.

Slowly, Biff crooked his finger at her, motioning for her to come to him. She would in time. Giving him the upper hand was not in the scheme of things for this evening. Why waste precious moments when she didn't have to. She wanted a partner tonight. Biff wanted to pretend she was Clare. That fact bothered her for a moment, a second only. After that she thought on what she would gain if he got rid of Michael's new wife for her. Michael might not want her after Biff took her to his bed. What he didn't know wouldn't hurt him.

Posturing for him, she put a hand on her hip. She touched her lip, pulling the bottom one forward. For a transitory instant in time, she thought he would leap at her. The bulge in his pants continued to grow. Biff was a big man. His member was large. Deep and raw she moaned in the back of her throat.

"What do you have in mind for tonight?"

She sidled up to him, placed a quick kiss on his lips before backing away.

He set his hands on her waist, tugged her until she stumbled against him. "Come, tell me how you plan on divesting Michael of his little wife. He never lets her out of his sight. I'll play with you as we talk. You will like everything."

"Sometimes he does," she purred while she pressed her ample breasts against Biff's chest. She stroked him from his shoulders to his groin, stopped at his arousal. "There are times when she's with Timmie."

His voice grew dark and dangerous. "Yes, some of her rides she is accompanied by Big Tom. We must be careful of Big Tom. Timmie is no threat to our plans."

He pulled the corsage of her gown down until the rosy tips of her nipples popped free. He bent low to suck one into his mouth. She arched against him craving his teeth against her flesh.

He moved back, watching her. Her breathing was fast. Her nipple was shiny from the moisture left behind by his mouth. She didn't want to wait. Neither did he. He caught her behind her knees, with his foot. Together they fell to the rug.

"Biff!" She lost control of the moment.

"Yes?"

He tasted her again, pushed at her gown until it pooled beneath her hips. He tore at the fabric until there was nothing between them except his clothing.

She swallowed hard, trying to slow the moment. "We just have to wait until it's Timmie who is her chaperone now won't we?" She purred softly in the back of her throat, pressing her hips against his soft belly. "You need to take your clothes off." She tugged at the laces on his shirt her breasts swaying and puckering in the chill.

"Suppose that would be the best." He pressed hot kisses down her body, laving more when he reached her stomach. "I've waited for more than two months. Don't have much patience now."

In the back of her throat, she moaned. "Plan on paying the man a visit in the next day or two. Have to wait until the water recedes a bit more. I'll get her for you."

"Raynard said the same. He didn't succeed, just managed to get himself into more trouble." He lifted her hips. He was between her legs, looking at her.

"The man's a fool. Decided his life was worth more than revenge. As far as I know, he left the area when the storm blew itself out. Glad to see the bounder leave. Wasn't fast enough as far as I was concerned."

He pressed his mouth against her while he watched her.

She didn't know how he could keep talking at this moment. He licked her swollen petals. She could barely speak. She twisted, moaning as she tried to speak. "So, it's up to you to get the girl. Michael wouldn't think…"

She touched his shoulders, her eyes wide, loving the way Biff stared at her breasts when she thrust them out. She was swelling with need just thinking about a man, even Biff driving inside her. "Well, Michael wouldn't believe you wanted her." She was panting now, wishing he would stop talking, cease with the questions.

Biff ran his hands along her legs. His look of chagrin surprised her. She groaned when he lifted his mouth from her. "I played my cards too soon. Thought she was dancing the same tune as her sister. Offered Flannigan a dollar for her when he was done."

She tossed her head back howling with laughter, forgetting the moment forgetting she wanted him inside her. "You did what? A dollar?

I doubt if the little slut is worth that much. Ah, well, suppose you will have to wait it out. Are you a patient man, Biff Gideon?"

He lifted his shoulders, "I wanted her. Thought the man would share. Busby was there with me. We were both more than willing to let Flannigan have her first. He didn't take too kindly to my thoughts."

He was just staring at her. With his fingers he parted her spread, her folds. When he finished his quest, he looked at her. His grin was wide. "Would you like your pleasure now?"

"Yes..."

"Ah, but I do believe you will have to wait a bit longer. You don't seem quite ready."

She tamped down her lust. This was her game to play. After a deep filling breath and a few seconds, she was able to speak again, "No wonder it's been hard to find the little harlot alone. With you and Busby acting like idiots then Raynard seeking revenge what else could the man do except protect what he thought was his?"

"I've got to have her."

His thumb massaged her, touched erotically upon her most sensitive flesh.

She closed her eyes then gritted her teeth, willing the waves of raw hunger to vanish. "Yes, I want Michael too. We'll put our heads together; figure this out in the next couple of days. What are you going to do after you have her?"

"Make sure there are no tales to tell. I've a plan that won't fail. After I take what I want, no one will ever see her again. You will be free to wed Flannigan."

With that said, he undid his trousers. A moment later he was deep inside her, pumping hard, frantic with his possession.

Chapter Eight

August turned into September. Everything was dry again. The stud farm was making money. They won more races as Timmie learned how to avoid other jockeys. Clare had a plan. In a few days they were traveling south to North Carolina. She was beyond excited. In her valise, she packed a pair of riding britches. When everyone was milling around, gambling and talking about the horses she meant to go to Duster. Timmie would never argue with her when she told him she would race. He would, however, search out Michael. She would wait until the last minute. By the time Timmie found Michael there would never be enough time to stop her.

The morning was glorious, the sky so blue the sight made a person think of long summer days. The scents were all familiar horse smells coupled with the beginning of autumn. She just returned from exercising Duster. Big Tom rode with her. She was brushing the big stallion thinking on her scheme, going over all the tiny details that could go wrong so she could mount a counter attack.

Michael was behind her, stoking her backside. "You understand the ideas you put in my head when you're showing me your deliciously rounded bottom? The sight makes me want to do things we can't do here where everyone can see us."

He picked her up. She found herself hauled beneath his arm toward the back of the stable as if she was merely a sack of grain. While he stopped in front of the door to the tack room, he swiveled. "Timmie!"

"Suh." His jockey stood beside him, a grin on his face. "What can I do for you?"

"Don't let anyone into the tack room. Do you understand? No one."

Only a few hours had passed since this morning when she shared the bath with Michael. He made love to her in the tub, water splashing over the sides so much so she was sure drops must have filtered through the floor boards. Now this. He was insatiable.

"No, Suh, no one will get by me. You two have fun now." He winked.

Clare wondered just how much Timmie understood. He was eighteen. He must have had at least one dalliance by now. Heat rushed to her face. Everyone would know what the boss was up to with the door to the tack room closed. Nonetheless, she understood once he started kissing her, she would no longer care a fig what anyone thought.

"Good then, I plan to be inside discussing a few things with my wife, very important things."

He tightened his arm around her waist giving her a gentle squeeze along with the knowledge as to what was about to happen.

Hah! There would be no conversations passing between them except when she whispered or perhaps cried out his name into his mouth. He shut the door with his foot. After that he hefted her up so she was pressed against him, her unfettered breasts against his chest. "I like it when you wear nothing beneath your shirt." His lips found hers in a long drugging kiss, all the while pressing her against him with one hand and adeptly opening her shirt with the other. He pushed the sleeves from her arms. Her breasts sprang free. The chill air from the dark room swept across them tightening the sensitive tips.

Before she could take in a deep breath of air, he shirked out of his shirt. He discarded her boots then her britches. She was naked, shivering with the myriad of sensations he generated. He had the wickedest look on his face, his eyes simmered and darkened just as they always did before they made love.

One more time he picked her up by her waist. He set her down, her elbows resting on a pile of hay, her bottom in the air. What was he doing? She recalled how Duster covered the mares. She groaned resting her cheek on her hands. He wasn't truly going to do this?

She jerked when he nipped her backside then nipped again, his teeth grazing across her tender flesh. "So adorable, so very sweet," he murmured, nipping then licking across the rounded flesh. His hands caressed the curve of her hip the other circled her breast, teasing and taunting until a moan of ecstasy slipped from her.

"What are you doing? You can't mean to..."

Oh, but she did know he would mean to do anything. She recalled when he brought her atop him, straddling him so she could set the pace. There was the time he brought her legs over his shoulders. He'd been so deep inside her she could barely inhale. Thinking about the way he felt, she moaned.

"Just like the studs covering the mares."

He nipped her hard on her shoulder then her neck. The hand on her hip slipped between her legs then inside her. He sent two fingers deep into her sheathe, moving, teasing her. She pushed back against him, wanting him inside her.

"You told me..."

His fingers now kneaded the sensitive hard jewel between her legs that sent her to a place of frenzy. "Yes, I did tell you I could cover you just as Duster does the mares." Suddenly, he thrust into her, deeper then deeper still.

She screamed with the pleasure of it. Moaned and heaved until she could barely breathe.

"Hush, you'll have Timmie or Big Tom knocking the door down believing I was hurting the little missy. We can't have that." Slowly as an expert lover could do, he moved inside her. She tried to get him to move harder and faster. With his hands on her hips, he controlled her.

"I can't hush. Only if you stop seducing me."

"Ah, but this is no seduction. You were ready for me before I coaxed with even one word. Why, I believe you are always ready for me. Is that true?"

She nodded. He changed the pace. Pulses wrenched her body, deep with aching hunger, vibrating, hot. Magic. The earth turned, shimmered in multitude of lights. Until everything he was doing to her took over.

Her cries filled the tiny room again as he drove harder and faster as she reached her climax. He exploded inside her, his body resting on top of hers. Sultry hot moments ticked by.

"Did you like that? I think you did. Nod your head if you want to play some more."

She nodded. He was still hard and deep within her body. Clare tried to swallow, attempted to answer. Suddenly, she was on her back. Michael was above her, his huge forearms beside her head. His eyes were a deep dark green simmer with the light of a man well pleased. His voice sounded murky and delicious as dusky as warm brown honey. She closed her eyes, dragging in air as her body calmed. Lightly, no seduction or coaxing in mind, his fingers traveled across her.

His lips molded over hers. They were moist and soft. He pushed his tongue inside when she opened for him. Now she felt his rod, still damp from their first lovemaking.

The tenor of his kisses changed. Her body jerked to life, recognizing the change. He kissed her and kissed her again. Kissed every part of her. "I like the tips of your breasts," he murmured as he moved from one to the other then back again. "They are so large and pink, larger now that I've sucked on them. Look at them." He told her as his mouth closed over one, sucked and sucked until her hips writhed off the hay beneath her. When he pulled away, she saw he was right. The nipple was elongated and hard. She'd never seen her nipples so huge and wet from his attention. He moved to the other breast. Minutes later, when it seemed he was satisfied with that endeavor he moved lower. His large hands were beneath her lifting her hips, moving her higher, higher still.

"Wrap your legs over my shoulders," he told her. "Just as you did the other morning when we couldn't get out of bed."

In this lovemaking she would always obey. She wanted him to do to her whatever it was he planned. Once again, he surprised her. His mouth closed over her intimately. He nipped and laved, bringing her to a high plateau. She squirmed and coiled. While his tongue drove inside her, she screamed again arched then tugged on his hair. A few seconds later, he drove inside her, one more time she reached that blessed pinnacle he so easily sent her to.

"Michael..." Her cry was soft filled with the exhaustion he always brought her to.

"You liked that, did you?"

When she finally opened her eyes, he was grinning at her. He kissed her nose then her forehead.

"You know I did."

"We should get back to work, unless you want to ride me. Three times is not too many for one short afternoon's delight coupled with a romp in the hay."

He ran his tongue along her lower lip. Beneath him she quivered. "Why?"

"Good question, work can wait. I want you to sit on top of me." He tugged on her lip with his teeth before he sent his tongue inside her mouth. "You are so hot. I like being inside you even if it's only your mouth. What do you think? Can we do this one more time?"

"You're still inside me."

"Hard as steal."

He kissed her again, his tongue playing with hers, fencing, dueling as if one could gain supremacy.

"No! Ma'am, no, you can't go in there,"

Timmie was at the door. His hastily spoken words permeated her liquefied body. Still, she couldn't move, not one part of her. Someone wanted to come into the tack room. She was naked. He was deep inside her. This couldn't be happening.

Clare pushed on Michael's shoulders. Suddenly she found her voice. "Michael! We can't! You have to stop now!"

"I will go where ever I please. Let me by!" The lady's voice rang out in a sneer. "Don't you dare lay your filthy hands on me, boy."

"No, ma'am, I've my orders. No one's goin' in dat room."

Clare heard a thud on the door. Good for Timmie, he was trying to keep the woman out. She seemed terribly determined.

"His orders are not meant for me," she informed Timmie in a haughty tone. "I'm going to see him. Well, Michael will want to see me. He will have you punished."

"No, he won't want to see you. If he does, it's not at this moment."

"What do you know?" The door handle turned.

Clare grimaced. Frantically she was pushing on Michael who just now seemed to be getting the gist of what was happening outside the door.

"Know my orders, Ma'am. Know Michael won't want you goin' in dat room."

"Get your hands off me! You're nothing. You're a slave."

"Free man now."

Another loud thud hit the door. Clare understood, as she was certain Michael did too, that Timmie wouldn't touch the woman. She was brazen. Clare would give her that. Whoever she was.

His lips thinned. She saw his anger surface. "Jillian."

Quickly, Michael grabbed a blanket then wrapped it around her.

"You know her?" She was incredulous, shouldn't be she supposed. Michael lived in this area all his life. Was born in Mayfair Hall.

"Unfortunately, yes. Wish I never set eyes on that woman. She's a complication I don't want to deal with. Seems I haven't a choice."

He turned his attention to pulling up then fastening his britches.

The conversation outside the door took place in less than a minute or two. Clare was glad he didn't entirely disrobe. If his lovemaking had gone on longer, he might have done that very thing. As it was, she burst into the room, pushing Timmie aside, her mouth agape at the sight in front of her, "Michael?"

She stared at him. Stared at his flat belly then lower. Her gaze turned to Clare. The realization as to what they'd been about in the room seemed to shake her. Shook her for less than a second.

Clare wasn't at all certain she saw shock. Now the audacious woman sashayed into the tack room as if she'd been invited.

Plain and simple, the woman ogled him. Clare shivered in disgust as she tried to sink into the corner. Realizing she'd not been caught doing something wrong, she tilted her chin, straightened her shoulders.

"Jilli, you're not welcome here. You need to leave."

It seemed she didn't pay attention to his order. Instead, she strutted forward, hips swinging until she stood over her. She pointed a finger at her in accusation. "Little slut."

Jilli's words took her back a few thoughts. Slowly, Clare rose, the blanket wrapped tightly around her nakedness. She shivered. She saw Michael shrug into his shirt then his boots. He took the lady's arm, ushering her outside. When they were out of the tack room, he closed the door behind him with a loud bang. The sudden jarring sound made her jump. Closing her eyes, she counted to ten then twenty. Thought perhaps she would have to count to thirty before she could garner the necessary control.

Very slowly, Clare let the breath she'd been holding whoosh out in a long sigh of relief even though she understood the respite would be short-lived. She was certain the woman would never vacate the premises quickly. Who the devil was that lady? Well, she didn't think the well-shaped blond woman was much of a lady. What did she mean to Michael. The woman possessed a predatory air when it came to her husband. Michael never mentioned another woman.

Once she was certain no one would barge into the tack room, Clare dressed. She understood, sooner or later she would have to face this Jilli person. Whoever she was. Meeting a past lover of Michal's wasn't something she thought she would be doing today. She wasn't pleased. It was not well done of Michael. She should have been forewarned. He should have at least mentioned this woman.

Obviously, he knew her. Maybe she wasn't a past lover.

Men...

Well, she would forgive him this indiscretion if he gave her a good explanation. The pair knew each other, that fact was blatantly evident. The woman was possessive, thinking she owned him, that fact was also unmistakable. She pulled out of her hair a few pieces of hay. After that she checked to make sure all the buttons on her shirt were fastened properly. She smoothed the fabric of her pants, wishing she wore a gown instead.

For more seconds than were necessary she rested her hand on the door latch. She tried to suck in enough air to fill her lungs. Perhaps the deed would give her courage. The ploy didn't work. With a bout of defiance and a willingness to see this through to the proper conclusion, she opened the door.

What she saw was Timmie's back. Jilli and Michael were near the front of the stable, seeming to argue. Her husband waved a hand in the air, slashing it back and forth several times. He was angry, furiously so. Well, she knew his temper was on the explosive edge before he left the tack room. Nonetheless, she'd never seen her husband quite like this.

She stepped up beside Timmie, her hand momentarily on his shoulder. "Don't worry about this. Don't believe a herd of stampeding horses could have stopped that woman. The fact she found a way to pass you then get into the room was not your fault."

"Massa's angry," he said his body seemingly frozen in the spot. "Dat woman's been here before. Before you came to Mayfair she showed up without invitation. Never liked her then. Like her even less today."

"Not at you, Timmie. Michael's not angry at you. He's livid because we were interrupted in something very private."

Also, he was angry because he didn't like this woman. Clare didn't know why. The reason was something Michael needed to tell her.

"I couldn't stop her," he berated himself one more time. "She just kept on as if going inside that room was her right. Couldn't tell her what I thought the two of you were up to." He flushed.

Clare almost laughed at his chagrin. Kept the smile from forming. "You did fine."

She stepped toward the pair, understanding she couldn't put the moment off any longer. She had to make a stand; show the woman she couldn't come here anytime she wished. Couldn't intimidate her.

Sun slanted through the open doors. The soft scent of wildflowers mingled with horse and leather caught the breeze. They were scents she was fond of.

When she stopped beside Michael, she didn't speak. His broad shoulders were stiff, his square jaw hard, set in a line of resolution. The small tick of his muscle on the side of his chin gave her a wealth of information, none of it good. He would not put up with whatever this Jilli had in mind.

"I came to see you, Michael," she purred softly batting dark lashes at him. Don't see why you're annoyed with me. You never were before when I came to see you."

Jilli directed her gaze toward her. She peered at her, a smug look on her narrow face as if she won something.

Clare knew the smug purr was for her benefit. Jilli's eyes were small just as Clare was sure the smallness matched her tiny character.

Surprisingly, Jilli glared at her as if she trespassed in her domain. Mayfair stable was hers. Well, no it was Michael's now. Nonetheless, Jilli had nothing to do with it.

Clare put her hand on Michael's arm. He set his atop hers, staking possessive claim. The gesture should be obvious to anyone looking at them. She felt warmth along with security by the gesture.

"As I told you before you're not welcome. I'm a married man. Even if I wasn't wed, your presence would not be welcome on Mayfair land. It would not be appreciated."

"You would rather spend your time with this little nothing, this nobody? She's a slut. Just as her sister was known as the harlot of Virginia she is also. The two of them had to run away to avoid scandal." Her voice turned whiney.

Clare's gasp of surprise at Jilli's accusations startled her. The woman was brazen as well as audacious.

"I'm no harlot," Clare spoke softly, tried to sound calm in the face of the ridiculous charges neither is my sister. She wondered if the allegations would ever cease. For a short time, her life was filled with peace. She was wed to the man she loved.

"You've no reason to call my wife a harlot. She was a virgin on our wedding night."

Michael proceeded on his course. He would defend her to the end.

Well, that wasn't exactly true. She was an innocent the night before they wed. The thought brought a small grin to her lips. He didn't need to share that but for some crazy reason she was glad he did.

Michael continued speaking, his hold on her hand tightened. He squeezed as if to give encouragement. "While you've slept with so many men, I'm sure you lost count by now."

One of Michael's hands was fisted at his side. He appeared ready to hit the insolent lady.

"I want you to leave. Don't ever wish to see you again. Don't come back to Mayfair. You're not welcome."

Jilli postured, one hand on a hip, her voluminous breasts pushed outward, as if that disgusting gesture would change Michael's mind. Clare didn't think the woman could do that, change what her husband was thinking. What she knew about Michael was that he rarely changed his opinion.

"Including you or have you forgotten? I've slept with you more than once," she shot out sending the intensity of her gaze toward Clare, flaunting the knowledge. When next she smiled, she spoke softly. "You loved my breasts, Michael. You sucked them deep into your mouth. You told me how delicious they were, so sweet, you could suck on them into eternity."

Clare felt ice form in her veins. She caught the small whimper of dismay in the back of her throat. Truly, she didn't want to hear any more of this conversation. The words were disconcerting to hear how he did the same thing to another lady that he did to her. Her chin tilted higher all the while she wanted to run someplace where she could hide. She needed to remind herself Jilli was in his past. She was his future.

Michael wrapped his arm around her, pulling her to him, sheltering her. The grip of his fingers tightened on her shoulder. "You spout unnecessary venom. We both understand you weren't a virgin the first time I had sex with you. You gave countless excuses as to why, none of them true. While your virginity wasn't entirely an issue with me at that time, the fact you continued to see several different men while you professed your love for me, did. You sicken me, Jilli. If anyone standing here is a slut, the woman is you. Clare is a sweet innocent woman who understands how to give her heart to a man. She would never cuckold me."

When Clare saw the flush paint Jilli's face she understood everything Michael said was true. He untangled himself from her. He stepped toward the woman. With his hand on her forearm, he led her to her horse. Just as he'd done with her the day her sister went back to England, he tossed her on the horse. When she was secure in her seat, he gave the mare a swat to its backside. The horse shot forward.

"Don't come back, Jilli!"

She watched the woman ride from Mayfair. The trembling she felt since the first realization they were about to be invaded calmed. "Who was that woman? What does she mean to you?"

"Suppose we do need to speak of her." He watched as the lady's horse slowly faded into the distance. "The night of our wedding she was one of the topics I had in my mind to discuss with you." He cleared his throat before continuing a slight flush staining his handsome face. "I got sidetracked with your buttons. Do you recall?" He was grinning now as if he remembered that moment with quite a bit of fondness.

"I'll never forget the way you made me feel, the way your hands caressed and thrilled me to my very soul."

She didn't want to think of this woman. Didn't want to remember her heated words that were tossed her way. She said them to hurt her.

"We are off track again. I'd like to go back to the tack room."

The heavy sigh he emitted left her with the notion that wasn't going to happen. "I would not like to be found that way again. Once was enough for my lifetime."

She stood on the tips of her toes then kissed him. She swept her tongue along the center of his mouth. He opened for her, sucked her tongue deep inside. His hands pulled her up, cupped her backside so she didn't have to strain to reach him.

"The possible discovery was quite stimulating." He grinned down at her then lower. "Didn't you find the imaginable discovery exciting?"

She punched him in the chest. "You were not stimulated in the least. What you were was angry."

"To true, a tale that will never be repeated. I do want you again. Jilli didn't do anything to ease the lust I feel for my wife."

When she pushed on his shoulders, he let her slide down the length of his big hard body. She was pleased with his words. "Tell me everything about this woman who you made love to, who you sucked her big breasts into your mouth."

He grimaced. "It all happened before I met you."

"I understand." I never believed you were a virgin. That state is not something a man covets."

His smile was broad with sudden understanding of her words. "You were jealous. That pleases me. She means nothing to me now. For a short time, perhaps a week, I thought I would ask her to marry me. I did not."

"We should take this conversation to some place more private."

She grabbed his hand then started to the house.

"My bedroom?" he asked, his grin wicked when she turned to look at him.

"That will never do. We would find ourselves sidetracked before you spouted out everything you know about her everything you did with her."

Suddenly, Clare thought she didn't want to know everything he did to her or with her. His lovemaking techniques were most likely quite similar with all his previous women. She craved to be his only woman. Knew one couldn't go back in time. As long as she was his only woman from this day forward.

"Our bedroom is the only place where we will have this privacy we need."

"Perhaps the parlor. We can tell the servants not to come in." She thought that would be just like the tack room. "That won't do either."

"We can send them all home for the night," Michael said as he waggled his eyebrows at her. "We'll have the entire house to ourselves. You know," he paused, "I haven't made love to you in every room. We should make that a mission. We could start in the kitchen."

"Old Suzzy lives in the house," she informed him of something he knew yet seemed to forget.

"She would be happy to stay in her room," he tossed out with a bland smile.

"She is no longer a slave. You cannot confine her to her room. Our bedroom it is. We will talk first. We can sit on the veranda. You won't take liberties until I'm satisfied as to your intentions where this Jilli is concerned. Hell, and damnation that cannot be her name. It's deplorable."

~ * ~

Michael wound his fingers through hers. He whistled, pleased with her jealousy. While he wasn't at all happy about the interruption or about the sudden appearance of Jillian Whitehead, he comprehended Clare's loyalty to him. When he handpicked Clare for his wife, he did a fine job.

Instead of heading straight upstairs, he stopped in the kitchen to order dinner to be served in an hour. He also ordered a pot of tea along with a couple bottles of the fine red Bordeaux as well as one of the Sauternes from Leslie Hall, which was his favorite for after he ate.

After dinner was taken care of, he asked Delilah to heat water for their baths. Clare still wore several pieces of hay in her hair. She looked adorable. He thought of her delectable and delicious backside. Thought of coming inside her so deep and hard he wouldn't be able to think. In the tack room, he'd been frantic, so frantic he couldn't get his britches off before he had to bury himself inside her silken depths.

They'd been married some time now. She could be with child, should be. So far there had been no indication to refute that. He made love to her every night as well as the days since the night before their nuptials. If she were to have her woman's time, it would be soon. If not...ah, they would be thinking about their first born in late March or early April. A spring baby would be nice indeed. He wondered when she'd tell him.

"Michael?" They stepped into the bedroom. He swept her against him, kissed her hard and deep. "Who gets the first bath?"

It seemed she didn't want a repeat of this morning. "You my dear, when you are done you can scrub my back." He was laughing at the look of chagrin on her face, all the while he plucked the remaining pieces of hay from her hair. "I'll wash your hair, your delicious backside then your charming front side."

"I think not." She stood away from him her hands on her hips. She was smiling though. "If any of that happens, we will not get to our conversation this evening. You must exhibit control. I wish to know who that woman is as well as why she showed up today, posturing as if you were still hers. Not for one moment did I like what she implied."

He purged himself of the breath he'd held in his lungs until she finished her tirade. "You do have a point. However, I want you now, this instant. I can't wait. Been thinking about this since we were interrupted."

She backed away. Her arms outstretched as if that tiny gesture would stop him. "No, Michael, you can't have me. Go out on the porch and have a cup of tea when Old Suzzy delivers the beverage."

He grinned at her then with a quick stride, he swept her into his arms twirling her around several times. He pressed a deep hard kiss to her lips before setting her back on the porch. "Put on that beautiful confection you wore the night before we wed. That would please me."

"I'm going to wear one of my virginal gowns that stretch from my chin to my toes. For further protection, I'm going to also wear the heavy brocade robe I keep for winter." She tossed her hair flirtatiously. So much of what came undone when they played in the tack room.

"What if I promise I won't touch you? Rather you wear—"

She poked him in the chest then frowned. "Don't promise something you are incapable of keeping. You know what will happen if you see me in that negligée."

They fell silent when Old Suzzy brought the food and wine onto the porch. Several other servants hefted the buckets of hot water to the bathing room. Ah, but he did love arguing with her. Her spice and vinegar were entertaining. Life would never bore him with his wife. She was so independent the fact scared him, frightened him to the tips of his toes.

This weekend was the next race. He knew she had something planned that he wouldn't like. He could read it in the set of her eyes when they spoke of the race. Being two steps or more ahead of his beguiling, intrepid wife was necessary. He couldn't bear it if she was hurt racing Duster or Gypsy. She was right about one thing; Gypsy would do better if a lighter jockey rode him. Maybe Timmie's little brother, Sirus, would be interested in the job. Both young men spent their lives around the horses at Mayfair. They both rode as if born to the saddle. He would make a mental note to ask them tomorrow morning.

While she disappeared into the bathroom to bathe, Michael poured two glasses of wine. When he felt certain she was naked and in the tub, he strode inside the small room. He pulled a small footstool to the tub then set the wine on the hard surface. For a few seconds, he stood back to look at her. His gaze ran the length of her. She was a delight, his delight.

Clare's eyes were huge pools of shimmering blue. They were opened wide in speculation. He swallowed the lump of raw hungry desire surging to all his masculine body parts. "Are you certain you don't want help washing your hair or your front? Perhaps your back. That couldn't be too dangerous?"

In answer she scooped water, tossed the liquid at him. Startled, he managed to step back to avoid most of the hot liquid drenching him. While wiping water from his face, he hooted with laughter. "You don't have to do your worst. A simple no thank you would get the point across."

"Go on, Michael, get out. Leave me in peace. We both understand a few words would not sway you from your purpose."

She covered her breasts with her hands slipping lower into the water.

He grinned. Her beautifully large pink tipped nipples didn't disappear before he saw enough that he wanted to taste. His groan vanished with the rising steam to be tamped down with his resolution to not touch until later. She was dead-on about Jillian. She had the right to understand the woman's motives. He wished he understood why she showed up today unannounced.

"Enjoy the wine. The next round of hot water will be here in fifteen minutes." He backed from the room.

He sighed heavily. A replay of this morning would have been nice. For now, though he needed to figure out why Jillian visited. Why for some reason she still believed she had a hold on his desires. The woman never did anything without a motive. He needed to discover that reason before he would come to regret it. Clare had to be part of her incentive. What the devil could she want with Clare?

Deep down, however, he comprehended she wanted him, not because she cared about him, because she coveted Mayfair Hall. Jillian Whitehead didn't care about anyone except herself along with her carnal pleasures. While that thought tumbled through him, he realized Jilli wished harm to come to his wife. This was a new twist he would have to be more aware of. He would inform Timmie as well as Big Tom there was a new threat looming on the horizon.

Michael didn't understand what he could do to convince the hateful woman he would never marry her. He would never make love with her again, Clare or no Clare. Jilli repulsed him. He felt that way before Clare arrived in Virginia a few months ago to turn his life upside down, to give him all the dreams he'd coveted since Brinkmeyer stole the plantation from his father. He'd never been more pleased when she agreed to wed him. Now, she might carry his child. A new dynasty would begin here. Flannigans belonged at Mayfair Hall.

He'd been leaning on the railing of the balcony mesmerized by the flow of the river, watching the currents play. Tonight, the setting sun was beautiful. It was almost November. Clare's birthday had come and gone. She was twenty-one, a ripe old age. It seemed so long ago that he was that young. As soon as the sun disappeared, there would be a decided chill in the air.

"It's your turn," she spoke softly from behind him, her hand finding purchase on his back. She stroked the length. He shuddered with a new wave of hunger. Raw desire surged between them with lightning speed.

He'd known she was there as he caught the scent of fresh gardenia on the air. When he swiveled to look at her, he grinned. "You weren't lying about your armor now, were you? Are you somewhere beneath all that heavy brocade? Ah, you would be naked, wouldn't you? I could enjoy slowly removing each piece. We could pretend each additional layer was a new button. Would you like that, Clare?"

Ignoring him for the time being, she poured herself another glass of wine not deigning to answer an obvious question. He didn't miss the tilt of her chin or the stiffness in her shoulders despite the air of calm serenity she tried to possess. He wanted one taste of her sweetness before he disappeared inside for his bath.

"Enjoy the view along with the wine. A hot bath will be nice. I'll hurry." Before he strode by her, he caught her in his arms. Beneath the robe, his hand unfastened several of the buttons then cupped her breast teasing the tip until she moaned softly. "Clare, it doesn't matter what you are wearing. If I want you and you are willing, I'll be inside you in a matter of seconds. It doesn't seem as if I can take my time loving you. Why don't you put on the other lingerie while I'm bathing? It will be so much more pleasant for both of us."

His mouth molded over hers, his tongue dipping and investigating inside her hot sultry depths. With no hesitation, he pulled away. He whistled while he strode to his bath. He did possess the strength of will to look but not touch, at least not to the point he wouldn't be able to resist.

In his mind, he went over everything he needed to tell Clare about Jillian. There actually wasn't a lot to say.

Michael settled his head on the lip of the tub. For a few relaxing minutes, he closed his eyes, enjoying the liquid heat pooling around him. Deciding it was best to get on with the evening, he washed then dressed in a pair of buckskins and a white lawn shirt. He left the lacings free at the top while he tucked the shirt into the pants.

Barefoot he padded silently onto the veranda. Quickly, he returned for a pair of moccasins that would serve to keep his feet warm. The dinner tray arrived.

"Should we talk first?" Clare asked as she sipped her wine, her eyes sparkling with something she wasn't telling him.

"Perhaps we could do both," he laughed at the thought. "I've done a great deal of thinking where Jillian is concerned. Imagine I should begin at the very start of our fledgling relationship, as I've no coherent thought as to why she suddenly showed up today.

"My impression was that she wanted to insult me. Didn't seem to me she had any other reason to visit."

Thoughtfully, she buttered a roll before taking a tiny feminine bite.

His plate of baked trout and squash between his forearms he leaned toward her. "She did insult you quite a lot. That could be one reason she visited Mayfair. I've known Jillian since I was about five. The Whiteheads own a plantation southeast of Mayfair. She has five older brothers. Our parents were good friends. Often, we saw each other. I remember one time before I turned fourteen, we went for a ride together. She is older than I am. She was fifteen at the time. Jillian was my first sexual encounter. At the time, I imagined myself in love. Came to find out the feeling was lust. Even then she was a little flirt. I wasn't her first. The fact she wasn't a virgin didn't make a wit of difference at the time. I was so enamored of her as well as innocent, I didn't care."

"Fourteen?" she asked, her butter knife still in one hand, the roll in her other.

Smiling at her amazement, he leaned back his arms resting on the chair. "Fourteen is not so young. She taught me how to give a woman her pleasure. Jillian was quite experienced even in her youth. I was an apt pupil."

Her eyes darkened while she ran her tongue across her lips. "I don't like thinking about the facts she spouted this afternoon. The fact that the way you make love to me...that she taught you."

His chuckle brought a plethora of frown lines to Clare's forehead. "You don't have anything to be jealous about."

"I'm not."

Her hasty denial brought another chuckle rumbling up from his belly. He quite enjoyed this bit of possessiveness.

"After that summer we drifted apart. Her father sent her north to New York to finishing school. She was supposed to become a lady instead of the wild hoyden she'd been when she left."

"Didn't do much good, did it," Clare said, her voice nearly cracking.

"No, we picked up where we left off after she returned. Only now she was older and I was dirt poor. Mayfair Hall was no longer my inheritance. At the time, I didn't understand why she professed to love me. We even spoke of marriage."

"Thank goodness you didn't wed that woman."

"All Jillian wanted from me was the sex. What she wanted from a husband was a plantation where she could be the mistress. She wanted money, lots of it."

He pushed his plate away. Sipped his wine instead of finishing the meal. With talk of Jillian, he was no longer hungry. The thought of her turned his stomach sour.

"What stopped you from marrying her?"

It seemed Clare finished eating also. She leaned on the railing, her adorable backside toward him totally covered by the brocaded armor she wore.

Michael couldn't help but think of this afternoon. She was wonderful and she was all his. He thought the time to end this conversation so they could move on to more enjoyable pursuits were just about here.

"I caught her with her legs spread for Biff Gideon of all people.

At the time though, he was a fine specimen, lean and well-muscled. They were in an isolated glen, a few miles from here."

When he said the words, his breath caught in the back of his throat. Biff, the man offered him a dollar for Clare. Jilli had history with the man.

When he looked at Clare, her face was drained of all color. The exchanged look between them cemented his thought. She realized what he was thinking.

"Do you think she's still seeing Biff?"

"Jillian seeks out any man who will give her what she wants; lots of sex as well as lots of money."

His bitterness crept into his words. He joined her at the railing, his shoulder touching hers.

A silver slip of a moon shone over the river. The scent of her filled his senses. An owl hooted somewhere in the dark. He set his hand on her back, ran his hand to the soft curve of her bottom then back to her neck. She turned to him, her face tilted toward his. Quickly, he brushed a light kiss on her lips.

"Biff wanted you. Suppose they might be plotting something. Jillian can't have Biff's plantation. She might believe that if you were gone, I would want her again."

"Do you?"

"Do I want to marry a self-serving bitch?" His voice was bitter. "Biff wasn't the only man who tasted her charms. As far as I know just about every available man in the area bedded her, married or unmarried. The woman taught me what love wasn't."

Biff was married. That fact never stopped him from visiting the whorehouse just outside of town. Rumors had it that for a time Raynard was holed up in one of Biff's outbuildings. Biff provided slaves for his entertainment.

"So, the three of them plot something neither of us would like," she spoke softly, shivering as his hand continued to move along her back.

"Yes, maybe. Raynard wants revenge against me. What better way to get his vengeance by forcing you?"

"This isn't all about me. He could also find his retaliation by harming Duster or stealing him. That would put the stud farm back. What he doesn't know is that Link would be more than happy to assist me in purchasing a new magnificent stud."

"True, to both."

Michael shuddered at both images. The stable was guarded night and day. Clare was guarded too. Despite the fact she resented his dictate, she didn't go anywhere without protection. He pulled her into his arms, held her close. His hand on her head she was nestled against his chest.

"I don't like this. Need for the danger to be over."

"Me neither," he told her as once more he ran his hand meant to soothe along her back.

She was so damn delicate, fragile. He needed to keep her safe from all the elements at play here. He hoped he was right. If he were, they would know where the danger came from.

He felt her withdrawal as she pushed away from him. "Let's go inside. It's getting a bit chilly out here."

"Dressed in all your armor you're cold?" One eyebrow arched toward the heavens.

She nodded. Old Suzzy was at the door. "Take everything except the wine, Suzzy," Clare said. She helped set the dishes on the tray. A few moments later Suzzy was gone.

Sitting in a chair in front of the fire, Michael stretched out his long legs. "This weekend..." he paused, twirling his glass by the stem. "This weekend you will not try to race. I won't allow you to do so. If you do attempt to disobey me, you'll regret the insubordination. A wife is supposed to conform to her husband's wishes."

Her little gasp of surprise didn't have the effect on him she would have wanted. When she spoke, he also wasn't surprised by her defiance.

"My riding abilities are good enough to race either Gypsy or Duster. You know that for a fact. This is an absurd tactic to assert your will."

He'd poured himself a glass of brandy. He was thoughtful. Wondered what he would do if she didn't listen to him. "Heed what I said. I'm on to your machinations. Don't expect me to go easy on you if you challenge my word in any way. I've given you a great deal of authority with the horses. Have allowed you to participate in many things no other husband would. Don't make me change my mind. If you disobey me on this issue, there will be discipline."

"All right."

All right? All right what?

He saw the darkening of her eyes. He would have to maintain a place that would be two-steps in front of her. As far as he was concerned, she wasn't going to court trouble or danger by riding in any race against men. She could be pregnant. Could carry their child even now. Indeed, she most likely was a couple of months along. Since they'd been wed, she had no monthly flow. Be damned he wasn't intending to bring that huge piece of news up to her. If she didn't know...that thought caused him to freeze, his mind in chaos for a moment.

"Clare, what are you saying? Are you telling me you've no intention of doing as you please?"

It seemed she studied her toes. She slid her hands along the length of her brocade robe. "If that's what you want to believe. I'm not telling you anything."

"Hell and damnation! You are planning to race. Mark my words, Clare." His anger growing, he pointed his finger at her. "Your racing will not happen. No, you won't sit Gypsy or Duster while we are at the race in North Carolina. What you will do is stand by my side, hold my hand. You will cheer Sirus and Timmie on to victory. We will mingle with the other horse breeders. We will investigate the value of their stables. You can help me make decisions about further purchases. That is all."

"If that's what you want. Truly, Michael, you cannot mean to stay by my side every second. I'm sure you will have to relieve yourself sometime."

She placed the glass to her lips, smiled sweetly then drank as if she didn't just admit that she plotted to disobey his orders.

He jerked with exasperation coupled with something else. She was playing her hand boldly. He'd never expected her to say something so vividly blatant. "I will take you with me. Lead you by your arm until I'm...relieved."

She flushed to the top of her forehead. Well, she did start this. He would figure out some way to end her proclivity, to make her way without his permission. He didn't know yet what he would do if she tried to race. He would think of something that would give her more than second thoughts about challenging his orders. He would make sure she had nothing she could race in if she attempted thwarting his wishes.

"You would do the same with me?"

Thinking that far ahead hadn't happened yet. Supposed he would have to do just that. He grinned the wickedest grin he could muster. "Yes."

For a moment her eyes crossed. "That," she swallowed hard. "That would not be gentlemanly."

"I'm your husband. Where your safety is concerned, I need not pursue that course. Clare, I touched as well as kissed nearly every white curvaceous inch of you. Nothing will deter me. Though, I could tie your wrist to mine. That would keep you close. Don't you think?"

The thought had brilliant possibilities. She was right. At the races, there could be hundreds of milling people. How difficult could it be for her to slip into the throngs then disappear until it was too late for him to stop her from racing?

"You wouldn't. Doing so would embarrass you as much as me." She sounded defiant as well as astounded.

Fingers tapping together beneath his chin, he shot her another grin. "Suppose you will have to wait and see. For now, should we have a glass of the wonderful Sauterne? After that I would like to explore what is beneath your armor."

"You are finished giving me orders?" Her voice was sultry and hot. "I'm not sure... I guess I might like your attention. However, I have a few things to speak plainly about."

"You do?"

"Yes."

"Well, what is it then?"

"If you discipline me for anything, I'll return the favor. You will be sorry. You cannot possibly think to tie me to you. I won't accept a child's punishment either."

This was growing amusing. He wondered exactly how she defined her words. "A child's punishment? What pray tell is that? A swat to your adorable backside? I would never wish to mar that beautiful white flesh with the red mark of my hand. Or..." he paused thinking along a different line, "perhaps I would place you in a corner with your nose to the wall for you to think about your wickedness."

Seconds later she was still studying her toes. "I would fight you. I'm not a child. I know my own mind as well as my body. I can make coherent decisions for my life." When she looked up, she was breathing hard. Beneath that heavy brocade robe, he knew her breasts were heaving.

"No, you are anything but a child. I would never hit you nor will I hit my children. What do you think of your nose to the wall? In any case, if I pursued that particular form of punishment, I doubt you would learn anything. No, my dear, I will need to think seriously on this important matter." He drummed his fingers. "The lesson must garner knowledge. You must learn that to do something if forbidden will not go well for you. You will suffer consequences."

"I'm not at all pleased with this conversation," she told him primly, her chin tilted ever so regally.

"Maybe I should come up with something more fitting. Perhaps even," once again he tapped his fingers together while he pondered the situation, "You should understand what will happen to you if you disobey me. Do you want to know what I will do?" He knew now what the perfect solution would be. He almost hoped she would try something. If she did, he would find a way to embarrass her to the tips of her tiny sweet toes.

He figured it out. The discipline would be delightful as well as enjoyable for both of them. She would also learn that he would not allow her to trample him into the dirt with her insubordination. He didn't intend to let her harm one tiny part of her delicious white flesh. Race, never in a million years.

"I would not like to know."

"I will explain very thoroughly."

He proceeded to do so. In the process, he was now delightfully positive she would still attempt to gainsay his wishes. No, she would just be more careful. He would have to be ever more alert to assume every possible precaution.

~ * ~

Jillian slammed the door to Biff's office behind her. She picked up a pillow off the chair facing his desk. Clutching it to her magnificently heaving bosom, she glared at him. Shamelessly, he grinned, enjoying her tantrum.

"What has you all tied up in a knot?"

Ah, he played with the pen he'd been writing with until her timely arrival. Biff had a good idea what was wrong. He wanted to hear Jillian say the words. After that, they would ease each other with a glass of wine and sex. Sex with Jillian was always one of his favorite pastimes. Mostly because she was insatiable. Tonight, the act would be exhilarating because she was angry. The chance of discovery waited in the wings. His wife might come upon them. It was a delightful possibility. He might have both of them at one time. He'd never actually thought to do that with his wife. The sex might be more interesting than ever. It was time he treated his wife the way she deserved to be treated. She would never refuse him again.

"Michael doesn't want me. Prefers that slut of a wife to me. How dare he flaunt her in front of me? You know they were in the tack room. She had hay in her hair." She leaned over pointing a finger at her chest. "They were making love while all the stable hands knew what they were doing. How dare he embarrass me like that?"

Biff saw the deep valley between her breasts along with the soft white curves. He wanted to bury his face between those immense rounded globes. He salivated remembering how she felt beneath him just last night. Perhaps having Jillian was better than Clare. Her breasts were much larger. Her nipples were an amazingly beautiful shade of pink. Very large, ripe for the sucking. Jillian knew what she was about, never failing to drink him dry. Clare was most likely an innocent. Better than anything he enjoyed experienced women. They never shied at anything he did. Some even had unique ideas of their own.

Yes, when he first had her she'd been fifteen. He was eighteen. She delighted him even then. Jillian wasn't a virgin when he tossed her skirts in the hayloft. Many times, he wondered who had her first. Once he asked her if Michael deflowered her. She shook her head. Nonetheless, she would not give him a name. So many years after the fact, he supposed who took her first was no longer important.

It didn't matter to Biff as long as she would grant him sexual favors whenever he asked even when he didn't such as tonight. He wasn't going to marry a woman who wasn't a virgin, as he wanted to know his children were his. Wouldn't marry a woman who dallied with anyone wearing pants. When William Brinkmeyer began selling Sophia's favors, he didn't fall in line. No, he understood what the man was up to. He wasn't going to lose his land to the greedy man. Well, with Sophia so obviously flaunting her favors, no one paid Jillian any particular interest. The woman did what she wanted until her father caught wind of what she was about then sent her to New York. Thinking of that time, he chuckled to himself.

When she returned from finishing school, she was more talented in the arts of pleasure than when she left. Biff had a standing assignation with her every Thursday night. He paid her quite well for that one night. All the other times were free.

"Why doesn't that surprise me? Michael was always the prude. Didn't want a woman who sold her favors. Too bad he's married."

"We're going to get rid of her." Jillian strode around the room swinging the pillow in one hand. "If I can't have the man, no one else will."

Too bad he had to tell her the truth. "Michael won't marry you, not ever. Doesn't make any difference if Clare is dead or alive. You should understand that before you do something foolish, something that could threaten your life. You wouldn't want to die because of her."

"Why not?" She stopped her pacing glaring at him. "I'm the perfect mate for Michael. We've known each other since we were just children. We both come from wealthy plantations."

"For the same reason I wouldn't marry you if I were to find myself single. Every man wants to know he's the father of his children. You bed every man you see. Don't want to get the pox either. It happens when you spread your legs for so many different men."

She threw the pillow at him. Hit him in the face. He laughed hard.

"You're a slut, Jillian. Admit to the fact. You've bedded more men than I have women. You delight in sex. You're unquenchable. Men don't want that characteristic in a mate, only a mistress. If you were my mistress, I would have to keep all the windows and doors locked to the house I rented for you otherwise I'm quite certain when I came to visit, I would find another man or possibly more in your bed."

"It's fine for a man to spread his seed around. However, a woman can't have multiple lovers. I always use protection. I've never had a child." She grimaced.

Biff was certain she detested children. It was a good thing she was careful. Jillian would make a horrid mother. No child deserved an upbringing by that woman.

"Ah, so you're that advanced in your sexual life. I believed only the women who frequent whorehouses would know how to prevent conception." He threw the pillow back. "You understand, of course, there are no guarantees. No method is one hundred percent reliable. You could even now be carrying my child. Last night I didn't withdraw from your precious body. My seed stayed where I planted it."

Sitting down she clutched the pillow tightly. She let out a long decidedly slow breath of air. "I wore a sponge. I didn't go to finishing school. Well, I did for two days. Couldn't stand the girls there. All they did was simper. There chatter went on endlessly about men and what happened when they wed. They whispered things about me from behind their hands."

Biff sat on the edge of his desk clearly intrigued by her revelation. "What did you do? You were gone two years."

A well-practiced look sent his heart tumbling, racing with immediate need for this woman. His body tightened in anticipation. Soon she would be on his desk her long white legs around his flanks. "A high-priced Madame took one look at me and reached the conclusion that I would bring her a great deal of money." She lifted her shoulders, "I enjoyed myself immensely."

"Did you now? Your father would have had apoplexy if he'd known."

Somehow, he didn't understand how Jillian managed the feat.

When she lifted her shoulders in an artfully delicate shrug, the corsage of her gown dipped lower. He stared at the white tops of her rounded jewels, soft globes of pure delight. From experience, he knew they filled his hands.

"That's a unique talent you have. You think I'll stop asking questions if I get a look at your pretty pink nipples. I've seen them many times. Why don't you partake of a brandy? You can tell me more if you like. You even have my permission to disrobe."

The way she walked was provocation enough to send him reeling. The talents she showed him last night didn't compare to this evening. Maybe he should let her take the lead to see where this sexual encounter would go.

"I also made a great deal of money, the fools parted with the coin so easily. Was paid fifty dollars a tumble, five hundred to spend the night. I had ten wealthy clients. One was a US Senator, another was a judge. They were all married. Said their wives didn't like sex." She tossed back the amber liquid then refilled her glass. "None of that makes a bit of difference. I want to know how we are going to get rid of little miss prim and proper."

"I've an idea. Perhaps I'll tell you after you accommodate my latest desire."

Biff locked the door. He grinned. She was already perched on his desk, the papers lying on the floor, her skirts pulled to her waist. She wore nothing beneath. He salivated.

Chapter Nine

Clare skipped alongside Michael keeping up with his long manly strides. The day was perfect for racing. Today she meant to prove herself to him. He would learn that she could ride as well as any man. He would never suspect she would defy his order. She also didn't think he would carry through with the punishment he told her waited if she challenged him. She meant to challenge him in every way possible, not just today but every day for the rest of their lives. The punishment be damned.

This afternoon there wasn't one cloud in the cerulean blue sky. The weather wasn't too hot either, perfect for racing. After all, this was November. Just as she hoped, throngs of people congregated along the racetrack. All she needed to do now was misplace the blasted man. Doing that was going to be more difficult than she previously thought. She understood that fact better than anyone. He was determined to keep her safe. She didn't need a man to do that for her. She was perfectly capable of looking after herself.

When she came up with the plan, she believed tricking Michael would be child's play. Because of the way he stuck to her, she now knew different. In the past, he always became too intense when the horses were racing. He would have never noticed if she left his side. If she slipped away, he wouldn't miss her until the end of the race. By that time, it would be too late for him to prevent her from riding. She meant to ride Gypsy in the mile race. Sirus wouldn't mind if she pulled rank. He would simply shrug. Timmie, however, if he discovered the ruse, would rush to tell Michael.

Timing was everything.

Since the night they discussed Jillian, he didn't mention this race. To Clare, it seemed he forgot about his dictate to her. He thought that after he described in explicit detail what he would do if she did as she pleased going against convention as well as his husbandly command, since women didn't race, she would simply put her notion aside.

He was very wrong. He would learn. This was her means to discipline her husband at its finest.

No, over the rest of the week she'd been the perfect wife. She accepted all his orders without arguing even when he was outlandish. By being submissive to his every whim, she lulled him into complacency. Hers was a fine trick. All this time she became more determined to have her way. They stopped in front the stalls holding the stallions.

"What do you think, Clare? Both Duster and Gypsy have a good chance at winning."

Michael fondly stroked Duster's nose. He didn't give her a second glance. He didn't pay a moment of attention to her. She had him. Not for one second did he think she would challenge his authority. Her simpering complacency worked.

"With Sirus on Gypsy, the stallion should fly around the track. Of course, he has to make sure no one gets close enough to push him into a ditch. If that happened, he could break a leg, or his neck."

"That shouldn't be a problem. Timmie has given him instructions. They practiced every day. Sirus knows how to avoid difficulties such as that as well as how to use his strop to intimidate the other jockeys."

"Hope it doesn't come to that," she murmured thinking about what she could do if the time came for her to use something other than defensive tactics.

For a moment though, she cringed. Even if she got a chance to race, when Michael saw her, he'd be furious. He would tie her to him for the rest of the day. Nonetheless, she would have succeeded in her dream. It was today or she might not ever get the chance again.

Now or never.

"No," he said stroking his chin. "Sirus needs to get out in front as soon as possible. That way he won't be in a position that needs defending. Gypsy enjoys taking the lead. He doesn't need to be pushed."

"Are you placing any bets?" she asked hoping perhaps he would leave her alone long enough to do so.

She needed to get to the place where she hid her riding britches then change her clothes before the race. Again, timing was everything. As the seconds quickly ticked by, it seemed to be slipping away from her.

"Not today. Want to see how Sirus does. Duster should win still..."

Michael rarely bet. There were too many variables he always told her. He wasn't a gambler at heart. No, betting wasn't his style. He liked to make his money by sure things.

"Come along," he told her, taking her hand. He headed toward the track. His grip was firm, too tight for her liking. She stumbled when he started off too fast. "Sorry," he told her then slowed his pace. "Seems I'm eager to find a good spot to watch the races."

Perhaps she'd been wrong about him. Maybe he still didn't trust her. This wouldn't do. No, she had to get away. He tugged on her hand now when she lagged behind.

"Michael?" She halted trying for an indignant tone. "What are you doing? I don't appreciate you dragging me everywhere."

He didn't answer. She wanted to cosh the man over his head. They stopped in front of another owner. "Mr. Jones." Michael nodded.

"See you brought Duster. He's a fine horse; fine, fine animal. Think you'll win?"

"Certainly hope so. Impeccable blood lines," Michael said smiling fondly at her now that she was huffing and puffing. "My wife's brother-in-law bought him for Clare to start up the Mayfair stable. She is always excited on race day. Aren't you dear?"

She didn't like the way he acted. He was never solicitous. They moved on, speaking to others, always idle meaningless conversations his hand tight upon her own. Wandering through the crowds they finally reached a spot where it would be quite easy to watch the races. Duster was in the third race. He and Timmie would be up next. Gypsy was in the sixth. She had more than enough time except it didn't appear that Michael was going to get himself lost in the crowd of people. Nor did it seem he was going to let go of her hand.

She never actually thought he would keep hold of her the entire day even though he threatened to do just that if she gave him reason. She hadn't. All week she'd been a meek biddable wife. For the entire week as well as this morning she acted complacent. Now his hand settled on her waist, his fingers tightening with excitement. The starting gun went off. Duster handled the group of horses expertly as did Timmie. While others jockeyed for a place, Duster was a length and a half ahead of the horse in second place. The stallion was amazing. She felt a beam of pride fill her. She…no, they owned this magnificent animal.

They were at the winner's circle when the fourth race started. Surely, he would let her go long enough to shake hands then accept congratulations along with the prize money. He did not.

"Why don't you hold onto the trophy along with the money?" He squeezed her shoulder. Nevertheless, he didn't let go of her. She needed to do something fast. Now, her hands were full. The fifth race was about to start.

One handed, he slipped the prize money into his money belt before covering the pouch with his jacket. A few moments later they left the trophy with Sirus who stood by the trailer. The fifth race began.

"I need to…" She swept her tongue across her lips desperate for a means to escape him. He said he would follow her there. "Need to relieve myself."

"You do?" He grinned before heading in that direction. "Well, then let's not waste any time. Gypsy will race soon. I don't wish to miss a moment of his race. I know you don't either. We've been looking forward to this moment all week."

"I can do it by myself."

She sounded incensed, felt piqued too. All her plans were unraveling if he didn't let her go. She had to get away from him.

"Can you?" He squeezed her shoulder then whistled. "We've just enough time before Gypsy races." He grinned at her while he waited for her, his arms crossed over his chest.

He was a cad. This was terrible. Silently she cursed him. When she came out, he stood in front of the door. When he smiled at her, she understood she had lost. The sixth race started without her.

Damn him.

They found a good spot to watch the end of the mile race. Sirus didn't get out in front like they hoped. However, he did well. At the very end, he shot past the horse in first to win the race. Once again, they were in the winner's circle accepting their winnings along with the congratulations.

"Hmm..." Michael looked at her, his grin all-knowing. "Let's find a quiet place where we can watch the remainder of the races. The fewer people the better. Doubt if I can find a spot where there is not a single person. Ah, well, if I did that it might take some of the sport out of watching, now wouldn't it?"

She shuddered hoping he didn't know what she'd intended. How could he? She straightened herself. She tilted her chin upward. "What are you talking about?"

"Discipline."

Discipline!

She closed her eyes. His hand on her upper arm, he led the way through the people. He found a spot overlooking the course. There were only ten or so others. The place was quiet. A soft breeze ruffled the oak leaves overhead. A squirrel darted up a nearby tree. He leaned against a tree. When he let her go, she wanted to run. Her feet wouldn't move.

"You can't mean to do what you described the other night. Michael, that's barbaric."

His grin was wolfish. He didn't reply quickly. He stroked the length of her with his gaze. She understood he would do just as he said. Before he spoke, he cleared his throat. "Discipline is important in a relationship such as ours. Punishment comes in many different forms. In my mind, the reprimand must teach a lesson otherwise the chastisement is faulty. A woman must learn where her husband stands on certain issues. In those cases, he must be obeyed. Our little discussion didn't seem to have the desired effect, at least not what I hoped for. You seem to believe you can proceed in whatever manner you choose. I will never stand by and allow you to hurt yourself."

"How did you know?" She was beside herself, backing away from him, feeling as if her eyes glazed over with apprehension. "How, Michael? You couldn't possibly have known. I was so careful."

"You understand if you run, I would catch you. If that were the case, I would have to contrive more discipline. Something with a bit more learning power than what we are about. After all, this punishment today is minimal. You ask me how I knew?"

"Yes."

She had a good idea. Maybe all he did was wait until he backed her into a corner and she admitted what she was about. She was a fool. By asking the question she told him her intentions.

He reached into his pocket, pulling out strips of fabric that had once been her riding britches. She felt her eyes widen with disbelief. He did know. This wasn't a bluff. Once again, she found herself shaking her head while she moved back a step. She swallowed hard. The thought of punishment sent her knees quaking. She was mortified to the tips of her toes. The embarrassment would be overwhelming.

His shoulders lifted slightly. "It wasn't difficult. I searched your valise. If you were intending to ride, they would have been there. But no," he paused touching his chin with one of his long fingers as he thought on what he intended to say, "you are smart, creative as well an extremely clever young woman. You would think of someplace else to put them. I searched the next obvious place."

She was shaking her head, wringing her hands, still thinking running was the only solution to this unexpected dilemma. There was nowhere she could hide. He would catch her. She didn't stand a chance. At least she wouldn't be around people. He would drag her wherever he wanted her. "You don't have the right to go through my things. You…" She ran her tongue across her parched lips. He had every right to search her belongings. He didn't find the britches with her valise because they weren't there.

"Your eyes are so very wide, even a tiny bit dazed. I do believe they are about to cross. I don't trust you when it comes to racing. Link told me as much. I've found he was right. Knew you wouldn't be so blatantly obvious as to put them in the most logical place for me to search. So," he paused, grinning at her as if he held the upper hand. Well, he did. "I made a point of searching both horses' stalls. Big Tom found your riding ensemble. He's on my side, you know. If he were your husband, he wouldn't allow you to do half the things I do. I'm very generous with your behavior, as I overlook much. I even believe a woman should have knowledge about birthing. Big Tom was more than willing to assist me in my endeavor to locate your britches. They were buried under some cleverly arranged hay."

"Michael, no, I won't do it again. I promise." She held her arms out as if she could ward off his advance even though he didn't make one move to reach her.

"Come here, Clare. You see that's the stickler. I don't believe you. Nor do I trust your word about this issue. After you realize I mean what I say, then I might take your word for the truth. However, when it comes to the races... I'll have to think that one over for a while. I'm not a dim-witted fool you can walk over, tread beneath your tiny yet adorable feet."

She was frozen to the spot where she stood. Understood completely if she didn't come to him, the ensuing moments would go worse for her. The fear that rose inside her, she gulped down. He wouldn't do what he told her. This wasn't at all fair of him. Well, if he did this to her, she would find some way to discipline him when he least expected her to do so.

"I'm waiting, Clare. Don't make me come to you. I won't be pleased if you refuse this husbandly request of mine. My patience is unraveling as we speak."

More people milled into the semi-secluded spot he picked. She didn't wish for anyone to be anywhere near when he inflicted his unique form of discipline. If she could, she would resist him. He couldn't make her do what he said. If she maintained control, her body wouldn't respond to his fervent coaxing. Clare comprehended she didn't have a prayer. Whenever he touched her, she melted to liquid heat. Her jaw clenched with determination. She stepped forward.

"Good girl, now turn around. Put your beautiful white arms inside your cape. Hold real still. Mums the word, you understand, not one sound from your pouty pink lips." He lightly nipped her neck, laved the spot, sending shivers down her spine. "This will all be over very soon. After that we can move forward."

"Michael, please not here. Not where there are people. You can't possibly..."

"You comprehended fully my intentions. Still, you decided to deceive me then do exactly what pleased you with not one thought to your husband's wishes. Now under my expert tutelage, you will learn a much-needed lesson in obedience. You will realize your husband always has your best interest at heart. When you realize that fact you will always do as I say."

Clare didn't believe that possible. Still…

Doing as he bade, she slipped her arms inside the cloak which was secured in the front. He fastened all the frogs until no part of her except her face could be seen. When he seemed satisfied, he slipped his fingers into the side openings. She felt his hands in front of her. Felt the bodice of her dress slowly coming unfastened. She whimpered. Her knees shook while her heart raced. Someone looked at her. She tried to smile. Unable to do so, she closed her eyes, silently willing this moment to end.

"Hush, Little Pigeon. Try to hold very still. You don't want to call attention to yourself. I know you don't. Just allow me to teach the lesson then we'll move on to something more private for both of us. What I've planned might even be enjoyable for you. After all I mean to see to your pleasure."

When he spoke, she'd allowed her lashes to drift upward. She closed her eyes again. Methodically, he pushed fabric aside then down her arms. So far there was no seduction or gentle coaxing. Michael seemed indifferent. He didn't touch her to seduce just to remove unwanted clothing. For the time being, his intention was simply to strip her of her clothing along with her pride. Perhaps she'd been too arrogant, too certain of her abilities. Maybe she possessed too much pride. Suddenly, beneath the covering of her cloak, she was naked from the waist up.

Her lips quivering, her voice barely a whisper, while her body thrummed with sexual need, "I promise. I won't try to race again."

His lips against her neck, his whisper teasing sensitive flesh, "Truthfully, Clare, do you think I'm an utter fool? An idiot male who you can manipulate through sultry sweet lies you've no intention of keeping? Your arrogance knows no bounds. The sooner you learn I am not a fool or an idiot, the better it will go for you. Also, the sooner you learn that you cannot manipulate your husband the discipline will end." His large warm hands cupped her breasts fondled them, squeezing each one, tugging on her nipples. At that instant, she thought she might swoon. Her eyes closed with pleasure.

She sucked in a long drought of air, a tiny mewl followed. She supposed the seduction would begin now. After that she tried to keep whatever sounds she made behind her teeth. She could not. It seemed for the time being he was satisfied with fondling her breasts. She swore and cursed to herself while she tried to hold back the raw hunger he generated. Her insides pulsed and heated, throbbing with need she couldn't deny. She knew her female parts were swollen, slick with moisture. His long fingers squeezed then plucked at her nipples rolling them between his fingers. She squirmed against his large form. Her body coiled with anticipation despite her efforts to tamp the potent hunger down.

He played her, toyed with her. For the entire seventh race he did nothing more except let his fingers dance over the sensitive pinnacles of her breasts. She could not bear much more. Her knees threatened to give way. The breaths of air she tried to inhale unable to reach her lungs.

"Do you like this, Clare? All these people don't know what I'm doing to your sweet jewels with the tight pink buds overflowing my large hands. They don't know how beautifully naked you are beneath the cape. Well, you are not naked yet. However, in a few more moments you will be quite stripped of all your clothing. Soon you'll climax right here in front of everyone. However, they won't know unless you give yourself away. Remember, not a sound from those sweetly kissable lips of yours. This one time I don't wish to hear you cry out my name."

Methodically, her skirt rose on her legs. His fingers brushed across sensitive spots. She didn't wear a petticoat. "How naughty," he said while he nipped her neck. "You wished to have as little clothing as possible to change out of before the sixth race. This of course, suits my purposes better than if you donned petticoats along with a chemise for me to divest. Too bad for both of us you still wear your drawers." His fingers found the waistband of the offending article. He tugged bending slightly.

"Lift your legs, Little Pigeon so I can remove this hindrance to my plans. I don't want anything to stand between you and my nimble fingers."

Still in denial, she was shaking her head. Stunned, though she bent each leg, did as he commanded. He stuffed her drawers into a pocket of his coat.

"Now your dress. Let me see how this will go." Slowly, he pushed the fabric down her body, sliding the material over her hips, along her thighs, his fingers brushing against her already aroused flesh. She almost cried out. He nipped her neck again, laved the spot with his tongue over and over again he continued the blatant seduction heating her to a level she'd never known before. He couldn't possibly have that many pockets. No, he left the torn britches on the ground as a reminder to her. He was telling her she must obey her husband's wishes. He dropped the gown. The fabric pooled around her feet. Quickly, he bent, forced her to lift each leg before he kicked the fabric to the side.

Go to the devil!

She was very nearly naked. Her stockings and her shoes along with the cape were all she wore. No, he was doing just as he told her he would do. She never thought for a moment he would go through with this wild scheme of his to discipline. He told her to believe him. Explained to her very carefully if she didn't, she would find herself regretting the hasty and ridiculous decision to challenge his absolute authority.

Truly she hadn't believed.

His fingers splayed on her belly, tightened, stroked then whispered softly along her heated flesh. Her throat was parched. She tried to swallow. When his hand cupped her mound, she nearly cried out, a whimper emerging with the sensual contact. Breath rushed from her lungs.

"Hush now. You don't want Mr. Chalmers over there to hear you. He might guess what it is we are doing, what it is you're experiencing."

Her head settled against his chest. She moaned softly wishing she could stop the throaty sounds from emerging. Mr. Chalmers who owned one of the racehorses stared at her, quirked a snowy white eyebrow toward the heavens then nodded as if he gave permission to carry on.

Michael looked up. Behind her he cleared his throat then spoke directly to the man. "She didn't feel so well a few minutes ago. That's why we walked up here onto the hill. She is hot, very, very hot blooded, so hot she had to remove her gown. The fresher air you know. Thought the slight breeze would make her feel better. She is much improved. With a bit more time, I'm certain she will be back to her normal self. Don't pay any attention to us."

Mr. Chalmers grinned then shook his head, a sly grin forming on his weathered face. Oh God, he knew. The man didn't believe the lie Michael told him. No, this couldn't be happening to her. Michael's feet pushed hers farther apart, nudged until he was satisfied. She was open to him. He lifted his knee between her legs, she felt the abrasion of his trousers. "Oh…oh…"

The contact vanished. So very provocatively, he slipped one then two fingers inside her, his thumb giving zealous attention to the most sensitive place on her entire body. She tried to think of something to get her mind off his wheedling fingers. Wildflowers came to mind as did riding Duster, the wind in her hair. Nothing worked. She was at a loss while his fingers danced in a primal enchanting rhythm over every sensitive inch she possessed. The mercuric feelings were intense and undeniable. She was lost to the sensations he created.

It seemed his hands were everywhere, his fingers moving in then out of her, slowly at first then faster, his thumb massaging that tiny spot where she could never deny. She gritted down on her teeth, pushing the sensations to the back of her mind. Trying desperately to ignore the inferno of raw hunger building everywhere. Her body began to pulse then beg for her release as she was on the precipice. She stiffened feeling the end of the perverse pleasure coming to a standstill.

It seemed he sensed the moment too. "Close your eyes, Clare. Mr. Chalmers is still staring at you. Don't want anyone save me seeing the way your eyes glaze over with fiery passion with your delightful climax."

She did. She cried out again, softly. However, she couldn't help herself. Her body writhed and seethed with the pleasure he gave her. Within his strong arms, she undulated, reaching for the ecstasy she yearned for. Suddenly replete, she fell limp against him. His forearm held her steady. She leaned her head against his chest. With startling finesse, he'd done her in.

"My wife is fine," Michael said softly. "Clare is no longer quite so hot. She will recover quite nicely. It was the air, the very fresh, cool air that helped her. We will walk back in a few minutes as soon as she gathers herself together."

Mr. Chalmers nodded again then strolled down the hill. He understood what happened. How dare Michael do this to her? *Hot? Hot body?* She vowed that she would get even. She would find some means to bring him down. He should be disciplined for this, just as he disciplined her. An idea began to form in her head.

"Are you ready to walk to the inn? We've dinner waiting us in our room. I for one am famished."

He was holding her up or she would be in a puddle at his feet. "I can't walk right now."

Truthfully, he needed to give her a few more minutes to recover from the wild sensations he single handedly created. She'd never felt this way, this sated. Of course, they'd never been standing up when he brought her to her climax. He didn't even come inside her. With so little effort on his part, he rendered her helpless, totally at his whim, unable to move or perform a coherent thought.

"In your clothing condition I can't carry you. Well, I've a different idea tumbling around in my man's brain. Since you seduced me without a thought for me, I'd like relief. It's not fair or just that you were the only one in this relationship who found ecstasy. As soon as you can walk, we'll try out something different I have in mind. It wasn't well done of you to seduce me in this manner, leave me wanting."

"I want my clothes put on me." She didn't want to go another second without her dress covering her. "I didn't seduce you!"

"No, no clothing. At least not yet. If I were to succumb to your wishes, well, then in a matter of a few minutes, I would have to remove everything again. You're in the perfect state for what I have in mind. No more punishment, Clare, at least not today. Have you learned the proffered lesson? No, don't answer that just say yes since I understand you will answer in the affirmative whether you mean the word or not. I'll wait and see what will happen the next time we are at the races."

"I've learned."

She thought for a moment that perhaps he was right. He should wait for confirmation. The discipline was not that bad. Indeed, it was a tiny bit enjoyable if she had to admit anything. Although he did manage to embarrass her quite thoroughly. The excitement of discovery was possibly an aphrodisiac. When she thought about what he did to her body, she didn't even mind that Mr. Chalmers guessed what Michael was about. Perhaps she could lull her husband into complacency.

"Come along now. I believe I will have to devise a more severe form of punishment for the next time. You don't seem as if you've learned anything. Have you, Clare?" He flung her dress over her shoulder. "You will need this later."

She imagined she hadn't as she still didn't understand why exactly he thought she could never compete on a level with the other jockeys. Though she wasn't about to tell him her thoughts. Deciding again not to answer she walked beside him. She felt the sway of her breasts against the fabric of her cape as the wool scraped her nipples. One of his hands was beneath her cape. His fingers rested on her hip. For the longest time, he didn't move his hand. Now, he caressed her side up to her breast, lightly touching the hard tip then back to linger on her hip. He flattened his hand across her belly teasing her.

"Michael what are you doing?"

"Walking with my wife," was his succinct reply.

The palm of his hand floated languidly across her nipples again, then again enticing her, heating her. The inferno began to simmer anew. He knew what he was doing. They were now at the stable where the horses were housed. He kept walking until they reached the back. It seemed he knew where they were headed. She wasn't certain. Nevertheless, she didn't believe she would protest whatever he had in mind.

He stepped inside a small room. She closed her eyes for a moment soaking up the silence as well as the scent. After he shut the door, he turned the lock. She waited, anticipating. Certainly, she guessed exactly what her husband had in mind.

"You quite seduced me a few moments ago. I need you, Clare. Here you can make all the noise you want, scream out my name, keep your eyes open so I can witness the hunger. I will quite enjoy that since you could not do so a few minutes ago."

With infinite slowness, he began to unfasten the cape. With half the frogs undone to nearly her waist, he pushed the cape open. With his teeth and tongue, he fondled and caressed the hard tight buds he adored. In a few seconds, his buckskins were unlaced. His finger found the pearl hidden between the swollen slick folds. She was panting, breathing heavily, so aroused again she wanted to howl. He could so easily do this to her.

She clung to him. Her back was pressed against the wall. "You know, Michael, I'm going to figure out some way to punish you for what you did today. The deed will happen when you least expect it. You will be surprised."

It seemed he ignored her words. "Wrap your long white legs around me," She did then he was deep inside her moving with a heated determined rhythm.

She screamed his name. He groaned. The mating was over almost before the seduction began. After he stopped moving, he pushed damp hair from her face.

"You are beautiful. You will punish me, you say? Will you tell me what you plan on doing? It's only fair since I explained everything in specific detail to you."

"No, what I have planned for you will be a surprise. Unlike the way you disciplined me, no one will ever know when the punishment will take place, Michael. Except for Mr. Chalmers knowing what you were doing to me beneath my cloak, the punishment or discipline as you named the deed was quite enjoyable. Even with him staring so blatantly, what you did was titillating. I'm certain he was also aroused. You might have done him a favor of sorts. Why would you possibly believe I learned some type of lesson?"

So much for luring him to believe she learned a much-needed lesson.

"You are a challenge to me, woman. A man can always hope the discipline he sets out to employ is successful. I will have to think of some other tool. Clare, when were you going to tell me?"

"Tell you what?" she asked blinking, wondering what he was expecting her to say now. "That I intended to race?"

His grin was charming. He had some tidbit of information to

share. She waited for an answer while he fastened his pants. "Your breasts are more sensitive, larger as well."

"All right. I'll give you that. Does this mean something?"

She still didn't know where he was taking this conversation. Slowly, he began to secure her cape. Before he covered her breasts, he tasted each one again. She didn't understand the man.

While he was still grinning, he adjusted the cloak over her shoulders finishing with the frogs. "You haven't had your woman's time since we were married."

"True."

Heat suffused her entire body.

"Clare, are you increasing? You don't intend to keep this a secret, do you? Would you harm our child?"

She hit him, a solid punch to his chest. "Of course not!"

~ * ~

Michael woke slowly. He felt different. To sleep heavy eyes, muted light slanted in through the balcony window. When he tried to stretch, he couldn't. Wanting to hold his wife in his arms, he attempted to turn. Still sleepy, he narrowed his eyes in a failed attempt to see better. His mind raced. *No!*

Suddenly, he bolted wide-awake. His eyes opened to see his wife, quite as naked as he liked to see her sitting beside him. The tips of her beautiful breasts puckered tightly with the early morning chill. She was ginning hugely, smug, proud of herself. In his mind, he registered the sight, realized the development for what it was. He was in her power. She would proceed as she wished.

It was almost that same moment he comprehended his wrists were bound to the headboard, his legs also bound to the foot of the bed. He found himself spread eagle in front of his wife, quite as helpless as the day he was born. This wasn't to be. Quite handedly, she'd done what she swore to do. He wished to applaud her. This was the discipline she spoke to him about. Of course, he could not manage the applause. He was open to whatever mischief she planned. He quite appreciated the thought as well as her strategy.

"How did you manage this without waking me. Usually, I'm a light sleeper," his query was deep, throaty as he was rapidly becoming aroused.

His sex was coming to life just thinking about what she had in store for him. In a moment his member would be standing at attention.

Her finger tripped along his jaw then down his neck. She hesitated at his pulse point just as he would have done to her. "Your punishment, Michael, is just beginning. You were a bad boy when you made me stand naked while you had your wicked way with me, while you fondled my breasts, touched me intimately. That was not something I could appreciate. It was what you intended though. I could have made a public display of your humiliation. I chose not to. Mr. Chalmers most likely had a bout of apoplexy when he realized what you were about right in front of him. Now, I'm going to do the same for you, teach you a much-needed lesson in comportment. Your blood will be hot too."

He considered that he liked this form of discipline. He could hardly wait to see what she would do next. This scenario was derived from his wildest imagination. Who would have thought his once timid wife would dream up this scenario?

Clare ran one finger down the center of his chest to his groin. She stopped without touching him even though he vividly sprang to life eons ago. He groaned as she bent over to bite one of his nipples then the other. The hard tips of her breasts sashayed delightfully across his chest. This was not what he expected. Her fingers danced along his body. She teased his legs with kisses and tiny nips from her small white teeth.

"A wife seducing a husband is hardly punishment."

He thought if he climaxed just now, he would be embarrassed to the tips of his toes. He didn't want to be unmanned in front of her. His sigh brought a realization that perhaps he'd done that to her, embarrassed her to the tips of her toes. Well, he had good reason. Maybe the discipline wasn't as good as he thought it might be. Next time, if there was a next time, he would have to make sure more than one man saw what he was doing without seeing her naked. That was the problem. Only one person witnessed her climax. If she tried to race again, more people watching would certainly teach her more thoroughly. No, that wasn't such a grand scheme. When that happened, in his mind the one man had been one man too many to witness something so tenderly private between them. He'd been sorely tempted to end the punishment before it reached the proper pinnacle. There had to be another way to drive his point home. He would think on the problem.

While she continued to kiss his entire body, the smooth softness of her hair slid across him, his chest, his legs, his swollen manhood. Everywhere the strands touched they burned with silken fire. He nearly jumped out of his body when her mouth closed around his sex. How the devil did she learn to do that? He was about to explode. If she didn't stop, he was bound to detonate. He would not be able to return the exquisite pleasure to both of them.

More than anything he needed to wrap his arms around her. He craved control. She was in charge, not him. Perhaps this was to be his discipline the loss of control. Maybe they both had things they should learn about each other. A man's authority was necessary for a smoothly run household as well as sexual pleasure. Or was it?

When she nipped, kissed as well as laved the length of his rod with her beautiful soft mouth, he thought surely he would ignite. Suddenly, his legs were untied. She sat atop him, straddling him. Her wet slick core touched down on his rod. She was so very hot. Forever, since his wedding night, he wanted her to ride him. Once more she assumed power. Gladly, for this instance, he would hand over the reins to this mating.

Slowly, exquisitely, she positioned herself so his member touched her core, slipping a hair inside. A firestorm pulsed around the tip. "Would you like me to sit on you?" Her voice was dark, sultry as well, honeyed, and sweet.

The sultry sound seduced him further. He felt her wetness, the slickness that invited him inside along with the swollen heat. He groaned then nodded. She took him inside then stopped to look down at their joining. Not for one second after the next second did she move. The pulses of her body stimulated him until he thought he could stand no more.

"Untie me."

His words were a command. He didn't think she would like the tone or the tenor. He understood he was right when she frowned at him, shaking her head, her hair dancing around her breasts, her tight pink nipples playing hide and seek among the long strands.

"That was not the best choice of words in this situation. You need to learn a bit of submissiveness. The lesson will not be learned unless you pay attention. A woman should have every right a man has. Don't you think? A woman jockey, although unusual, should be allowed to race if she is competent. Don't you think? Her physical strength should not be an issue if she can control her mount."

Once more she stared at their joining then back to meet his gaze. She made an erotic picture, one he meant to keep firmly planted throughout eternity in his poor man's brain.

Good God, did she consider him her mount? The thought held an interesting ring to it a certain appeal. Time to see this scenario to the most proper conclusion was upon him. "Clare!"

His hips jerked up when she moved upward. Slowly, she slid down his shaft then again and again. Each move was precise, sending him exactly where she wanted him to go.

She enticed him, brought him to the brink of no return over then over again. His nipples seemed to fascinate her. Her fingers played with them, fondled them, flicked across them. He didn't want to answer her since she was totally wrong in her assumptions. She could not hold her own with the strength of the men who would race against her. If the race was simply a race and not a contest of brute force, at times he might agree with her. As the situation stood, he could not. Nothing she could ever do would change his mind.

"You crave control, Michael. You are not pleased unless you dictate to everyone."

She bent over. Her lips molded to his. Her hands framed his face as she swept her tongue inside. He met her head on, fenced with her. Her tiny mewl of pleasure pleased him. She was seducing herself. That was exactly what he did at the race.

He closed his eyes against the waves of pleasure that were almost there but not there. She would cease her teasing when she thought him close to spewing his seed inside her depths. He needed to touch her, bring her to her release before he erupted with the ecstasy she created. If he didn't agree with her, he might remain in this position the rest of his life.

Admitting to something he couldn't concur with was not tenable. "A man needs to rule his household."

He watched the tilt of her chin, the small lines running horizontally along her forehead. Knew she'd won this bout with him.

"Do you take me for a fool? An idiot? A woman unable to make decisions concerning her life?"

She moved just a hair then froze. One fingertip touched his lips. She leaned forward to kiss him again. This time the caress was feather light not meant to coax or even wheedle a reaction. The touch was hardly enough to be described as a kiss. In the process though the pretty pink tips of her breasts touched upon him. The coolness of her hair glided smoothly across his overheated body. He was a man damned simply because he could not, would not ever let her hurt herself.

Between his teeth he gritted out the best answer he could come up with. Most of what he told her he believed wholeheartedly. He needed ease from this untenable position she had him in. "What I believe is that you're undoubtedly the smartest woman I know as well as the best horsewoman."

"A calculated answer meant to alleviate your situation," she murmured softly. "While the compliment is pleasing, the words are not what I wish to hear at the moment."

He bent toward some new ideas, perhaps a few words that would ease her mind about him. "In woman things you certainly can make fantastic decisions. I have complete trust in those decisions."

Daintily, she cocked her head to the side, her hair once more sending a silken wave of fire across him. "What pray tell is a woman thing?" She moved slightly, up then down. The gesture was not enough. "Perhaps I should leave now. I don't appreciate your answers. You need more learning time. Thinking about your answers along with what they mean is imperative. Maybe you need to contemplate some of your archaic male thoughts."

"No!"

He wanted to put his hands on her hips. Needed to touch as well as kiss every sweet inch of her. He thought his hands might be getting numb, his fingers unmovable.

"Woman things..." He swallowed hard, clenching his numbing fingers searching for an answer that would appease. "Are about cooking and sewing. They are about babies and raising children as well as running a household, planning menus. Don't women sit around knitting as well as speaking of their children?"

He was becoming more and more baffled with each second that passed. He didn't understand her. She never did woman things. He had the reluctant thought that he might have just insulted her.

"Why can't woman things be racing horses? Why can't woman things be something other than the stereotype put out by men? Men want women to wait on them hand and foot."

She lifted herself from him. Sashayed her adorable bottom to the tray that must have been set on the table before he woke.

"Because she is delicate, needs protecting. Women are fragile."

He was desperate to put an end to this. Nonetheless, he seemed incapable of lying so that she would untie him.

With a butter knife held in the air, she pointed it at him, at his sex. "A woman does not need protection. This is not the Middle Ages. Perhaps that might have been true then. It is not now. You will have to reassess your ways."

"Because you are pregnant, damn you, with my child!" He had not meant to lose his temper. He was at the end of his patience. She would do what he commanded when he did so.

Not now, when she has the upper hand.

"Well then, when I'm not increasing you will allow me to race?"

She lifted an eyebrow, which infuriated him. It was a damn masculine gesture. She had no idea. He wasn't going to fall for this trap she set.

"I didn't say that," he ground out. "You will not ever race. I will keep you constantly pregnant."

"Constantly pregnant? I don't like that, Mr. Flannigan. Sounded to me like you said I could race when I'm not pregnant. If not that, what did you say? I will never race? You're wrong. I will find a means to satisfy my female needs. I was born to race."

"I'm going to punish you for this. You will not find the discipline enjoyable. This is hell, Clare You have to see that my way is the right way."

She sat down then crossed her legs. Her breasts moved softly. Her nipples were so beautiful and large, larger now because she carried his child deep inside her. He wanted to suck them deeply into his mouth. Wished to fondle them then tug them to tight hard buds.

"As soon as you tell me what I wish to hear, I'll give you your freedom."

She smiled at him, took a bite of the scone she'd just buttered. She moved so he could see her most intimately. The blasted woman knew what she did to him. She teased ruthlessly. He was more aroused now than when she left him.

"I can't do that, tell you what you want to hear, Clare. Eventually, Old Suzzy will find me then she will get rid of the bonds holding me here. When she does that, I will find you. That's a promise I will damn well keep!" He wanted to yowl with his frustration along with his fear for her. "You don't understand that even though most jockeys are slight, they are men, they are stronger than you."

"Hmmm...who has you tied up and at their mercy? It is me, a mere woman who doesn't have the strength to protect herself from the male species."

"You do," he admitted grudgingly, "however you tied me up when I was asleep, took advantage of a circumstance. The feat was accomplished by guile and stealth. In the real world you will rarely have such an opportunity. You would not be able to accomplish such a feat if I'd been awake."

She sighed then, her beautiful huge nipples beckoning him to taste as they wavered. "You are much larger than me. Take Sirus, he must be only slightly larger. He would only be slightly stronger if at all."

"I would guess he's a few inches taller and outweighs you by a hefty thirty pounds, possibly more. Men are hard, possess more muscle per pound. If you discovered that truth, would you capitulate, Clare?" He felt a moment of exhilaration. She might give in, might be receptive to the argument put forth.

"You think so?" she blinked a few times.

Nevertheless, she made no move toward him.

"Yes, untie me. After we've played this out to its proper conclusion, we will get the scale along with the measuring stick. If he is larger than you then you will give me your word that you will not race."

"All right. What if I'm larger than Sirus?"

"You are not."

She stiffened, however, she walked toward him. "I'm certain that I must outweigh him. He is such a stick."

"We will see. The two of you could arm wrestle," he grinned as she pulled the strings that held his wrists in place.

Before she could say another word, he set her atop him. After that he brought her to a climax she would remember for the rest of her life. Instead of outside her, he wrung himself out inside her sweetness. This time he did not embarrass himself.

~ * ~

As it turned out, Sirus was a good three inches taller. He also outweighed her by thirty-five pounds of solid muscle. She promised, grudgingly. Michael understood this would not be over until she proved herself on a racetrack. He decided then and there, he would find some innocuous race where she could easily win astride Duster, a race where he could pay the jockeys to leave her alone. His sigh of desolation rang through him. If he did such a thing, she would just grow bolder either that or she would figure out what he did. He didn't wish to contemplate the retaliation.

This morning Clare left for a ride. Big Tom went with her. He spent the morning training Gypsy. Damian Andrews along with his son Jess, arrived midafternoon. They brought two beautiful bay mares. Duster would cover them tomorrow.

Damian was leaning against the railing of Gypsy's stall. "When did you say your wife will be back? I'd like to get a good look at your stallion before tomorrow."

"Soon, she left a few hours ago. In fact, she should be here now." Michael wiped sweat from his forehead with the back of his arm. He worried, always worried about her. Big Tom was with her though. All would be fine.

"Raynard has not been seen for over a month now," Michael murmured the words, was surprised he said them aloud.

"Raynard?" Damian asked as he stroked Gypsy's nose. "The man poses some kind of problem for you? Why?"

"He was the overseer of the slaves here at Mayfair. Fired him back in July. The man swore retribution."

Michael watched Jess Andrews stroke the foals who were now a couple of months old. The young man possessed a tender hand. He would be a great horse breeder.

"Heard in town when we were asking directions to Mayfair you freed the slaves. My own are also free. Though the only slaves I purchased were given their freedom as soon as they worked off their purchase price."

Michael told them the story of Juney, the little slave girl who was whipped along with Clare's part in her rescue. When he finished, he shaded his hand over his eyes searching up river, the direction Clare rode this morning.

"Would you consider selling either of these young foals?" The question came from Jess.

Michael turned his attention from Clare's tardiness. He chuckled softly. "No, along with Duster, those two are the basis for the stud farm. The mares have immaculate bloodlines. There ancestry cannot be disputed. You have good taste as well as a good eye for horse flesh."

"Just thought I'd ask," Jess said, a wide grin on his boyishly handsome face.

He was the mirror image of his father. This boy would crush hearts as he was certain Damian had.

"We've thoughts of racing too. None of my horses have bloodlines dating back to Fearnought or Byerley Turk. How did you get Duster?" Damian asked, his curiosity seeming to be peaked.

"Clare's brother-in-law purchased him for her. He wanted to see her succeed in this endeavor. We are doing quite well with the cover fees along with the winnings from races."

Ah, Michael thought of the punishment and discipline meted out in the last few days. He thought on the way his wife pleaded with him not to caress and fondle her in front of the people. If he wasn't mistaken, even though she enjoyed the climax, she did learn a valuable lesson. He hoped he wouldn't have to think of something else. He didn't want to hurt her. He prayed that he would always be a few steps ahead of her plotting.

"Timmie," Michael felt as if he waited long enough. "Would you saddle three horses?"

He turned to Damian. "Would the two of you enjoy a ride along the river? I can assure you picturesque scenery is quite beautiful this time of year with all the autumn colors on display. The ride is also beautiful in the spring when the wildflowers begin to bloom. We'll go as far as the cave." Ah, now spring made him think on their first kiss. After that, the second one when he fondled her breasts for the first time. She was so very passionate.

"I'll ride Jingle Bells. You two can flip a coin for the pleasure of riding Gypsy."

Michael laughed at the look in Damian's eyes when he mentioned the mare's name. "My brother-in-law has his cherished ones. They are children he has rescued from abuse. It is my most learned opinion that the children named both mares. The other one is Maid Marion."

"Jess can ride Gypsy. Midnight is quite the mount for me today."

They started off at a canter. Michael yearned to gallop the horses all the way to the cave. He didn't think they would go there. Big Tom hated that cave as did Clare. Told him there were abundant supernatural stories about the place. He wouldn't ever go in that place.

"Sounds like just the spot," Jess laughed as he pulled even with Michael as well as his father. "I like to explore caves."

They turned down the lane heading toward the river. Michael's heart was in his throat. He had a bad feeling about this. Somehow, he knew something had happened to Clare. The hairs on the back of his neck stood on end. It wasn't like Clare to be this tardy. He recalled the last time she went missing. The result was a dislocated shoulder along with bruised ribs as well as one that was broken. Midnight might have died if not for her quick thinking.

"I'm certain all is fine. We'll most likely find them walking the horses or..." Damian's voice trailed off as they looked west along the river.

"Perhaps we should hurry a bit more." It was Jess speaking this time.

When the explosion rocked the ground sending shock waves pulsing through the air, with nothing said between them they gave the horse's free reign.

"Clare!" His heart pounded to his throat.

~ * ~

"No, Jillian we won't do anything about Clare. I don't want the chit enough to risk my reputation or this plantation. No woman has that much worth. Don't want to go against the law. She would cry rape simply because to have her, I would have to force her. It would be inevitable. I'll have to satisfy myself with your favors until a riper creature comes along."

The pair were drinking brandy. She sat on his thighs while his hand explored the length of her leg. Biff's wife visited relatives up north in Philadelphia. Coupled with Jillian he had the house to himself. While it was fun to find sexual pleasure in unique places, one's bed was always nice.

"I don't understand you, Biff. I thought...well I believed you would do this for me."

She postured for him thrusting her breasts out as if the blatant gesture would cause him to change his mind.

"It's too early for an argument. Let's go for a walk. Perhaps that secluded glen would be quite the place. I'll carry a blanket."

"Why, Biff? Not the glen now, want to talk about the doing in of the Flannigans."

"Numerous reasons come to mind. The best and most persuasive is that Raynard wants vengeance. Revenge is the dominant thought in his head. He assures me both Clare as well as Michael will get what they deserve. All I wanted was to bed the girl not kill her."

"You believe Raynard? Even I know he is a deceitful evil man."

She tossed back the remainder of her glass. When she pushed off his lap then stepped to the window, she pulled back the draperies looking out onto the vast expanse of lawn in front of the plantation.

"Yes, spoke with the man three nights ago. He is bent on doing this."

Biff appreciated the slim line of her back. She was tall for a girl. Her long white legs when wrapped around him were quite delightful. Her hips curved pleasantly, her fanny soft, rounded just right for his hands.

"He won't find Clare alone. We tried that route when you weren't so cowardly, Biff. Now you don't have the balls to take a risk. She's never left to her own devices. If not accompanied by Michael, Big Tom is guarding her."

"No, she isn't. That's precisely why Raynard had to come up with a plan. This will work. After the last accident, her roaming habits are predictable. She always rides along the river. Never goes into the wooded area. Raynard will be there today, on the river. He will pretend to need help. Believe he has a dog in mind that needs rescuing. The man much preferred to borrow one of the young slave girls who have been seeing him. Quickly, I put an end to that idea."

"How?" Jillian looked as if she didn't believe what he was saying had a prayer of a chance in its success. "How is a dog going to help achieve his ends? Surely, the two will recognize him then run the other way. Whoever she has riding guard duty will not allow her to get close."

Biff tossed his head back then hooted with laughter. "From everything Raynard has told me, the little missy is impulsive. Despite the possibility she might come to harm, she will come to the poor creature's rescue. She would not let another animal suffer."

"Big Tom will follow. He wouldn't be able to allow her to go to the animal's aid on her own."

Amused by this scenario, Biff grinned. Perhaps he should have allowed him to use one of his slaves. "He might still use Juney, one of Flannigan's freed slaves. That would be the perfect tool to use against Clare."

"So, they will go to help the dog or perhaps the enticement will be Juney. What then? In any scenario overpowering Big Tom would be difficult even though Raynard is not exactly small."

Biff lifted his shoulders, still feeling the merriment cavort through him. "He'll shoot the man, render him unable to come to Clare's aid. Clare will be his to do with as he pleases."

"That might work. Is he shooting to kill or render helpless?" Jillian asked walking toward him now, one finger flirtatiously touching her lips, her well-rounded hips swinging delightfully, her long hair sliding down the length of her.

Biff wanted to caress them, frame her buttocks with his large hands after that explore more thoroughly.

"He says just to render the large man unable to come to her aid. Where Raynard is concerned one never knows. She is most likely riding her favorite stallion, Duster. Raynard plans to steal the horse, perhaps to start up his own stable."

"Well, that will set the stud farm back a bit."

She laughed while she ran a finger along Biff's jaw. Her eyes darkened. "What is he going to do with Clare? Steal her as well?"

While he wanted to toss her skirts this instant, Biff was a patient man. He would see this through. He wanted her in that secluded glen. Wanted to see her white flesh caressed by sunlight.

"No, Raynard would find that the Stewart clan would bear down on him. I'm not at all sure about his plans. When I asked, his grin turned evil. Perhaps he didn't want to tell me."

She snorted disbelief in her eyes. "They are all in Scotland. Months would pass before they could do damage to him. By then his trail would be cold. America is a large and in places uncivilized land. Though it is best you don't know what the man plans."

His hoot of laughter surprised her. America was uncivilized in just about every city and state.

"True about the Scotland part. You're also right about the travel time. It would only take a few months both ways for them to unite here in Virginia. Raynard wants to head west, start as the overseer on another plantation. He believes there are others that would appreciate his ways of dealing with the slaves. He will take Duster with him. He will somehow do away with Clare without leaving her body where the corpse can be found. What do you think? Is his plan a good one?"

Her eyes widened as if she came to the same conclusion as he did. "He's putting Clare in the cave. How will he keep her there? I suppose he could bind her then go deep inside. I've heard that cave is vast. With all the twists and turns, she might get herself lost." With glee she rubbed her hands together. "I will have Michael all to myself."

Biff told Jillian enough times Michael would never have her. He wasn't going to say the words again. In time, she would learn as well as accept the truth. His only regret with this plan was that he would never have Clare beneath him. He would never feel her soft breasts or see all that lovely white flesh of hers. No, he would have to make do with the whores who plied their trade outside of town, Jillian as well.

Regrets. I will have to deal with each and every one of them.

Disappointments could so get in the way of one's life. He understood if the girl lived, he wouldn't have that pleasure either. Michael would continue to keep her well and truly to himself.

Ah, his thoughts shifted to the present. Jillian didn't like it when they made love in the outdoors. She would pout prettily. Complaints would frolic from her lips. He didn't care how she whined. With her hand inside his as well as a blanket tucked over his arms, he headed for the secluded glen, carnal pleasures with this very willing lady at the forefront of his mind.

He thoroughly enjoyed the walk. She held back, acting true to form, complaining about the dirt along with the nasty bugs. The way Jillian pouted when she didn't get her way, sent lust to every manly part he possessed. At this moment, he was hard as steel. Today would be a completely enjoyable tryst with his accomplished lover. Momentarily, he'd been surprised when she divulged her brief stay in New York.

She told him she meant to move to Williamsburg in a few weeks. Ah, he would miss her. Perhaps he could see her every month or so. No, he would never pay the exorbitant fees she charged. When she visited here, he would have her free of charge. He could wait. There were senators along with judges living in the capital city who would pay her handsomely for her favors. A few weeks ago, she decided she would set up her business just as the madam in New York had done. She would be rich as Midas.

When the blast rocked the ground beneath them, Biff was deep inside Jillian. He laughed then lost his seed inside his fetching paramour.

Ah, he would miss her. Nonetheless, there would be others to take her place.

Chapter Ten

Clare heard the cries of pain. The girl was screaming now. She saw Juney curled into a tight ball, her hands over her head. She lay close to the water's edge, waves lapping against her. Raynard stood over her his whip in hand, lashing her while she shrieked. Blood dripped from the girl's back and buttocks. It seemed he didn't leave one place untouched. Raynard yelled at her to get up. She whimpered, her soft cries wrenching Clare's heart.

All this time she was certain Raynard would come for her. Instead, he wanted the sweet black girl who'd done nothing except refuse his advances. Clare learned later he did force her. He just wanted a reason to beat her. Maliciously, Raynard enjoyed inflicting pain. The girl wouldn't fight. She didn't know how to do so. Her entire life she'd been trained to be submissive.

Clare spurred Duster to a gallop. She raced forward, unthinking straight to the man. Juney was too small, too frightened to resist to put up any kind of defense. She would do whatever Raynard wanted. Michael would be furious with her. His fury would have to wait. Whatever he wanted to tell her, she would accept as fact. He would be right. Nonetheless, she couldn't watch then not do anything.

"Stop, Little Missy! I'll go get her!" Big Tom yelled out while he reached for Duster's reigns in an attempt to keep her from flying into the midst of what would be a battle. He missed. He cursed. "Don't!"

The pounding of Maid Marion's hooves echoed behind her as she flew forward intent on one thing. Her heart pounded in her throat reverberating in her ears. Before she reached the couple, she had second thoughts. She remembered how the whip felt across her back. Recalled the agony, the healing time. Over her shoulder, she looked for Big Tom then thought better. Only fear was getting in her way.

None of that mattered now. Juney mattered.

When she was close, she pulled the big stallion to a sliding halt then leapt from his back. In a moment, she was atop the overseer, hanging on to his arm, kicking at him. Her toes met his knee. The violence was met by a yowl of fury.

"Stop! Stop this instant!"

He tossed her off. Clare flew through the air to land on the soft dirt along the bank. Her head felt dazed, lines blurred in her head. After she lay sprawled on the riverbank, he lifted his gun then pointed the muzzle at Big Tom who charged forward.

Big Tom yanked on the reins. The horse reared, startled by the sudden change of command. The horse's hooves came down on the soft riverbank. Big Tom slid off the mare. He froze as he stared at Raynard, holding his hands outward. "Now, ya don't want to do dat. There are witnesses. You'll have to kill all of us."

Raynard grinned, his slightly yellowed teeth showing. "Fell right into my plans the two of you did. Knew you would come to the rescue of the little slut. She's not what she seems." His finger pulled on the trigger seeming to delight in the fear he created. "Killing all three of you? Well, that's a good suggestion. Wonder why I didn't think of it."

"No!" Clare raced toward him, reaching him and jerking his arm just as the gun fired. "No!" She turned to see Big Tom. She looked back to Juney who was still curled into a tiny whimpering ball. For a moment, only the softly lapping water on the bank's edge could be heard.

Big Tom yelled at her then his knees seemed to buckle. He fell on the ground in a heap.

Ignoring Raynard, she directed her attention to her friend, her guard. "You've killed him."

She reached Big Tom. Heard the moan of pain. Saw the blood pooling from his shoulders.

No, he isn't dead. She looked to the sky. *Thank you.*

"I'm fine, Little Missy. Just a small wound, nothing to worry over. Take care." He closed his eyes then fell limp.

Raynard stood over her. One hand fisted. "Damn you to hell and back. You ruined my shot!"

He hauled back his fist. When his knuckles hit the side of her head, she slumped to the ground. For a moment she saw the blackness, bright lights floating around her then nothing.

Clare blinked a few times as she started to regain her senses. Her ears were ringing, blood pounded, taking each breath more difficult than the last. Blackness surrounded her. Her head pounded horribly. She decided she must be in the cave. She finally opened her eyes then searched the immediate area for Big Tom. He would be afraid. The big man thought these caves held supernatural spirits. He might have died trying to protect her. Oh god, oh god no...she acted so damn foolishly. Michael was right about her. She didn't have one ounce of common sense in her head. She couldn't fight a man. She wasn't strong enough. She should have learned her lesson the first time she tried.

Now this.

Within a few seconds she found him, trussed up tight, his arms bound behind his back. His feet were tied as well.

"Are you alright?"

Stupid question. She saw the blood on his shoulder before Raynard hit her.

"I be fine. You jus' worry about yourself. Got to figure out a way to get out of here.

"I can do that. I know how to get us out of the cave."

Her fingers fumbled with the knots. She sat back on her heels trying to remember what Michael showed her when they visited the cave so many months ago. First things first, she needed to finish untying him. Groping, she managed to unbind his hands. With his hands freed he managed to undo the rope around his ankles. They were impossibly tight. Beneath her breath she swore. She was afraid, horribly afraid. Darkness closed in upon her weighing down her chest. She had to remain calm and steady. More than anything she wanted Michael here with her, as she needed to feel his strength. Deep in her mind she repeated his directions knowing this saving business was up to her, no one else.

"No need to do dat, Little Missy. You'll think of something," Big Tom said. "I trust you."

Michael told her how to save herself just in case something

happened to her in the cave. She laughed at him then. There was no laughter now, only grating terror. How could he possibly know this would happen? Well, she would have to recall all the instructions. First though, she would have to find the lantern a long with the fire sticks.

"Dat man closed up dis cave. He was laughing, talking in gibberish. He mad crazy dat man is," Big Tom said, his voice trembling, his terror showing in the quaking of his voice. "Sent all those rocks tumbling to the ground. I couldn't do anything for you. Juney is here too, just a bit down dat way. He wants all of us to die. Raynard is an evil man, wicked all the way through."

With her eyes shut for a moment, she tried to remember. Juney was here. She half expected Raynard to take the young girl with him. Well, it didn't matter that she shut her eyes. In the cave there was no light. She ran her hands along the wall. The stone was rough to her touch. For several feet she traveled in one direction.

"What you lookin' for? Maybe I can help."

"Oh, if I don't go far enough, I won't find the tiny niche where the lantern is. If I don't go the other way..."

She thought she was mumbling to herself. It was the only way she could keep the terror at bay.

"You want a niche?" Big Tom, asked the sound of his voice seeming to improve. "Unlike you, I was conscious when he drug me inside. You're going the wrong direction. Keep talking to me so I know where you are. What are you looking for in this niche?"

She appreciated the help. If Big Tom knew where to look, perhaps they would have light. "Michael has a lantern along with a few other things stashed in the small opening somewhere in this wall. He showed me where it was. If I could only see even my hand, it would help."

"I'll be your eyes. You just keep chattering. I'll know just where you are. We'll have that lantern in no time," Big Tom said with a soft chuckle. "Imagine me being eyes and ears for you."

She felt as if she heard his smile. A grin from Big Tom would be unexpected. He must be keeping his fear at bay to help her. She was afraid. She'd never been so terrified and helpless in her entire life. Clare understood how to save all of them. All she need do was find the damn lantern. Nonetheless, the cave wasn't getting any lighter.

She spoke of nonsensical things as she moved slowly along the wall. She tried to think of things to tell them that would give hope. "Michael will look for us. Juney," she paused, "you alright?"

She whimpered softly. Clare had not had time to look at her back. She'd seen the blood though.

"Y-yes..."

Well, for now that would have to do. Juney would have to be able to walk unless Big Tom could carry her.

"Don't think he or anyone else will be able to remove those rocks. We're going to die in here. Doesn't make no difference about ghosts and witchcraft workin' their spells in here or findin' a lantern. We're all going to die."

What he said wasn't a question, more of a statement. Clare didn't want to hear his fear. Now, she heard Juney moan. Up until now her life had been carefree and easy. She supposed she should tell them about the second opening. It would never do any good unless she found the lantern along with the fire sticks.

"No one's going to die today or anytime soon. How is your shoulder?" She thought she remembered seeing a few bandages in a small tin box near the lantern where the fire sticks were. Michael did tell her there were other things.

"A lantern is not going to keep anyone alive," Big Tom said as if he was now resigned to that fate. "Unless there is a second way out of this place, we're going to die."

"You didn't answer me about your shoulder." She tripped on jagged rock, cursed softly.

"No, Little Missy I didn't. The way I see dis, my shoulder is the least of our troubles. I haven't lost much blood. Suppose dat's a good thing. I'm not weak. When we got us some light then we'll look for 'nother way out."

"Do you think you can carry Juney? He must have whipped her more than the last time."

She worried about both of them, wished she could see how bad they were hurt. Big Tom didn't sound terrified. Nonetheless, she knew he was. Juney only moaned and whimpered. What she recalled when she dashed crazily to save the girl, the bodice of her dress ragged hanging on her shoulders in thin strips that did little to conceal.

"I can walk," the tiny voice quivered. "I can walk. It's just dat it don't seem as if dere's a reason. Where do you plan on walking?"

"As soon as I light the lantern, I'll show you. After that we can be on our way out of here. I know where there is another opening to this place."

She didn't want to get any hopes up too high. Lighting the lantern then finding the marks leading to the opening at the river seemed to be monumental tasks at the moment. Raking her mind, she tried to recall everything Michael showed her.

When she finally reached the hollowed-out section where the lantern was supposed to be, she fell forward scraping her face and hands on the rocks. Nonetheless, she was pleased with her find.

Fumbling on the floor with her hands, she found the lantern, then the box that held the fire sticks. With the lantern lit, she stepped back, proud of herself. She held it high. Big Tom was pale from the loss of blood. Juney was still curled into the tight ball shivering. She didn't know how either of them was going to walk very far, let alone swim if they had to swim.

That brought another problem to mind she had not thought of. With a deep breath afraid she knew the answer. "Can you swim, Big Tom?"

"No, 'fraid of water."

Well, she wasn't surprised. "Juney?"

"No one ever taught me."

This plan was going from bad to worse. She meant to look on the bright side. Happily, she gazed at the lantern. Never before had she been so pleased to see light. Clare didn't think she would ever take light for granted now that she knew how deep blackness felt.

"We should get going. Come along both of you. I'm going to get you out of this nasty place. Michael showed me several months ago how to go about saving myself."

Clare decided then and there she didn't like caves any more than

Big Tom. This time she felt like whistling. She didn't. They weren't out of the cave yet. If she missed even one of the marks, they might be hopelessly lost. If that happened, it would take a miracle to find them.

She helped Juney to her feet. Juney struggled hunched over. Nonetheless, she walked on her own. Big Tom pushed from the floor of the cave, a strange look in his eyes. It seemed he might finally believe her about the second opening.

"D'ere is another way out of dis here place?" He sounded hopeful.

For a few seconds he leaned against the side of the cave as if he tried to steady himself. "Jus' catching my breath. Must have stood too fast."

"Yes, I'm going to get us out of the cave. Come along."

She held the light as high as she could for as long as she could. After several turns, she allowed the beacon to swing in her hand. They would have to make do, at least the light showed against the floor.

"I can hold dat if you like, Little Missy."

Big Tom stepped up. He smiled at her. "Must be heavy for that scrawny little arm of yours. My wife wouldn't have one bit of trouble holdin dat lantern high. She's a big woman though. Got to be big enough for me."

He took the lantern from her. The light bounced off the walls as well as the floor.

Clare grinned. His wife was tall, broad of shoulder too. He was right. She was big enough for him. The trio started on their way again as she marked each place to turn. Big Tom walked beside her, Juney behind. The atmosphere of cold silence didn't bother her. She knew she saw every mark, made every turn correctly. They would find the opening soon. She counted five turns. That was exactly how she remembered.

Reaching the opening of the cave seemed to take a lifetime. When she traveled the tunnels with Michael, the distance didn't seem so far. She had not been terrified for her life on that day. Today, her heart thundered while her breaths rasped in and out of her lungs. She shook either from the damp cold of the cave or fear. She supposed the reason made no difference. They were walking down tunnels then suddenly blue sky beckoned. The light blinded her until her eyes adjusted. They weren't lost.

The pool of rushing water was high. Beyond the opening the current appeared treacherously fast. Her heart skipped a beat in delight then fear at the rapidly moving water.

When the river was low, usually in the summer Michael told her one could walk out. At this time of year, the water was brown, filled with silt, runoff from the recent storms as well as too high to walk from the cave. Walking out today would not be possible. She would have to swim to shore then walk back to Mayfair Hall. Michael would have to bring a boat for the other two.

Did he even know she was missing?

It seemed to her Big Tom read her thoughts. "Dat husband of yours will be searching for you. He knows you always ride along the river. I'll bet if he showed you dis here cave, he's coming for you as we stand here lookin' outside. He would have heard dat explosion. Your man would hightail it right here to see what happened."

That was all true. However, he was busy with the Andrews men talking horses. He might not even be aware of the time. At least it wasn't dark. If the sun had set, she would have had to stay here until daybreak. This was good. Yes, sunlight was good. She brought in a deep breath of air, readying herself for the cold swim.

"Are the two of you going to be all right here without me?" she asked as she looked from one to the other.

Protective feelings surged within. While she didn't want to leave them, she didn't see another choice. "Remember, Big Tom, ghosts don't haunt this place. You've just heard too many far-fetched tales. There is nothing to be afraid of now that we know we can leave."

She understood he was thinking that was easier for her to say than for him to do.

"What you got in mind?" Big Tom asked, his curiosity seeming to get the better of him.

The look he slanted her told her would most likely object when he heard. He would believe she was going into the river. It was true. She couldn't wait for someone to miss her. She wasn't about to delay a moment. If she did, the sky would turn dark. No one, not even Michael would attempt a rescue in the dark.

"Don't worry about me. All will turn out just fine."

She smiled then touched his shoulder. The gesture was meant to reassure. Clare was certain her gesture had the opposite result.

His features turned to a grimace, scowl lines forming along his broad forehead. He shook a finger at her as if that would help him make his point. "You need to just sit here tight, wait for dat man of yours to come for you. You know he will," Big Tom said while shaking his head. "You can't go into dat water. If something happened to you, Mr. Flannigan will skin me alive. Like my skin just the way it is right now."

"He won't do anything of the sort. He will be pleased you protected me from Raynard. I promise you nothing will happen to me. I'm going for a short swim that's all. After my swim, I intend to walk to Mayfair Hall. I'll bring back Michael along with Timmie. They have a boat so we can get the two of you out of here before nightfall."

"Can't let you do dat." Big Tom was shaking his head, his hand stretched toward her as if he meant to keep her from swimming. "Can't let you go into dat swirling water. It's deep and it's runnin' fast"

"I'm a strong swimmer," she countered thinking about his words of warning, a threat that was out of character. Trying to reassure once more, "Nothing will happen to me. I promise you that."

So, for a moment the statement took her aback. If Big Tom chose to do so, he could physically restrain her. He could keep her here on dry land. No, a recently freed man would never possess the audacity to hold a white woman captive. This notion was absurd. She would continue on, as if she didn't want to spend another moment in this cave waiting for rescue that might or might not happen. Besides she was hungry. She had not eaten since early this morning.

"You have no choice in this. I'm not going to sit here through the night waiting for someone to save us, which might not come. I'd like to eat dinner with my husband as well as our guests. I want a glass of wine or two or maybe even three after what has happened today." She needed the lecture over and done with before she went to bed. Clare braced herself for what she knew Michael would tell her. Perhaps there would be more discipline. She wondered what form that would come in. If he made love to her, she didn't care what he did. Besides, there should be no punishment when she did nothing wrong. She rode with his permission. Big Tom accompanied her.

Big Tom was still shaking his head, "Too dangerous, too dangerous, Mr. Flannigan will have my hide if I let you get into dat water. No suh, I can't allow dat to happen."

Clare was smiling now, grinning from ear to ear thinking to pat his shoulder again. She held her hand back. "Rest assured, I will protect you from my husband. Now, it might be prudent if you turned your back. I'm not swimming in all my clothing. The weight of them would surely drag me down."

She almost laughed when his dark skin paled at the mention of her disrobing. No, Big Tom would not stop her. He would give her the privacy she needed.

She meant every last word. With her spleen vented, she began with the fastenings on her shirt. Weighted down would not be a good way to go about swimming in the river. She was heartily pleased she wore her riding britches this morning. She could tie everything around her shoulders then put her clothing on when she reached dry land. Nothing would hinder her arms and legs or drag her down.

"Now, will the two of you survive if I leave you? You won't do anything stupid like run back into the dark cave?" she teased, smiling at the colorless faces in front of her.

"Don't go," Juney said, as she reached out her hand to stop her, the girl's eyes wide with fear. "You wait for your husband like Big Tom says. He will surely be here."

Hell, and damnation, if she had to wait for a man every time, she wanted to do something, she would positively die of boredom. Clare chose to ignore Juney's plea. She walked to her, picked up her hand, held it for a moment. "Juney, I'll be back within the next couple of hours. I'll most likely have to walk back to the hall. Well, I won't be back. I'm positive Michael will not allow me to do so. Nonetheless, you will be rescued hopefully before the sun goes down. The two of you will be home to share dinner with your families."

She wasn't going to wait longer. If Big Tom wanted to protest further, she wouldn't argue. She took everything off down to her chemise.

The sleeves of her riding shirt were tied around her neck, as were the legs of her pants along with her shoes. She was ready to swim if the water was too deep to wade.

When her toes hit the water, she nearly cried out. The river was cold, damn icy. Of course, the water was frigid. This was the first of November. With her shoulders squared, she continued forward. By the time she reached the mouth of the cave the water swirled around her shoulders. She looked behind her hoping to send them one last word of optimism. Clare didn't want to admit to herself she was terrified. Walking out of here was one thing; swimming on the other hand was something entirely different. She was a strong swimmer. *I'm strong.*

"I'll be back in no time."

Well, most likely she wouldn't be back. Michael would never allow that. The bottom dropped away from her feet. She rounded the corner and started swimming. As her husband told her, the distance wasn't far. Less than ten minutes passed and she was striding up the bank. She'd been half afraid Raynard would be there waiting for her. Even though the thought was ridiculous, she couldn't rip the idea from her mind.

The devil, she was cold. A stiff breeze blew from the north. She rubbed her arms in a feeble attempt to warm herself realizing what she needed for warmth was a hot bath or Michael's arms around her. Quickly, she dressed then wished for dry clothes. This situation couldn't be helped. She couldn't have done this any other way.

Praying she wouldn't run into Raynard; she started along the riverbank to the hall. Her legs were tired. Her head still throbbed from where Raynard hit her with his fist. She was terrified she would encounter either Raynard or Biff. With Big Tom in the cave, she had no one to protect her. There was still a ringing in her ears. Funny how she didn't notice the pain from the blow to her head until now. She staggered, gasping for breath. Forced by the agony to her hands and knees, she heaved in air.

Clare sat. She decided to rest for a few seconds before continuing. Her eyelids fluttered closed. She jerked herself awake. This wouldn't do. With determination she stood. She walked, staggering more with each step thinking she must look like a drunken sailor. When she passed the cave opening, she saw the rocks. A chill swept down her backbone. At that moment, she saw the men. The breath rushed from her lungs in a long silent whoosh of air.

"Michael!"

She smiled then slipped to her knees. Relief filled her. They were safe now. She didn't need to walk further. He was racing to her. She couldn't move, yearned to hold out her arms to him. In a moment, he wrapped her in his strong arms then ran his hands along her body. After that it seemed he reassured himself she was alive as well as unhurt.

"Big Tom?" he asked softly. "Is he alright?"

"In the cave. He's afraid of the water. Juney is also there. She doesn't know how to swim. Got to get a boat to them."

She gasped for air while the information they all needed tumbled out. He ran his hand along her back, up then down. She felt the soothing motion while she leaned into him. Tears filled her eyes. She'd never been happier.

"That's what we were just planning. We figured someone was sealed into the cave. We heard the blast," Michael said softly.

His arm was wrapped around her shoulders. It seemed he didn't want to let her go. She didn't want him to either.

"Did Duster come home? He's safe, isn't he? I think Raynard wanted to steal him."

He swept her into his arms. His long strides brought him to Jingle Bells. He was about to help her onto the mare.

"Take her home on Gypsy," Jess said softly. "I'll trade you mounts. Get her home and dry."

Michael nodded at Jess. "Thanks, Timmie took Duster back. It seemed the horse objected in some way to Raynard. We'll most likely never know. We saw the rocks. We were just going for the boat."

"Thought for sure Raynard would have taken the stallion. He wanted us to die. He didn't know there was another way out of the cave. The cavern was so dark I couldn't see my hand. The walls seemed to close in around me. Big Tom helped me find the lantern. I remembered how you showed me to get to the opening." She sounded like a blathering idiot.

"Raynard shot Big Tom. The bullet hit his shoulder. He's going to be fine, at least that's what he says. Juney was whipped again. He used Juney to get to us."

"All three of you are safe. That's all that matters."

She heard his thoughts about what she did. Understood how he was holding his fury back. "Big Tom tried to stop me. I know you're going to be angry. I had to try to keep Raynard from whipping her. I couldn't let him hurt the girl again."

"Furious?" He pulled her tight, his chin resting lightly on her forehead. Against her back, she felt the trembling of his big body. "Furious doesn't even begin to describe my emotions. Thought we'd been over this too many times to count. You don't have the physical strength to go up against a man." Michael gritted out the words while his hands tightened around her, bringing her flush against him. "I could have lost you today." He shook her slightly. "How do you think that makes me feel?"

Clare supposed he was right. She wasn't going to admit to anything though. Perhaps he'd discipline her again. A grin Michael couldn't see formed. No, all she wanted was to be home safe and in his arms. She wanted him to make love to her in their big bed.

They rode up to the house. Damian, Jess along with Timmie were going for Juney as well as Big Tom. They would be home safe in another hour. Sirus saw to Gypsy. In the house Michael called for hot water. Thankful for the bath to warm her she also wanted to feel clean again. The muddy river water stuck to her skin.

Old Suzzy met them, all business as she saw to their needs. "Bring hot water along with wine and food. Don't believe Clare has eaten since this morning. Tell Mammy Jo that Juney was whipped again and that Big Tom was shot in the shoulder. Let Big Tom's wife know he's going to need a great deal of tender loving care for the next few days."

In the bedchamber, he stripped her of the wet clothing. "You didn't try to swim in your clothes, did you?"

Michael didn't wait for an answer. Instead, he covered her in one of his robes. The fabric held his scent, all male and spicy. She wanted his arms wrapped around her to feel heat soak from him into her. God, she wanted to be warm.

When the tub was ready, he watched her slip into the heated water then sigh with the pure pleasure of the heat. He brought her a glass of wine. She realized she was hungry too. The sun was beginning to dip below the horizon. The evening might be dark before they returned. She prayed not.

"Are they going to get them out before the sun gives up the daylight?" She was afraid for Big Tom. "Tom might be terrified in there after the sun slips behind the hills. He is so afraid of ghosts along with other nonsense. How can a man so huge be afraid of something that doesn't exist?"

"I believe so. Drink your wine, Little Pidgeon. They will be back soon. I'm certain of it."

He smiled at her, his voice holding a wealth of different tones.

She didn't like the quality of his voice. There wasn't a doubt in her mind that a lecture was forthcoming. While she bathed, he watched seemed to study her. He brought her a nightgown along with the matching robe. She wanted the armor she wore the night before their wedding.

Meaning to finish this before she became a bundle of seething nerves, she began pointing a finger in his direction, "No matter what you say, I will do the same again. I don't regret my actions."

"Thought you would say that." He sighed pushing his hair from his face. "Slowly, I'm beginning to understand your sense of justice and fair play. They are fine as well as noble. The very real problem revolves around the fact you have no idea what your physical abilities are in comparison to a man. You believe sincerely you are capable of meeting all obstacles on your terms. The fact remains, you cannot. I don't like you putting your life as well as our baby's life in danger."

"Would you want me to allow that man to beat her? Just ride on by as if I didn't see them?" she tossed the question to him, even though she understood what he would say.

Once, not so long ago, she heard his opinion.

"We've been over this before. The answer is still, yes. Nonetheless, just as last time, I would have expected you to come for me. He wanted you not Juney. His was a ploy to send you to him so he could leave you in the cave either that or force you to his will. The other people, Big Tom especially might have been all that held him back."

"In that you're wrong. Raynard still wanted to force that girl. He's wanted her for the longest time. Even though he took her before, he still wants her. Don't believe he cared about me. The only reason he took me was to hurt you. He was thwarted twice. Do you think he will try again?" That thought was too much for her, way too much. Despite the newfound warmth her body shook as shivers iced down her spine. She didn't want to be afraid any longer nor did she wish to remain confined by guards. If he thought Raynard remained in the vicinity, she would continue to feel restrained.

She didn't like the feeling.

"No, if the man is smart, he will cut his loses here. With ease he can get a job elsewhere. Someone will be as mean a cur as Raynard. Might even applaud his methods of keeping the slaves in line. Don't doubt that fact for a second."

~ * ~

Even while he held her gently against him, Michael wanted to shake her until she understood then accepted everything, he told her. He didn't understand how he could make his point. Hell, Clare did comprehend. She didn't listen. Perhaps the problem revolved around the fact she didn't agree. What more needed to happen to her for her to accept the fact she was a woman? She could never do battle against a man.

Now they were wrapped in one large quilt sipping the Bordeaux, quiet for the time being. The veranda was cool. They should go inside before she took a chill. It seemed to him that Clare would always rather sit on the balcony than inside. Before they found themselves on the porch, he built up the fire. They could still watch for the return of the others from inside. Perhaps he should move her close to the fire. She must still be freezing bone-deep.

"I believe the river froze my very soul. I feel the cold bursting from the inside out."

She touched his cheek. Love shone in her eyes. He wished she would tell him how she felt.

He wanted to hear her tell him she loved him again. Instead, if she said anything she would speak only of lust. He guessed that was his fault insisting that he didn't love her that what he felt was simply lust as well as hunger for her. She accepted that fact, took his words to heart.

"We should move inside."

Just as he said the words, the men along with Juney crested the hill in front of Mayfair. He saw Damian give a thumbs up sign. "There they are."

He turned to her. "Just as you hoped, they made it home before sunset."

Earlier he ordered dinner for his guests. The plan for this evening was for all of them to eat together. At this moment, all he wanted was time with his wife, minutes to hold her that would turn into hours. He needed to clasp her safely in his arms for the entire night. It was a reaffirmation of life that he craved. Today had been harrowing at best. The blast stretched every nerve to its snapping point. Before he could spend more time with Clare, he needed to remove himself to the stable to take care of unfinished business. Mammy Jo would be waiting for Juney as well as Big Tom. They both would need healing time.

He was grateful for the protection Big Tom gave his wife. Thanking him again was imperative. He would toss in a small bonus for his loyalty, no perhaps a large bonus would be more the thing. Although, from what he understood so far was that if Raynard wanted, he could have killed all three. Ah, but the man thought he did just that by sealing the cave.

Michael looked heavenward, sending a silent prayer that the man had not succeeded. Clare was still here, very much alive.

Once Clare was settled on the big brocade wing chair in front of the fire, her legs curled up beneath the voluminous robe, a glass of wine along with the bottle on the table beside her, he kissed her tenderly on the lips. Unable to draw away from her, he ran his knuckles lovingly along her cheek. He didn't want to leave her tonight. There was nothing for it. There was so much at Mayfair that needed tending.

"I'm going downstairs until everything is settled. I'll be back as soon as I can. Don't fall asleep." He stepped back, her auburn hair curled endearingly around her shoulders. He yearned to bury his face in the silken strands. Her cheeks were a soft peach probably from the chill of the night. Fire glow shadowed the room casting a warm and romantic ambiance on her delicate features.

His long sigh seemed to catch her attention. She tilted her head toward him, questioning. Her soft, trusting smile sent myriads of emotions coursing through his body. He didn't have one clue how he was going to control his impulsive wife. At the moment, he wasn't doing the job. Unfortunately, she was in charge of herself along with her irrational and dangerous decisions. He could not hover over her every second of the day. That thought was made obvious by her spontaneous behavior this afternoon.

While he walked slowly down the stairs to the main floor, he passed Old Suzzy. In the kitchen when he exited out the backdoor, Delilah was busy with dinner preparations. He thought on his wife upstairs curled up in front of the fire. That was where he wanted to be. Tomorrow, Duster would cover the two mares Damian brought from his home in Maryland. That would earn this stud farm another four hundred dollars. The Andrews would stay two more days until they were quite certain the mares would have been impregnated.

With another win at the races, he would discuss with Clare raising the stud fee to two hundred fifty dollars. The winter crops the freed men planted were doing well. Some of the more enthusiastic farmers took the crops to market coming back with money in their pockets. This was something new to these men. Most appeared eager to improve their lot to make money that would help support their families. The schooling of the children as well as the adults was going well also. So far only two families chose to leave. Much to Old Suzzy's delight her children with their families all decided to remain at Mayfair Hall.

It was November. Clare still didn't act as a woman should who was increasing. Just last night when he touched her belly, he felt the slight baby bump. He would have to continue with the lectures until long after their child was ready to see this world. The babe would be born late March or early April. As he walked, he thought on ways to keep her safe. Now, with Raynard gone, he would have to keep her protected from herself. He wished Raynard would never show his face in these parts again. Truth be told he prayed the man would die a slow agonizing death.

When he started down the porch steps, he breathed in the fresh clean air from the river then looked around the farm seeing all that was his. The breath he seemed to be holding rushed out as he watched Mayfair people come to the aid of Big Tom as well as Juney. The scene in the yard in front of the stable could only be described as chaotic at best. Several of the men brought stretchers for Juney along with Big Tom. Mammy Jo gave out orders doing as good a job as any competent drill sergeant. Damian along with his son leaned against the stable, arms crossed in masculine stances that conveyed amusement to Michael's lips as he broke into a broad grin. Ah, they were two of a kind. Jess was the spitting image of his father. Michael wondered if his son would look like him.

He spoke with Mammy Jo first. The healer for the small community assured him that both Big Tom as well as Juney would be taken care of. They would be fine. Big Tom was just a big whiner. He enjoyed the attention. At the moment, his wife fretted over him, soothing his darkly feathered brow, then running her hand down his chest. The sight gave him more reason to grin. He thought Clare might do the same for him if he were injured. He didn't intend for that to happen.

He stepped up beside Damian and Jess, seeing there was little for him to do. The family and friends came together in team-like fashion. "What do you make of all this?" Michael asked when he found all the bedlam winding down with the exit of the people to their respective homes.

Damian lifted his shoulders while he turned his attention to him. "From what I've heard the men are in the process of forming a search party. They are so angry. I doubt if the man, Raynard, stands a chance in hades if the men find him." He paused, stroking his chin in obvious thought. "How is your wife? Seems as if she did a foolish thing today. Ah, but my wife was much like that in the beginning. I've found a few ways to restrain her enthusiasm in certain endeavors."

"Care to give a newlywed man advice?"

Honestly, Michael didn't believe anything would curb her

impulsiveness. Her spontaneity was who she was. Most times her recklessness delighted his sense. He was certain Link had always allowed her to do pretty much as she pleased. Why should she curb herself now when she was an adult woman?

"Not really." He grinned.

Michael didn't want to leave it at that. Desperately, he needed some helpful hints to give him a lifeline here. "Clare wants to race Gypsy. Told her a flat-out no. She hid a pair of britches in Gypsy's stall."

Michael continued with much of the rendition of that afternoon.

He remembered caressing her so very soft naked body, which of course he left out of his explanation of the events of that day. Thought of how she squirmed and jerked with each persuasive caress of his fingers. Afterward, when she wrapped her long white legs around him, he thought he died, been sent to paradise. She climaxed almost as soon as he thrust inside her. Ah, she reached that heavenly pinnacle twice in less than fifteen minutes. He thought on waking up tied to the bedframe the morning after they returned home. She sat beside him just as naked, her beautiful white breasts swaying slightly with each movement. This type of spontaneity he loved.

He supposed he didn't want to curb all that beautiful impetuous nature. In some things he yearned for more. What she would do next, left him guessing as well as breathless with eagerness.

"Truly, you don't have advice?"

He longed for some bit of information he could hang onto perhaps tuck away for the next time he knew she meant to defy him.

Damian arched a dark eyebrow. "Give her what she wants most or give her children. With a brood of children to occupy her time, she'll be too busy to entertain thoughts of racing. Although, from what young Timmie told me this afternoon before the explosion, he believes she could hold her own in a race. Told me she's smart, knows how to get away from the other racers. Timmie also told me Gypsy is fast, likes to take the lead then never give it up."

"In a race against men? Do you have any idea what goes on in these horse races? There are no rules. There is no punishment for running another racer off course. The racetrack is bedlam. I would never allow that. She could get hurt."

Damian showed even white teeth behind his broad grin. "If not that, why then you will have to make sure she has more than enough children to keep her mind off racing. Children are a great deal of work." Damian slanted his gaze toward his son. "They also have their rewards."

Michael thought of the baby bump he felt this morning. "Believe we've started on that course. In another few weeks, she'll agree with me that she has no place on Gypsy during a race."

"Clare is increasing? Well, congratulations are in order. If she's anything like my Amorica, she'll think of the child she carries before she gives into her impulsive wishes. Women are like that. Their children always come first in their attentions."

He thought on the advice along with the information. Hope for the future gave him reason to feel some respite from his fears. Still, he would guard her well during the races.

"Thank you, the two of you must be famished. Delilah will have dinner ready in about twenty minutes. I hope you don't mind if I forego dinner downstairs to one with my wife in our bedchamber. We originally planned to spend the evening with the two of you. Now, however the circumstances have changed. Tomorrow night we'll have a dinner together."

"Of course not, go be with her. I'm certain the two of you have things to speak of," Damian said softly his grin widening with each passing second.

"We started on that much needed discussion before we saw the entourage riding home. Clare thinks of it as me lecturing her. She doesn't listen. I will see you first thing in the morning. Let Old Suzzy know if you need anything." He held open the door for the men as they entered, "By the way. I hope it doesn't offend either of you if I allow Clare to watch the process tomorrow."

He had not been certain how to approach the delicate subject.

Jess laughed as he walked past the two men. He didn't send his thoughts either direction as to the topic. Michael had the distinct impression the young man would have no protests.

"No, no complaints whatsoever. Once had that conversations with my wife, Amorica. She won out. Told me a woman should understand all aspect of life. Since they are a part of mating, they should not ever be left in the dark. She said other things too, things I'd never share. Showed up at the event wearing her man's clothes, her hair bound under a hat believing I would think her one of the hands come to watch." Damian grinned as if the story was to his liking. "We had an interesting time. While she watched, I showed her how things could happen to a young woman who watched the two animals mate."

"Have the distinct impression there is more to this story than you're willing to tell. Believe I've been in the same place the first time I let her watch the mating. She was quite the innocent at the time. Believe one could say her eyes were wide open during the event."

With that said, Michael left whistling remembering how he made her feel that day. She loved his attentions. He hoped she was still awake. Oh, but perhaps if she wasn't he could think of some way to surprise her when she did open her eyes. Tying her to the bed was out of the question. He would never restrain her. He would ponder over the possibilities. Delighted, with the notions forming in his man's brain, he rubbed his hands together.

She would like what he planned.

Maybe not tonight, her ordeals from today would leave her exhausted. When he stepped inside, the fire in the grate was burning low. He put another log on the dying flames. He turned to the wing chair to speak to his wife.

She was sound asleep. Her dark lashes fanned softly across her cheekbones. Damn, he would have liked to talk to her or perhaps just sit with her watching the flames dance in the fireplace while sipping the wine.

Old Suzzy left a dinner tray for them on the table along with another bottle of wine. She stopped drinking the wine a few days ago. While drinking the lemonade, she told him she didn't believe the wine could be good for the baby.

Perhaps she had a point.

He sat in the chair next to hers, the table separating the space. From the new log, flames caught, burning brightly. The soft glow filled the room. She moaned adjusting herself on the chair.

Clare should wake up as well as eat. Kneeling in front of her, he ran his knuckles along her jaw then down her neck. He thought of opening her robe. When he touched the fasteners, she swatted his hand away before changing positions. He wasn't going to give up with her delicately feeble gesture. Slowly, he untied the bows of her robe spreading the fabric.

A sudden gasp left his lips. Beneath the robe she was naked. Her beautiful breasts easily revealed as he pushed the fabric aside. The palms of his hands feathered across each nipple. He sipped air into his lungs realizing he would soon make love to his wife. The food would come later. Enticing his body to harden more, she moved again. The twin globes moved slightly, the tips hardening with the touch of cooler air against them. He was hard as steel. Lust, there was something to be said for hunger and throbbing passion. Once again, he didn't want to think about love.

Truly, he thought she must be too exhausted tonight to partake of his manly needs. When her eyes opened, she smiled. Her hand fluttered for a moment before she tenderly touched his lips with a fingertip. "Should we eat? I'm famished. It was all I could do to wait for you."

Her gaze focused on his mouth where the tip of her finger touched then lower, lower still. His wife wasn't hungry for food.

"Food can wait."

He realized Clare was made for him, just him. He knew also he loved her as well as lusted for her. After Jillian he never thought to love a woman. Clare was his though. He wouldn't bend her to his will. He would give her everything she needed to be independent of him.

"Michael?"

"Yes, Little Pigeon. Would you make love with your husband?"

She wound her fingers through his hair, tugging him close to her lips. She whispered, "No, however I will make lust."

His gut tightened. He didn't like her words. The word lust certainly didn't please him. No, it didn't please him at all. However, he understood until he was willing to say the word love to his wife, she would never tell him what he yearned to hear from her sweet mouth. She said the word love, once. Much to his chagrin, he immediately replied that for him love didn't exist. All he understood about love was what it wasn't. No, at the time he felt lust. That was all. He would make no excuses for his blunder. Now, he understood what love was.

He moved back, kneeling on the beautiful blue and white Aubusson carpet. It was time for him to admit the truth. Love was the emotion he felt for his wife. She swept her tongue across his mouth before pushing against him. With no second thoughts, he opened for her. All thought left his feeble man's brain behind. For him, everything was physical. His fingers played with the soft pink crests that moved fetchingly for him. Heat burned, flamed.

She unfastened his shirt. He shrugged it off his shoulders. This was too much for him. He wanted to take her in front of the fire. Sweeping her into his arms, he carried her to the floor. In a breath his clothes fell to the wooden floor along with her robe. She was on her back. He spread her legs seeing all of her, all that he possessed. His manhood was hard and throbbing needing her more than he could ever imagine.

"You almost died today, passed on to another world," he murmured softly as he enticed her until her beautiful body succumbed to all he yearned for. She writhed then arched. His fingers found the hardened treasure that brought her so close to her climax. She would be there soon.

I love you, Clare.

He thrust inside her, holding still for a few seconds, feeling her sheathe kissing his length, pulsing against him, tugging him farther inside. She cried out accepting him into her. Her fingers dug into his shoulder. He spent himself.

Sprawled atop her, he struggled to breathe. His body cried out for more from this beautiful woman. He yearned for the words of love she once gifted him with. The admission of love was not to be. He would always regret letting that moment go.

"Lust is such a wonderful sensation. Don't you think?" she murmured to him; her eyes closed.

Angry with himself, with her, he pushed away, looking down on her thick dark lashes that fanned softly across her pale white cheeks. She opened slightly glazed over eyes, still hungry with desire.

Hell and damnation, he didn't think lust was wonderful at all, at least not without words of love to be spoken with the lust. He felt a soft fingertip run across his face, down his neck, to touch a nipple. He bucked. His member grew steel-hard again.

He placed her hands above her. Clare's eyes were still closed. There were tears spiking her lashes.

"I didn't hurt you. Did I?"

She shook her head in an attempt to tell him no. "Not physically."

Swamped with confusion he needed to get inside her head. That feat was damn near impossible when she wouldn't speak, refused to tell him how she felt. "How then?"

Her body was so still. She didn't move. Slowly she opened her eyes. "It is nothing, nothing at all. Don't worry. There is nothing wrong. I just had a moment..."

Like hell, he would worry. He didn't want to hurt her in any way, as he didn't think he'd abused her. "What did I do? What didn't I do?"

Michael understood he had to have an answer before this continued any farther. Her lips thinned. He understood that look quite well. She wasn't going to tell him anything no matter how much he demanded her to do so. He could give orders or stamp his feet and yell. She wouldn't tell him what bothered her. He let her wrists go, while he rolled off her.

The tray of food, no longer appeared appetizing. Yet, he knew Clare needed to eat. He didn't think she'd had food since this morning. It was well past nine in the evening.

"You will eat?" He lifted an eyebrow into the air.

"I'm not hungry."

"For the baby."

He pulled out his best weapon, encouraged by Damian's advice. After that he held up his hands. "I understand the child is a wee tiny thing now. Nonetheless, it would not do for the mother to take sick, now, would it? We both understand that whatever goes into your stomach also nourishes the child." Now he thought his argument brilliant, no more than magnificent.

"You don't pull any punches, do you? All right, I will have something. Do you think one glass of wine would harm the baby?"

Truthfully, he had no idea. This instant, the baby was barely there. It had been her notion that the alcohol might not be good for the unborn child. He lifted his shoulders. "I don't know. Why don't you see how a glass makes you feel?"

She nodded. When he handed her the glass, she sipped. "It's fine. I feel as if so much happened today, I need to relax. When I close my eyes, all I see is the blackness enveloping along with the pain. I never heard the explosion."

He felt the same. "Tell me about the tears," he spoke softly, watching the reaction on her expressive face.

"They are nothing, just a naïve girl's need to feel more than lust from the man she is wedded to." She paused.

To Michael it seemed she was thinking. With a tiny lift of her shoulders, it appeared to him she made up her mind. "From the very beginning of our relationship you made the fact perfectly clear to me that you couldn't or wouldn't ever love a woman. I understand. The tears formed because of a second of weakness. We could also blame the tears on the baby. Can we not?" Her smile brightened the room along with his heart. "Will you forgive my moment of weakness? I never planned to wish for more than was possible for you to give."

More than anything he yearned to give her the words she craved. His smile didn't reach his heart or his soul for that matter. He was afraid. Terrified of his feelings for her.

Since Jillian, he never intended to become vulnerable to another human being let alone a woman. At that time, he hardened his heart. Told himself he would never say words of love to a woman even a wife. Once again, he held the words she needed to hear back behind his lips.

The food seemed to turn sour in his stomach. She picked at the pieces he put on her plate. The wine seemed to go down without effort. He was afraid she would regret her indulgence in the morning.

"There is nothing to forgive. You only lust for me. I understand.

Lust is nice. Hunger. Passion. Raging desire. They are all…nice."

The words landed like a rock in his heart. He pulled in a long draught of air hoping the effort would lend him courage to explain his feelings.

It did not.

Epilogue

The weather was unnaturally chilly for the first week in April. Clare watched her two-day-old son nurse at her breast. His eyes were a deep green. She didn't believe for a moment they would change color as Old Suzzy told her they might. What little hair he possessed held a reddish tint. He would be the spitting image of his doting father.

"There you are. Timmie and Sirus just returned from the race in Richmond. Both won. Thought you would like the good news."

He sat down next to the bed, let his son enclose his finger within his tiny hand. His grin was wide, endearing to her. While she still yearned to hear the words of love from him, she also understood why he could never say them. Jillian was at the root of his problem with love. He understood she wanted to hate the woman but she didn't"

"That's good news."

She flashed him the beautiful smile that won his heart a year ago. He felt certain he'd fallen in love with her the moment he saw her lips form into the radiant grin. Even though he'd been unable to give her the words of love she wanted to hear, he doted on her.

This woman, Clare, was made just for him. He understood he needed to tell her so. For the life of him he didn't know why the words were so very difficult to say. During this year she became part of him. She was his. He most certainly did love her.

"Your son will look like you. You see that don't you?"

She reached out to touch his face. She was so dear to him. So precious as was their son. He wanted another child as soon as possible. He wondered what she would say to that. The doctor told him he should wait at least six months, that a year would be better, to have another child.

"I would love a girl that would have your astoundingly beautiful blue eyes, ones that simmer darkly when she is angry."

"She would never be angry," Clare laughed the sound so pure and sweet the sensation stole his breath from his lungs.

"If she was anything like her mother, she would be impulsive. When she didn't get her way, she would fight back with fury. I would love her to death. I would also shield her from all harm."

"Are you going to be as autocratic with the daughter you don't have yet as you are with her mother?"

She smoothed the downy red hair of her babe nestled in her arms.

"I'm domineering with you. I merely know what is best for my wife." He kept the grin behind his teeth at her look of disbelief. "I will also know what is best for all my children, male or female."

"My point exactly."

The babe was finished with his meal. She handed him his son. "You will take care not to jostle his head."

He stared at her milk white breasts, the nipples elongated because of his son's attention there. He wanted to attend to those hard pink crests. She wasn't ready for sex. Michael chastised himself for his eagerness to be with his wife. She closed the robe, quickly, fastened the material as if she understood his thoughts.

With his child in his arms, he walked around the room. The boy stared up at him with vivid green eyes.

God how he loved his son.

Loved his wife too.

When the boy's eyes began to close, he set him in the crib near the window. Sunlight filtered through the white lace curtains on to his son's little face.

With trepidation in his heart, he sat down beside her. He was afraid. Terrified of the words he was about to spew. He'd waited so long. He could wait no longer. She tilted her head slightly as she looked at him. Curiosity evident in her eyes.

"Is something amiss?" She reached out to touch his hand.

He enclosed her small fingers within his. After that he cleared his throat. "This has been a long time coming," he spoke softly. "I should have told you this as soon as I understood the depths of my feelings. When it comes to words, I'm not a brave man."

"Michael?" She appeared worried, apprehensive that he might give her bad news. "What's happened?"

For a moment he breathed in then out. He recalled how badly he'd done when he told Old Suzzy she was a free woman. Didn't do much better when he tried the next time. What if he failed? His tongue seemed to be tied up in knots the inside of his mouth parched.

Running his tongue along his lips, he blurted, "I love you, Clare. I've always loved you from the moment I saw you. More so from the first kiss we shared. I was angry with you, too, because you possessed Mayfair Hall. Nonetheless, I loved you."

Her smile filled him with pleasure. For a few moments she closed her eyes. "I wanted you to love me for the longest time. When you told me what I felt for you was just lust, you hurt me deeply. Even though I loved you I felt a deep need to hurt you in return. You truly thought that though. I understood you were sincere in your belief. I didn't know how to change your feelings for me."

He nodded. She looked at their entwined fingers. "You were made just for me, only me. Just for Michael is a lovely thought."

"You are mine, Michael. Only mine."

Prologue

London 1823

Memories. Bobby didn't want to remember that part of his life. Didn't want to relive the nightmare. Six-years-old, that was when it started when his life turned topsy-turvy, the day he became a different person. His gut curled thinking about the day so long ago.

When he closed his eyes, he saw the horrific picture, blood everywhere. The sight he vanquished from his head these last twenty or so years was vividly clear today. With the summons to the Duke of Richmond's townhouse, everything rushed back into his mind with a vengeance. His father, as he watched the enfolding scene, his eye blazing with impotent fury while he hung from a rafter, his hands tied above his head. He'd been helpless to prevent the tragedy.

Bobby hid while Sherry violated his mother. When he and his men finished with his mother, they killed both parents. They killed them because his father refused to play a part in the scheme to steal the heirs of wealthy lords so the second sons could inherit. The fourth marquis of Stonebridge was dead. Bobby, Robert Wyatt Munroe became the fifth marquis on that day.

"Lord Robert?"

His name spoken from the Duke of Richmond goaded him from

his musings. "Yes?" If he could run from this, he would. These two dukes would probably follow then drag him back. He was doomed now to a life he wanted no part of. Doomed to become something he didn't know how to be. He possessed no lordly skills. Was trained to pick pockets and to break into homes to steal the gent's blind. At that time, he possessed the fastest hands and feet of anyone who lived in St. Giles parish.

Drake Montgomerie, the Duke of Richmond, was running his fingers over his jaw as if in thought. "You will have to go to Scotland to reclaim your inheritance, Glasgow to be exact. Leslie Stewart, the Duke of Southcliff, will accompany you as well as guide you in your decisions. If you have questions, he will answer them. He will also point to solicitors as well as advisors whom you can trust.

Impatiently, Bobby waved his hand in the air. "My life is fine as it is. Don't want to be a marquise. Don't want the responsibilities. Don't want to move to a city or the country estate my parents once owned. After all this time, hasn't some distant relative come to claim the inheritance along with the coveted title?"

Montgomerie's fingers formed a steeple beneath his chin. "No one. You've not a brother or sister for that matter. Your father was an only child as well. You must suck it up. This is what you were born to be. As it stands, here is no choice for you."

The Aubusson carpet was bound to have a hole worn in it where he was walking in skinny circles. He stopped, swirling on a boot heel to meet the gazes of both dukes. "Has Scarface been caught? Am I walking into this with blinders on? My father was murdered because he didn't want to have anything to do with baby stealing. Told Scarface along with his minion, Sherry, no."

"Avery Bainbridge, the man you knew as Scarface, fled to France. We can't touch him there. No, he has not been caught. It's been three years. Who knows, he might grow bored and return. He would be foolish to do something so reckless."

With his hands behind his back, Bobby rocked on his heels. "Piper was stolen as an infant. Her father was murdered that night giving his brother the scar that runs across his face. His attempt to protect his daughter was foiled though."

"You mean Portia Leighton?" Leslie asked, his voice soft. "Are you thinking there might be more children who were stolen?"

"Scarface was the second child of an entitled family. Thought he should have become the duke instead of his older brother. He stole Piper for revenge only because the older brother, Roc Leighton, was guarded too closely. Who's to say there are not more children under Jocko's tutelage who should be heir to a title?"

"Who is Jocko?" Leslie asked, seeming to take great interest in the tale woven here this day. "Would like a *wee* bit of clarity."

"Scarface dumped me on Jocko's doorstep right after my parents were murdered. He was the reigning thief in St. Giles Parish. Had the most clout along with the largest territory, still does. It wasn't long after that day that Piper was handed to him then Billy. There were other babies too. However, Jocko took special interest in the three of us. Billy and I were told we weren't ever to let Piper be alone. As we grew up, that was near impossible though. We got older. Our working hours were at night. Hers were during the day."

"I've heard when Brett MacLachlan caught her picking his pocket, she was disguised as a boy," Leslie said while he sipped the brandy Drake poured for him.

"True enough. Didn't take Brett long to discover the truth then fall in love with her."

"Back to you," Leslie turned the conversation around. "Once in Scotland, I want you to go see Scarlett Gordon. She runs an escort service. However, she will also tutor you in the ways of a titled aristocrat as well as help you find a young debutante to become your wife. During the interim, she will accompany you to balls and whatever else you need."

"A woman? An escort? Whatever for?" Bobby wasn't ready to court or see any women, especially not a debutante. The thought made him shudder with revulsion. Didn't want a virgin in his bed. Didn't understand what was happening here.

"She will get you ready to become the Marquis of Stonebridge," Montgomerie told him pleasantly. "Know this right up front, Scarlett is no whore. She doesn't sleep with her clients. The woman, simply put, helps men when they need a woman by their side."

An escort... Bobby mused. The thought sounded delightful, perhaps even a bit sinful. His future seemed to be looking up.

Chapter One

Robert Wyatt Munroe, fifth Marquis of Stonebridge, stood across the street from a three-story home near the outskirts of Glasgow. His palms sweaty he rocked back and forth on the balls of his feet. With his boots planted firmly apart he wiped his hands on the black trousers that fit him like a second skin. His manservant, Fitzmeyer, fixed his perfectly tied cravat as he also made sure his hessians shone until light danced from them. Bobby, his preferred name, held the sides of his dark blue frock coat.

Despite the fact he held the title for nearly two months, he didn't feel anymore comfortable now than he did when his parentage was made public. He denied the fact was true simply because he didn't want to become part of the aristocracy. This was a part of his life he thought would remain in the past. After the things he'd done, he could not be the son of a marquis. Bloody eyes, but he spent his younger years picking pockets in Vauxhall Garden. When he was older, he robbed houses of gents like himself. The roof over his head was whatever he could find in St. Giles Parish.

The few friends he had urged him to find a wife. Told him he should court a debutante. The only way to do that was to come to Glasgow for the season. He was a fish out of water in the mansions with others of the peerage, as he would be expected to dance as well as comport himself in the manner befitting his station in life. Was expected to have genteel manners.

He, Bobby Munroe, knew nothing about courtly manners. Had never possessed a last name until two years ago. Put him in a crowd of people where he could relieve anyone of their purse, he would be at ease. Sweat beading on his brow, he looked across the street. Inside that house was the woman, he was told, who could teach him how to be a gentleman. An impossible task if anyone bothered to ask him. No one did.

Scarlett Gordon, his breath caught in the back of his throat.

He checked her out a few days ago. Followed her when she attended to some errands. She was the most beautiful woman he'd ever set eyes on. While he never got close enough to see the color of her eyes, her hair was deep mahogany. When the light caught the strands, it shimmered a myriad of colors. She wore it piled atop her head. He watched her as she swore and pushed away the tendrils of hair that wouldn't stay put. Her nose was pert, her lips generous. He was sure he could span her tiny waist with his hands. He wanted to see what was beneath the dress. Wanted to taste all of her.

Today, if he summoned the courage to enter into her domain, he would discover the color of her eyes. That was the problem. All signs of courage vanished as soon as he saw the house. His breath hitched in the back of his throat while his heart bellowed beneath his breastbone.

She would teach him what he needed to know. Bloody eyes but he needed to learn so damn much no one could do the job. When it came to dancing, he had two left feet even though in a race to get away from the constables, he could out run one and all. No one in St. Giles and the surrounding area was faster afoot. One look at a dinner table with all the tiny silverware, plates and cups and whatnot, his gut turned sour churning in displeasure. He wouldn't make just one mistake. No, he was positive his blunders would be in the multiples.

No human being, no matter what kind of saint, could teach him enough so that people would believe he was a marquis. He had to learn by Saturday next. The first debutante ball of the season was only a few days away.

You best get on with it old bloke. Not going to learn anything standing on the street, starin' at the house. Wishful thinking never got you anywhere. Take action.

You and I both know I never wanted this. Was quite happy being Piper's bodyguard, living in the highlands. Had everything I wanted. Didn't need marriage or heirs. Had fun with the willing lasses around the MacLachlan estate.

Go across the street, coward.

Bobby swallowed, however the act didn't chase away his fear. Didn't do anything to dry his damp palms or the moisture beading on his forehead. He wished he remembered to wear his gloves Fitzmeyer set out for him. Wished...

There were too many bloody things he wished for. None of them involved learning how to dance or wed a debutante. He liked to have fun with his women, liked them willing and passionate. Everything he heard about debutantes belied that notion.

They were all virgins. What the devil would he ever do with a virgin? Heard they expected the sex act would be done with clothing on. What kind of fun would that be? He didn't think Miss Scarlett was going to teach him about lovemaking. He wondered if she was a virgin. Wanted to say it didn't matter although it did. He wasn't in the mood for untried maidens. Made a point of avoiding them.

Yet...

Perhaps...

Miss Scarlett Gordon might not be a virgin. Her escort service allowed sex if both partners were willing. He was willing, more than willing. All he would have to do would be to coax her to readiness or his way of thinking. Didn't need lessons in sweet-talking. He was a master of the fine art of seduction.

His sigh was heavy even as he almost turned around to come back later. At his interview, her bodyguard made a point of telling him if she was going to be his escort she would never partake of sex with her client.

She didn't give out her favors.

Ever.

He wanted Scarlett. Wanted her the first second he saw her. Not one of her other ladies would do. Bobby wanted to know her story from the beginning to the present. A lady, and she was a real lady, wouldn't sell herself as an escort of any kind. So, what were the reasons for the transgressions? His informants he assumed were accurate. The information they brought him well documented. Miss Scarlett didn't have sex with her clients. That made her an even bigger challenge for his charms.

Scarlett Gordon was the daughter of an earl who passed a few years ago. Her stepmother was a beautiful woman who was seen at high society functions. Other relatives, an uncle, he heard about, was a wastrel who frequented gaming hells as well as whorehouses. No one had anything good to say about the man. In Bobby's mind that fact didn't condemn him outright. He knew lots of men who spent hours in both places.

The lady in question stepped out on the porch. Her arms were wrapped around her slim waist as she searched the area as if looking for her new client. A smile crossed her features when she saw him. She tilted her head to one side, a picture of serenity. It seemed she was capable of reading his mind, seeing his fears.

He nodded. His time for prevaricating was up. Heaving in a deep breath of air, Bobby strode across the street. His heart lurched upward to lodge in his throat. He wiped his palms on his trousers wishing once again he thought to wear his gloves.

When he reached her, he placed her hand in his then gallantly bending at the waist brought her hand to his lips.

"Good afternoon, Miss Scarlett. It's a fine day is it naught?"

She pulled her hand away. "You're a tad bit late, Lord Munroe."

There was a hint of censure in her voice except her striking green eyes twinkled with what he hoped was humor. She was teasing him. He liked that along with the flirtatious slant to her lips.

"Been across the street for a half hour. Was thinking of your pour feet and the battering they're going to take when we dance."

She laughed. The sound of her laughter sent ripples of pleasure down his spine. The sound was deep and pure. It was honest, uncontrived. One more thing about her he admired. Honesty in a woman was rare. Piper and Molly possessed that innate quality. Women who didn't lie scarcely existed.

"I'm sure my feet will be just fine," she said with a half-smile casting a rosy sheen to her complexion. "Care to come inside? We won't dance until after our meal." She looked at his arm. "You need to offer me your assistance."

He did so. "Not sure why, nonetheless I have seen men and women walking like this. Who needs to be held up, you or me?"

"No one, the gesture is simply impeccable manners. Now, when we step inside, we will be announced. The same will happen Saturday night at the Richmond's ball."

Her voice was soft, a little bit throaty. He liked the sound of her voice almost as much as her laughter. When she was close to him, he caught the scent of vanilla.

He liked the way her fingers felt surrounding his arm as he placed his hand over hers. The door was opened for them. Inside, she stopped.

"The Marquis of Stonebridge, Robert Wyatt Munroe. Accompanying the marquis is Miss Scarlett Gordon," one of her ladies announced. The pair stepped forward.

"Smile," she told him.

When she let go of his arm, he stuffed his fingers through his hair. She grinned at him. "You don't want to do this do you? We can curtail the lessons at any time. Just say the word."

"It's not that. I just don't see any hope for me. Who's going to want to marry a pickpocket and house robber from St. Giles, even though he's been pardoned and he's a marquis? I'm not what would be termed a decent catch."

She didn't seem to comprehend what he just told her. "You'd be surprised. The title coupled with the wealth you possess now will bring young debutantes along with their doting mothers to you as if you were the King of England. You will have to make sure you are not duped. I've the distinct feeling in this circumstance that would not be easy. From your past, you must have an uncanny sense of a person's worth."

"They won't want me for me," he told her realizing he wanted a woman who didn't care about the title or wealth. Ever since Piper found Brett, he wanted the same kind of love they shared. He didn't see how that would ever be possible as he was thrust into this situation where, as a person, he didn't make a difference. All that mattered was what he could bring into a relationship.

She laughed again, only the sound wasn't pure although he had a strange thought that the bitterness he heard in the tone was honest. "In this town you'll have a hard time finding a woman like that, especially a debutante. Although I do know a few couples who seem to love each other."

"What about you?" Bobby asked as Scarlett led him into the dining room. "Do you love anyone?"

The question wasn't his business. He expected to be put off or a polite set down to be her answer.

"Love is for fools. Not me. Don't want anything to do with men in that way," she spoke softly.

Bobby suspected it was from the depth of her heart. Still, he wanted to understand what drove her to escort men when she didn't like them. He wanted Miss Scarlett to like him.

She obviously didn't want much to do with the male species except their money. Groats for services rendered. He supposed that placed her in much the same category as the other women he'd be meeting. With a sudden thought he came to realize most women were dependent on men in some way for their livelihood. Miss Scarlett tackled this in the only way she understood.

She wasn't in the same category as the other women. He knew it. Decided he would do whatever he could to change her misconceptions about men, in particular Bobby Munroe. Didn't truly care if she liked other men. Just wanted her to appreciate his finer points.

He was at first pleased she didn't have a lover then disappointed. It didn't appear she wanted one. He yearned to change that. Wanted to be her lover. The only man in her life.

If not more.

"Shall we eat?" She stopped at the door to the dining room where an array of plates and silverware were set out.

His quick drag of air surprised her enough to look his way. Her eyes were wide. In the fading light of the evening very green as well, not the usual hazel but they were vividly dark green.

"What is it?" she asked, a small smile spreading across her face as if she knew the answer to her question. "What makes you gasp in surprise?"

"I'm a simple man. Ran a violent, wild life until the last few years. Ate from vendors on the streets with my fingers. Sat down to a few meals in the kitchen with Billy and Molly when I was Piper's bodyguard. Never seen anything like this."

She set her hand on his arm again then quickly withdrew it. For a moment she looked away. "At the ball on Saturday," she paused for a second, her smile finding its place again, "you should hide any surprise you have behind your teeth. You don't need to give your critics fodder for gossip. Believe what I say, you will have critics."

"In other words, don't show emotion. To save my soul, I'll try. Does that mean with you also?"

She failed to hide her surprise behind her beautiful mouth. He grinned wickedly hoping she would, in time, soften toward him. How patient was he? Well, he'd never been known for his patience. What he discovered since meeting Piper was that patience would most likely be rewarded. He hoped it was true with Miss Scarlett as well.

"When you eat at extravagant affairs such as this one, you should make sure you eat very little of each course. They will vary. Don't imbibe too much. It will make your mind fuzzy. When you are meeting mamas and their off spring, a man doesn't want to be fuzzy-headed."

Bobby tossed his head back with unrestrained laughter. "Bloody eyes, I'm no innocent, Letty..."

"Scarlett."

He grinned widely scarcely believing he found a small niche in her armor. "I'm no innocent. Know what drink does to a man's thinking. Wouldn't have survived in St. Giles Parish as long as I did if I was a drinking man. Sure, as I'm standing here, I'd be in Newgate."

She dropped her gaze to the tiny little shrimp in the bowl in front of her. He watched her swill in a deep breath of air, the softly rounded tops of her breasts just showing above the modest cut of her gown turning a pretty pink. Then she looked at him, "Neither am I. Was trying to teach, to..." she paused for another draught of air. "I don't know you, Robert Mu..."

"Bobby," he corrected, all grins as he watched her blush deepen.

"Robert, you must learn to go by Robert. It's more marquiseish," she flushed again. "I think it's time for the first round of dance lessons."

"Rather pursue this conversation." He looked around, "Have we finished with the meal?"

"No."

"Then...?"

Letty didn't strike him as a woman who flustered easily. Somehow, he managed to quite unintentionally fluster her. "I need to eat something more than one tiny piece of shrimp."

"Of course, it's what you are paying for. Forgive me."

He reached across the table to place his hand over hers. "Letty..."

"Scarlett."

He would give her this one. Clearing his throat, "I promise to do better. I won't tease or flirt while we are still at the table. Won't make promises for the dance floor or after that. Shall we get on with the food? I starved myself the entire day so I could eat all you told me would be put in front of me. Don't intend to go away hungry."

Course after course was set in front of him. With each course there was a different wine. He understood what she tried to tell him about sampling but not truly eating. By the time they finished the meal he felt sated, ready for a nap as well as bit bleary-eyed.

She smiled at him. "See?" She lifted a small finely shaped mahogany colored eyebrow toward the ceiling.

"I did try to control my appetites. Never been good at it."

As the meal progressed his appetite for Letty grew. Every little movement she made intrigued him. His curiosity flourished. Their conversation held little meaning while he tried to probe unsuccessfully into her past.

She remained silent.

There were those in this town who knew her history. A few well-placed groats along with the right questions never hurt. He would discover a few more facts about his escort tomorrow.

"Are you up to trying your hand at dancing?" She pushed back from her chair.

"Shouldn't you be waiting for me to help you from your seat?" he asked as he wiped his mouth, carefully setting his napkin on the table. He focused on her, waiting for her to say something. She lowered her lashes.

Another blush swept across her lily-white skin. "Yes, I forgot. I've never seen why a man should help a lady from her chair. My apologies for overlooking the next step. You are to be the perfect gentleman. Do believe you're learning quickly."

"I am. I have to overcome my past, a past that was my life. If I want to be the perfect gentleman..." He wedged his hands through his hair. "This wasn't my idea. Want to be me the same person I was before I inherited a title that means nothing to me."

"As we all do. We want to be ourselves. You say you need an heir..." Scarlett tapped her chin as if in thought. Bobby would pay for those thoughts if they were for sale.

He waved a hand in the air, frustrated sensations flooding him. "The people I know and care about tell me I need an heir. What does a man from St. Giles Parish, St. James Street know about such things? Heir?" He drug in a rattling breath of air. "You don't want to hear any of this. I'm ready to step on your feet if you're prepared for uncounted bruises. Let's go upstairs if that's where the dance floor is located."

She smiled at him, a dazzling smile, one that started the melting of his soul. He felt an urgent surge of lust.

Her tenderness amazed him, stole another tiny piece of his heart. Letty was, by far, the gentlest creature he ever met. A man could count himself lucky to have a woman such as she in his life.

"Come."

She led the way out of the dining room to a grand staircase he never noticed when he first entered the house. He walked behind her watching the gentle and very provocative sway of her hips as she made her way to the third floor, certain she had no idea how stimulating and intoxicating her movements were. Her mere presence enticed wicked thoughts. It wasn't difficult for Bobby to imagine the gentle curve of her hips or the length of her leg beneath the gown that concealed so much while doing nothing to reveal. The gowns modesty set his imagination on fire.

One of the ladies, the escorts, sat at a piano playing a tune, a waltz if he wasn't mistaken. He assumed he was supposed to dance to that music. His toes twitched. In his mind he was shaking his head. Before he left MacLachlan's estate, he watched Brett and Piper dance the waltz. Brett was debonair. She was a wee bit clumsy.

Bobby scoffed inwardly at his second and third thoughts concerning the viability of this activity. "I would not dance," he murmured thinking if he tried, he'd make a bloody fool of himself.

"You will. Just make sure you only dance once with any lady. If you partner more than once with a debutante, it will send a message that you prefer that particular woman. Which in turn will start the gossips running their tongues about a possible marriage. If you dance three or more times with one woman that is an announcement of an engagement."

"I would only dance with you."

"That would also generate rumors as all who attend these functions know who as well as what I am."

"Perhaps I should find the most expensive brothel then sire my heir there. That, in the end would be far more enjoyable than attending balls. Bruising young women's feet is hardly my idea of fun."

He was surprised when she closed her eyes for a moment but when she opened them, she was smiling. "Just like a man to prefer no commitment over a wife."

He felt his hackles rise. "From what I've heard, I don't believe you should be talking about commitment."

She stiffened. Her lips thinned to a narrow line. Her brows did the same. The small chin he admired tilted defiantly upward. "What have you heard?"

He relaxed. Didn't understand why. "A great deal of things. You are a constant as far as conversation goes. There are rumors. Innuendos. Many things about your life, about the men you escort. I'm sure what the men have to say is far from the truth. Much of it is flippant and denigrates your character. However..." He placed two fingers on her chin, turning her to look at him. "I find your character impeccable, beyond reproach."

"What the fashionable people think of my character matters not to me. I've made my choices in this life. I'm satisfied with the outcome."

Her rebuff of her character as well as his defense miffed Bobby.

She turned, lifting her skirts. Without looking back to see if he followed, she made her way to the center of the ballroom. When she turned to beckon him forward, she was a replica of her earlier self. The anger if it ever was there vanished.

He stood in front of her when she faced the door. A tiny gasp escaped her lips. He ran his knuckles down her cheek. Wishing to break through the stiff façade she managed. "Your character makes a difference to me. You bristle when your past comes up. What is it that you hide?" He had his guesses. Thought perhaps in time she would tell him.

Perhaps not.

With information he would be armed. Perhaps he should pay a visit to her step mama tomorrow. From what little Letty told him, he was sure the woman could shed some light on the situation.

"Don't worry about me. I can take care of myself," she told him before turning to the piano player. "You may start."

He didn't have one doubt in his mind about that.

She held one of his hands with hers. "Put your other hand on my waist. We will waltz. Think one, two three, one two three…"

Scarlet closed her eyes as if she didn't need to see him. She explained what their feet would do. Slowly at first, she began the dance.

He followed.

Stumbled and swore.

She laughed softly seeming to enjoy the dance.

Two hours later they were laughing. Bobby was holding onto Scarlett whose head rested against the hollow of his shoulder. They were both breathing hard. He felt the softness of her breasts pressed against his chest. Felt burgeoning lust. Let his hand slide to the small of her back then a tiny bit lower as he pressed her against him.

Immediately, she stiffened. Slowly, she pushed away. "Don't do that again."

~ * ~

"Lord Robert Munroe likes you," Torra giggled. "No, I'd say he's crazy over you. One can tell just by the way his eyes shadow you around the room. He never stopped looking at you."

Scarlett didn't want to listen to the notion. Didn't want anyone to be crazy about her, especially a man who could rip her freedom and independence right out from under her feet.

The truth was Robert did something to her self-control no other man could do.

She didn't want a man, any man.

With his steady and oh so persistent flattery, he began to melt her heart. With his gentle smile and outlandish behavior, he made her laugh. She didn't remember the last time she laughed, a real laugh a belly laugh. He also made her uncomfortable in too many ways to count.

When his hand settled on her waist, she thought her heart wouldn't stop racing. She gasped for air. When he eventually picked up the simpler steps, they flowed around the ballroom as if they were made for each other, as if they were one and the same.

She waved her hand in the air in denial, "Nonsense, he needs a debutante not a long-in-the-tooth spinster. Must have a wife so he can sire an heir. A twenty-three-year-old matron will not do for a lord of the realm."

"From what few words I overheard; he didn't seem so eager to find a debutante. No, his focus was on you," Torra said as she settled back into the big chair and sipped the tea that was more milk and sugar than tea. She looked over the rim of the cup as if waiting for an answer.

She wasn't going to get one.

"What did I miss?" Muira, one of Scarlett's other ladies, waltzed into the big drawing room. She poured herself a glass of sherry then sat down across from the other two ladies. "The two of you look as if you're sharing secrets. Care to let me in on them?"

"How did your evening go?" Scarlett asked wishing to keep the conversation on anyone but herself.

Too many questions twirled around in her head about Robert, turning her brains into mush. He intrigued her. She didn't like that fact. Sent her heart thrashing around in her chest so hard she didn't know how to restrain it. When she thought of him dancing with one of the simpering debutantes searching for husbands, it sent a debilitating wave of jealousy from the tips of her toes straight on up to her faltering brain.

"You know Lyle Cummings. His hands are everywhere. What he wants is a whore not an escort," Muira said while she pulled off her slippers and stockings. "My feet hurt so badly. He stepped on them at least ten times each dance. Never an apology from his lips and he held me too close. I had an instant urge to slap the silly grin off his face."

Scarlett's laughter bubbled up despite her attempt to stop it. "Robert was just learning. He stepped on my toes just once. He truly did catch on quickly."

"Getting back to Lyle Cummings. You *dinna* have to go with that man. If you told him no, he wouldn't keep bothering you," Torra pointed, shaking her finger at Muira, reprimanding.

Muira lifted her petite shoulders. She was tiny and fragile with the look of a porcelain doll. Her deep brown eyes narrowed as she ran her hands down the length of her skirt. "He pays well. While I *ken* he wants to take me to his home then to his bed, he doesn't push or force. Someday he'll wed. I'll have to move on then but for now he suits. I can count on him to want an escort once a week, sometimes more. He keeps me in spending money, likes to give expensive gifts."

"You don't have to try new men," Torra said. "If Lyle Cummings is suitable, who am I to criticize?"

"Where men are concerned one never knows what you're going to get," Scarlett added with a visible sigh. "Even though they are screened by Tristan." Tristan was their in-house bodyguard. He did look over Robert's credentials. He was given the okay by two dukes, two men who were known to work for the English government.

When she closed her eyes, all she could think of was Robert. All she could see was his innate power, all confined in his body seeming to want to burst out. He was tall, much taller than her. She reached his chin. With most men she looked straight into their eyes. Her uncle called her an abomination of a woman, a big gangly thing with no female charm. That thought didn't stop him from forcing her when she turned thirteen.

Moisture welled in her eyes.

She pushed the hated tears away with the backs of her hand, wishing Torra and Muira didn't notice. It seemed tonight at least luck was on her side. They were both so caught up in their personal lives they didn't see the gathering tears that even now spiked her lashes. With her thumbs she pushed them away. She drank deeply of her lukewarm tea.

"Tell us about the marquis. Is he handsome as sin or just wealthy with a title? Would you like to take him to your bed?" Muira asked as she wriggled her toes.

The downstairs maid, Lydia, brought her a hot bath with Epsom salts to soak her feet in. "Ah..." she sighed as her feet sank below the water. "This is truly heaven if one exists."

"All of the above except the part about the bed. You all understand I don't do that," Scarlett said thinking perhaps in this case...no. She sipped a breath of air before she continued. "His eyes are silver blue. Most of the time more blue than silver. When he laughs the outsides turn even bluer."

"He's *bonnie*," Torra put in. "The man is taller than Scarlett. In comparison he makes her look tiny."

Scarlet felt heat rush to her cheeks. "I'm not that tall," she protested knowing her words were in vain.

For a female she was very tall. A tiny woman, a delicate woman, that's what she always wanted for herself. She envied women like Muira who were fragile, who appeared as if they needed a man's protection. If she'd been fragile, she would have never survived her younger years. It was her strength of will coupled with her size that eventually acted in her favor. The last time she was assaulted, she was able to break free. She remembered the moment clearly. Once she coshed, him over the head, she ran. Never returned home.

Still...

"I'm not a giant nor am I the largest woman..."

"I'm sorry," Torra leaned forward taking her hand in hers. "We know you're sensitive about your height. You are not a large woman. You're so slender why a strong wind might blow you away."

"Hardly." Scarlett's sarcasm could not be missed. "In any case, what I was trying to say is that he is larger than me. That fact is nice for a change. Not that it matters. I'm helping Lord Munroe discover his future wife. He must find a debutante. There is no place for me in that scenario."

"There is no reason why you couldn't be his wife. Everyone knows your father was an earl. Your pedigree is just as fine as the marquis," Muira said leaning back. "You have all the requisite skills to run a household as well as the knowledge to see the man through rough times.

"You all *ken* I won't marry. Won't be under a man's control. Ever." Scarlett's voice took on the same strangled emotion it always did when she spoke of men.

Images of her uncle, naked, his rod pushing from his groin flooded her brain. Closing her eyes never vanquished those horrible images along with the worst ones where he forced himself inside her. "No, I'll never let a man into my life or my bed," she murmured softly cringing while the hated pictures slowly faded for the moment.

"That's a shame. You've got so much kindness to give," Torra said. "I'd wager your Lord Munroe knows a thing or two, maybe three about giving a woman her pleasure. Being with a man that way is not all hurt and shame. I should know. I've experienced both." Torra leaned forward. "Don't be a coward all your life. Take a risk. If the man offers to bed you..."

"I will say no."

"If he doesn't ask and finds a way to coax your favors from you what then? Will you give love a chance?" Muira put in a few words too.

"Sounds like two different things to me. Coaxing is tantamount to force. It just makes the woman want you so bad she doesn't *ken* how to say no," Torra said while she fiddled with the teacup's handle.

Muira tipped up her glass emptying it. "I'm going to bed. You two don't stay up too long talking. The regrets will come in the morning when you're trying to open up eyelids that don't want to cooperate. I'm going to accompany Lyle to a lecture at the university. Says he will look good to his colleagues with me on his arm. Hah, they all know what I am. Don't understand that man. Never will."

"I'll heed your advice and go straight to bed. Tristan told me there is a man who would like to meet me tomorrow. Needs an escort to a family gathering in Edinburgh of all things, not too sure about going out of town with a new man." Torra laughed turning to Scarlett. "What about you?"

"I'm not tired, nevertheless I'll retire soon. Lord Munroe and I are going on a picnic tomorrow if the weather holds. I assured Lord Munroe that would be a proper outing to take a debutante who catches his eye. I will make sure he understands what is proper as well as what is not."

"I think you protest over much. You've already caught the gent's eye. All you need do is reel him in." She held up her hands. "I know. You don't want to wed. Ever. As an afterthought, do you truly think you can teach that man what is proper? Seems to me he'll do what he pleases."

"That's ridiculous. He's not infatuated if that's what you're implying. I've only met the lord today. It's impossible to feel what you're speaking of in such a short time," Scarlett said as she tried to ignore all the warning signs blaring in her mind.

"Mark my words," Torra was shaking her head as she walked up the steps. "He will find some way to catch you on his terms. Take care or you'll be in over your head."

Thinking on all the girls said, Scarlett finished her tea. She strode to the front porch. A calm evening breeze swirled around her cooling her heated cheeks. A sliver of a moon hung low in the sky while a few scattered dark clouds traveled across its golden warmth. She wrapped her arms around her waist. It was colder than she thought it would be. She was chilled to the bone. In one meeting, Lord Munroe brought promises as well as untapped fears into her life. She wasn't sure she was ready to explore them.

He would challenge her to do so.

She remembered watching Robert while he stood across the street debating to come inside. Clearly, he'd been nervous despite his title and his standing in the community. She understood. Lord Robert Munroe believed he was a fraud. Had heard gossip about his kind as well as how they shouldn't be allowed to associate with true gentry.

Just as she was a fraud, they had that fact in common. What other similarities did they share?

There was nothing true and honest about Scarlett Gordon, daughter of the earl of nothing. Her father was dead to her the moment he wed Lydia Robin. The woman brought into the home that had once been filled with love. Her relatives, Uncle Baron to be exact, had ruined her life, changed it forever. After he finished with her, nothing would ever be the same. She shivered. The man turned up here a week ago asking for an escort. Told her she owed him. No, she already paid the man too dearly for words.

Scarlett knew what he wanted. She would never willingly give anything to that man let alone her body. She paid the price too many times to count. Until she managed to flee, she'd been at his beck and call. No one believed her when she told them he raped her.

The deep breath she inhaled was filled with scents of spring purging the stench of her memories. Daphne bloomed around the front of her porch. The hoot of an owl then an answering one could be heard. She wondered what Robert was doing right now.

"*Nay*," she murmured softly admitting that she was truly a coward, afraid to take chances in this life, forget about Robert. A man will only bring pain and suffering. A man is not for the likes of you.

Still, it seemed she remembered the touch of his hand on the small of her back then lower when he took liberties she didn't give. She liked the sensations he evoked. The man's hand resting on her buttocks sent heat simmering through her body joined with an ache to that place between her legs where Baron violated.

Remembering the pain would never end. If she could forget, she would. Too cold to stay outside, too restless to go to bed, she followed the stairs to the ballroom. She hit a note on the piano with her finger.

Thought of the dances they shared. He would do well at the ball. She liked the nearness of his body, recalled the heat.

Once the tutoring ended and he found a wife, she wouldn't see him again. She didn't understand the pang in her heart. *I've only known him for one day. I'm a fool to think he could ever be more than a client.*

A bloody fool.

Torra was right. She did need her sleep. Robert told her he would pick her up at noon. The time was well past midnight now. She had things to prepare before she could tutor Lord Munroe in the fine art of a picnic. Everything needed to be proper. He would probably prefer something bawdier than what she planned.

Finally in bed, she punched and pounded the pillows as she attempted comfort. She pulled the covers up then tossed them away.

Her legs were wound around the sheets when the sun peeked in through the window.

"Good heavens," she murmured staring at the tangle of bedding she was sitting on. Her dreams haunted her, touched that part of her she kept hidden from everyone. Robert would ask about her. Already intimated that he would learn all he could about Miss Scarlett Gordon. There were people who knew. People who denied the truth. She shivered. She realized Lord Robert, if that was his wish, would discover everything she meant to keep secret.

Scrambling from the bed, she pushed the nightdress she wore so it hung below her knees. She rang the bell for a bath and breakfast. The meal would have to be small. The ormolu clock sitting on the mantel chimed ten times. Her heart raced. Two hours until he picked her up. The minutes would fly. She had so much to accomplish in so little time.

She should have listened to Torra. Should have gone to bed before midnight. She only had herself to blame.

What more could go wrong?

By the time noon came around she'd worn herself out with all the preparations for the picnic. She knew exactly where they would go. The park was semi-private. There would be people on foot, possibly some on horseback. There might even be other people with a picnic in mind who could be seen. The place was perfect to take a young debutante who didn't have a chaperone, a place where the lady's innocence would remain intact.

She smiled when the carriage with the Marquis of Stonebridge's crest on the side rolled to a stop in front of the house. Robert leapt from the door, his powerful legs eating up the short distance to the porch in a matter of seconds. Eager to see him, she opened the door before he could knock. Today, he didn't stand across the street garnering courage.

"Good afternoon, Letty." He kissed her hand. "You look beautiful today. A fine picture of a woman."

"Scarlett. What do I have to do?"

She didn't pull her hand away suddenly mesmerized by Robert's smile along with his well-formed lips. Her gaze drifted to the silver-blue shimmer of his eyes. She swallowed hard tamping down the unruly nerves and sensations that fluttered through her.

"Nothing." He grinned showing even white teeth behind his perfectly formed lips. "Nothing. I've chosen the name I prefer. You are Letty to me. As eventually you'll call me Bobby. When I see to your woman's pleasure, I don't want to hear you calling out a name I *dinna* recognize."

"You're incorrigible, Robert. We'll have no more talk of a woman's pleasure and my calling out names. While you employ me to teach, you are Robert to me. We won't hear of anything else."

He leaned so close to her ear she felt the whisper of his breath across her cheek when he asked with a wink. "What does incorrigible mean?"

Pulling away, wary of his quick advances, she spoke, "Never you mind. I don't want to speak of such things. Shall we?" She flashed him the largest smile she could then accepted the proffered arm.

Unlike yesterday this man flashed an aura of confidence.

"I won't stop asking. A man has to further his education. Especially a man such as myself who just recently learned to read and write. I've street smarts. Can pick a pocket with ease. Can run from constables. Can enter a gent's home and divest him of his silver and valuables. Reading and writing is new to me." With his free hand, he picked up the basket and blanket. At the carriage the driver brought the steps for her.

"All that?" She wasn't sure what exactly to make of his statement.

How could that be? Stealing from the rich? Picking pockets? He might have said something about that yesterday. Her mind had been in the clouds.

Scarlett set herself down. Bobby took the seat opposite. "Your green eyes are flecked with gold this afternoon. I didn't see that last night. Is it the sunshine or are you pleased to see me?"

"Is that a compliment?" she asked then couldn't help but smile at him.

He had this air about him. Robert was a flatterer. He had a way with women that could not be denied.

"Are you pleased to see me?"

"Of course, but it must also be attributed to the sunshine. No one has ever said such a thing about my eyes."

"Indeed." He moved on to another topic, "The dress you chose is a bit severe for my taste though. I'd like to see the tops of your breasts. Yes, that would be nice, just a hint mind you. I wouldn't want to share what is going to be mine with anyone else."

The heated flush rose. She was sure it would be on her face for the rest of the afternoon. "There *ye* be doin' it again. Incorrigible *ye* are Robert Munroe." He challenged her in ways she didn't understand.

"If my being that way keeps the rosy blush on your features, don't believe I'll be stopping' anytime soon. Pink on your cheeks becomes you."

"I forgot. We need to tell the driver where to go." She pushed her head out the window as if to tell the man up top.

His strong hands about her waist, Bobby pulled her back, "Hush, I already told him where I want to take you. No need to confuse the poor bloke."

"But..."

"But?" he asked his grin widening.

"I wanted you to see where you should take a debutante, a place where a chaperone isn't needed. You won't know where to go." She began to feel a tiny wave of dizziness descend.

"Don't want to be any place a gentleman would take a debutante. Don't want a debutante. What you have to remember is that I'm no gentleman. Deep down in the deepest part of my heart and soul I'm a rogue. I love to be with women yet I don't consider myself a womanizer. When it comes to a woman's delight, never take anything for granted. Today, with you, we will be alone. As I said, don't want to share you." He held up his hands to stop her speaking. "Just alone. I'm not taking anything from you. I *ken* you're not a willing lass or a *bricky* one either. Someone, a man, scared you. We're going to have to work on that setback. Can't go through life living in fear. Don't want you to be afraid of me. This is just so we have ourselves to ourselves with no interruptions. Maybe get to know each other better. What do you say?"

She sat back with a tiny mew. On one hand wanting to tell him to turn around and take her where she determined while on the other hand yearning to discover what it might be like to be with a man such as Lord Robert Munroe, pickpocket turned marquis.

Alone with a man.

She didn't want to be a coward. She wasn't a *bricky lass* either. *Oh dear.*

Nerves twitched.

Could a man be gallant, see to a woman's needs unselfishly? Could a man be with a woman and not hurt her. Torra and Muira thought some men could be that way. She stared at her feet. Wiggled her toes inside her slippers. Blinked a few times as her mind wandered farther afield than his question. Wandered to places she was afraid to go even while she longed for them.

"Letty?"

Her head popped up. "Scarlet."

"Will you go with me?" His eyes narrowed, as did his lips as he waited, his fingers tense and stiff resting on his knees. "Will you go with me to a place where it will just be you and me."

"Yes, I'll go with you." She sounded unsure yet for the first time she felt a burgeoning confidence. Some would say because of her work, her escort service, she was overconfident.

She wasn't. She always made sure the girls as well as herself were protected. She screened her clients. Tristan, her bodyguard, stood in attendance when they were interviewed as well as the first excursion. The men had to be recommended by customers or people she trusted.

Both the Duke of Southcliff and the Duke of Richmond

recommended Lord Robert Munroe. His credentials were impeccable. He didn't lie or prevaricate about his time on the streets. He didn't mistreat women. What more could an escort want?

He leaned over, his muscled forearms resting on his thighs. He picked up her hands rubbing gentle circles on the inside of her wrists. Her heart raced. "You're cold. They are so tiny."

Cold, yes, she was cold. "Tiny?" she squeaked unable to wrap her mind around what he said as she tugged slightly in a feeble attempt to remove her hands.

He chuckled softly, "Your hands as well as the rest of you. Tiny." He set her hand palm to his palm. "See, my hands overflow yours. Tiny. Delicate. My fingers overlap your wrist."

She cleared her throat. "Until now you haven't lied to me. There is nothing about me that is tiny." Again, she tried to tug her hand from his. For a few seconds he hung on then let go.

"I'm sorry. Didn't mean to hold your hand so long. Thought I might warm you up. Letty, compared to me, you're tiny. I'm a big man in case you haven't noticed. Don't like to have to bend too far to kiss a *lass*."

Unable to meet his gaze she looked out the window. When she finally brought her attention back to him, he was grinning broadly, his even white teeth showing. "Thought you'd never come back to me. Why? Why do you think I lie?"

"I'm taller than most women," she blurted realizing he could make an argument to refute her statement. In fact, he already did so.

"True but not taller than me. Letty, you don't reach my chin."

"I weigh..."

"Hush." He set a finger against her lips. "I could pick you up and carry you without straining myself or gasping for air."

"I..."

He settled against the back of the seat, stretching both arms across the width. his legs extending at an angle to the other side. He closed his eyes, opening them slowly to look her over. He perused her from the tips of her slippers to her eyes, lingering for a few seconds on her hips then her breasts. She warmed all over.

"If we were lovers, I would reach over and lift you up so you would be sitting on my lap. Would you like to sit on my lap, Letty girl?

Have my hands resting on the gentle curve of your hips."

"Are you going to talk naughty?"

She was breathless from the thought of sitting on his lap, from his hands resting on her hips as well as lower as they did yesterday when they danced.

"Talk naughty? Never heard it put that way. Suppose so because once you were on my lap, I'd touch my lips to yours, nibble the corners of your mouth, your eyes, the tip of your nose then that very sensitive spot behind your ears. If we were lovers, I would continue," he spoke softly.

She touched behind her ears feeling as if her eyes were crossing. "Is it sensitive there?" She didn't realize she spoke out loud.

"Should we find out?"

His wicked grin sent her heart into a tailspin. "No," her voice wavered on that single word as she thought she might like to discover the truth of his statement.

"That no didn't sound convincing."

"No," she spoke bolder.

"You could be a *bricky lass*. I promise you it would be like butter on bacon if you wanted to sit on my lap." His voice was husky smooth, created an unknown havoc deep inside. Chaos she didn't have a foggy notion how to deal with. "No." She could lose everything she worked for if she couldn't stay strong in this endeavor. He was a devil. Only touching her with words, he generated scalding heat.

"No?" A long whoosh of air left his lips, "Well, if you were my lover mind you, there would be other more fun things to explore. Once I kissed your lips over and over again until sweet, little sounds rippled from your lips, charming sounds that told me you were enjoying yourself and I was giving you pleasure I would continue down your neck to that point right there." He touched her where she felt her pulse pounding furiously.

She jumped, startled by the heat of the touch, by the rough callouses on his finger.

"I know you would beg for more."

"More?"

"Ah, I see you want to learn what I would do next." He sat back again, seeming to think. "It's debatable. I would either unfasten the hooks at the top of your gown until I could see the sweetly rounded globes of your breasts along with the pink tipped nipples or I would slip your shoes off your delicate feet then explore your legs. You've rather nice legs I imagine. Since you are so very tall, they must be long. Would you wrap them around me when we make love?"

When he mentioned her breasts, she felt her eyes grow wide as she clasped both hands at the base of her throat as if that gesture would protect them. "S-stop..."

"Ah, I see I've given you things to think about."

"We shouldn't. You shouldn't be saying things like that. It's not proper."

He tossed his head back, laughing, "Proper? There is nothing at all proper about us along with what we want."

"I *dinna* say I wanted what you want."

"How are you feeling?" he asked looking smug and so very pleased with himself.

She was sure he knew. Didn't know how he knew.

Without thinking she blurted, "Hot and... *Nay* I will not say it."

"I'm pleased that you're hot and wet. That means all the naughty talk made you excited. Perhaps ready for more ecstasy. Are you a naughty girl for listening? For growing hot and wet when all I did was talk. When we are together, you will be pleased. I will make sure you're delighted. You're a passionate woman, Letty Gordon. There is no need for you to hold yourself back, not for the right man."

She had no words as she stared at the perfectly aligned floorboards in the carriage. Nothing what he said rung true for her. She didn't feel the ache between her legs. When her uncle mauled her then forced her, pain, it was only pain she felt. How could she believe he would be so very different? That what he said he was going to do wouldn't hurt.

"You cannot be sure I would be delighted." Her voice hitched with a soft waver of doubt. "You know nothing about me."

"I can," he whispered. "When you've the courage, I'll prove it to you but not until you are willing to give all of yourself over to my capable hands..." he paused gazing at her tenderly. "You won't regret your decision and be assured I want to learn all I can about you. I won't stop until I know you inside and out."

"I think we're here."

When the carriage stopped, she rushed through the open door then to the ground without benefit of the steps. She was so in over her head with this man. Drowning, that's what was happening to her. What would he do or say next to set her teeth rattling and stretch her nerves until she thought they would snap? To make her long for what he spoke of. Even now she wondered what his bold touch would generate inside her.

She ran to the edge of the small river flowing over rocks to find its way down into little, swirling pools. The clear water looked crisp and cold coming from snow melt higher in the crags. Her hands were clasped together, her focus on a spinning eddy in front of her when his hands rested on her shoulders. They were gentle contradicting the innate strength of the man. She kept the surprised gasp behind her lips.

"You don't need to fear me, Letty." His voice was deep, soothing yet exciting at the same time. "We will do well together you and I."

Oh, dear Lord, what was she to do?

~ * ~

"Didn't know the lad's identity was discovered. Suppose it had to happen sometime. Would rather have had it happen on my terms." Avery Bainbridge paced the tiny apartment room in Paris where he met his second in command, Jocko.

Avery, or Scarface as he was known in the dregs of London, fled England three years ago with the law after him. He understood he couldn't resurface anywhere near London or Glasgow except he needed to take care of urgent business. Jocko was afraid now that Bobby obtained power and wealth, he would seek to take his place in the organization. Once a criminal always a criminal.

Leslie Stewart working with Drake Montgomerie discovered the true identity of Bobby, one of Jocko's street urchins. Two children twenty-two years ago were abducted from their parents or guardians. The third one, Bobby, was the son of one of his minions. Jocko was the man who raised Bobby, Billy as well as Piper. He was the man who made sure they survived the streets.

The marquis, Bobby's father, wanted out of the organization. Didn't agree with Avery, the leader, both in Glasgow and London, or want to be part of his plans. Didn't like the blackmail as well as the kidnapping of the babies. So, Avery had the lord murdered, after his wife was raped in front of her husband then murdered also. He took their son, Bobby, under his wing. Gave him to Jocko to keep safe. Avery made sure the lad was kept in the bowels of London, made sure Bobby learned the trade. The boy was an apt pupil. In his own way he took care of the boy planning on reinstating him as the leader in Glasgow when the time was right. Those three, two boys and a girl lived in abject poverty for the first years of their lives. There were others, nonetheless these three were the most important to him.

He lost out on the revenge he sought when Piper was caught nabbing a gent's purse. The Scottish laird, Brett MacLachlan, who nabbed her, ended up wedding her. She was reunited with her mother, a formidable woman known as The Duchess. He regretted their reunion. For a little while the revenge tasted so sweet.

The Duchess was his sister-in-law. He was the second son so he inherited nothing. Avery killed his brother, the duke, then kidnapped the baby girl. The duke, his older brother, defending himself slashed him from his forehead to his chin. That was when Avery became Scarface. He took great delight in knowing the little girl was true nobility, his brother's daughter when he watched her picking pockets in Vauxhall Garden.

Now he had Lord Robert Wyatt Munroe to contend with, to bring him over to his side. The task wouldn't be an easy one. He needed to find something to hold over the man's head. At this time there was nothing he could use. When Bobby regained his title, he also gained a pardon.

"Bobby has employed an escort to teach him how to be a proper lord," Sherry, Jocko's emissary in Glasgow said. "We'll see how that goes. She's supposed to teach him how to be a gentleman."

"He will have to learn a great deal if he's to survive the gossip along with the defamation of his character," Avery mused thinking of all the young man had done while working in St. Giles Parish, while the boy increased his fortunes with the stolen booty. He understood one day his identity would be revealed. What happened next was up to him.

"Do you want me to return, keep an eye on the two of them, the escort and the marquis?"

Avery thought for a few seconds. "Jocko can do that. You think there might be something between them?" Avery was slightly amused at the thought. "Who is this lady who calls herself an escort? I would learn more about her."

"Heard tell she's the daughter of a wealthy earl. Dead he is. Scarlett Gordon is her name. For some reason no one speaks of, she left home when she was fifteen. Want me to learn more?"

"Yes, Jocko has enough to do in London. Stay in Glasgow. Send messages from here on out. If I think it's safe, I might show up in the city. Not like anyone would recognize me there."

After Sherry left, Avery sat down with his mistress and a glass of brandy. She was good to him, loyal. He truly should marry her. If he traveled to Scotland to oversee this situation, he would see to that. When he fled London with her three years ago, he considered marriage.

Just didn't get around to doing so.

"You're going to risk it all to return to England," she said her eyes filling with moisture.

He heard no question in her voice. Understood she was resigned might even travel with him. "I miss the excitement."

"You don't have to do that. You've men who can accomplish what needs to be done."

"Will you marry me?"

Avery didn't get down on one knee. Would never lower himself to something like that, especially with a woman.

"You don't think you're coming back..." Her voice trailed off. She turned away as she stared fixedly at the window.

"I don't have a death wish," he told her stepping closer, nuzzling her neck. "Come to bed with me. We can speak of this later."

Avery sensed her reticence. Didn't want her to draw away from him. Couldn't lose her. Despite his horrific scar, she cared for him. Love he didn't know nor did he question.

"I don't want you to go." Her rigid voice sent a sharp stab of pain into his gut.

"But will you marry me?"

"If you promise not to leave."

"Can't do that."

"Then..."

He placed a finger on her lips. "Hush. If I don't come back, I need to know you're taken care of. You'll have enough funds to live wherever you want. Returning to London is a possibility for you."

She capitulated. Avery knew it was something she wanted. "Yes, Avery, I'll become your wife."

Once a McClellan lass

Beautiful, naughty and audaciously daring, young Nickie Gray is a McClellan princess through and through—as wild and reckless as the most incorrigible of her male cousins. Now that she has reached a marriageable age, Nickie has set her amorous sights on a most unsuitable male—the notorious rake and womanizer known to all mamas on the debutante scene in London as dangerous. When her chaperone tells her all rakes are off limits, she finds the challenge one she sets her mind to.

Always a McInnis rake

Not expecting to find a ravishing woman throwing herself at him yet blatantly willing to accept whatever overtures she makes, handsome Collin McInnis is thrilled by the brazen escapades of this naïve creature and is willing to experience her high-spirited advances with no expectations of commitment. On the high seas, he is bested by a vivacious beauty whose love of freedom and adventure rivals his own...and by an inescapable tidal wave of passion that threatens to engulf them both.

A few days shy of All Hallows' Eve Connal McKenna, Laird of

Clan Chattan stands on the parapets of his castle. Bonfires line the hillsides while his clan prepares for the upcoming festivities. Drawn by the whispering of the wind, Connal McKenna feels a strange restlessness in his soul. Setting out to discover the wickedness that is calling to him, he discovers his mate. With gentle words and sensuous kisses, the auburn-eyed highlander conquers his mate, the beautiful, defiant Wynnie Adair who he comes upon during an evening ride. She must ultimately put her trust in the only man who can save her from the ruthless plans of her father and succumb to his gentle coaxing.

In Brady's Arms
Sweet McKenna Book Two

Forced to run from the only home she knows, beautiful, headstrong Lillian Townsends seeks shelter in the wild highlands where the McKenna clan live. Trying to avoid a betrothal contract signed by her stepfather to an aging lord, she is desperate to find a means to sidestep the inevitable, including a marriage to the oldest son of the laird. Lilly is enamored of the young lord who pursues her with unrelenting determination flashing his devilishly handsome charms. She is hard pressed to resist.

Besotted from the first moment Brady McKenna sees Lilly, he is determined to find a means to coax her into his arms and bed. With only the promise of carnal pleasure as his mistress, Brady relentlessly pursues the woman who has unwittingly forged a place in his heart. She is like no other woman, proud, defiant and enchanting. Despite his father's advice to stay away from her, he cannot. He boldly seeks her out and makes her his own.

Nobody but Walker
Sweet McKenna Book Three

The Highland Lass...

She was brought up, adored and loved by a doting mother and father ardently protected by her brothers. She was everything sweet and innocent until she was faced with betrayal and an unexpected and out of wedlock pregnancy. When she gave her love to a man who couldn't return her passion and commitment, she was left devastated and furious. Faced with the loss of her child if she didn't comply to his demands, Crissie McKenna followed him to Belfast then on to his country home to discover he was already married.

...The Irishman

Stunned to find out his one and only encounter with the woman he wanted to love forever created a child, Walker Endicott, Earl of Briarwood, claimed his child as his only heir. Walker threatened all her previously held values even while he thrilled her senses. From the moment he first saw her to the second she ran after him begging him to make love to her, his captivating masculinity held her fascinated. In his arms she would know tempestuous passion, bitter despair, and a soaring joy that would humble them both before the power of love.

Roby's Moonlit Night
Sweet McKenna Book Four

Once she'd been a pampered child with high expectations for her future blessed with love. Then she became an innocent pawn in a terrible game of greed and power. Now, with a noose around her neck, Pippa was to hang before she had the chance to unveil the men who drove her from her home, before she had the chance to live.

Roby McKenna was a man blessed with endless charm and wit. While he searched for his eternal love across the Atlantic in a new land, he would have to come home to find her. His silver blue eyes could sparkle with amusement or harden to steel gray with displeasure. He had all the women a man could want or need. As he grew older, mistresses were not enough. A quirk of fate brought him to the gallows, a spark of destiny made him claim the condemned Pippa as his bride.

Made for Houston
Sweet McKenna Book Five

Leah Kennedy is as wary of people as she is strikingly beautiful. However, the shocking death of her father that forever changed her girlhood has left her terrified of the very love she desperately longs for. Only in the untamed splendor of the Scottish crags does she feel safe from the feelings she stirs in men and the cruel mockery of Selkirk's villagers.

Debonair, well-educated doctor Houston Stuart has turned his back on social privilege along with professional honors to set up a medical practice in the lowlands of Scotland. There, serving those who need him the most, he hopes to forget the bitter memories and disillusionment that disturb his days.

Coincidence brings the cultured doctor and this fey mountain girl together. Something as bizarre as destiny disrupts the obstacle of birth and breeding, stubborn pride and fear which has kept them apart...as each seeks to heal the other's wounds with a raw passion neither can deny and all the odds against them cannot defeat.

Say You Love Kit
Sweet McKenna Book Six

Fascinated...

When the woman stepped through the door of the pub, the sun setting her fiery red hair glowing around her delicate features, Kit Stuart finds himself captivated by the sight. The moment he sees her he knows she will be his. Convincing the fire-haired lady of that fact isn't easy. After she calls out another man's name when he kisses her that night, he is instantly enraged as well as jealous. The road they travel is fraught with secrets that neither can tell. Trust is an elusive quality that neither can give.

Intrigued…

Forced to run for her life, desperate and afraid, Aila MacDuff willingly enters into the Kinnel Stones, a mysterious place where people disappear then appear magically in different times. At the first sight of Kit, she finds herself inexplicably drawn to him. She's been told to search for her mate and that she will know when she finds him. Aila doesn't know what this man's name is or what he looks like. Nonetheless, she is certain he will be similar to her mate from one hundred years earlier. Despite the fact she is falling in love with Kit, he can't be her mate. Her mate is a shifter. Kit is not.

My Sweet Broc
Bad Boys Book One

He's a bad bad boy...

Broc Wallace is a fun-loving rake who never thought any beautiful woman could melt his heart. He lives life in the present enjoying the camaraderie of his friends and the pleasures of his mistress. When Bliss races into his life, he is ill prepared to deal with her secrets or give up the tenor of his life. When the truth is revealed, he finds himself unable to forgive and forget the betrayal.

...but she's sweet for him

Bliss MacTavish knows she's playing with fire when she refuses to tell this bad boy her name. He tempts her with sweet whispers of seduction knowing her innocent nature will be unable to refuse all he yearns to give her. Deciding to follow her heart, she finds the repercussions more than she bargains for when she gives herself to this bad boy.

Crazy for Cam
Bad Boys Book Two

He's a bad bad boy...

Lord Cam MacEwen, Viscount of Rosehill, tries his best to be proper and court the lady of his dreams in the acceptable way. The feat proves impossible when the lady in question uses every means at her disposal to tempt him. He fights his jealousy for another man as well as the need to make her his own, finally giving in to her irresistible passion.

...but she's crazy for him.

Chelsea MacTavish wants the bad boy she fell in love with and kissed just before her eighteenth birthday. With feminine wiles and irresistible allure, the sensuous lady plans to best Cam at his game of hearts and make him forget his need to court her properly.

Falling for Flynt
Bad Boys Book Three

He's a bad, bad boy...

Fascinated by Hope's loss of memory yet haunted by her sultry beauty, Flynt is irresistibly drawn to the stoic miss—and into her troubles with the sultan who wants her for himself. When he discovers she is the sister of his best friend, his pride keeps him from pursuing her and making her his.

...but she's falling for him.

Raised in a harem but now penniless, alone and without her memory, Hope must discover a way to remember all that she has lost. She finds a way to continue with her life as a servant in Flynt's home. The first sight of Flynt steals Hope's breath as well as her heart. Can she overcome her fears and give herself to the man she fell in love with.

Dancing With Donal
Bad Boys Book Four

He's a bad bad boy...

Once a bad boy always a bad boy, Donal Chamberlin's carefree ways come crashing down around him when he meets the ravishingly beautiful Daryl MacTavish, the innocent little sister of one of his best friends. He is determined to win her heart as he sets his sights on marriage and an heir. His past gets in the way of his quest when a woman he once loved threatens Daryl's life.

...but she's dancing with him.

Daryl has seen the control her sister's husbands hold over them. She yearns for a life where she makes decisions for herself. No man will have power over her. But no man kisses her the way Donal does. No man can make her forget all her goals leaving her helpless to give up her dreams. Yet Donal is determined to dance through all the barriers she thrust in front of him, pursuing her until she says yes.

Loving Leslie
Bad Boys Book Five

He's a bad bad boy...

Leslie Stewart, Duke of Southcliff is stoic, set in his ways, a spy who is used to having his life well ordered. He expects life to continue on in this perfectly conventional fashion. He assumes his bad boy status while keeping mamas and debutantes at arm's length. An heir is needed but Leslie has every intention of finding a woman who doesn't covet his wealth and tittle. He is irresistibly drawn to the headstrong young lady who becomes more beautiful as she develops into a woman.

...but she is loving him.

When Leslie kisses Lacie MacTavish, she knows even at the tender age of fifteen this is the man of her dreams. Forced to wait until she comes of age, Lacie withdraws into herself. Now she is eighteen and Leslie has returned from a mission for the British Government ready to claim her as his bride. She refuses him and he must find a way to seduce her and in the process create a burning passion within her, which she cannot deny.

Pleasing Arie
Bad Boys Book Six

He's a bad bad boy...

Arie Demir has never been denied anything in his life. He takes what he wants. What he undeniably yearns for is the beautiful redheaded spitfire he sees in a restaurant in Glasgow. At every turn, she confuses him by disputing his power over her. Alison refuses to accept the fact he owns her. While Arie tries desperately with patience and tenderness to drive her wild with new sensations, his scorching kisses ignite the fires of her very soul to make her understand he is all she will ever want.

...but is she pleasing him?

Alison Fletcher never expected to find herself kidnapped and sold to a whorehouse then bought by a Turkish sultan to become his slave. She vows to never surrender to the arrogant man who believes he owns her. She is stunned by the magnificently handsome man who awaits her compliance. Unexpectedly, she finds Arie the lesser of all the evils. The hidden depths of his mesmerizing dark brown eyes hold her into their power; his muscular embrace makes her weak with desire. She is his to do with as he wishes.

Graham's Wicked Kiss
Bad Boys Book Seven

He's a bad bad boy...

Graham Chamberlin is stunned to find three young boys dangling from the trees lining the drive to Runningmead Manner. On further inspection, he is astonished at their obsession to protect a young woman who has been brutalized by her pimp. The woman he discovers hiding in a third-floor attic room is gravely injured. He takes the silver haired stowaway under his wing. Clearly, Graham's new guest is a lady with many secrets. He is determined to unlock all the mysteries surrounding her.

...But she can't resist his wicked kiss.

The years since Ria left the convent where she was raised have been a nightmare. Her secrets are dangerous—as is the powerful man determined to find her. Handsome Graham Chamberlin is clearly a gentleman with secrets of his own, but staying with him could mean the difference between life and death for Ria. With each passing day, her handsome host turns Ria's convalescence into an increasingly sensual escape. Now her greatest challenge may be imagining anything less than a future in his arms.

Feeling Etienne's Love
Bad Boys Book Eight

He's a bad bad boy...

Etienne Dubois is the son of a wealthy vineyard owner who craves the excitement of putting his life on the line. Working with the French government and as a confidant of King Charles X give him reasons for living. An encounter with a beautiful young woman in a plush bordello in Paris has him rethinking his roguish ways. Etienne never expects to become a father especially from one encounter with an innocent prostitute who whispers his name and has him rethinking his well-ordered life.

...But she can't help feeling his love.

Elisa Moreau, the only daughter of Angelique Moreau, the owner of an exclusive bordello in Bordeaux, France, has loved Etienne Dubois since she was six. Unfortunately, until an unexpected encounter at a brothel in Paris puts the two of them in the same room, Etienne doesn't even know she exists. Confused but wanting Etienne and this chance meeting to never end, Elisa gives herself to the man who has held her heart in hands for what seems like her entire life.

All I Want Is Link
Bad Boys Book Nine

He's a bad bad boy...

Merry Stewart is wildly unpredictable. Left alone to run wild over the Bordeaux and Scottish countryside she becomes impetuous and daringly bold. Over the years, she's found she can bedevil her softhearted brothers into allowing her exploits to go unnoticed. As a young woman she has learned she can do as she pleases when she pleases. Now, Merry has set her amorous sights on the Duke of Weston—a man she has never met but has every intention of marrying. No other suitor will satisfy her—especially not the exceptionally striking, horse breeder, Devlin Mathews.

...she's the woman of his desires.

Posing as commoner Devlin Mathews to escape a potentially fatal confrontation, Devlin is enthralled and infuriated by the audacious, duke-hunting dark haired vixen. Bedeviled at every opportunity, he finds dealing with the tiny she-devil exasperating as well as intriguing. Without revealing his true identify, the infamous rogue pledges to thwart Merry's plans to wed the man of her dream-never imagining the bewitching strategist would turn out to be the only woman he would ever dream of marrying.

Devlin's Angel
Bad Boys Book Ten

He's a bad bad boy...

Merry Stewart is wildly unpredictable. Left alone to run wild over the Bordeaux and Scottish countryside she becomes impetuous and daringly bold. Over the years, she's found she can bedevil her softhearted brothers into allowing her exploits to go unnoticed. As a young woman she has learned she can do as she pleases when she pleases. Now, Merry has set her amorous sights on the Duke of Weston—a man she has never met but has every intention of marrying. No other suitor will satisfy her—especially not the exceptionally striking, horse breeder, Devlin Mathews.

...she's the woman of his desires.

Posing as commoner Devlin Mathews to escape a potentially fatal confrontation, Devlin is enthralled and infuriated by the audacious, duke-hunting dark haired vixen. Bedeviled at every opportunity, he finds dealing with the tiny she-devil exasperating as well as intriguing. Without revealing his true identify, the infamous rogue pledges to thwart Merry's plans to wed the man of her dream-never imagining the bewitching strategist would turn out to be the only woman he would ever dream of marrying.

Foolish for Piper

The pickpocket...
Piper has spent her life surviving the streets of St. Giles Parish in London, a den of iniquity and crime. Masquerading as a boy she escapes the whorehouses the young girls are sent to as they come of age. The day she encounters Brett MacLachlan begins the same as every other one. When she picks his pocket, she has no idea her life is going to change irreversibly.
...and the mark
Handsome aristocrat Brett MacLachlan has come to London for his amusement only to find his world turned upside down by a thief and her dog. From the moment he spots her, Brett knows there is something intrinsically wrong. In his arms, Piper discovers passion and joy. Yet secrets of her past haunt her, and a scar will tell the true tale as well as her identity.

Taylor's Destiny

She traveled to another time and place to change destiny...

Enjoying a day of sailing, Taylor Maxwell never expected after a suffering a concussion she would wake up in another century. A resilient independent woman in the twenty-first century, the blond beauty is ill prepared for life in the 1800s. Her first sight of the naval captain who rescues her makes her heart stop, giving her hope for her future.

His life is transformed by a woman who appears from nowhere...

Born to a life of ease, Reid Stewart defies the dictates of those born to aristocracy and chooses a life of adventure in the navy and as a spy for the crown. When he discovers a nearly naked woman on the bow of small sailing ship, his heart warms. His love for Taylor and his need to protect her from a man who pursues her might cost him his life as well as hers.

Caitlin's Duke

She played a fiddle in an Irish pub...

Caitlin O'Shea Is the most beautiful woman Roc Leighton has ever seen. With her blue violet eyes and long black hair she captivates him. In turn he mesmerizes Caitlin. Caught in the power of his gaze as he watches her, she is wise enough to know he desires her but will never give his heart to her. Caitlin has vowed to never be any man's mistress.

And fell in love with an English Lord...

Roc knows the first time he watches her play the fiddle and dance around the pub, she will be his next mistress. Despite her protest, he will find a way to convince her that her place is with him. While Caitlin's determination to keep her vows, fate takes a cruel turn and she is forced to seek refuge with Roc.

Catching Meara
Book One in the McKenna Clan Series

Meara Thorton was a feisty, world-class computer hacker—cornered by the FBI and shockingly given the chance to be their newly acquired technical analyst. Brilliant and intuitive, yet aching with the loss of everyone she has cared about, her restless heart led her to discover a love she fought and a world she didn't know could possibly exist.

Sweet Sexy Sadie
Book Two in the McKenna Clan Series

From the first time Sadie's eyes met those of Brody McKenna in the hot Sierra Madre Mountains, theirs was a potent attraction—not gentle, slow, and easy, but hot, hard, and all-consuming. The daughter of a dysfunctional family, Sadie had dreams no man could wrench from her with hot sex and an all-consuming passion. She'd challenge this alpha male with all the strength she possessed. But her red hair, fiery temperament, and indomitable spirit obsessed Brody...and he knew he had to find a way to show her he was more than he appeared and convince her to make a life with him.

Sweet Misbehavin'
Book Three in the McKenna Clan Series

Cast adrift after fleeing the home of Jokul, the ice demon, Atantsi, a firestarter, grew to womanhood as she moved through time to keep the demon from finding her. Though stubborn and courageous, she was ill prepared to use powers she had not been taught. Her first sight of the intoxicating Carr McKenna left her breathless, and her second encounter gave her hope for a future she never thought she had.

A playboy, a second son and a shifter, a man who thought his life would be carefree, Carr McKenna was shocked to discover the woman he'd paid as an escort is a firestarter who is running for her life. He is the leader of all the McKennas around the world and that he has multiple powers. His passion for Margo and the need to defend her might cost him his life as well as hers.

Sweet Talkin' Sugar
Book Four in the McKenna Clan Series

Lyonesse McKenna, was dreaming, or was she? From the instant Lyn saw Deacon McClain across a black jack table in a crowed Las Vegas casino the unmistakable attraction sent Lyn's senses flying into overdrive. Her family of shapeshifters believed in soul mates. She'd always been skeptical yet she couldn't help but question the way her heart sped when he looked at her.

When Deacon appeared in Las Vegas he knew his first job was to save Lyn from a Sea Demon, but the next order of business was to convince her he would someday mean more to her than she'd ever expected. But her stubborn nature and unbendable spirit consumed Deacon...and he had to chase away all the demons real and imagined in order to win her heart.

Sweet Surrender
Book Five in the McKenna Clan Series

Ripped from her family at the top of Infinity Cliff, Kimi McKenna finds herself thrust somewhere into the future. Dark elements threaten to destroy the earth unless Kimi can work together with the white witch to stop the destruction. Confused by her mate's role in the conspiracy, she refuses to acknowledge the connection. But amidst raging fire and attacks on the people she is coming to hold dear, she allows Maska O'keefe into her heart.

Maska O'keefe has loved the beautiful shapeshifter for years. Unable to save her life years ago, he vows to watch over her as he is given a second chance to convince her that even though he is a witch and not a shifter, they are indeed soul mates. Kimi's divided loyalties between her family and the cause she is now a part of will determine their relationship. Only the part she plays as the messiah can bring this to a conclusion in the final battle.

Dakota's Bride
The first book in the Lakota/Pinkerton Series

When Emma St. John received her brother's letter imploring her to escape her stepfather's vengeful scheme and to trust Dakota Barringer with her life, she was willing to chance it. But the handsome, brooding riverboat owner Emma found in Natchez a danger of another kind. For Emma soon found herself surrendering to an unrelenting desire.

Raised by the Sioux when his parents were killed, Dakota had been betrayed once before by a white woman. He wasn't about to trust another, especially one claiming that her stepfather, a powerful U.S. senator, had framed her as a murderess. But he couldn't let Emma's intoxicating effect on him. Now Dakota would risk his very life to protect the innocent beauty who had seduced him with her tender love.

My Angel
The second book in the Lakota/Pinkerton Series

A BEAUTY IN BUCKSKINS
When her father decided to send her to a finishing school back East, Angela Chamberlain refused to be confined to stuffy drawing rooms. Instead, the daring spitfire who could shoot like a man and ride like the wind longed for a life of adventure and romance—and she knew exactly who could give it to her. Devil Blackmoor was a hired gun with a dangerous reputation. But Angela was willing to go to the ends of the earth to capture the handsome devil's heart.

A DEVIL IN DISGUISE
He'd come to America looking for excitement, but Devil Blackmoor got more than he bargained for when he encountered a beautiful rebel who answered his kisses with a wild innocence that touched his very soul. Yet standing between them were more obstacles than either ever dreamed. For Devil had strapped on a gun for the wrong man. And that made Angela his enemy. Now he'll have to choose between his duty and the woman he loves more than life.

The Locket
The third book in the Lakota/Pinkerton Series

The year is 1894. Seeking revenge for crimes against his family, Misha Petrovich follows a path that leads straight to Ariel Cameron's boarding house in Mist Harbor, Oregon. A family heirloom in Ariel's possession leads Misha to believe she is guilty. The locket has been handed down to the oldest girl in the Petrovich family for generations. Ariel is innocent of wrong doing, but her father is not. Misha is torn by his feelings for Ariel and his need for restitution against her father. Knowing that the relationship between them is fragile, Misha does everything in his power to protect Ariel's father. His efforts are to no avail when her father is shot. Ariel comes to realize Misha's steadfast courage and determination to protect her and her father despite what has happened to his family. Ariel's love and devotion heals Misha's heart.

The Talisman
The fourth book in the Lakota/Pinkerton Series

Running from a marriage that lasted one night, Dr. Moriah McKeown discovers the land she has settled on is coveted by determined and lawless men. Yet the proud young woman who once vowed never to abandon her home has second thoughts when her adopted children are threatened. Her only recourse is to enlist the aid of a dark, dangerous gun for hire.

Haunted by the past and a betrayal he will never forgive, Ian Civanovich uses his fast gun and his reckless courage to forget the faithlessness of a woman in his past. He will trust no female—nor will he rest until the threat hovering over Moriah McKeown is put to rest.

Forever His
The fifth book in the Lakota/Pinkerton Series

Struggling to come to terms with the part she played in Jacob St.

John's death, Etta Barringer resigns from Pinkerton Agency and seeks peace and solace in a Rocky Mountain Cabin.

Jacob has vowed to discover the reason Etta has betrayed him, sold him out to his enemy and left him for dead.

Isolated in their cabin, they discover their love for each other and learn to trust. But the trust is shattered when Jacob learns she is married to his sworn enemy; the man who left him in the desert to die.

Allura's Secret
Twelve Dancing Princesses Book One

Allura McClellan is horrified by her father's decision to take out an ad in the Times awarding her to the man strong enough and smart enough to win her hand and uncover her secrets. She's an intelligent young woman who takes great delight in the freedom allotted to her by her father. She's well aware that marriage would effectively curtail the adventures she's shared with her sisters and cousins.

Hunter Gray is nothing like the other men who've arrived to vie for Allura's hand in marriage and everything that goes along with it. However, he is the first to refuse to concede defeat and pursue her despite her attempts to disguise her true appearance. It's her temperament that is of more concern to him than her looks. Hunter has worked all his life with the hope of someday owning his own land. Now that it looks like there's a very real possibility that everything he's ever wanted is within reach nothing is going to deter him – including Miss Allura's disagreeable disposition.

Amorica's Wager
Twelve Dancing Princesses Book Two

Amorica Hepburn was sent to London to find a husband. Finding a man was the last item on her agenda. With her two cousins, Amorica wagers she can dissuade her suitor before the others. Despite her efforts she discovers a chemistry that cannot be denied. Suddenly she is the arrogant man's wife, pledged to a marriage neither desire. But swept off to his ancestral home above the Dover cliffs and into his strong embrace, Amorica is soon possessed by a raging passion for the husband she had vowed to despise...

Damian Andrews couldn't afford to trust the emerald-eyed spitfire who happened upon his secret. Amorica's hatred of all men of his kind only inflames the war that rages between them. Still, he can not control the intense desire his stubborn bride inspires, or make her surrender to his will until he has conquered the headstrong beauty on the battlefield of love...

Ravyn's Marriage of Inconvenience
Twelve Dancing Princesses Book Three

A REGAL BEAUTY

When the duchess decides to wed her to a wastrel and a fop, Ravyn Grahm takes matters into her own hands and declares her engagement to another man. Instead of fessing up and telling her great aunt what she has done, she goes through with the pretense. Ariec Lakeland is the bastard son of an earl and has a dangerous reputation. But Ravyn is willing to do most anything to keep the duchess from discovering the lie.

A DEVIL-MAY-CARE SMUGGLER

He'd bought land in America, looking to put down roots and end his life of adventure, but Ariec Lakeland got more than he bargained for when he encountered a beautiful heiress who made a promise she didn't want to keep. But the promise could not be undone and standing between them were more obstacles than either ever dreamed. Ariec had made plans to spend the rest of his life in America and that was at odds with Ravyn's plan of living in England and running her father's estate. Now, he'll have to choose between his dreams and the woman he loves more than life.

Christel's Sunrise
Twelve Dancing Princesses Book Four

He Made Her An Offer...

Life has thrown Christel McClellan some experiences that could have devastated a less determined woman. Beautiful, self-assured and fiercely independent, she is trying to forget the loss of her stillborn child. But is the child alive?

She Couldn't Deny...

Life is carefree for Ryder MacLaren who loves to see what is on the other side of the sunrise. Laird of Clan MacLaren, he is wealthy, handsome and happily unencumbered...until stunning Christel McClellan enters his life. When he hears her story, he believes the child she thought dead has been sold to a wealthy buyer.

Storm's Passion
Twelve Dancing Princesses Book Five

SHE MADE A PROPOSAL...

Life strikes Storm Graham a shattering blow when she learns her father has bartered her to a man she detests. Storm is beautiful, self–assured and fiercely independent, and refuses to be a pawn in her father's schemes, yet she can find no way out of this bargain made in hell. Going on the offensive she asks the wealthiest man on the eastern coast of England to marry her, never believing she might fall in love.

HE TRIED TO REFUSE...

For Hadden Johnston life has provided everything he ever wanted, including a sanctuary for homeless children. He is wealthy, handsome and happily unencumbered...until stunning Storm Graham marches into his life and proposes a marriage of convenience. Yet this type of marriage to a woman who inflames his senses is far from acceptable. If he's going to be tied down, he will move heaven and earth to have this woman warming his bed.

Gotta Have Fayth
Twelve Dancing Princesses Book Six

A regal beauty with raven hair and piercing blue eyes, Fayth Graham is unwilling to parade herself in front of the wealthy Lords of England during the season. Seeking a means to dissuade any man wishing to wed her, she seeks a way to ruin herself for marriage. When she unexpectedly meets a man with sparkling gray eyes and an infectious grin, she decides this is the man who will keep her from agreeing to obey.

He returned from six months at sea, looking for a few nights of pleasure with a willing lass, but Jarret Kinsley got more than he bargained for when he met a beautiful debutant who responded to his kisses with a wild innocence that touched his heart. Yet the obstacles looming between them might rip them apart. Both had vowed never to marry, so when consequences of their dalliances got in the way, Jarret would have to choose between the life he's always desired and the woman he loves more than life.

Ella's Pleasure
Twelve Dancing Princesses Book Seven

A WHISPER OF PLEASURE
Ella Hepburn was an auburn haired debutant from the harsh Scottish coastline—a wild innocent to be seduced and tamed. A spirited beauty, she captivated Drake Montgomerie's jaded heart—while succumbing to the smoldering desire she felt for her unyielding suitor.

A WHISPER OF DANGER
In Drake Montgomerie's glittering world of money and privilege, young Ella discovered passion and desire could overcome everything she'd been taught to resist—entangling Drake, the heir apparent, in a lethal coil of aristocratic family intrigue. But grave peril would only nurse the sparks of a love that knew no limits and a magnificent ecstasy that would not be denied.

Eveleen's Seduction
Twelve Dancing Princesses Book Eight

A WHISPER OF SEDUCTION

A brutal attack on Eveleen Hepburn's cherished island off the Scottish coastline leaves her shattered and bewildered. Learning a man she once trusted can kill as easily as he can breathe even though the deed saves her life, creates questions that need answers. An innocent beauty, she enchants Logan Maxwell's cynical heart—giving in to the raging passion she feels for her mysterious suitor.

A WHISPER OF INTRIGUE

In Logan's Maxwell's world of espionage and privilege, young Eveleen discovers truths about herself she never expected, and a need for passion and love can overcome all her fears if she learns to accept certain truths. She finds herself entangled in a lethal battle for land that was once owned by French nobility, taken from them during the revolution and sold to Maxwell. But grave peril would unleash the flames of love that simmers, creating a magical union that cannot be refuted.

Tavia's Deception
Twelve Dancing Princesses Book Nine

WHISPERS OF DECEPTION

When her father decides to send her to London for her season, Tavia Hepburn resolves to see the world instead. The raven haired beauty decides to disguise herself as a lad and find employment on a ship bound for Barcelona as a cabin boy. But she never bargains on finding passion and love to a red haired sea captain who rescues her from certain death.

WHISPERS OF MURDER

For James Macmurra, the world is black and white until he meets a young debutante, who turns his world upside down. He's unable to deny Tavia's intoxicating effect on him. In a match tense with obstacles, unwillingness to divulge secrets, and unforeseen peril, irresistible desire and passion grows into undeniable love. James would risk his life to shelter and protect the innocent debutante who seduces him with her sweet love.

Larena's Fascination
Twelve Dancing Princesses Book Ten

WHISPERS OF FASCINATION

Fiery, free spirited Larena Graham never wanted to marry a duke. She is thrilled to be in love with the fourth son of an aristocrat, Gavin Broon. But when it seems Gavin ignores her, she set her sights on politics and bettering human life. Unsuspecting intrigue and a plot against her, she continues her dangerous plans despite Gavin's wishes.

WHISPERS OF TRUST

Gavin has every intention of properly courting the beautiful Larena until he must leave the city in order to put his affairs in order. Returning to London, he finds the woman he means to make his own is embroiled in political protests that could lead to a prison ship. Larena must learn to trust the handsome Scotsman whose most pressing mission is to protect her and keep her from harm.

Tira's Education
Twelve Dancing Princesses Book Eleven

WHISPERS OF EDUCATION

Learning how to build ships is Tira Hepburn's only dream until she meets Jamie Lundin and her world is turned upside down. With her raven black hair and vivid green eyes, she tempts Jamie and pushes him to defy his vows. She never bargains on finding an irrevocable love and a passion to a man who cannot fulfill her dreams despite his burning desire for her.

WHISPERS OF A BARGAIN

Arrogant and self-assured Jamie is brought up short when Tira captures his heart. All his carefully made plans are put to the test when he decides to teach her the art of ship building if she will spend a week with him alone on his ship. He is unable to deny Tira's intoxicating effect on him. When Tira leaves him behind unwilling to live with him without the benefit of marriage, he races after her. Jamie will risk everything to shelter and protect the innocent debutante who seduces him with her sweet love.

Aidan's Love
Twelve Dancing Princesses Book Twelve

Whispers of Love

Aidan McLellan has loved since she first set eyes on him as a young girl. Spontaneous, wild and eager to grow up, Aidan haunts his waking thoughts day and night, insinuating herself into his life. With her fiery red hair and sparkling sapphire eyes, she seizes Blade's heart even while he tries to resist the innocent child until she becomes a woman.

Whispers of Courage

Blade has waited what seems a lifetime to claim the woman who captures his heart as a little girl. Claiming his inheritance before his younger brother takes what is rightfully his, Blade must convince Aidan of his sincerity after years of avoidance and wed her before his father dies so he can return home, securing his rightful place. Everything is put to the test when his life as well as Aidan's is threatened by the man who once called him brother.

Don't Hustle Letty
Good Girls Book One

She's a good girl...

As tempted as Scarlett was, she had too many secrets to let

someone enter her world—secrets that would send any reasonable man to the farthest ends of the earth. Bobby was far from reasonable and despite her desperate attempts to hold him at bay, he would not let her past destroy their future. With her escort service, Scarlett used men and their insatiable lust for women to capitalize on the means to survive and prosper. She vowed to never wed, to never put herself in the control of a man.

...nonetheless he has other ideas.

Lord Robert Munroe, with his newly acquired title of marquis goes to Scarlett's for training on how to comport himself. The marquis, better known as Bobby, knows how to pick a pocket as well as get into a bloke's home to steal them blind. What he doesn't know is how to be a gentleman. When he sets his sights on the prim Miss Scarlet, Letty, to his way of thinking, he decides she is the woman he wants to call his wife. He tempts all that she is with sweet words and tender coaxing until she is unable to refuse all he hopes to give her.

Only Caro's Baby
Good Girls Book Two

The Scheme

Genius botanist with theories of inherited traits, Caroline Kenworth desperately wants a baby. Finding a suitable father won't be easy. Caroline's super-intelligence makes her feel pushed aside, unwanted as a woman. As a bluestocking she is determined to spare her child the suffering that plagues her life. Which means she must find someone very special to father her child. A person very...well...ignorant.

The Target.

Duncan Murray, the Earl of Downsberry, well known for his lack of intelligence as well as his rakish ways with women, seems as if he is the flawless man to fulfill the role. His amazing good looks and Scottish brogue are misleading. Caro learns too late that this debonair earl is a lot smarter than she first thought—in addition he's not about to be used then abandoned by any woman who has schemed to steal his sperm.

The Detonation

A dazzling solitary woman whose desires to learn what it would be like to become a mother... A man who is in control of all he does never allowing anyone to usurp his role will settle for nothing less than surrender... Can lust coupled with physical attraction drive two strong-minded yet vulnerable people to a completely unforeseen love?

Twelve Days to Love

When Archer Steele shows up at Calanthe Durand's failing plantation with an alligator over his shoulder, Cali thinks she's never seen a more handsome man. During the war she had to defend herself and her servants from both union and confederate soldiers. Independent and self-sufficient, she vows to never marry.

But Archer Steele has different ideas. The first time Archer sees Cali in town, he feels an instant attraction. He decides he will do everything and anything to convince the beautiful Miss Durand he is worthy of her love. During the weeks leading up to Christmas, he gives her twelve gifts in hopes she will fall in love with him. Yet they are faced with challenges they must overcome before Cali can commit to a marriage.

Door to Heaven

Jessica Lawrence is the stepdaughter of a woman born in the twentieth century transported back in time to the year 1868. An acclaimed suffragette, she raises Jessica to believe in the equality of women. Jess Law believes everything she was taught, and when the time is right she becomes a private investigator. Courageous and impetuous, Jess finds danger in her quest to save all women from white slavery. Her passionate mission results in a wedding to Roc Newman, a man she knows can steal her heart...

Roc can't trust the sapphire-eyed spitfire who invades his home in search of secret papers and knocks him flat with her karate moves. Jessica's refusal to obey his wishes serves to inflame the war between them. Still, he cannot control the intense desire his reluctant bride inspires, or make her surrender her independence, until he has conquered the headstrong beauty on the battlefield of love...

Rebel Heart

HER REBEL SPIRIT DEFIED HIS OUTSIDERS SOUL...She was velvet and silk, eyes the color of a summer storm and amber hair. Victoria DeMontville, because of a promise and a codicil to her father's will, was forced to marry one man to protect her from another. She hated Cameron Savage with a fierce passion. But to hold on to her genetic research and find a cure for the deadly Signe virus, she must pretend to love the enemy at her door, come with weapons of fire to melt her icy heart...

HIS OUTSIDERS TOUCH IGNITED RAGING PASSIONS... He wore a mask, disguised as the Phantom, a true legend come to life. Even as war and debate over new genetic research engulfed them all, he would find his greatest adversary in the beauty who'd branded him an outsider and barbarian, the woman he was born to possess, his soul mate.

Safari Moon

Solo St. John, a wildlife photographer, is preparing for a trip to Alaska. Suddenly, Solo finds women of all sorts invading his privacy, his home and his office, all cooing nonsense words and blatantly throwing themselves at him. Solo doesn't know why, and he has no idea how to rid himself of the persistent women. He finally decides to beg a favor of his best buddy Nyssa Harrington.

In love with Solo for the past ten years and knowing he doesn't return her feelings Nyssa doesn't want to talk to Solo. She knows if she accepts his phone call, she will not be able to resist the temptation to hope again.

Straight to Heaven

Running from demons, Alexandra McMurdie stumbles into Forbidden Ground where up is down and elements of nature are contested. Though a strong independent woman in the twenty-first century' she is unprepared for life in the 1800s. Her first site of the formidable James Lawrence makes her heart skip a beat, giving her cause to reconsider her desperate need to find a way home.

Born with a silver spoon, James' life was torn apart during the War Between the States. Moving west he vows to put the life he once knew in the past. When he discovers a half-frozen woman near Gold Hill, his heart begins to thaw. His love for Alexandra and his need to keep her from a man who has pursued her through time might cost him his life as well as hers.

A Valentine's Anthology

The Lending Library-a fantasy by Christie L. Kraemer
Faeries try to fit into the human world when the forest where they make their home is destroyed by a mysterious enemy.

Chasing Rainbows-a contemporary romance by Genene Valleau
An eccentric aunt, an inventive uncle, a mother who wears poodle skirts, and a brother who wears pearls provide a hilarious backdrop for the courtship of a young woman who yearns for a "normal" family.

The Gift-an historical romance by Christine Young
A man and a woman on opposite sides of the Civil War get a

second chance at love after one final battle returns soldiers to their war-torn homes to rebuild their lives.

A St. Patrick's Day Tale
Christine Young, C. L. Kraemer, Genene Valleau

Tumble through time...

...to Ireland in 1817, when tensions are high between Protestants and Catholics and fae people guide the fate of villagers. A lovely Catholic lass stumbles upon the weakly ritual fisticuffing between Irish lads. She falls into the lap of a handsome young Protestant. Family ties, grudges, and two conniving faeries threaten their budding love. But the faeries outsmart themselves when they hijack a time machine that has mysteriously appeared in their forest and are whisked to...

...Eugene, Oregon in the 20th century, amid a property feud between the local faeries and night elves. The conniving faeries from Olde Ireland try to stir up more mischief. However, a warrior gnome convinces the magic folk to control their own destiny, and forces the intruding faeries to take refuge in the time machine again, spinning their way toward...

...A modern day castle in western Oregon. An eccentric inventor is determined to reclaim his wayward time machine and save his beloved wife from her latest misadventure. If only they can travel safely past the black hole...

a May Day Anthology
Christine Young, C. L. Kraemer, Rosemary Indra, Genene Valleau

Highland Miracle — Christine Young

HURTLED THROUGH TIME, Sean Michael Sterling, landed in the midst of a May Day celebration he didn't understand, assuming the role of Laird Sterling.

ILLIGITAMATE CHILD OF NOBILITY, Reagan Douglas searches for a way out of her half brother's house.

Defying the Odds — C.L. Kraemer

The night elves on the hill aren't happy without their magic. They concoct a plan to punish those who were involved in the act that rendered them almost human. Meanwhile, Uther, the rogue night elf, has returned to woo the Librarian to be his eternal mate.

Love in Bloom — Rosemary Indra

When childhood friends reunite it takes two fairies and a matchmaking daughter to help them admit their true love for each other.

No More Poodle Skirts — Genie Gabriel

After drifting for years in the innocent age of the 1950s, a woman struggles to join today's world by finding a career and a new love, with some help from her zany family.

Once Upon a Christmas Moon
Christine Young, C. L. Kraemer, Genene Valleau

TWELVE DAYS TO LOVE

When Archer Steele shows up at Calanthe Durand's failing plantation with an alligator over his shoulder, Cali thinks she's never seen a more handsome man. During the war she had to defend herself and her servants from both union and confederate soldiers. Independent and self-sufficient, she vows to never marry. But Archer Steele has different ideas. The first time Archer sees Cali in town, he feels an instant attraction. He decides he will do everything and anything to convince the beautiful Miss Durand he is worthy of her love. During the weeks leading up to Christmas, he gives her twelve gifts in hopes she will fall in love with him.

BOOTS AND BLADES

An ancient evil from the old country has arrived in the high desert of Oregon. Gnome children are vanishing then re-appearing, showing various stages of traumatization. Tiamoon, warrior gnome, will put her skills to use alongside Killian, a handsome warrior, also in need of a cause.

CHRISTMAS PAWSIBILITIES

With their world destroyed and their space ship malfunctioning, the dogizens of Planet Canid have little choice but to crash land on Earth. They face tortuous experiments at the hands of the Geeks in Green...or they can trust an eccentric inventor and his zany family to deliver the Canine Queen's puppies and help them celebrate new lives.

www.ingramcontent.com/pod-product-compliance
Lightning Source LLC
Chambersburg PA
CBHW060353260626
47160CB00006B/2292